A Passionate Woman . . .
A Bold, Reckless Man . . .
A Wild, Exquisite Love

The warrior's back was turned to her, so Tara had yet to see his face. He was tall, dark-haired, dressed in buckskins. He ignored her presence as if he'd forgotten her existence.

When she could stand the silence no longer, she inquired softly, "Why have I been brought here?"

At the sound of her voice, Star-runner turned around, and Tara gasped. "Grant!"

Before he could stop himself, he was seeking her mouth, and God help him, he thought, as he drank in the sweet taste of her. He wanted to take her tenderly, but she didn't want to wait. She opened herself like a flower in the lifegiving rain, in the storm of their need . . .

As long as the snow kept falling, they had all the time in the world . . .

"Let it be a long winter," Grant whispered . . .

Call Down the Moon

Joyce Thies

POCKET BOOKS

New York   London   Toronto   Sydney   Tokyo

This book is a work of historical fiction. Names, characters, places and incidents relating to non-historical figures are either the product of the author's imagination or are used fictitiously. Any resemblance of such non-historical incidents, places or figures to actual events or locales or persons, living or dead, is entirely coincidental.

An *Original* Publication of POCKET BOOKS

POCKET BOOKS, a division of Simon & Schuster Inc.
1230 Avenue of the Americas, New York, NY 10020

ISBN: 0-671-63094-6

First Pocket Books printing April 1989

10 9 8 7 6 5 4 3 2 1

POCKET and colophon are trademarks of
Simon & Schuster Inc.

Printed in the U.S.A.

*To Janet Bieber, for listening
as the chickadee listens,
and to Irene Goodman,
who felt my heart and understood.*

Preface

Before the aristocratic house of Collingswood rose to glory in England, before the fierce Armstrongs claimed their isles in the Scottish highlands and the Wainwright family was accorded any prominence in Connecticut, another noble clan reigned supreme over a vast and beautiful kingdom. Calling themselves simply "the people," they enjoyed a superb freedom, adventure, and happiness.

They were one with the universe and all of its powers. They knew that the Great Spirit was at the center of life, that all things were his works, and that his center was everywhere, within each one of them. Therefore, they had only one inevitable duty—the duty of prayer, the daily recognition of the unseen and eternal. For the sun, the earth, the wind, and the water, they gave thanks.

The Great Spirit blessed them for their constant devotion, and they grew and prospered into a mighty nation. Out of this realm came many tribes, and one of these was the Absaroka, Children of the Raven. They believed that they were two-legged as the birds were because the birds leave the world with their wings, and they would one day leave it in the spirit. Known to the white man as the Crow, they lived wisely and well in the sacred mountains of Montana.

Unlike their Indian brothers—the Sioux, Blackfeet, Gros Ventres, and Cheyenne—the Crow accepted a philosophy handed down by the wise men of their tribe. Everything changes during a man's lifetime, and when change comes to any created thing, it must accept it; it cannot fight but must change. Eventually, the Crow accepted the knowledge that they could not fight the white man, and, hence, they survived.

Plenty-coups, war chief of the Crow, said it best: "I want my people to learn all they can from the white man, because he is here to stay, and they must live with him forever. Riding with the whirlwind instead of opposing it, we shall save the heartland of our country."

And so they did.

Prologue

Absaroka Mountains, 1849

The night was dark and clear, the moon unnaturally bright. A sharp wind hurtled crystal shards of snow down the sheer mountain passes. Below the timberline, jackpines leaned away from the frigid blast, granite boulders were reshaped by relentless fingers of hoary frost.

It was the winter of the big snow, the night of the icicle wind.

An unending volley of boreal flakes blew against their lodges, but the Children of the Raven didn't feel the cold. The earth was their mother, and they lived upon it like good children in a mother's house. Their lodge poles were cut from strong cedar that would not buckle under the wind. Thick buffalo hides lashed with leather covered the walls of their tepees, holding out the cold and the snow. Those inside the sturdy walls were warmed by the fire burning in the center of the packed dirt floor, by their heavy buffalo robes and the wisdom of their elders.

The company fell silent as Mountain-lion, a wise man and chief of sixty moons, prepared to speak. "Listen," Mountain-lion said as he lit his pipe. "It is time that I tell you of the medicine dream I was given. Young men, pay heed, for my time of dreaming is done, yet I have still dreamed. I was walking from my lodge and looked into the sky. The night was westward, for the star that does not move had turned around the seven stars. I heard a voice and saw a white buffalo bull pawing the moon, and even as I looked, the bull turned and wished to speak with me."

Abruptly, Mountain-lion shivered, and his voice reflected the reverence and awe felt by all his listeners. "The white bull has told me of a great warrior who shall come among us. The winds, the thunders, the moon, and many stars, all the forces of nature, will give him much strength, bravery, and cunning."

Otter's-heart, a boy of only six snows, shocked the company by standing and proclaiming loudly, "Perhaps I am this great warrior."

"No!" Mountain-lion intoned.

"Who then, Grandfather?"

Normally, the company would have chastised the small boy for interrupting an elder, but they were so disturbed by Mountain-lion's vision that no one corrected him for speaking out of turn.

"This warrior will look like nothing we have ever seen," Mountain-lion predicted. "He will be marked with the sign of the raven and will have the power to call down the moon. We will sing of his great skill and daring in our lodges, yet he will not truly be one of us until he fulfills his destiny."

Split-nose, chief of the clan, a man whose brave deeds were shouted in every lodge, dared to inquire, "And what is that?"

Mountain-lion gazed into the fire, his tone mysterious, conveying the wonder of dreams. "He must go on a quest that none but he can fulfill. To do this, he will be compelled to chase the stars."

None among them had the capabilities Mountain-lion had ascribed to this warrior. Would the one who was coming be a man, or one of the all-powerfuls disguising himself to test their mettle? Perhaps Mountain-lion had misinterpreted his vision.

"To chase the stars, he must run like the wind," Otter's-heart burst out, expressing the confusion and doubt felt by all.

Mountain-lion drew on his pipe. He didn't speak again until he was certain all would listen. "No. Star-runner will chase the stars across the great wide waters and not return for many moons. When he comes to our village again, he will be cleansed and ready to protect us in our time of need."

Swift-bear, a youth of fourteen snows, could be silent no longer. "What time of need, Grandfather?"

Again, Mountain-lion waited for the speculation to die down before he gave his answer. "The white buffalo has shown me an enemy intent on stealing the heart of our people. His cruel warriors will redden the earth with the blood of high chiefs. When Star-runner returns from his sacred journey, he will roam the rivers and valleys in search of this fearful enemy."

For long moments, fear drained the company of their voices, but then Split-nose threw off his robes and stood before the fire. "Hear me, Absaroka! To save our hearts, we must pledge our fealty to Star-runner."

One by one, the other warriors threw off their robes and joined the young chief. To a man, they vowed loyalty to Star-runner, the great warrior who was coming to lead them. Aligned with him, they would be like an angry buffalo, which never retreats, which nothing can stop.

It was the winter of the big snow, the night of the icicle wind—the beginning.

PART
1

Chapter

One

St. Louis, April, 1864

At eventide, the mighty Mississippi was wrapped in silence, a wide silver ribbon that stretched across the Missouri hills. As the moon ascended the sky, the moving gulf of glimmering water rose ever higher and eventually spilled over its low banks. It was the first season of high water. The next would not come until June.

On the wharf, a Missouri River packet tugged at its hawsers, impatient to commence the great two-thousand-mile race to Fort Benton and Montana riches. The waterfront gaslights blinked yellow at dawn, and the *Ophelia* opened her decks for provisions. She would be the first to embark on the hazardous journey upriver and the first to return to St. Louis with her holds filled with gold.

The *Ophelia*'s bow took the form of a huge serpent rising up out of the water from under the boat. The serpent's scaly black head darted forward and towered as high as the upper deck. While in passage up the river, its open mouth would vomit smoke, shielding the brass field pieces that were mounted on the wheel carriages. Once under way, a stream of foaming water would come from beneath the stern, dashing violently against the lower deck.

No machinery would be seen, no wind or human hand appearing to help this serpent swim upwater. To ignorant, pagan eyes, it would seem a monster of the deep, carrying a boat on its back, lashing the river waves with violent exertion. To pass safely through Indian territory, the *Ophelia* would need such illusion.

By midmorning, the cobblestone streets of the waterfront were alive with activity. A row of soot-rimmed warehouses lined the levee, belching cargo through their yawning doors as steadily as their chimneys spit smoke. In the crowded alleys, black-skinned roustabouts hoisted heavy crates to their sweat-slicked backs. They formed a parade to the river, singing mournful songs of labor as they mounted the gangways and carried the last of the *Ophelia*'s cargo on board.

Up and down the wide wharf, farmers, gamblers, fur traders, and ill-smelling wolfers roamed freely, exchanging tales of the adventures that surely awaited them in the vast northern territories. Newly recruited soldiers complained about the glorious Union victories they would never see and the unsung battles with savage Indians that were yet to come. Merchants and miners, befrocked missionaries and full-blown strumpets strolled along the levee without a care. They boarded the *Ophelia* with light, easy steps, shouting, laughing, and praying for the shortsighted folk they would soon leave behind.

A wildly assorted crowd, they were free to come and go as they pleased and did so at their leisure. Taralynn Armstrong was not so lucky. Her presence among them would immediately draw all eyes. No matter what her purpose, the waterfront was no place for a lady, especially one who didn't wish to be found.

Hiding behind a large wooden barrel of flour, Tara peeped out at the crowded wharf and immediately took a tighter grip on the small derringer hidden in the deep pocket of her twilled cotton skirt. He was still out there! Mutton-chop whiskers, bright plaid coat, foul-smelling cigar, and beefy red face, the dogged Mr. Snedeker was almost as easy to spot as she was.

She'd deliberately dressed in dark clothes and wore a

prim, high-necked traveling dress that paid little compliment to her blooming complexion or dainty figure. Her poke bonnet was a nondescript gray, but it did nothing to subdue the flaming red curls that framed her face. Nor did it hide the vivid green of her eyes. Those same Scot ancestors who had passed down the courage she needed to embark on a perilous trek to Montana Territory had also bestowed on her the distinctive coloring that severely hampered her chances of ever getting there.

From Connecticut to Missouri, Amos Snedeker had been after her like a blooded hound after a fleeing fox. To throw off pursuit, Tara had taken a roundabout journey, a coach to Bridgeport, then a ferry across the Long Island Sound, but it was as if Snedeker could pick up her scent over impossible distance.

On the streets of New York, he had dogged her steps from one hotel to another. He'd missed the train she'd taken to St. Louis, but not the next, and he'd begun combing the city for her the moment he arrived. Tara had barely managed to elude him this morning when she left the lodging house she'd chosen specifically for its nondescript appearance and back-street location.

If it hadn't been for the handsome sum she'd conferred on her hackney driver, the pertinacious detective would have finally caught up with his quarry. Then she would have been dragged aboard a train heading east, forcibly escorted back to Laurel Glen Farm and the Wainwrights.

Tara closed her eyes, willing back all emotion. She no longer had any ties to Laurel Glen, not the land or the people. She was better off without the gracious home, fine clothes, and expensive jewels she had left behind—and those who had provided them. From now on, all she had gained from her past must be used to ensure her future with her rightful family. She was through living a lie.

She was a fighting Scot Armstrong, not a blue-blooded Wainwright. Her home was not a white stone mansion in Connecticut but an isolated ranch in Montana Territory. Once she was there, Margaret Wainwright would no longer have any power over her. Once there, she would be safe.

A whistle warned of the *Ophelia*'s imminent departure. If Tara didn't take action soon, she wouldn't be aboard when the boat left the landing. But how was she going to get through the crowd without being spotted? Snedeker, always Snedeker, right behind her, breathing down her neck.

She'd come so far and was now less than five hundred miles from Nebraska Territory and safe sanctuary. As soon as the *Ophelia* turned westward past Mobile Point into the swelling tide of the Missouri, she would breathe easier. Once she was north of St. Joseph, had crossed the Platte River, the authorities would lose their jurisdiction. Snedeker would then have no choice but to go back to Connecticut empty-handed.

Tara edged slowly around the wide wooden barrel. What she needed was a man, a strong, protective husband who would laugh in Snedeker's face if he accused her of being a thief and tried to take her into custody. She took a deep breath and plunged into the crowd, frantically searching for a good candidate for the role. He had to cut an imposing figure but must be a gentleman, a man who would do a lady's bidding without asking a lot of questions. Of course, any man with a gun in his back would take some direction, but she needed one who wouldn't attempt to dissuade her until she was free from pursuit.

"Where ya goin', girlie?" a man in oily buckskins inquired as she hurried past him. "I got me a twenty-dollar gold piece and more where that came from. Throw in with me, and I reckon we'll have a right good time."

"Whoa there, honey!" A heavyset merchant in a shiny store-bought suit grabbed hold of her arm. "If you're bound upriver, I'm goin' your way."

Tara jerked out of his grasp, her fingers trembling on the pearl-handled pistol. "I am bound to my husband, sir," she warned. "Let me pass."

The man took a step backward, her scathing manner having the desired effect. Relieved, Tara forced herself not to run as she continued her progress toward the wide-planked gangway. It wasn't that far away. Maybe she could get on board before Snedeker caught up with her. She looked over her shoulder and panicked. The eagle-eyed man had spotted her, and there was no way she would escape unaided.

Whether it was fate or luck, the next moment brought her

a glimpse of salvation. Young and tall, he was less than five yards ahead of her, striding toward the gangplank. He was dressed in a Prussian blue frock coat and fashionably tight fawn trousers. She recognized the style of his tapered top hat as the latest thing from the haberdasheries of London.

His cravat was snowy white, indicating the care he took with his person. Wellington boots of finest leather marked him as a man of some wealth. Though cut overlong, the sheen of his blue-black hair was natural, not the result of any perfumed pommade. Tara couldn't see his features, but she didn't much care what he looked like. Time was growing dangerously short. Snedeker was still a good distance behind her, but he was moving up fast.

Tara quickened her step until she was walking beside her target. Then, gathering all of her courage, she slipped her arm through one of his. She could sense the man's startled surprise and spoke hurriedly. "Here I am, dear. Did you think you had lost me?"

"What . . . ?"

When he would have stopped, Tara slipped her free hand inside the front of his coat and jammed her small pistol into his ribs. "If you value your life, sir, you will keep walking," she ordered beneath her breath as she smiled with false affection into a pair of cobalt-blue eyes.

Tara emitted a tiny gasp at the sight of his handsome face. Such a hard set of features, the prominent cheekbones and unyielding jaw darkened by the sun. Long hours of exposure made his skin look like copper, a permanent polish broken only by the tiny etched lines beside his eyes and mouth. His mouth could have been carved from smooth stone, but then his lips twitched and his teeth flashed white against his dark skin. Tara gulped. Amusement was not the emotion she wished to inspire in him.

"I . . . I'm not averse to using this gun," she stuttered. "And I will, if you don't do exactly as I say."

He gave an indolent shrug of broad shoulders. "Perhaps."

In return, Tara gave him a sharp nudge with the derringer. "No perhaps about it."

They took several more steps. Tara glanced back, searching for Snedeker. He was pushing his way through a platoon of soldiers. "Walk faster," she ordered her captive.

The long legs took two giant strides before Tara realized she'd never keep pace. She felt like an anchor that couldn't hold its depth. "Slow down!"

Obediently, the man did as he was told, and Tara took heart. For all his size, he was proving tractable. "Listen closely," she advised with renewed bravado.

Leaning into him, she rested her head for a moment on his upper arm so he could better hear what she had to tell him without being overheard by those around them. "I'm your wife," she stated softly. Hard muscles tensed beneath her touch, a powerful surge that shook her composure all over again.

To reinforce her superior position, she reminded him a bit desperately, "If you give me any trouble, sir, this small gun will put a very large hole in you."

"Very large," he agreed pleasantly.

"You there!" Amos Snedeker shouted over the heads of the milling crowd behind them, forestalling Tara's hope that her escort would be fully prepared before the inevitable confrontation.

"I am your wife," she decreed once more, tightening her grip on the man's arm as she jabbed him again with the barrel of the pistol. "We are traveling together today on the *Ophelia*. We have been married for several months, and you have no knowledge of the girl that man hailing us will question you about. What's your name?"

"Grant Collingswood. And yours?" he inquired lazily, as if being on the wrong end of a loaded gun was an everyday occurrence. He had a slight accent, possibly English, but Tara didn't waste time trying to place it. It didn't matter where he was from, as long as he played the role she required him to play.

She blurted the first name that came into her head, "Henrietta. Henrietta Collingswood."

Grant chuckled. "Too much name for such a little bit of a woman."

"You're in no position to judge," Tara advised in a biting tone, trying to match the challenge in his eyes. "This gun more than makes up for whatever I may lack in size."

"It does give you a certain advantage," he allowed graciously. "Still, I'd never marry a woman named Henrietta

12

even if she held a gun to my head. Henriettas are big-boned, with gargantuan breasts and fat hips.''

Cocking his head to one side, he ran his eyes down her diminutive figure. "You are definitely not a Henrietta, hardly any bosom at all.''

"See here!" Tara choked out, face flaming. "You don't seem to understand—''

"You there in the blue coat!" Snedeker was upon them. "Stop, I say! I demand that you stop.''

Tara went cold. The charade had begun, and all she could do was pray that Collingswood would hold up his end of things. She opened her mouth to speak to their accoster first, but Collingswood didn't give her the chance. "What you have to say had better be important, mister. My wife and I are supposed to be boarding, and I don't appreciate this delay.''

Tara let out her pent-up breath. The man was still cooperating. Evidently, little or no, her hand on the derringer concerned Grant Collingswood more than he'd been willing to let on.

"Your wife?" Snedeker looked taken aback for a moment, but then renewed suspicion gleamed in his pale blue eyes. "I get it. She paid you off. Well, Amos Snedeker ain't sidetracked that easy. I was hired to find her, and I aim to collect the bounty for doing the job.''

"Bounty?" Grant asked, a surprised glint in his eyes as he glanced down at the diminutive woman at his side.

"Didn't know you were protectin' a criminal, now, did ya?" Snedeker spit out his cigar and ground it under his shoe. "Ain't no kind of pay worth the fix you'll be in if you don't turn her over to me. This li'l gal's done wrong by some mighty powerful folks, and I'm obliged to bring her to justice. Mister, whatever she paid you, you don't need her kind of trouble.''

Tara shrank away from the belligerent look on Snedeker's face, unconsciously pressing herself closer to Collingswood. She could tell that Snedeker wasn't going to give up his prize easily. When Collingswood slid a protective arm around her waist, she was so grateful for the added security that she didn't realize what he was doing until it was too late.

Within seconds, the derringer was forced from her hand

into his and pocketed in his trousers. In the blink of an eye, he pulled a long-bored revolver from his belt and aimed it at Snedeker. "I'm sorry to use this means to convince you otherwise, my good man, but my darlin' Mathilda and I don't have time to argue the matter further. The *Ophelia* is about to pull out, and we're going to be on her."

Tara was too frightened to utter a sound. The man she'd waylaid with a tiny pistol had been carrying a gun the whole time! A very large, deadly-looking weapon, it seemed very much at home in his strong hand. What kind of man was he? She frowned. *My darlin' Mathilda?*

She looked up, and then as quickly down. One glimpse into those intensely blue eyes was enough to tell her she would be wise to stay silent. For better or worse, Grant Collingswood had taken control of both her and the situation.

"Mathilda! I tell you, her name ain't Mathilda," Snedeker insisted, but he took a step back, less wary of the gun than of the man holding it.

Tara couldn't blame him. Snedeker had undoubtedly seen what she'd missed. Beneath his fashionable clothes and a veneer of gentlemanly charm, Grant Collingswood was pure danger. If she hadn't been so caught up in her own predicament, she would have recognized that he posed an even greater threat to her than Snedeker. She'd been incredibly stupid to judge him harmless simply by the expert cut of his clothes. His arm about her waist was like a manacle that tightened imperceptibly whenever she tried to pull away.

"She's the one I'm after," Snedeker hissed in frustration. "She matches the description exactly." He pulled an oval frame from his pocket and showed Collingswood the small oil portrait it contained. "See? I don't know what story she gave you, but that's the truth of it. If it's money you want in exchange for her, I'd be willin' to split my share with you."

"I repeat. My wife's name is Mathilda, Mathilda Pauline Collingswood. She has rarely been out of my sight since the day of our marriage," Grant declared shortly, gathering Tara closer against him. He gazed down at her face. His eyes, a blistering blue, branded her his possession.

Tara was stunned by that look and terrified by the prospects of what might happen to her once Collingswood had dispatched Snedeker, which she was now certain he would do. In an attempt to escape one trap, she'd walked blindly into another. "I . . . eh . . . I don't mind going with Mr. Snedeker if it will help clear up this confusion," Tara offered, the quaver in her voice matching the quaking in her limbs. "We still have a few minutes before they'll give up our cabin to someone else."

The man holding her stiffened, but, instead of letting go, he gave her an affectionate squeeze and a lethal smile.

"Really, dear," she insisted, desperately trying to pull away from what she now saw as the fire, in order to jump back into the much safer prospect of the frying pan. "You . . . you just go ahead, while I speak to Mr. Snedeker.

"Please," she whispered, a shudder of dread shaking down her spine as she felt his fingers curve possessively over her hip. At his touch, she flinched, scorched by a heat that wasn't physical yet burned like fire.

"I won't hear of it, my sweet. You belong with me," Collingswood vowed lovingly, before shifting his focus back to Snedeker. He replaced the gun in his belt, challenging the man with nothing but the cold warning in his eyes. "Doesn't she, Mr. Snedeker?"

The visual exchange lasted less than five seconds, and in that short span of time, Snedeker appeared to shrink. "Sorry. My mistake," he wheezed like a large, deflating balloon. But before disappearing back into the crowd, he blustered weakly, "You ain't seen the last of me, young lady."

Grant Collingswood dismissed his threat with an uncaring shrug, then offered Tara his arm. "Shall we go, *Mrs. Collingswood?*"

Chapter

Two

"I'm not going anywhere with you." Tara twisted out of Grant's grasp, swallowing hard.

"You would disobey your husband, Mathilda?" Grant shook his head in mock resignation. "What a troublesome little baggage you are turning out to be."

About to take hold of her again, he was distracted by a loud, shrill whistle from the *Ophelia*. It was the final calling. Those members of the crowd who were bound upriver but had yet to board swarmed the banks, pushing and shoving their way toward the gangplank. Within seconds, Grant and Tara were engulfed in a rushing stream of humanity, and Tara was jostled out of his reach. Another steamer wouldn't be en route to the Montana boom towns for weeks, and those who suffered from gold fever couldn't contain their greed for even that long.

As soon as the rumors of rich strikes at Alders and Last Chance Gulch in Montana Territory had filtered down to the states, wild-eyed men had left their wives and children. Zealous Union and Confederate soldiers had cast off their uniforms and deserted their posts. Enterprising merchants had closed up their shops in order to supply a clientele who would pay double, even triple, for their provisions. All sought tickets on the first steamer headed for the Upper Missouri. Love of family, honor in war, satisfactory profit in business—none of these could compete with the expectation of colossal riches.

Glaring, Grant watched as Tara was carried away by the advancing tide of exuberant passengers. Amid bright unfurled banners and waving arms and an ear-splitting swell of shouted farewells, he caught one last glimpse of her triumphant green eyes and a victorious toss of red curls before she disappeared from view.

Grant swore with frustration but without any real anger. His plans for the girl could wait a while longer. A swift smile transformed his face as he pictured how she'd react to their next meeting, but it fled almost as quickly. The mere thought of another confrontation with her heated his blood to a fever pitch, and he hadn't reacted that strongly to a woman in years, especially not one so young. The little spitfire looked to be barely out of the schoolroom.

The aching tension in his loins took Grant unawares, and he didn't like being caught off guard by the reactions of his own body. Controlling his emotions was part of his stock-in-trade. As a gambler, he enjoyed taking chances, but not before he knew what was at stake and had calculated all the risks. What was at stake if he got involved with "Mathilda Pauline"? She was an extremely beautiful woman yet, according to Snedeker, a criminal with a price on her head.

Grant's jaw went tight. Why should that knowledge only enhance his interest in her? He didn't need trouble, especially not the female kind, yet he couldn't help being more than a little intrigued.

Where women were concerned, he held his cards close to his chest. They had a place in his bed but not in his life. When he saw one he wanted, he played out his hand with measured skill, never revealing what he was thinking or feeling as he sized up his opposition. If the woman raised the ante, he sweetened the pot with a few suggestive words, a heated look, and usually found it was all that was necessary to beat her at her own game.

With "Mathilda," however, he wasn't positive that would be the case. As soon as she'd pulled a gun on him, Grant had realized that she could give him an interesting run for

17

his money. And the higher the stakes, the greater the pleasure in winning. Yet, even if he'd felt no desire to take her to bed, her fate had been sealed the moment she mentioned having a cabin.

With unhurried strides, Grant entered the flow of human traffic surging toward the gangway. Unlike his fellow travelers, he felt no need to rush. Unlike most of them, Grant knew what awaited them all at the headwaters of the Missouri and in every direction—an awesome gathering of summits, each higher and more impregnable than the next. Fortune seekers might think the mountains were carved of pure gold, free for the taking, but far too many would pay a deadly price learning otherwise. For centuries, this natural stronghold had effectively guarded its hidden wealth with the brutal weapons of ice, wind, and snow, marauding animals, and fathomless forests. Grant had no doubt but that it would go on doing so throughout eternity.

Any man who thought differently was a fool. Grant knew that the majority of eager prospectors heading out to the goldfields thought that bloodthirsty Indians posed the greatest threat to their success, but they would soon discover their folly. More miners would perish at the cruel hand of nature than at the hands of the red man. Without tracking experience, dependable gear, and proper weapons, such useless deaths were inevitable.

No, Grant judged as he stared at the dark currents beckoning to the savage wilderness, there was no need for him to rush. What awaited him in those mountains would wait forever.

Pressed in between a black-coated priest en route to save the heathen and an unsaintly-looking woman who had the opposite in mind, Tara leaned over the crowded bull rail. She'd done it! She was standing safely on the *Ophelia*'s main deck, waving goodbye to those left behind on the St. Louis levee. After three nerve-racking weeks as a fugitive, the odds of making it to Montana were now in her favor, and they would increase with every port the boat passed.

The stern-wheeler backed out into the Mississippi channel, swung about to the north, and picked up speed as it headed for the Missouri River junction. As Tara watched the shoreline recede, an exhilarating sense of freedom welled up inside her. Luck had been with her all day and was with her yet.

All things considered, her choice of protector had proved to be a wise one after all. Grant Collingswood had thwarted Snedeker's attempt to waylay her, and, with the help of the crowd, she had successfully managed to elude Collingswood. At least for the time being. He was a passenger, and therefore chances were high that she'd run into him again. However, after replaying the whole episode in her mind, that prospect didn't frighten her nearly as much as it had during her panicky flight up the gangway.

Looking back on it, Tara realized that the man she had cast in the role of her husband had only done what she'd asked him to do, nothing more. Of course, after dispatching Snedeker, he'd expected her to make some sort of an explanation, but that huge gun he'd been wearing and the possessive look in his eyes had erased all other thoughts from her mind but that of escape.

In retrospect, considering where they were bound, it was perfectly logical for Collingswood to have been armed. In the penny novels she'd smuggled into her bedroom, she had read many terrifying accounts of the bloodthirsty savages who roamed the wilderness and preyed upon those who encroached on their territory. As for the look of ownership Collingswood had bestowed on her, how else was a new husband supposed to view his bride? The man had done his best by her, and, foolishly, she'd been taken in by his convincing act as much as Snedeker.

When she saw him again, she would thank him very prettily for helping her and apologize for involving him in her troubles. If he were any kind of gentleman at all, he'd let matters go at that. After all, she'd not committed any serious crime against him. If he felt otherwise, she would listen penitently to whatever tirade he cared to make, humbly plea his pardon, then go out of her way to avoid him.

She was far more concerned with what awaited her at the end of her journey than with any unpleasantness that might occur during it. On her flight across the country, she'd gathered as much information as she could about what to expect during her passage up the Missouri River, but no one could tell her what to expect from the people who resided at journey's end.

In little more than two months, she would be meeting her father, Angus Armstrong, and her three brothers, Robert, Neal, and James. They were her closest living relatives, her own family, but she had never met them. Up until a few weeks ago, she hadn't even known they existed.

What's more, they knew nothing of her coming, knew nothing about her at all.

Tara shuddered, the boisterous crowd gathered on the lower deck blurring before her eyes. She had no idea what her real family would be like or if they'd welcome her. Would her father accept her as his daughter? To do so, he'd have to acknowledge that his only brother, Lachlan, had been a spineless liar, a traitor to his family, and that Lachlan's wife, Margaret, was a self-seeking tyrant who would do anything in order to achieve her own ends. Yet, without any tangible proof of this, how was Tara going to convince her father she was telling the truth?

Her greatest fear was that he would scoff at her story and angrily send her away. Then she would have nowhere else to go, no home, no family, nothing. What would she do then?

She could never go back to Laurel Glen. The agents her aunt had hired could track her to the ends of the earth, but she'd rather die than go back there. For eighteen years, she'd been the victim of a cruel lie, robbed of her rightful heritage. She would never be a Wainwright and would never forgive her aunt for what she'd done to her.

Woefully, unaware that the blood of Scottish chieftains surged through her veins, she'd spent her entire childhood trying to be someone she was not—a genteel member of cultured society. To please her aristocratic "parents," she'd struggled to behave circumspectly and suppress the wild, impetuous tendencies that had come so naturally. She had never been wholly successful and had suffered accordingly.

Her explusion from Miss Franklin's School for Ladies in New York had been proof of her failure in Margaret Wainwright's eyes. Intending to break Tara's irrepressible spirit, Margaret had banished her to that bastion of straitlaced convention on her tenth birthday.

On the first day, Miss Althea Franklin had sternly warned

Tara that there was not a hoyden alive she couldn't mold into a well-mannered young lady. In Tara's case, the woman's usual methods failed. Within a month, Tara had been relegated to a solitary room on the fifth floor so that she couldn't influence others to join in her mischievous pranks. For neglecting her lessons, her free time was severely curtailed. For insolence, she was thrashed about the legs with a willow switch. For running away, she was locked in her room at night and punished with a steady diet of coarse brown bread and weak broth.

For six years, the school had been her prison, but eventually she had driven her stiff-necked jailer to drink. The day Miss Franklin's penchant for spirits was discovered by a shocked trustee was the day Tara had been deemed hopelessly incorrigible and escorted back to Laurel Glen.

Thankful to be free, Tara had suffered through her "mother's" scathing censure, endured two years more of the woman's scorn, and prayed for a miracle, certain divine intervention was the only way she'd ever become the refined woman of quality the Wainwrights desired her to be. Her fervent prayers had gone unanswered.

Once she'd learned the truth about herself, however, she realized that there was no need for further prayer. In that way the shocking news had come as a blessing, for it meant she could finally stop fighting her true nature and be content with herself. In another way, however, the information had completely disrupted her life.

Three weeks ago, aware that he was dying, Lachlan Wainwright had confessed his part in a conspiracy that had begun when Tara's real mother, Ellen Armstrong, had died while giving birth to her daughter. Upon his beloved wife's death, Angus had felt free to leave Laurel Glen and seek a place of his own, one that more closely resembled the home he'd been forced to leave in the highlands of Scotland ten years earlier.

Placing the infant Tara in the care of Lachlan and Margaret, he had taken his three sons and headed west, promising to send for his daughter once he'd established a proper home for her and she was old enough to undertake the arduous journey. Long before that had happened, Angus had received word from Margaret that Tara had not survived her first year.

The barren woman wanted a child, and since it was unlikely that Angus would ever return to Connecticut and dispute her claim, Tara could be hers. They informed friends and relations who knew Angus that he and his sons had perished at the hands of the bloodthirsty savages who occupied the territories. It was now their sad duty to raise his orphaned daughter as their own child. By the time she was out of her infancy, Tara was considered a Wainwright by all who knew her.

Throughout her childhood and adolescence, her domineering "mother" had groomed Tara for the role she must play if the Wainwright line was to continue as Margaret saw fit. Although Lachlan was aware of the harsh treatment Tara met at his wife's hands, he never attempted to countermand her orders. But then, just in time to prevent Tara from marrying Louden Wainwright, a distant cousin and Margaret's hand-picked choice for Tara's husband, Lachlan had revealed the truth.

For his share of his wife's coffers, Lachlan had sacrificed everything in life that held any meaning for him—his pride, his honor, even the proud family name of Armstrong. As weak as that made him, he couldn't doom his brother's child to the same fate. He had loved Tara as much as he was capable of loving anyone and could not go to his grave knowing that because of his cowardice she would be trapped in a marriage as loveless as his own had been.

To make amends to Tara for his part in the plot, Lachlan had given her several jewels and a generous amount of money. Telling her to seek sanctuary with her real family, who had emigrated to Montana, he had arranged for her to escape Laurel Glen a few hours before her wedding to Louden had been scheduled to take place. With her uncle's help, Tara had avoided the fate Margaret Wainwright had planned for her, but it was still too early to tell if she could avoid the wrath her defection had inspired.

Tara had read the notice Margaret had placed in the newspapers. It said that Taralynn Rachel Wainwright was not only an ungrateful, rebellious daughter but a thief whose actions had broken her father's heart and caused his untimely death. Lachlan Wainwright's grief-stricken widow promised a huge reward to any man who could find Tara and bring her back to answer for her sins.

To prevent anyone from claiming that reward, Tara realized she had to stay alert. Snedeker might be only the first of many men who were after her. Still, considering how successful she'd been in eluding capture thus far, she felt more and more confident that she could continue doing so.

At long last, she was free of all the constraints she'd been under since birth, and, whatever it took, she intended to stay free. From now on, she would be true to herself, not others. Whatever expectations Angus Armstrong might hold for young women, specifically his daughter, she'd try her best to live up to them, but not if it meant sacrificing her soul. She was done with that kind of pain forever.

Chapter

Three

"I see you made it safely aboard."

Recognizing the deep-timbered voice, Tara whirled around, her expression wary. On a deck that was close to two hundred feet long and teeming with people, Grant Collingswood had made his way straight to her. "As did you, Mr. Collingswood."

Grant inclined his head politely. "I'm happy to see that your survival instincts haven't declined any since last we met."

Tara tilted her chin a fraction more, acutely aware that in order to meet his gaze she had to look up a considerable distance. Staring into his startling sky-blue eyes, she was again aware of the peculiar effect Grant Collingswood seemed to have on her. She had noticed the strange fluttering beneath her heart the first time she looked into his face but had put it down to fear. This time she wasn't so sure that was reason enough for her reaction to him.

Tara's mouth felt full of cotton, her skin tingled, and her blood raced as his gaze traveled over her. "I . . . I beg your pardon?"

"You have stationed yourself by a priest," he observed, and he shrugged his broad shoulders as the cleric ambled

24

away from the rail. "A wise choice, but what will you do now?"

"Choice? Do? Do about what?" Tara asked, not comprehending.

"How do you intend to reach your cabin without being accosted?"

While Tara grappled with that unexpected question, Grant returned the smile of a shockingly dressed buxom woman who sidled up to him at the rail. After what Tara felt was an embarrassing exchange of interest in each other's physical attributes, Grant gave a short negative shake of his head. The woman's face fell as she turned and walked away.

Grant grinned at Tara's shocked expression. "She was asking." He gestured toward the crowded forecastle. "They won't."

Tara followed the movement of his hand. For the most part, her fellow passengers appeared to be not only male but a scurvy-looking lot. As her eyes darted from right to left, she noted fearfully that several men were indeed leering at her. Realizing that the only reason she hadn't yet been approached was Grant's presence beside her, she stammered, "A-are you offering yourself as my escort?"

"Why not? You do need someone, Tillie." Grant used the nickname he had bestowed on her and chuckled at her irritated frown. "I'd be happy to substitute another name if you would care to divulge what it is."

Tara thought for a second and decided it was still a wiser decision to keep her real identity to herself. There was no telling if those chasing her had been advised that she might now be calling herself Tara Armstrong. She felt somewhat safer aboard the *Ophelia*, but she couldn't be positive that Snedeker was the only agent on her trail. Margaret Wainwright had enough money to hire a hundred agents just like him. "My cabin is secured under the name Mary Cooper."

Tara missed the satisfied gleam in Grant's eyes as he teased, "I prefer Mathilda Pauline. At least it shows some imagination."

"You don't believe I've given you my correct name?" she asked, trying to look properly insulted.

"Liars are not believed even when they speak the truth,"

Grant observed mildly. "Besides, a name like Mary is about as suitable for a little firebrand like you as Henrietta."

"Think what you will," Tara retorted indignantly, turning away to hide the guilty color in her face. This man was far too clever for her liking. Until she was safely out of the states, it would be better to avoid answering a lot of questions. Lies had a way of backfiring, and she'd already told too many.

On the other hand, considering her alternative escorts, she couldn't risk offending the man. He had pointed out a very real danger that she had naively neglected to take into account. An unescorted woman was considered fair game by unscrupulous men. Grant Collingswood might be an insolent rake, but he did show some semblance of manners.

"I wish to thank you for helping me, Mr. Collingswood." Tara forced herself to speak the ingratiating words. "I don't know what I would have done without you. Will you accept my apology for forcing you to come to my aid?"

"Apology accepted, of course," Grant replied, more graciously than Tara had expected. "Now, may I escort you to your cabin?"

Tara agreed at once and gratefully slipped her arm through his. "I am in your debt, sir."

Grant tipped his hat courteously and forged a path for them to follow along the crowded deck. In the midst of the crush, Tara's sensitive nostrils were assailed by a variety of odors, all equally foul. The strong fumes of hard liquor mixed with the rancid smell of stale perspiration and unwashed flesh. She held her breath, keeping close to Grant as he shouldered his way through a large group of French fur traders who reeked of alcohol and looked as if their skin were composed of putrid grease.

Trying not to appear intimidated by the salacious interest of these uncivilized men, Tara took a firmer hold on Grant's arm as they headed for the nearest companionway. Once they were inside the passage, she wondered which cabin Grant occupied, hoping it was close to hers. To be practical, she had to acknowledge that if she wanted to stroll freely on deck, she might have to prevail upon his services more than once.

"Thank you again—and now I must bid you good day,

26

Mr. Collingswood," she said, coming to a stop before her own accommodations. Drawing the key from her pocket, she glanced at the number on the door and then at the matching one on the brass key. "Yes, this is my cabin."

"Our cabin," Grant corrected silkily.

Tara's mouth dropped open. "What!"

"Since we are man and wife, where else would I stay?" he inquired curiously.

Tara paled at his intent expression. He was serious! "You know very well that business was just a ploy to get rid of Mr. Snedeker. I already admitted being in your debt, but surely you can't expect me to share a cabin with a total stranger . . . a man?"

"Can't I?"

Tara ignored the implied threat in his question and fought down the blush that rose in her cheeks. "If this is your way of demanding restitution, Mr. Collingswood, then I shall be happy to pay you whatever you feel your service to me was worth."

"Do you know what it's like to travel in steerage, Tillie?"

"Don't call me that, and no, I can't say that I do."

"How would you like to sleep on an open deck with a group of men who'd just as soon knife you as look at you?"

Tara cast a knowing eye at his expensive clothes. "From the looks of you, I doubt very much that is your circumstance."

"Unhappily, that is exactly my circumstance, for I am booked in steerage. It is true that I have the money to pay for better accommodations, but I only arrived in St. Louis today and found all the cabins were already taken. Lucky for me that you came along when you did, isn't it?"

"You are not sharing my cabin," Tara insisted heatedly.

"As your husband, it would seem very strange if I did not," Grant said, placing two fingers over her lips to prevent the inevitable protest. "Believe me, Mathilda Pauline Collingswood, you're going to need a husband on this trip. I suppose you might have been able to outrun Snedeker without securing my help, but on a steamboat there's no place to run. You had a good look at our traveling companions. Compared to most of them, you must admit that I'm a saint."

Tara slapped his hand away. "I admit no such thing, and for your information, I can take care of myself."

Grant snorted. "Like a helpless lamb among wolves."

To prove his point, he reached into his side pocket, pulled out her derringer, and dangled it on the end of one finger. "Do you think this poor excuse for a weapon will stop a man who's intent on having you? If so, you don't know one thing about male lust."

Tara bit her lip, trying to appear panic-stricken as she measured the distance between her hand and the gun. The hateful man was doing his best to frighten her, but after all she'd been through recently, she refused to be cowed by mere words.

"Look how easily I disarmed you," Grant continued. Noting her pallor, he assumed he was gaining ground and pressed his advantage. "Most any man could do the same. I'm offering you my protection, Tillie."

To further assure her, he added, "I don't know who or what you're running away from, and, frankly, I don't much care. If you extend me a like courtesy, I won't ask any questions. I promise."

With the quick agility she had displayed earlier, Tara's hand shot forward and snatched the gun away. "Thank you very much for your concern, Mr. Collingswood, but I'll take my chances."

She couldn't help but laugh at his startled expression as she took aim. If he thought to have her quaking with fear, he'd greatly underestimated her. Now that she had made it this far, she would find the means to foil him or anyone else who tried her mettle.

"Give me that thing before you hurt yourself," Grant bit out, incensed when she made no move to comply with his order. "I'm warning you, Tillie. I didn't like it when you pulled a gun on me before, and I like it even less now."

Tara laughed again, a tinkling sound of pure enjoyment. She, a tiny bit of a woman, had robbed this tall, muscular man of control. It was a heady feeling, a new and exciting feeling that she found very gratifying.

"It is not I who will be hurt if you persist with this nonsense," she tossed off airily, trying to sound like Wild Mary McGee, her favorite heroine from the dime novels she'd consumed. Mary was a woman who backed down from no man. "And I couldn't care less what you like. I no longer must answer to anyone but myself."

Grant's eyes narrowed on the gun and slowly traveled upward to her face, but Tara didn't collapse beneath the ominous menace of his cold blue gaze. None of her courageous ancestors, man or woman, would have retreated from this miscreant's challenge, and neither would she. "I appreciate what you did for me and regret any inconvenience my actions may have caused you, Mr. Collingswood, but now I insist that we go our separate ways."

"Come, come, Tillie. I beg you to be reasonable."

Tara was completely unprepared for the sudden alteration in Grant's tone and taken aback by the humble entreaty in his voice. "I've behaved badly, I know, but you are cruel to dismiss our marriage as if it were naught but an inconvenience."

Blue eyes dark with appeal, an agitated hand rubbing across his strong jaw, Grant looked sincerely wounded. Tara didn't quite know how to take this new tactic, and she simply stared. "After all," he went on, "it was you, not I, who demanded we be wed."

"I did no such thing," Tara sputtered, still not sure what he was trying to accomplish with this ridiculous speech. But she was sure of one thing. The damnable man was a very good actor, although why he had chosen to play this pathetic role was beyond her. Such heartfelt pleading would have no effect on her whatsoever, and he would soon find that out.

Waving the gun at him, she commanded, "Will you kindly remove yourself."

"If you had not pressed me so, demanded I do the right thing by you," Grant whined beseechingly, "I would have been content for you to remain my mistress. Please, sweetheart. Don't throw me over for that scoundrel."

"I reckon you should just pick her up and take her to bed, mister," a booming voice sounded from behind Tara, making her jump. At the same moment, a huge, pawlike hand reached over her shoulder and plucked the derringer away from her. Tara gaped as a gigantic barrel-chested man tossed her weapon over to Grant.

"Your gal sure is a high and mighty one," the giant

declared. "But the worst thing you can do is to beg a woman like that. Her kind don't respect a man lest he beats her so's she plays dumb, and fucks her so's she's blind to any other."

That said, he lumbered past Grant, calling back jovially over his shoulder, "I gave you your chance, young fella. Now take her inside and do one or t'other. I favor a good beatin' myself."

"You wouldn't dare!" Tara gasped, retreating as swiftly as Grant advanced.

"Sounds like good advice to me," Grant confessed irritably, closing the space between them in two strides. With the fingers of one hand curled over her wrist, preventing her escape, he pried the key out of her closed fist with the other.

"Let go of me!"

Grant shook his head. "You can scream if it will make you feel any better, Tillie," he remarked conversationally, dragging her unwilling body the few feet back to her cabin. "I can't wait to hear what suggestions we'll get from our outspoken fellow passengers should you try that."

"What kind of an animal are you?" Tara cried out in desperation as Grant unlocked the cabin door and thrust her effortlessly inside.

After closing and relocking the door, he turned around and looked at her, his flinty blue eyes boring into her anxious green ones. "Where are you headed?"

"Fort Benton," Tara admitted without thinking, trying hard not to reveal her trepidation.

Upon hearing her response, Grant expelled a resigned breath and spoke in a low, raw voice. "In two thousand miles, my dear wife, you're bound to find out exactly what kind of animal I am."

Chapter

Four

"Why are you doing this?" Tara backed farther into the
cabin, staring at the man who blocked the door. In her haste
to put more distance between them, she almost tripped over
a large wooden trunk of her belongings that she'd paid in
advance to have transported aboard and which was now
sitting in the center of the floor.

To hide the trembling in her legs, she sat down abruptly
on the trunk. "You can't do this," she revised, shakily.

"It's already done," Grant replied with finality, surveying
the simple furnishings of the cabin as he pocketed her key.
The room was paneled in knotty pine and held a double
berth, washstand, large cherry wardrobe, and three-drawer
chest all anchored to the narrow-planked floor. A small table
and two chairs were placed beneath the transom window.

Nodding his head in satisfaction, he said, "These accommodations should serve us both very well."

"They will serve me very well," Tara persisted, telling
herself that her best defense was in acting as if she still
occupied a superior position. Anger also helped to defuse
her fear, and if she meant to hold her own with this high-
handed scoundrel, she couldn't give in to that debilitating
emotion.

Grant tried not to smile at the picture she made. She looked like an affronted princess regally perched on a makeshift throne, about to order his immediate beheading. Mathilda Pauline, the name he had called her, meant "small, queenly warrior," and it suited her perfectly. He wondered if her real name fit her as well. He also wondered what she'd say if he told her that part of his name meant "determined protector."

The smile he could no longer resist creased his lips as he thought about his unexpected association with her. Perhaps their meeting had been predestined. He had good reason to believe in fate. "Portraying your husband should prove highly interesting."

Tara shivered as Grant's eyes delved into hers, but her tone was still challenging as she said, "You shall never know, Mr. Collingswood."

Grant admired her pluck. It gave her a dimension that more often than not he'd found missing in members of her sex. Her fiery nature intrigued him almost as much as her provocative beauty. Watching her face, a spear of desire stabbed through him. Very soon he would have this tiny bundle of womanhood naked in his bed.

He savored the thought, but his smooth expression didn't alter. "You'd be wise to accept this situation and me." He pronounced the words like an edict, knowing she would fight him, and surprised at how much he was looking forward to the fight.

Mathilda challenged him in a way no woman ever had, presented a puzzle that with each passing moment he was more anxious to solve. One moment she acted the lady, and the next she was a beautiful but devious adventuress with far more daring than sense. He perceived a wildness inside her that would incite any man to tame, yet also an innocence that called for soft handling. Under present circumstances, he decided it would be to his advantage to begin with a gentle hand and save the taming for later.

"This solution will solve both of our problems," he pointed out equitably.

"Yours, perhaps," Tara retorted in precisely the tone Grant expected. Fists clenched, she hopped back to her feet, her small body vibrating with frustration. "But not mine, so

I suggest you leave before I summon the captain and have you thrown out."

A crackling tension gathered between them as they searched each other's face for any sign of weakness. To his astonishment, Grant realized that the deadly stare that had struck fear in the souls of many a stout-hearted man was having little or no effect on the feminine slip of outrage who stood before him. Indeed, if the daggers shooting from her eyes could cause physical damage, he would lie mortally wounded. She didn't realize that she couldn't win against him no matter what she tried.

"You need me, Tillie," he persisted, but his patience was wearing thin.

"I don't."

Grant suppressed a powerful urge to shake her. "You do!"

Her eyes denied him, flashed mutinous fire.

"Shall I prove it?"

Tara gaped at him, all of her nerves screaming in alarm as she felt his gaze rake insolently over her body. She analyzed the chiseled contours of his face, the determination in his eyes, and the queer fluttering inside her breast gave way to something else. She was frightened of his challenge, but in some deep corner of her soul she was completely unafraid. For a brief moment, she sensed that in dealing with him, all that was feminine in her was not a weakness but her only strength. Unfortunately, that feeling fled the moment he stepped closer.

"Touch me and I'll . . . I'll . . ." Tara's threat trailed off into nothing. If he chose to attack her, how could she stop him? What could she do? He was so big, so strong. Much stronger than . . .

Grant nodded as her expression changed. "Now you're beginning to understand the import of what's going on here."

"All I understand is that you're an arrogant, deceitful coward, so low you'd take advantage of a helpless woman," she blustered, throwing insults at him since she could find nothing else near enough at hand to throw.

When that tactic failed, she tried to appeal to his sense of honor. "You may speak like a cultured gentleman, but if you lay one hand on me, you'll be no better than those filthy, uncivilized men on deck.''

"Since you speak like a cultured lady but don't behave like one, I may have to lay both hands on you," Grant taunted silkily.

"You're . . . you are—"

"Yes? What else am I?"

As she stood toe to toe with him, Tara's throat went dry. "It's not fair!" she cried out. "If I were a man, you wouldn't attempt something like this."

"If you were a man, there'd be no need." Grant reached for her, keeping her in place with his hands on her arms. "Men respond to logic."

Tara's eyes locked with his as she geared herself up for battle. Then, when she saw there was nothing threatening in Grant's gaze, her muscles relaxed and her mouth dropped open. Grant's blue eyes were full of warmth, his lips curved upward in an indulgent smile. Her own eyes widened in surprise.

"Any man would want you, Tillie," he murmured softly as his arm came around her waist. "Would want much more from you than I am prepared to take to prove my point."

Tara's heart began pounding so loudly she could feel it in every limb. He was going to kiss her, she knew. Inexplicably, instead of being afraid or outraged by his arrogance, she was avidly curious. How would a man like Grant Collingswood kiss?

At the first touch of his mouth on hers, she realized she had never been properly kissed before, not even by her fiancé. Grant made no concessions for her youth, her inexperience, or the difference in their size. Yet, strangely, she wasn't repulsed by his attentions. He was giving her an in-depth sample of male passion, and Tara found that she liked it. He caught her lips as if they had been created solely for his pleasure and launched a thoroughly intimate exploration. With his tongue, he traced the soft flesh he had captured, seeking, caressing, tantalizing.

Tara gasped as her lips tingled and burned, then parted in pleasure. For the first time in her life, she experienced invasion, could feel a man's tongue searching that which, before this moment, had been the inviolate sanctuary of her mouth. Her reaction was wholly instinctive and as shocking as the thrusting feel of him inside her.

She felt the pounding of her heart in her breasts which were pressed against Grant's chest. She felt it in the heated rush of blood racing through her veins. But most of all, she felt the wild, wonderful sensation in that secret, shameful place between her legs. As the hot, moist pulsing intensified, she felt an aching weakness in her limbs, a strong urge to melt against him, prop herself up with his strength.

She didn't think to struggle, forgot that each spurt of pleasure she was experiencing was an insult not to be tolerated. She gave herself up to these wondrous new feelings, her lips clinging to his in convulsive response. Her fingers spread across his chest, tingled with the heat of his body.

Grant ended the kiss abruptly, dropping his arms and thrusting her away without any warning. Tara blinked up at him, bemused for an instant. She bit back the whimper of protest that hovered on her lips when he took a hasty step backward.

Grant cleared his throat and shoved his hands into the front pockets of his coat. Good God! The woman was lucky he didn't take her right now. "How old are you?" he growled.

"Eighteen," Tara mumbled, staring dazedly at the hard mouth she still wanted, the blue eyes that burned into her face with a fire she still felt throughout her being.

Grant clenched his fists. His attempt to prove that she needed him had backfired right in his face, and if she didn't stop looking at him as if she were dying for more of his kisses, he was doomed to give them to her, no matter how young she was. And if he touched her again, he wouldn't be content with just her mouth.

Irritated by his fierce physical reaction to her, Grant spoke in a harsh tone. "This boat is carrying close to two hundred passengers, Tillie, most of them men. What I just did is nothing compared with what some of them would try. Do you still think you can prevent an assault?"

Too shaken to reply, Tara stumbled away from him. Covering her burning face with her hands, she sank down on the berth. She hated to admit it, but Grant had just proved, and very effectively, that she was indeed fair game for any unscrupulous ruffian who made up his mind to have her. He had also proved something else that she found even more daunting.

In one respect, Grant was the least of many evils, but in another the greatest threat of all. He had kissed her to demonstrate her vulnerability where other men were concerned, yet with all of her being she yearned for him to kiss her again. She couldn't understand what had happened to her. How could she have responded so wantonly to a man she hardly knew and certainly didn't trust?

"The only way you'll be safe for the remainder of this journey is if I move in here and our fellow passengers think you belong to me." Grant made no attempt to approach her again, sensing she would eventually give in if only he could alleviate her anxiety concerning his motives. To do that, he was prepared to lie through his teeth.

"All I want in exchange for my offer of protection is a decent place to sleep and somewhere to store my belongings where they won't get stolen. You'll be perfectly safe."

Tara forced herself to look at him, to respond to his brusquely spoken statement. "You've done nothing to prove I'd be safer with you than anyone else. Why should I believe anything you say?"

She was right to worry, Grant knew, but he replied, "All I can say, Tillie, is you're damned lucky you chose me instead of someone else for your foolish antics today. If you didn't like my little demonstration, believe me, you'll like the real thing even less. Think of how I might have reacted to what you pulled on me today, then consider what I've actually done. You have to admit, you've gotten off very easy."

Tara knew he spoke the truth, but she still didn't trust him. Beyond the obvious problems she could foresee if they shared a cabin was the discomfiting knowledge that all he'd had to do was kiss her, and she'd taken total leave of her senses. The thought of how she might react if he kissed her again scared her to death. As she considered one humiliating possibility after another, she nibbled on her lower lip.

Grant assumed she was wavering. "All I want from you is a share in these accommodations."

Tara's flush was painful in its intensity. "And you . . . you wouldn't . . . ?"

"At thirty, I have neither the desire nor the patience to tutor an untried virgin," Grant lied, guessing the trend of her thoughts. "When a woman comes to my bed, she knows not only how to receive pleasure but how to give it. I'm well past the age when I'd find it entertaining to seduce a child."

"Oh!" Tara was stung by his scathing assessment of her. It was true she was young and had a limited knowledge of lovemaking, but she wasn't a child. Perhaps she had responded naively, but Grant's assault on her senses had taken her unawares. As great as the relief she felt that he didn't consider her behavior wanton was the damage sustained to her feminine pride.

Not just Louden but several other handsome young men had paid court to her after her coming out, and none of them had insulted her as Grant just had. They had been grateful for her slightest touch, had begged for the honor of bestowing a chaste kiss on her cheek.

It was painfully apparent that after stealing a kiss that could never be called chaste, Grant wasn't the least bit enamored of her charms. Still, what other choice did she have but to accept his offer of protection? It was either that or risk being brutally assaulted.

Her decision was given in a sullen tone. "You'll have to request a cot unless you want to sleep on the floor."

"Fine." Grant strode toward the door so she wouldn't see the triumph in his eyes. "I'm going to retrieve my belongings from the purser. Bolt the door when I leave, Tillie, and don't open it again until you hear me knock three times."

"Surely I'll be safe in my own cabin!"

"You'll be safe when you start doing exactly what I say." Grant's lips thinned with annoyance. "At the midday meal, we'll establish you as my wife. Until then, you'll stay in here with the door locked."

Tara didn't care for his arrogant tone, even if she could see a certain wisdom in his plan. She'd already taken quite enough orders from him today. "I'll do that, but not because you have any right to tell me what to do. Don't forget, you have yet to prove yourself to me. How do I know this pretend marriage of ours will have the results you suggest?

I've noticed several men aboard who look perfectly capable of breaking you in half without the slightest exertion.''

That wild flare came into his deep blue eyes but was quickly extinguished. "We'll discuss your rights and mine when I return with my baggage," Grant promised caustically, fists clenched.

"Yes we will," Tara shot back with equal spirit as he wrenched open the door, stalked through it, then slammed it closed with a vicious backhand. Eyes wide, Tara stared at the trembling door frame for a long time.

He had a violent temper! Apparently, her intimation that he might come out a poor second in a fight with another man had highly provoked him. What other things would she learn about him in the next two months?

"Tillie!"

Tara jumped at the hoarse bellow. She got to the door just before it opened and Grant thrust his head inside.

"I told you to bolt it!" he ground out. "What the hell are you waiting for?"

Tara arched an imperious brow, her voice dripping acid. "I'm waiting for you to leave, and there's no need to curse. Any man who intends to portray himself as my husband will behave as a gentleman or find himself minus a place to sleep."

"Why, you—" Grant bit off the furious words he was about to utter. To put up with her, he was going to have to acquire not only the virtue but also the patience of a saint.

"This time, lock the door," he suggested wearily as he withdrew his head.

It took almost a full minute before he heard the bolt slip into place. The sigh of relief that escaped his lungs irked him almost as much as the woman who had inspired it. If she had this strong an effect on him after an hour in her company, what kind of shape would he be in after two months?

He was still grumbling to himself as he reached the stairs winding down to the lower deck. He needed a cabin but wasn't sure he could contend with the willful woman who came with it. He couldn't afford any distractions from the course he'd set for himself on this trip, and Mathilda was proving to be just that.

What infuriated him more than the intense desire he had

to endure whenever he looked at her was that he'd known she was trouble from the very first, and he'd still chosen to get involved with her. Not only that, but he would probably enjoy every minute of it. He'd relished that confrontation with Snedeker far too much. When he'd curled his fingers around the smooth handle of his revolver, he'd felt a familiar blood lust singing in his veins. It was a good thing for both of them that Snedeker had backed off when he had.

Moreover, he knew, even if Tillie didn't, that the odds of his being called upon to act on her behalf again were very high. Rather than putting him off, he took real pleasure in the knowledge. He was a gentleman by name, a gambler by trade, but neither by nature.

Grant shook his head in self-disgust. After spending eight years in England, enjoying the peaceful life of the landed gentry, Grant had to admit that his appetite for danger didn't appear to have diminished one whit. Nor had he changed his mind concerning the roles men and women should play in the world. No matter how modern society viewed things, it still came down to survival of the fittest. The way he saw it, a beautiful woman like Mathilda should be awarded the man who could demonstrate he was the fittest of all.

Grant took a deep breath as he came to a stop before the purser's cabin. Such thinking was dangerous. Not in thought or deed could he reveal that he was anything but what he appeared to be on the surface—a ne'er-do-well gentleman gambler who had something in common with the majority of other men on board, a greedy eye looking out for Montana gold.

Chapter

Five

Tara removed her bonnet and washed her heated face and hands at the washstand. She was about to open her trunk in order to hang up her dresses in the wardrobe when she noticed a list of regulations tacked up on the back of the cabin door. The rules were mainly directed to gentlemen, but since there appeared to be so few of them aboard, Tara doubted they were much heeded.

According to what she read, "gentlemen" were forbidden to lie down in berths with their boots on, to appear coatless at the table, to whittle or otherwise damage furniture, or to enter a lady's cabin without that lady's consent. When, a few moments later, three knocks came at the door, Tara was tempted to test that last rule and forbid Grant reentry, but she couldn't dredge up the courage.

"They have sounded the dinner gong," Grant announced as he walked into the cabin and dropped two large leather satchels on the floor next to her trunk. Straightening up, he saw that she had removed her bonnet, and the sight gave him pause. Swiftly, he averted his eyes from her glorious ringlets of flame-colored hair, fighting the sudden urge to release it from the confines of its tight chignon and comb his fingers through it.

"Shall we go, my dear?" he inquired tightly.

Tara ignored the endearment and nodded, very relieved to put off the time when they would be confined together inside the small cabin. "I am famished," she declared truthfully.

"It has been a long morning," Grant agreed, noting her wary gaze on his belongings and understanding her unease. To prevent her from dwelling too long on the intimacy of their upcoming living arrangements, he gallantly offered her his arm. "We won't find the gracious fare available on the Mississippi packets, but neither shall we starve."

As they made their way through the unsavory crowd on the lower deck, Tara was grateful for Grant's presence beside her, but once they'd entered the equally crowded dining salon, she realized that she could take all of her future meals alone without fear of being accosted. The full-fare passengers were of a much better class than those roaming the decks in steerage, and other than a few polite nods, her entrance prompted very little notice.

The salon itself served as a combination dining room and parlor and was decorated in a surprisingly ornamental manner. It had an air of spaciousness because of its height and vaulting, although it was not very wide. The ceiling was decorated with frescoes and rosettes, all painted in rich colors, and every few feet there was a hanging lantern. The side walls were walnut inlaid with ebony panels. A cluster of sturdy chairs and several gaming tables were placed in the foresection. Off to the right of the tables was a bar, presenting sparkling glassware, liquor bottles, and a huge cracked mirror.

In the stern of the saloon was a currently unoccupied section with a sign that said it was reserved for ladies. In contrast to the masculine accoutrements at the head of the room, this narrow portion was decorated with light rosewood furniture and a bright floral carpet. Hanging over the partition to the ladies' section was the religious inscription, "Where Will You Spend Eternity?" cut out of stained glass.

Tara glanced over at her escort and murmured feelingly, "A highly pertinent question."

"What is?" Grant inquired.

Tara gave a dismissing wave of her hand, disregarding his intense scrutiny as he guided her between tables. Locating one that didn't have any other occupants, he declared, "This will suit," not bothering to ask her opinion, which only increased Tara's estimation of his supreme arrogance.

"I see no reason for us to continue this sham any further," she stated heatedly as soon as they were seated. "You have misled me into believing that my virtue would be in constant danger throughout this trip. Yet I can see by our present company that this is obviously not the case. If I remain among these gentlemen, I shall be perfectly safe."

"Perhaps," Grant conceded, tired of arguing the same point with her again. "If you want to take chances with your very delectable person, go ahead."

Flustered by his impertinent comment, she retorted, "I don't see that the risk to my person would be any greater than the one I'm taking in agreeing to your indecent proposal!"

Completely unmoved by her indignation, Grant shrugged. "Very well. If you need more proof, after we have eaten, you can return to our cabin alone."

"So I shall," Tara declared. "And if I have no trouble getting there, I will expect you to find other accommodations."

Grant agreed to her proposal without the slightest protest, and Tara's confidence swiftly diminished. It was plain that he didn't think he had anything to worry about, which made Tara think that she did. "Surely the captain of this boat has taken measures to ensure that his female passengers won't be attacked."

"You can make up your own mind about that, Tillie," Grant said as he stood up to greet the man approaching their table. "Captain Cyrus Randolph, allow me to present my wife, Mathilda Collingswood."

Tara was about to deny Grant's introduction of her as his wife when she heard a vile splat and realized that the captain had just spit a mouthful of tobacco juice perilously close to her shoes. Startled by the man's uncouth manners, she remained speechless as he dragged a nearby chair across the polished maple floor and sat himself down at their table. Well past fifty, Randolph had a leathery face with full jowls, thinning gray hair, and yellowed teeth. The rest of his robust body was clothed in a soiled, mis-buttoned wool uniform which looked as if it had been purchased before the man had gained his majority.

"So this is the new bride. Glad to have you aboard, ma'am," he boomed loudly, reaching across the table to pick up her hand. He shook it with a vigorous pumping motion that made her whole body vibrate, his brown eyes seemingly fascinated by the jiggling movement of her firm, young breasts. "Your man tells me you're going clean up to Fort Benton. Cain't say as we've ever had a real refined lady like yourself signed on for the whole trip. 'Ceptin' for the homesteaders' wives, most womenfolk leave off by St. Joe. The going gets pretty rough past there, and I cain't see to their creature comforts like I do on the early part of the run."

"I'm sure I'll be very comfortable." Tara tried to retrieve her hand, but the man held fast.

"Well, don't say I didn't warn ya, little lady," Randolph advised gruffly. "Once we cross the Platte, this here room is open to all and sundry. I cain't hardly bar a man from coming in when he's providing our food, hauling wood for fuel, and tuggin' on a line to get us off the mud. Gotta count on my passengers, cuz no river's worse to travel than the Big Muddy where the water's too thick to drink and too thin to plow."

At long last, he dropped her hand to smack Grant roughly on the shoulder. "Yup, you done yourself right proud with your bride, young fella. But if you've a mind to keep her 'til the Fort, you'd best make sure your pistol's always loaded."

In a conspiratorial aside, he whispered, " 'Case you're wondering, I'm referrin' to the kind that shoots bullets."

With a last hearty chuckle, he scraped back his chair, spit on the floor, and departed for the next table. Grant acted as if he hadn't noticed Tara's appalled reaction to the captain's behavior as their waiter arrived and served them a plate of cold sliced pork, a portion of navy beans, and two bowls of curdled rice pudding, but her face was still ashen when he handed her a cup of thick black coffee.

"Drink up," he suggested. "It looks like you could use a strong dose of intestinal fortitude."

Tara had gulped down half of the nasty-tasting liquid

before she found her voice. "H-how could that . . . that vulgar man ever qualify for his commission as an officer?"

"He's not in the navy, Tillie, and we're not on the high seas. Anyone with enough money to buy a boat can set himself up as a riverboat captain. Randolph doesn't have a master's license or even a certificate of rating. Nevertheless, as soon as we left port, he became the legal authority over all passengers and crew."

"Saints preserve us," Tara breathed incredulously.

"I am trying," Grant reminded her, his mouth split in an audacious grin.

Tara fought down an answering smile. Besides being the most handsome, Grant Collingswood was the most conceited man she'd ever met, and she refused to add even more size to his head. "I may know little or nothing about you, Mr. Collingswood, but I do know that you are no saint."

"Then we are well matched, Mrs. Collingswood," Grant said, still smiling. "For though I know equally as little about you, I highly suspect that you are no angel."

Having spent many frustrating years trying to behave like one, but with little success, Tara was surprised to be so pleased by his assessment. Maybe it was because his blue eyes revealed such open admiration. Even though she took his words as a compliment, it wouldn't do to let him know it, so she hid her reaction behind a contemptuous question. "Besides telling the captain that we are newly wed, what other lies have you told him?"

"None greater than those you wished me to tell Mr. Snedeker."

Tara flushed at his rebuke, knowing she deserved it. "Fair enough," she acknowledged meekly, and she lowered her eyes to her plate. For several uncomfortable minutes, silence prevailed between them until Tara could stand it no more. "*If* I decide to go along with this charade, I should know more about you."

"I'm sure that between the two of us we'll be able to concoct a plausible-sounding story."

The man was as closed-mouthed as she was, Tara realized, and her curiosity about him increased. "Might I ask why you are making this arduous journey?"

Grant took several bites of his meal before answering.

"For the same reason as most everyone else. I intend to seek my fortune in the goldfields."

Tara's brow furrowed skeptically. "You don't look much like a miner."

Grant inclined his head. "And you don't look much like an escaped fugitive."

"I'm not!"

"Then why are you being chased by the likes of Snedeker?"

Unwilling to disclose more about herself until she knew more about him, Tara lied, "The man obviously mistook me for someone else."

"Obviously," Grant drawled mockingly.

"I am not a thief!"

"If you say so," Grant replied with an uncaring shrug that left Tara fuming. Silence prevailed again, but this time she was determined not to be the first to break it, and she wasn't. After his request for more coffee was met by the waiter, Grant continued their aborted conversation.

"I suppose there are some who might call me a thief as well," he admitted. "I'm a gambler by trade, and those who dislike acknowledging my greater skill often complain that I've purloined their money."

"You're naught but a riverboat gambler!"

Grant's brows rose at her horrified outcry. "And what manner of woman are you to pass judgment? In our brief acquaintance, you have yet to demonstrate any close association with those of lofty principle. As far as I know, you're naught but a light-fingered, scheming adventuress."

Tara was about to respond to his insulting accusation when she felt a cold, creeping sensation raise the hairs on the back of her neck. Turning her head, her eyes swiftly scanned the transom windows that lined the cabin walls. As if pulled by the power of a magnet, her searching gaze found the beady eyes of Amos Snedeker.

"Oh no!" she gasped, turning back around before the detective could see how strongly his presence affected her.

"Oh yes," Grant snarled, unaware that she was reacting to something other than his denouncement of her morals. "And until you prove otherwise, I will continue to act on that assumption."

Tara fought to control the fear that coiled in her stomach like a viperous snake. Somehow, Snedeker had managed to pay his way on board! For a time, only first-class passengers were allowed entry into the main salon, so he couldn't confront her now, but eventually he would find some means to waylay her. Moreover, if the man could convince Captain Randolph that she was a wanted criminal, she could be taken into custody and escorted off the boat at the next port of call.

Terrified by that prospect, Tara knew she had no choice but to plead for Grant's help. "When we get back to my cabin, I'll tell you anything you wish to know," she promised.

Grant was taken aback by her sudden need to be more forthcoming. "Anything?"

Tara nodded, then challenged, "But only if you can guarantee my protection for the remainder of our journey."

"Haven't I told you I would?"

Wondering how many other men might be chasing her, she replied, "It is not your willingness I question but your capability."

Beneath the table, Grant's hands clenched into fists. He had no idea why this woman continually questioned his ability to protect her, but he could see by her dubious expression that she did. Since he'd told her of his occupation, he'd obviously lost respect in her eyes, and apparently her lack of regard now extended to his physical prowess as well. If she knew the number of men he had killed with less cause, she wouldn't have dared insult his manhood like this.

Standing up from his chair, he stepped across to her side of the table and took a firm grip on her arm. "As your husband, I would have a sworn duty to protect you," he informed her through gritted teeth.

"As your wife," Tara said, reluctantly accepting both aspects of his offer, "I will expect you to uphold that vow, though you have yet to prove that you are equal to the task."

Grant guided her, none too gently, toward the door. Once they were back inside the cabin, he seated himself on one of the chairs and posed his first question. "So what did you steal?"

Green eyes glittering with vexation, Tara burst out,

"Nothing that wasn't mine. I sold some of my jewelry to pay for my passage, but the pieces were mine to sell. The accusations against me are just a ruse made up by my . . . mother to prevent me from escaping the despicable fate she has arranged for me."

Hearing her melodramatic tone, Grant suspected that he was about to be handed another pack of inventive lies by this lovely, deceitful young minx. Prepared to be amused, he kept his expression bland. "And what fate would that be?"

Wringing her hands together, Tara sat down on her trunk. As yet, she was afraid to tell him the whole truth behind her flight from the wealthy Wainwrights of Connecticut, afraid to admit to the small fortune she had hidden in the false bottom of her trunk in case Grant revealed himself as a totally dishonorable man. Considering his disreputable profession, he might not be able to resist the urge to stake himself with some of her money.

Still, if he had one shred of male integrity, even half of the story she intended to tell should arouse his sympathies, and with Snedeker on board she desperately needed Grant's help. Forcing a shimmer of tears into her eyes, she began her tale of woe.

"My name is Taralynn, Taralynn Wainwright, and I'm the only child of a very wealthy Connecticut family. My—"

"Taralynn," Grant interrupted her. "Mmmm . . . Mrs. Taralynn Collingswood. I like that much better than Tillie. Much more refined, don't you think?"

Exasperated, Tara snapped, "My name hardly matters!"

"On the contrary," Grant disagreed. "As Cervantes said in *Don Quixote,* a good name is better than riches. Of course, now that we've called you Mathilda in front of the captain, we'll have to continue calling you that."

The man was well read, which should be a point in his favor, Tara supposed, but at the moment she wasn't inclined to commend him on anything. She was attempting to outline her pathetic plight, and he could at least have the good grace to listen. "Do you wish to hear the rest of my explanation or not?"

Grant noticed that the shimmer of tears in her eyes had

quickly changed to the glow of temper, and he couldn't suppress his grin. "Oh, I do," he insisted.

Doing her best to bring back the distress that had marked her features and tone before being so rudely interrupted, she passed a trembling hand over her brow. "My . . . my parents were forcing me to marry a man I despise, a distant cousin, simply because he is the only living male who yet carries our family name."

Voice breaking pitifully, she continued, "Louden is old and fat and incredibly pompous, but my parents don't care about that or about me. All they care about is ensuring that our family estate will always be occupied by Wainwrights. They would sacrifice all for this cause, but I can't spend the rest of my days tied to a man I can never love, especially when I . . ."

Concealing the fact that her former fiancé was neither old nor fat but young and almost as handsome as Grant, she folded her arms defensively over her breasts. As she went on with her story, however, her shudder of revulsion was real and added truth to her claims. "I feel nauseated if Louden so much as touches me. His hands are cold and clammy . . . and he . . . frightens me. I couldn't marry him. I just couldn't, so I ran away."

Tara closed her eyes. She didn't have to fake the fear and humiliation that washed over her as she remembered the last time she'd been alone with Louden. He'd drunk far too much brandy at their prenuptial dinner, and she'd agreed that a walk outside would help to sober him. They'd strolled farther and farther away from the house until they reached the isolated gazebo in the center of the vast estate gardens. Apparently, since their marriage was only a day away, Louden had suddenly felt free to take liberties he'd never tried before. All during their lengthy courtship, he'd been gentle and polite, so tender in words and circumspect in behavior that she'd begun to question if he desired her at all. That night, he'd put an end to her questions.

It was as if the alcohol he'd consumed, combined with the sight of her firm breasts rising above the green satin bodice of her gown, had unleashed all his moral restraint. Pulling her into his arms, he'd planted a very wet kiss on her mouth, then whispered words that had shocked her to the core.

48

Pale blue eyes gleaming with lust, he'd promised drunkenly, "Oh, yes, once I have you naked and on our marriage bed, I shall teach you the full meaning of pleasure. When you're hot enough for me, I'll thrust inside you, branding you as my property."

Lips frothing with moisture, he'd brought her closer, grinding his pelvis against her as he squeezed her breast painfully. At the feel of his cold hand groping her, reading the intent in his eyes as he lowered his head toward her bosom, Tara had recoiled from him in horror and pulled out of his arms. "No, Louden! You can't!"

In a cruel tone that he'd never used before, he'd taunted, "From now on, I can and I will do whatever I like to you. You are bought and paid for, my dear, sold to me by your loving mother."

As she'd turned away toward the house, Louden had laughed and called after her, "Tomorrow night, you shan't run, my fiery little virgin. Tomorrow night, you will lie still like a dutiful wife and open your legs to all my very special attentions."

That night, she had learned more than one horrifying truth about Louden. He not only possessed a streak of latent cruelty, but he had never loved her, only the fortune she represented. Once they were married, all she would be to him was a possession to do with as he willed, and he'd left her in no doubt of his intentions. No, she couldn't go back to Laurel Glen. Not ever!

Opening her eyes, she said, "I have relatives in Montana Territory who will take me in. If I can reach them, I'll be safe from Louden and my parents."

Having watched the vivid emotions pass over her face as she recalled some frightening experience, Grant found himself half believing her story. "My offer still stands," he assured her. "As long as we're together, no one shall harm you."

"Thank you," Tara said softly, then cleared her throat to make her tone more forceful. "But you might not feel the same way when I tell you that Snedeker followed me on board. I saw him staring at us through the transom while we were eating. He will try to have me removed from the boat before we pass out of his jurisdiction. He's been paid a great deal of money to drag me back to Laurel Glen.''

Grant shrugged, and Tara couldn't tell what that meant. Either he didn't consider the matter his concern, or he didn't find the prospect of another confrontation with Snedeker much of a threat. For all she knew, Grant might decide to assist the detective in having her removed from the boat so he could have a first-class cabin all to himself.

''I'll pay you more to make sure that he doesn't succeed,'' Tara tacked on hastily, fearing the worst.

When all she got in return for her generous offer was a blank stare, she opened her reticule and drew out a velvet bag. She tossed it in the air so he would hear the heavy clink of gold coin. ''This should be enough to stake you at the gaming tables from here to Montana and back again.''

Grant shook his head. The naive little fool had no idea how dangerous it was to flash her money around like that. If he was anything like a goodly number of the other passengers, he'd have relieved her of both her purse and her virginity by now. And she was a virgin, a very high-spirited, defiant virgin but an innocent nevertheless. He was even more sure of that now than he'd been when he'd kissed her.

Standing up from his chair, Grant held out his palm.

Tara stared at it, then gazed up at his face. ''You're agreeing to my offer?''

''Exactly how much is in there?''

Suddenly, Tara realized that she had no guarantee that after she gave the bag of coins over to him, he wouldn't turn her over to Snedeker. Slipping her free hand inside her reticule, she searched for her derringer, then remembered that he'd taken it away from her. Whatever he chose to do now, she was completely defenseless.

Donning a cloak of false bravado, she replied shortly, ''Enough to pay you five hundred dollars for your services.''

Grant strove to appear impressed by a figure that could be won or lost in the first few rounds of a game of cards. ''That much?''

Assuming she had managed to trap him with his own greed but still not sure if he could be relied on to hold up his end of the bargain, she proposed, ''Yes, and I will pay half now and the other half once we reach Fort Benton.''

Grant's lips twitched as she hopped off the trunk and stood toe to toe with him once again. She really was a feisty little thing, and he couldn't help but admire her courage. It was such a rare trait in a female. "Agreed," he announced, fighting laughter. "You may consider me in your employ."

Tara heard the amusement in his voice and didn't like it, but there wasn't much she could do about it since she needed him so badly. As businesslike as possible, she opened the bag and counted out two hundred fifty dollars' worth of gold coins into his palm, then let him know that she still didn't trust him one whit. "Then, as your employer, I would appreciate it if you would escort me to the purser's cabin. I wish to place the rest of my funds in his safekeeping."

Grant offered her his arm. "A very wise decision. One never knows what kind of unsavory types might be aboard. Being temporarily short on funds myself, even I might be tempted to request a loan against my future salary."

Tara's knowing sniff was so slight she didn't think Grant would hear it, but he did. "Of course, by journey's end, I'm sure to find other compensations for whatever I may lose at the tables."

Tara's spine went stiff at his suggestive words, and her pulse jumped at the feel of her arm pressed against the hard wall of his chest. "I'd advise you not to wager too much on that assumption, Mr. Collingswood."

"Don't worry about me, Mrs. Collingswood," Grant admonished, patting her hand. "The only games I enter are those I stand a good chance of winning."

Chapter

Six

Late that night, Tara stood at the transom window of her cabin and stared out at the moonlit river. Only the ripples of water breaking on the shore disturbed the quiet of the evening. Tara's thoughts were not nearly so restful.

Since river travel was far too treacherous after dark, the *Ophelia* had been anchored for several hours, but Grant had still not returned from the main saloon, and Tara knew she wouldn't be able to sleep until he did. She was far too fearful of what he might do once he joined her. It was true that they'd struck an agreement that made him her employee, but the terms of their contract cast him in the role of her husband, and throughout the remainder of the day he had thrown himself wholeheartedly into the part.

As they strolled the upper deck, he had used any excuse to hold her hand or drape an affectionate arm over her shoulders. When introducing her to people, the expression on his face had been nothing short of adoring, and at supper his attendance on her had prompted several envious stares from the other wives. While in public, Tara had agreed to play the loving bride, but in private she expected Grant to keep a respectful distance. Unfortunately, the amorous gleam in his eye whenever he looked at her made her doubt that he would hold to that expectation.

The cabin held only one berth, and though Grant had unpacked his valises and stored his belongings next to hers in the wardrobe and chest, as far as she knew, he had made no provisions for a cot to be set up in their room. Tara didn't dare change into her nightgown or even close her eyes until she made certain that Grant wasn't planning to share a bed as well as storage space.

Unfamiliar with Missouri River travel, Tara had no idea that the first night out was a time for revelry. While she paced away the evening hours in their cabin, Grant was happily imbibing from the cask of contraband whiskey that the crew had broken open just for the occasion. Though a government edict prohibited the introduction of liquor into Indian country, it was far and away the most important cargo on upriver boats. Indians wanted firewater and would trade with anybody who supplied it.

By midnight, Grant was drunk enough to require nothing more than a few hours of peaceful oblivion before the next day began, but to make sure that his lustful urges were completely doused before he returned to the cabin, he tipped a few glasses more. He had gone far too long without a woman, but if he didn't want to lose his right to a cabin, he must do without a while longer. First, he had to inspire a little trust in his "new bride." Unfortunately, whenever he thought about Tara, he was overwhelmed by the need to make love to her.

An hour later, he lurched down the passageway and stumbled into the cabin. His eyes registered the provocative sight of his curvaceous cabinmate outlined in the moonlight, but his whiskey-logged brain was too benumbed to respond. He heard an outraged gasp, but, wanting nothing more than relief from the dizziness that plagued him, he quickly sought his bed. In moments, he was fast asleep.

Tara stared at him, unable to believe what she was seeing. As if the hard wood offered him the comfort of a soft feather mattress, Grant had stretched out full-length on the floor, fully clothed. With a brief, satisfied snore, he turned onto his side, and then his breathing became deep and regular. Obviously, he was too drunk to know what he was doing, but he would pay for his folly in the morning with some painfully stiff muscles and a crick in his neck.

"And it will serve him right," Tara judged unsympathetically as she gingerly stepped over his supine form. After her last encounter with a drunken man, she heartily disapproved of any form of drink. As far as she was concerned, Grant deserved any and all of the suffering he would endure for his overindulgence, but at least her worries were over for one night.

The next morning, however, Grant was the first one up, and, according to the light in the cabin, it was still early. Completely exhausted, Tara had slept so soundly that nothing could have roused her until after sunrise. Assuming that Grant's slumber had been prematurely interrupted by a bout with nausea, she rolled over in the berth and hid her smile in the pillows. When she heard him pouring water into the washbowl, she peeked through her lashes at him, amazed when he immediately turned around to face her.

"So you're an early riser, too," he declared cheerfully, not exhibiting one sign of stiffness or pain. His blue eyes were clear, without the slightest streak of red, and his complexion wasn't sickly at all. He bent over with ease and washed his face, then began applying the lather he had mixed in his shaving cup onto his stubbled cheeks.

"I'm glad you're not like those women who find it fashionable to waste the better part of each day languishing in bed," he complimented her before turning back to the mirror hung over the washstand.

Coming more awake every moment, Tara saw that Grant's hair was still wet from a recent washing, and he had already changed his clothes. Today he was dressed much more casually in a loose-fitting white shirt rolled up to the elbows and dark breeches that enhanced the look of his well-muscled legs. His feet were bare. Involuntarily, Tara's gaze ran over his body.

With his wide shoulders, narrow hips, and long legs, Grant Collingswood was the embodiment of every schoolgirl's romantic dreams. His hair was as black as gleaming ebony and had a tendency to curl when wet. The planes and angles of his face were elegantly carved. Above a determined chin was a sensual mouth that prompted some less than maidenly dreams about kissing. And, of course, there were his eyes. Set beneath thick black lashes that any female would envy, they were as devastatingly blue as the sky and equally as beautiful.

Tara's face grew hot as she envisioned what he might look like without a shirt. The exposed skin of his throat and arms was dark, and she wondered if it was the same shade all over. Thinking how it might have gotten that way intensified her blush, and then, to her horror, she glimpsed his face in the mirror. Grant was watching her, and his smile was knowing.

Tara was suddenly overwhelmingly aware of how alone they were and how often they would repeat this morning ritual over the next two months. As if she truly were his wife, she would be witness not only to his morning toilette and his sleeping and eating habits but to several other domestic intimacies as well. No matter how she dealt with this situation, by the end of this passage, at least physically, she would know all there was to know about this man, and he would gather the same knowledge about her!

Self-consciously, Tara lifted her hand to her hair, trying to tame the riotous red curls she knew were sticking out all over her head. She must look a sight! At almost the same moment, she felt the need to dive under the covers. Never before in her life had she appeared before a man in nothing but her nightclothes.

"Don't be embarrassed. You look very fetching with your hair down, and that high-necked gown covers everything else you've got to offer," Grant scolded as Tara dragged the quilts up to her neck.

"I . . . I have nothing at all to offer you!"

"Since I'm naught but your lowly employee, I suppose I must abide by that opinion," Grant allowed as he blotted his cheeks with a towel.

Tara wasn't the least bit reassured by his words, but Grant was seemingly unaware of her anxiety. Dropping the towel on the floor, he rolled down his shirtsleeves, then strolled across the room and sat down on the edge of the berth. As Tara propelled herself backward as far as the bedstead would allow, Grant bent over to pull on a pair of ribbed stockings and brown Hessian boots.

Ignoring her action, he stood back up and stamped down on his heels. "Since you're obviously reluctant to get out of bed this morning, I could order breakfast in. Until we reach St. Joseph, first-class passengers are allowed that luxury, and since we're supposed to be newlyweds who are probably tired from all our lusty exertions of last night, it's expected that we would do so. What would you like?"

"Since we are nothing of the sort, I would like for you to leave so I might get dressed!" Tara replied in a breathless, high-pitched tone, her brain reeling with the erotic images his words brought to mind.

Mischievously, Grant dropped back down onto the mattress. He smiled when Tara nervously shifted her legs to avoid touching him. "If I thought the trembling in your body was out of fear for your modesty, I might comply with that request, but we both know that's not what's bothering you. You want me to leave you alone because you can't stop imagining what it would be like if I didn't. Would you like me to tell you or show you?"

"Neither!" Tara squeaked, her face burning hotter and hotter as she reminded him, "Ours is strictly a business agreement."

"True enough," Grant said, prying her clutching hands away from the quilt. Considering that she'd slept contentedly while he'd spent the wee hours of the morning with his head hanging over the chamber pot, he took perverse pleasure in her discomfiture. "But no one will believe we are man and wife if you cower away from me like this whenever I come near you. I can see that in order to play your part convincingly, you're definitely going to need some more practice."

"Don't you dare touch me," Tara warned, but his fingers were already secured around her wrists, and his grin told her that he would dare anything.

"But you want me to. Don't be ashamed of your feelings, Taralynn," Grant drawled, pressing her shoulders back against the pillows with the weight of his body. "I don't know what you've been taught, but they are entirely natural. Such passion in a woman is a virtue, not a sin."

Tara shook her head in denial of his words, showing both her youth and her straitlaced education. "Such feelings are

wicked, and you . . . you are a very wicked man for even
saying such a thing to a lady.''

"But then, you are a very wicked young lady," Grant
teased, just before his mouth descended.

It was worse than the first time he'd kissed her, Tara
thought, for this time a quivering started deep in her belly
and worked its way down her thighs, all the way to her toes.
Crushed against his chest, her breasts ached, pulsing with a
feeling that was like nothing she'd ever known, a feeling that
was so good it had to be sinful. And yet, when she felt his
tongue stroke over her lips, then slide gently inside to run
over the smooth surface of her teeth, she shivered with the
delicious wonder of it.

His mouth felt so warm, so right against her lips. Without
her even realizing that he'd released her wrists, her arms
came up to twine around his neck. She was well beyond
thinking, beyond anything but the molten, spiraling energy
that gathered strength inside her with every kiss and touch
and caress. And he was touching her in places where she
had never been touched, taking greater liberties than Louden
had attempted, and she was letting him.

Somehow, the ribbons at her throat were loosened, and
the tiny buttons down the front of her nightgown were
undone without her uttering a single protest. Tara could feel
his warm fingers lingering over her bared breasts, could feel
her nipples aching with a tension that made her cry out. She
arched her back, instinctively asking for something she knew
only he could provide. Though she should have been suffering from acute shame, when his palms closed over her naked
flesh, she whimpered in pleasure, feeling none of the revulsion she'd felt when Louden had touched her.

Grant swallowed hard as he viewed her naked breasts.
When was the last time he'd felt this burning hunger? he
asked himself. Sexual desire had become nothing but an
irritating itch that needed to be scratched occasionally, and
normally he felt nothing for the women he chose to relieve
it. But now, with Taralynn, it was different.

Kissing her, touching her, watching her slender body
shiver in response, made his head spin. She aroused strong
emotions, both positive and negative, that he simply couldn't

blunt. His jaded senses were alive with feelings and sensations he hadn't experienced since . . .

Grant gave his head a slight shake to clear away the memory. No, it could never be like that for him again! He wanted this woman to want him as badly as he wanted her, but that was all he wanted or needed from her, all he would ever want.

With that resolution firmly in mind, he set himself to the task of giving pleasure. "You're beautiful, Tara," he complimented her, his fingers continuing their sensual play with the sweet feminine curves exposed to his admiring gaze. "Your nipples are such a delicate shade of pink."

Tara drew in a shuddery breath, his shocking words sending currents of heat straight to her most secret places. As his thumbs flicked lightly over the hardened tips of her breasts, she throbbed and squirmed, her brazen body pleading with him to do more, even though her brain knew that what she wanted from him was wrong. She bit down on her lower lip, trying to muster her spinning senses, but then his hands shifted to cup her, testing her weight in his palms.

"Please," she moaned when the kneading motions stopped.

Immediately, Grant caught her nipples between his fingers and gently squeezed. "Do you like that?" he asked, not needing an answer. The frantic beating of her heart told him all he needed to know, and he was quick to increase his advantage.

"Yes, oh yes," Tara moaned as her taut flesh was drawn down the length of his fingers. Then, through a blaze of pleasure, she watched him lower his head, and before she'd recovered from one shockingly pleasurable sensation, he was showing her another. His mouth enclosed one nipple, and his tongue rasped circles around the quivering bud.

Tara gasped at the pulsing spirals of feeling that radiated from her captured nipple. As his teeth punished it with a gentle nip before guiding it deeper into his mouth, her whole body writhed in torment, and her insides turned to liquid as his fingers continued to caress its twin. Tara kept her eyes tightly shut. What she felt was so good that she tried to pretend she wasn't pushing her breast against his hand with wanton need, arching her back to increase the pressure of his suckle. But then that wondrous pressure was suddenly gone, and her eyes flew open.

Grant was staring down at her breasts, his expression unreadable as he slowly lifted a hand to touch a nipple with a gentle forefinger. The pink bud was already so oversensitized that Tara couldn't hold back an agonized moan. "You're amazingly responsive for a virgin," he murmured incredulously. "I didn't expect that, but it's certainly going to make your first time easier. I wasn't looking forward to hurting you. Now I know I won't have to."

Tara felt the fiery color creep up her neck at his words. Because of her indecent behavior, he'd concluded that she was willing to become his mistress! After what had just happened, how could she possibly disabuse him of the notion? Somehow, she would have to.

Avoiding his eyes, she sat up and hastily rebuttoned her bodice. "You won't hurt me, because I won't let you," she whispered miserably. "No matter what you think, this . . . this sort of thing shan't happen again."

Grant frowned at her bent head. "This sort of thing?"

Tara nodded, thoroughly humiliated. When Grant brought his hand up beneath her chin, she flinched away from his touch.

Grant's frown deepened, and, despite her reaction, his hand returned to her face. Holding up her chin, he stared down into eyes swimming with moisture. Her response to him had been so full of passion, he'd almost forgotten how young she was and how innocent. "My dear, little sweetling—"

"Don't call me that!" Tara cried, jerking her chin away. "I am not your dear little anything!"

"But—"

"I am your employer and nothing else," Tara insisted, refusing to cry. Suddenly, she was ragingly angry with him. Realizing that fury was a welcome antidote for the shame that threatened to overwhelm her, her voice rose. "Allowing a man like you to . . . to take such liberties was an unfortunate mistake that won't be tolerated again."

"Is that so?" Grant inquired, rapidly becoming as angry as she.

"Yes, it is. And if this unholy breach in our agreement is ever repeated, I shan't pay you another cent!"

Standing up from the bed, Grant fought the urge to take her as she deserved to be taken. She'd loved every minute of this so-called unholy breach, pleading with him to touch her. And now she was threatening to punish him if he gave her what she wanted? It had been a mistake for him to think she was different from other women. She might be young, but she'd already learned to deny her own passions. "If I remember correctly, you were the one who was begging for it."

Grant was speaking through his teeth, and this time there was no mistaking the savage flare in his eyes. It took every ounce of Tara's courage not to quail beneath that look and all of her willpower to admit, "Be that as it may, only a despicable rounder would be so unkind as to remind me."

"Be that as it may, let me remind you of something else," Grant threatened as he stalked toward the door. "If I win at the tables tonight, I'll have no need for the second half of my salary."

Chapter

Seven

Fortunately, Tara was able to waylay a passing steward, who escorted her to the dining saloon in time for the midday meal. For fear of running into Snedeker, she hadn't dared to walk on deck alone, but after hours of frustrated pacing, she had realized that Grant wasn't coming back to fetch her. Apparently, as far as he was concerned, she could spend the entire day confined to their cabin.

As soon as she saw him, Tara planned to express her displeasure at his desertion of her and also tell him what he could do with the threat he'd tossed at her before stalking out the door that morning. If he ever made advances toward her again, he'd risk more than the last half of his salary. At the very least, she'd blacken both his eyes!

To her frustration, Grant wasn't seated for the meal, and no one she spoke to had seen him. She ended up sharing a table with a loquacious elderly lawyer, Martin Thorp, and his equally talkative wife, Eileen, who were returning to their home in Independence, Missouri. Coming up with a reasonable-sounding lie to explain her "groom's" absence only increased her irritation with him, and after listening to the Thorps outline the shortcomings of each of their four son-in-laws in boring detail, her temper was running even higher than before. It didn't improve any when she had to prevail upon the couple to escort her back to her cabin.

Like it or not, Grant had accepted her terms for employment and was obligated to abide by their agreement. Tara was fully prepared to tell him such when she pushed open the door, but the sight that greeted her left her speechless. Grant was searching through her trunk!

To her astonishment, he thrust a piece of paper under her nose and glared at her as if he were the wronged party. "According to this birth certificate, your name is Armstrong, not Wainwright—Taralynn Rachel Armstrong, daughter of Angus and Ellen Armstrong."

With a disgusted snort, he flung the paper down on top of her opened trunk. "That heart-wrenching tale you told me to get me to help you was just another one of your lies, wasn't it?"

Tara's first instinct was to scream at him for daring to go through her personal things, but the look in his eyes was so intimidating that she didn't have the courage. Indeed, when he began walking toward her, she found herself backing away. "It wasn't a lie exactly."

"Then what exactly was it?"

When his hands clamped down on her upper arms and she felt the power in each individual finger, Tara found herself telling him all that had happened to her in the last few weeks. In truth, it was a relief to tell someone, even if that person had strong-armed her into it. By the time she concluded with "So my real family believes I'm dead," Grant's grasp on her had lessened considerably, and his expression had softened.

"So your father has no idea that you're coming?"

"None at all."

"And you plan to journey all that distance by yourself?"

"I made it this far on my own. I'm sure I can make it the rest of the way."

Grant dropped his arms and stepped back. "Not without help you can't. The *Ophelia* can get you only as far as Fort Benton. The Gallatin Valley is over two hundred miles south of the fort, and to get there you'll have to travel by wagon over the mountains and through Indian territory. How in hell do you plan to manage that?"

Tara lifted her chin proudly. "I'll find a way."

Grant shook his head. Now that he knew the truth about her, it changed everything. Tara was as safe from him now as if she were a nun, a damnably enticing nun whom he was going to be cloistered with for several more weeks. "I wish to God you'd told me all this straight off."

"I couldn't risk telling you because I knew that my aunt's agents were still after me . . . and . . . and I had no reason to trust that you wouldn't turn me over to them for the right price."

"I wouldn't do that for any price," Grant ground out harshly, disliking her low opinion of him even though he knew that he'd fostered it himself.

"You . . . you wouldn't?"

"No, I wouldn't. I've still got some scruples," he informed her gruffly, and Tara didn't know why, but she believed him.

"Thank you."

An odd expression came over Grant's face as he gazed down into her eyes. "I'd advise you to keep your gratitude until we make it safely to Fort Benton."

"Then . . . then you're still willing to hold with our agreement?"

"To the letter."

Recalling how he'd kept to it this morning, Tara queried cautiously, "To the letter?"

His reply was fierce, and once again she believed him. "You no longer have anything to fear from me, Taralynn Armstrong. I promise you that. Nor from Snedeker. I won't let him get near you."

Late that night, Grant stole out of the cabin without making a sound. Tara was asleep when he left, but she woke up immediately when he returned. Since she didn't know he'd gone, her first reaction to the sight of a tall, dark form moving stealthily toward the berth was to scream, but then she recognized her intruder. Even in the shadows, she could see Grant's wolfish grin, and when he sat down beside her on the berth, she greatly feared what it might mean to her. The last time he'd smiled at her like that, he'd kissed her senseless, then bared her breasts and kissed them, too. So much for his promises.

"It's only me," Grant told her as she bolted upright in the bed and held up her arms to ward him off.

She felt rather foolish when Grant lit a candle, then folded his arms across his chest and scolded, "There's no need to behave like a scared rabbit. I'm not going to pounce on you."

Still wary, Tara snapped, "Then what, pray tell, are you doing in my bed?"

"On it, not in it," Grant corrected, a muscle leaping in his jaw as he noted the fear in her eyes. With an exasperated sigh, he stood up. "I just thought you'd sleep better if you knew that Snedeker has left the boat."

This news was so totally unexpected that Tara didn't know how to respond. Then she recalled the predatory smile Grant had been wearing when he walked through the door and the way he'd handled the man once before. "You didn't!"

"Didn't what?" Grant asked, his expression amazingly innocent, considering the vivid sparkle in his blue eyes.

"You tossed him overboard!" Tara accused, knowing she was right even though Grant denied the charge.

"I did no such thing. He disembarked quite voluntarily." That said, Grant sat down on a chair to remove his boots. A few seconds later, he blew out the candle and stretched out on the floor. He went to sleep instantly, but Tara didn't let him sleep for long.

"What if he drowned?" she shouted. "If anyone learns of this, we could both be accused of murder!"

With a long-suffering sigh, Grant rolled over onto his side and propped himself up on his elbow. He'd dispatched Snedeker to alleviate one of Tara's problems, but it had been a mistake to admit his role in the man's departure. He wouldn't be allowed a moment's rest until he'd answered all of her anxious questions. "Snedeker didn't drown. A man can't drown in three feet of water."

In an unrepentantly cheerful tone, he elaborated, "He may have gotten a bit muddy and a bit wet, but that was his own fault. I offered to lower the gangplank for him, but, apparently, he didn't feel like waiting."

"I wonder why?" Tara questioned dryly, not really expecting an answer, astonished when she got one.

"I can only assume that the man preferred jumping ship

to accepting my gracious offer,'' Grant said. "For some reason, he had the impression I might do him a bodily injury if he didn't immediately comply with my suggestion that he seek another mode of transportation upriver.''

"You drew a gun on him!''

"I was unarmed.''

"Then you threatened him in some other way.''

"Evidently he thought so,'' Grant admitted smugly. "Though all I did was tell him that you would remain under my protection throughout our journey and that I would frown upon any man who made trouble for you. The words were barely out of my mouth before he threw himself over the rail.''

Hearing the relish in Grant's voice, Tara could understand why the detective had taken those seemingly mild words as a death threat. Several times in their brief acquaintance, she had sensed the violence in him, and if he'd directed the full force of those savage lights that came into his eyes on poor Mr. Snedeker, she knew very well why the man had thrown himself over the rail. Tara had suspected there was much more to Grant Collingswood than could be seen on the surface, and after what he'd accomplished tonight, she knew it for a fact. She was thankful he was on her side, for with a few words and the mere force of his eyes, he had permanently gotten rid of the man who had doggedly followed her footsteps across six states.

A cold shiver ran down Tara's spine as she contemplated what Grant might do to her if she ever placed herself on the wrong side of his anger. She already knew she had sorely tried his temper on more than one occasion, but as yet he hadn't lost it completely. If he did, would she live to tell about it? After all, what did she really know about him?

"Taralynn?''

In her fearful state of mind, the sound of Grant's voice felt like a knife thrust through her heart. "What?'' she managed to squeak between palpitations.

"I've never deliberately hurt a woman. You don't have to be afraid of me.''

Amazed that he had ascertained so much by her silence, Tara swallowed hard. "I'm not the least bit afraid of you.''

"I'm glad," Grant murmured with a smile, then rolled over onto his back and went promptly to sleep.

After that night, their relationship changed in a way that Tara couldn't understand yet didn't dare question for fear Grant might revert to his previous, far more aggressive behavior. In the days that followed, he only touched her when he was acting in the guise of her husband. At all other times, he was ever the courteous employee, never the audacious rake.

Whenever they were alone together, he seemed to go out of his way to avoid the slightest physical contact with her, and hours would pass without any but the most mundane conversation between them. He spent his evenings at the gaming tables and didn't return to the cabin until she'd retired for the night. His winnings were ample, but he never again threatened to take advantage of her, even though she was well aware that he no longer had need of the remainder of his salary.

The more distant Grant's behavior became, the more curious Tara grew about him and the more mysterious he seemed to her. For one thing, he never did request a cot but continued to sleep on the floor. For another, although he talked and behaved like an experienced man of the world, a devil-may-care gambler, and an outrageous womanizer, he never appeared before her unless he was fully clothed, and he went out of his way to preserve her modesty. After kissing her, fondling her, and making no attempt to hide his desire for her, he'd suddenly started treating her like a younger sister, or perhaps it would be more apt to say like a sister of the church, remembering the one time he'd come upon her before she'd finished with her evening's toilette.

She'd stayed up much later than usual that night, and Grant had found her wearing nothing but a thin chemise, lace drawers, and long white stockings. He'd apologized to her so profusely and backed out of the cabin so fast that Tara had almost been offended. The only part of her body that had been exposed to him was her neck and shoulders, and he needn't have appeared so horrified by the sight. Perversely, she had pulled on a nightgown that had left the same amount of bare skin exposed, but Grant hadn't returned to the cabin before breakfast the next morning, so she didn't know what his reaction might have been to such a brazen exhibition.

Eventually, all the unanswered questions she had about him got the better of her, and when he left her alone in the cabin while he spent yet another night at the tables, Tara decided to search through his things, just as he'd done with hers. The first leather satchel that had contained his clothes was totally empty, but in the second, smaller one, she found a bound sheaf of papers. As she read the first page of legal documents, her eyes grew wider and wider.

She was so engrossed in her reading that she didn't hear Grant come in. "What the devil do you think you're doing!"

Tara gasped as the papers were snatched out of her hand, but she wasn't cowed by his thundering tone. "You're an earl! A titled lord! All this time you let me think you were a wastrel and a dandy or . . . or worse, when in truth you're a member of the British peerage. And you berated *me* for being a liar!"

Grant slammed the cabin door, then stuffed the bundle of papers back into his satchel and kicked it beneath the berth. "What I am is none of your business."

"If you expect me to keep this information to myself, it is," Tara warned, gratified by his livid expression. She'd been right to think he didn't want anyone to learn of his true identity. But what possible motive could he have for portraying himself as a ne'er-do-well? Why would he want people to believe he was bound for Montana to seek his fortune when, by all rights, he already was an extremely wealthy man?

Fists clenched, Grant fought for control of his temper. It was stupid of him to hold on to those papers, but after signing them he'd been overcome by a surprising attack of sentimentality. And he'd certainly never expected to share this journey with a woman who'd already asked him more questions and received more answers than most men dared to expect. Even more surprising was the knowledge that he didn't see himself taking steps to ensure that she wouldn't demand even more from him in the future. He was securely trapped in a snare of his own making, and all he could do now was make the best of it.

Willing his features into smooth lines, he said, "I'd consider myself in your debt if you would keep this discovery to yourself. It has been my experience that men don't begrudge losing their money to a professional card shark nearly as much as they do losing it to a titled English gentleman, and until I strike it rich in the goldfields, gambling is my only means of livelihood. If you had read farther, you would have seen that I've given up the title, so in truth a gambler is all I am.''

''And what of the fortune that goes with such a title? Have you given that up, too?''

Grant laughed at her suspicious expression. ''I realize that you Americans assume that titles and wealth go hand in hand, but in my case that just isn't so. What little is left of the Collingswood holdings will barely support my brother and his family, though George is beginning to make some progress in restoring our depleted coffers. He might be the second son, but he takes his family responsibilities far more seriously than I ever could. I have no interest in maintaining appearances out of some sense of misplaced honor, and I never will, which, of course, makes me the black sheep of the family.''

With a nonchalant shrug, he continued, ''I much prefer my life here to the one I had in England, so it was better for everyone if I passed on the title to George. Since I intend to stay in this country, he'll have far more use for it than I ever would.''

''You're never going back?'' Tara asked incredulously. ''Not even to visit your family?''

Grant shook his head. ''I no longer have a family.''

There was such sadness and pain in his tone that Tara couldn't bring herself to probe any further. It was obvious that he'd given up far more than just his title when he'd left England, and her heart swelled with compassion. Placing her hand on his sleeve, she murmured, ''I'm sorry, Grant, and please forgive me for prying.''

Grant gazed down into her shimmering green eyes and was instantly aware that he'd revealed much more than he'd intended. ''No harm done,'' he replied gruffly.

''And you have my word that I'll never tell anyone about your title. You shan't lose your livelihood on my account.''

Everything she felt was in her face, and Grant was

shocked by what he saw. He'd done absolutely nothing to deserve her sympathy, but it was his nonetheless. He felt a surge of emotion strong enough to knock the breath out of him, and his body was suddenly, achingly hungry for hers. Not for sex alone but for something he hadn't experienced since the day he'd lost his wife. He wanted the kind of comfort only a loving woman could provide, to lay his head on her soft breast and feel her gentle fingers soothing his brow.

As soon as that thought came to him, Grant cast it away. Eyeing the small hand on his sleeve, he stepped out from beneath Tara's touch. "Then, since you're finished snooping, I'm free to return to the tables and make up for what I lost last night."

Knowing she'd just been deliberately snubbed, Tara's response to this announcement was less than gracious. "You're quite free to do anything you like, as am I."

Grant looked as if he wanted to say something vile, but then his jaw clamped shut. "I'll be back in time to escort you to breakfast."

Chapter

Eight

Two weeks out of St.Louis, the *Ophelia* crossed over into Nebraska Territory. Firmly established as Grant's wife, Tara didn't have to worry about walking the deck alone, at least not the hurricane deck which housed the crew. She suspected that she might even be safe on the cabin deck. She didn't quite know how Grant had accomplished it, but the only males who ever approached her now were members of the crew.

With the threat of Snedeker out of the way, leaving the states wasn't as great a milestone as it could have been, but as the boat traveled upstream from Omaha, Tara still felt as if she were entering a new and exciting phase of her life. Though she realized that standing outside in a driving rain wasn't particularly good for her health, Tara wanted to witness this passage into the unknown for herself. She'd crept out of the cabin at first light, and, luckily, she hadn't disturbed Grant. Since he now acted more like her father than her husband, he probably would have prevented her from venturing out in such miserable weather.

Pulling the hood of her gray woolen cloak more securely around her face, Tara breathed in a lungful of the brisk northwest wind, knowing she would soon be in the great wilderness from whence it was coming. For the first time in days, she felt exhilarated, and after all the time she'd spent cooped up in the cabin alone, she didn't even mind the cold rain. Another few weeks, and she'd have her first glimpse of the Rocky Mountains, see for herself what life in the vast open territories would be like instead of reading about wilderness adventures in the penny novels she'd smuggled into her bedroom.

It was probably her imagination, but as Captain Randolph headed the bow out into the channel, Tara thought the current felt different, faster and wilder. It was almost as if the river were aware of the invisible boundary that marked its freedom from the ties of civilization and was celebrating. The *Ophelia* had worked up a good head of steam, but the current kept sweeping it backward as if the large boat were a chip of wood in a millstream.

Tara heard the captain shout, "Full steam ahead!" She saw the smokestacks belch sparks and felt a surge of power as the engineer opened up the throttle. Beneath her feet, the wooden deck shivered and groaned, but slowly the boat began to move forward. Then, with a final burst of speed, it thrust out into the middle of the churning river like a log propelled out of a chute.

"Thank heavens we made it," an excited voice exclaimed from nearby. "My pa says this is the same spot where three boats went down last season. Put under so much pressure, their boilers up and exploded, killing everyone on board. Pa said some of the bodies were blown two hundred feet out on the bank."

Startled, Tara whirled around, surprised to discover that her companion was a pretty young woman about the same age as herself. Displaying less concern for the miserable weather than Tara, she wasn't even wearing a cloak. Bareheaded and barefooted, she stood at the rail in a simple homespun dress that was already wet and clinging to her slender body, her long blond hair dripping water onto a face as serene and lovely as a cameo.

"Let's hope we continue avoiding such an awful fate," Tara replied, folding her arms across her breasts as a cold shiver ran down her spine. She had read accounts of such

accidents and didn't like being reminded that exploding
boilers occurred far too often in hazardous upriver travel.

The young woman stepped closer, her blue eyes shining
with a mixture of mischief and watchful interest as she
studied Tara's face. "I hear tell we've got plenty else to
worry about besides this rampaging current. Ice floes and
snags and floating cottonwood sawyers are supposed to be a
constant menace, and farther along we'll be up against wild
Indians after our scalps."

Glancing at the damp fringe of red curls that showed
beneath the hood of Tara's cloak, she continued dramati-
cally, "I bet they'd love to hang a bloody hank of your hair
from their belts. They've probably never seen a color like
that. Your scalp would be considered quite a prize."

Realizing that her constitution was being tested, Tara's
reply was matter-of-fact. "What about yours? I'm sure those
savages would be even more fond of your silvery blond locks
than my red, especially since your hair's so much longer
than mine."

"You could be right at that," the girl said with an admiring
giggle, then thrust out her hand. "When I saw you come up
here, I knew you couldn't be as prissy as you look. Besides,
you're just about the only other person on board who is
anywhere near my own age, and I was getting bored con-
versing with older folk."

Smiling back, Tara shook the outstretched hand. "Thank
you, I think."

"My name's Rose, Rose Dunn. My family's signed on to
Fort Benton. My pa's purchased some land in Montana, and
that's where we're bound. We're all excited to get there,
what with all the tales of gold we've heard. How about you?
How far are you going?"

Tara had never had a close relationship with another girl,
but there was something so appealing and honest about Rose
Dunn that she thought they might become good friends. She
hated to start off their relationship with a lie, but, circumstances being what they were, she had little other choice.
"I'm Mathilda Collingswood, and my husband, Grant, and I
are signed on for the entire trip."

Tara was startled by Rose's woebegone expression. "I
knew it was too much to hope that you two were simply

good friends sharing the same cabin,'' she sighed, blue eyes twinkling with amusement as she noted Tara's shocked expression. ''Such things do happen, you know. If you don't believe me, look to that couple in the fourth cabin. Ma says they're living in sin, but that don't . . . doesn't seem to bother them a whole lot.''

''But that woman is a . . . a . . .'' Tara sputtered.

Rose nodded sagely. ''A harlot, I know. Isn't it exciting? If we hadn't come on this trip, I probably would never have met one. We don't meet many ladies of ill repute on the farm, or gamblers, either, for that matter. Of course, I can see you're not a farm girl. You're so refined and all, but then, refined girls don't usually marry gamblers.''

''I was born and raised on a horse farm,'' Tara told her, leaving out the fact that Laurel Glen was one of the most successful breeding farms in New England.

''You were! Then however did you meet that gorgeous husband of yours? And is marriage to a gambler as thrilling as I imagine it would be? After living on a farm, don't you just love all the traveling and adventure?''

It was true that Grant was gorgeous, but traveling with him was hardly an adventure, and for some perverse reason, Tara wanted Rose to know that. ''Actually, this is our first trip together, and I don't plan to take another,'' she stated truthfully. ''So far, as you said, it's been extremely boring. Grant spends most of his time in the gaming hall, so I rarely see him, and even when he does come back to the cabin, he usually goes straight to bed.''

''You mean to sleep?'' Rose exclaimed. The disappointment in her eyes was so great that Tara almost burst out laughing. Apparently, it was assumed that a man who looked like Grant must be an insatiable lover. He very well could be, but to Tara's growing frustration, she had absolutely no proof of that.

''Ever since we left St. Louis, all Grant ever does is play cards and sleep,'' Tara agreed sadly, beginning to enjoy herself as she noted Rose's astonished expression.

Clearing her throat to prevent a giggle, Tara elaborated on her tale of marital woe. ''He always says he's too tired for . . . well, you know . . . but then, I probably should have guessed I'd have this problem before we were married.''

Rose stared at her. "Whyever for?"

"Well, Grant is much older than I am," Tara admitted with an unhappy sigh. "He just doesn't seem to have the stamina of a young man. This was supposed to be our honeymoon, but . . ." She trailed off meaningfully.

"Why, you poor thing," Rose sympathized.

Delighted by her new friend's reaction to this information, Tara was struck by another idea. Perhaps Rose could be counted on to relay Tara's dissatisfaction with her "husband's" neglect of her to someone else, who would pass it on to another, until eventually word got back to Grant. If that happened, he just might feel obliged to pay more attention to her and less to the good-time girls seeking work in the goldfields.

"To you, it might seem as if my life is exciting," Tara said. "But the truth is, I'm alone for hours and hours at a time. Grant is well past the age when he's all that interested in romance."

"Why, that's no better than marriage to a farmer," Rose complained. "They work in the fields all day and drop off exhausted as soon as they get back to the house." With a disgusted sigh, she went on, "From what you say about gamblers, I guess I'll just have to stay an old spinster. I absolutely refuse to get married if it means I'll be ignored."

"I doubt anyone could ignore you," Tara replied enviously, her depression increasing when she considered how easily Grant found it to dismiss her. She'd tried everything to regain his attention, flirting outrageously, dressing in clothes that showed off her figure to its best advantage, but nothing she'd tried thus far had made the slightest impression on him. It was maddening, and the more Grant backed away from her advances, the more relentless her need to pursue him became.

Rose saw Tara's frown and shook her head. "Forgive me for saying so, Mathilda, but your man can't be all that bright if he's neglecting you like that. Why, you're just about the prettiest woman on this boat. All the men think so. Only last night, my brother, Zeke, told me he would probably keel over if you so much as smiled at him."

"He did?"

"Yes, he did," Rose insisted, tucking Tara's arm through

hers as she led the way belowdeck. "Now, the way I see it, a woman has a right to expect her romance to keep going even after the 'I do's' are said, and it wouldn't hurt your marriage any if you gave your husband a little something to think about."

Since he was losing to the man for the tenth time in so many days, Slade Plummer found some pleasure in asking, "Ain't that your wife dancing over there, Collingswood?"

Grant looked up from his cards, his eyes following the direction of the grizzled prospector's hand to the other end of the saloon, where the fiddlers were playing a catchy tune. What the hell did she think she was doing? Grant asked himself as he saw Tara whirling around in the arms of another man. To make matters worse, she was wearing that shimmering blue satin dress of hers that cinched in so tightly at her tiny waist and dipped immodestly low in the front, showing off the perfection of her figure.

The first time she'd worn it, it had taken all of his willpower to keep his hands off her. Fortunately for her dancing partner, Grant recognized him as Zeke Dunn, a young, innocent farm kid who wouldn't do anything more than drool over her. Even so, as Tara laughed up into the boy's flushed face, Grant felt a surge of jealousy so strong, it made his teeth clench.

Striving to appear unconcerned by the spectacle his "wife" was making of herself, Grant tore his seething gaze away from her and back to his cards. "Mathilda has always enjoyed dancing. I'm glad she's found some means to enjoy herself while I'm otherwise engaged."

Having heard the rumor that had been circulating around the boat all day, the three other men at the table exchanged knowing glances. Jack Baker, a wealthy merchant who disliked losing even more than Slade Plummer, stated snidely, " 'Spect it's hard for you to keep up with a young gal like that, what with your being so much older and all."

Captain Randolph wasn't nearly as subtle. "Naw, that ain't his problem," he said with a lusty chuckle. "I'm a pretty old rooster, but I can still get my cock up when a spring chicken struts by. My guess is he visited one whorehouse too many somewheres along the line."

"That would explain it," Plummer agreed with a mocking grin.

What the devil? Grant had been willing to shrug off Baker's comment, but he couldn't let Randolph's crude remarks pass. All evening, he'd sensed a strange undercurrent in the atmosphere around the table, but he couldn't put his finger on what was wrong. Now, as his gaze traveled from one man to the next, he realized that they'd all been silently laughing at him since the poker game began.

Intent on finding out why, Grant placed his cards face down on the table and suggested softly, "Okay, which one of you gentlemen would like to tell me what this is all about?"

Seeing the dangerous look in his eyes, both Baker and Plummer backed off, leaving it up to the captain to pass on the gossip they'd heard. "Now, don't get your back up, Collingswood. You know what it's like on these here riverboats," Randolph chuckled. "Living in such close quarters, we're bound to find out each other's business, and the word about you is that you ain't been doing your marital duty by your pretty li'l wife."

"Mathilda said that?"

Randolph shrugged his shoulders. "Cain't say that for sure, but my guess is she must have been complaining to one of the other ladies. The way I heard it, she thinks you're too old to perform to her liking."

"Too old?" Grant repeated in a strangled tone, his irate gaze shooting across the room to his "wife." He'd restrained himself from bedding her as a matter of honor, but it was clear to him now that Tara didn't deserve such consideration. No woman belittled his manhood and got away with it.

"If you gentlemen will excuse me," he managed through clenched teeth as he scraped back his chair, "I believe I'd like the next dance."

"Be careful you don't tire yourself out," Randolph challenged jovially, and he scooped up the pile of chips in front of him. Baker and Plummer did likewise, just in case Grant decided to come back and finish out the hand. If the look on his face when he'd risen from the table was an indication, any man who went up against him was destined to lose, no matter what kind of cards he was holding.

Tara saw Grant striding toward her, and her mouth went dry. She'd expected him to be irritated if he heard the rumor that she'd started, and she'd hoped to inspire a bit of jealousy by dancing with Rose's handsome older brother, but she'd underestimated Grant's reaction. She could tell by his eyes that her foolhardy actions had unleashed a savage rage.

Then, as the musicians stopped playing and an awful silence fell over the room, Tara realized that every person present was waiting to see what the much maligned husband was going to do to his errant wife. Knowing she was about to suffer the worst humiliation in her life, Tara cringed and turned her face into Zeke's shoulder, praying he would protect her if Grant resorted to violence. Even as she sought shelter, Zeke dropped his arms and stepped away from her, deserting her in her hour of greatest need.

An atmosphere of tense anticipation permeated the room as Tara called on all of her courage and turned around to face what she knew was coming. Instead of Grant, however, she found herself standing about two feet away from six bald-headed Indians with painted faces. Naked from the waist up, they were wrapped in smelly blankets, but their cloaks didn't hide the knives and tomahawks hanging from their leather belts. They all had coal-black eyes, and every one of those eyes was fixed on her. Speechless with fright, Tara couldn't do anything but stare back.

"Again, flame-haired woman," the tallest of the six demanded in a guttural tone, gazing insolently at her breasts. "Again."

"Make cry music," another ordered, gesturing at the fiddler to begin playing.

When nobody moved to follow their terse orders, the tall one stepped forward, apparently as fascinated by the color of Tara's hair as by the shape of her breasts. With black, greasy fingers, he picked up a silk curl and felt the texture, then turned back to his companions and grunted something unintelligible.

Nearing the point of panic, Tara was certain he was staking his claim on either her body or her scalp, but then he turned back to her and ordered, "Four-bears say, again, flame-haired woman! Make dance!"

Arms crossed over his chest, Grant leaned back against a table and watched the proceedings with amusement. Tara, along with everyone else who was unfamiliar with Missouri River travel, was terrified out of her wits, but Grant knew these Potawatomie warriors didn't intend any harm. As far as Grant was concerned, they couldn't have timed their entrance any better or chosen a more perfect female to intimidate. For what she'd done to him today, Taralynn Armstrong deserved exactly what she was getting.

Before any of his nervous passengers got it into their heads to pull out a firearm, Captain Randolph rushed forward to greet his uninvited guests. "You're a vengeful bastard, ain'tcha?" he muttered to Grant as he passed by him. "Your poor missus is that close to faintin'."

To Grant's intense satisfaction, his "poor missus" broke out of her paralysis at that exact moment, emitted a tiny scream, and came flying toward him. For a woman who found him so sadly lacking as a husband, she certainly didn't hesitate to seek him out for protection, and their interested audience couldn't help but notice. As Tara cried out his name and threw herself into his arms, Grant felt somewhat vindicated. After this telling display, it was no longer necessary for him to make a public issue of her indiscretions, but once they were alone in their cabin, she wouldn't be so lucky. It was high time she learned that she couldn't flirt with danger without experiencing it.

"There's no need to carry on like this," Grant assured her. "They like what they see, that's all." But his words had no effect on Tara, who still clung to him like a limpet.

"They want my scalp . . . or worse," she whispered fearfully into his shirtfront.

Grant laughed scornfully, forgetting himself for a moment. "Potawatomies don't take scalps anymore. Those weak old women are here to beg for food and a barrel of firewater."

The certainty in his voice brought Tara's head up, perplexed by his mocking tone. "You sound as if that angers you."

Annoyed with himself for making such a slip, Grant searched his mind for something to say that would distract her. Tara was much too quick, and he'd be wise to remember that in the future. "Maybe if you lost all your hair, folks would understand why I don't share your bed as often as you'd apparently like me to."

Tara gulped beneath the censure in his blistering blue eyes, suddenly more frightened of Grant than she was of the Indians. "I . . . I shouldn't have—"

"No, you shouldn't have," Grant agreed, wrapping his arm about her waist in an iron grip. "But it's too late for regrets now. To salvage my damaged male pride, I'm going to oblige your wishes, Mrs. Collingswood, and make sure you are so thoroughly satisfied that all these humiliating rumors are laid permanently to rest."

Chapter

Nine

Grant escorted Tara toward the side doors, but before they were halfway there, Captain Randolph called after them. "Wait up, Collingswood. Chief Four-bears and his boys here are aimin' to make a real nuisance of themselves if your wife don't give 'em that dance. They brought us some cut wood, and now they expect to be entertained for their trouble."

Glancing back over his shoulder, Grant replied, "You'll have to pay them off with something else, Randolph. My wife and I are retiring for the evening."

After a short considering pause, Randolph spoke up again, "Sorry, but that ain't gonna solve our problem. You see, the chief wants to watch her dance before he makes an offer to buy her, and he ain't leavin' 'til then. Says he needs a new gal for his tepee, and he likes the look of yours."

Tara gasped in horror when she heard that, but Grant merely laughed. "Well, madam, it appears as if these heathen savages are even more impatient than I am to watch you dancing to their tune."

"I won't do it," Tara insisted, her eyes telling him that the Indians weren't the only ones who shouldn't expect much cooperation from her.

Blue eyes twinkling wickedly, Grant drawled, "As your

husband, I say you will. Four-bears is thinking about buying you, and considering what I've had to put up with from you lately, I just might pay heed to his offer."

"No! You have no right!" Tara cried out in outrage as Grant pulled her unwilling body back toward the dance floor. Every step of the way, she felt six pairs of obsidian eyes crawling over her person, and before she had gone much farther, she whispered frantically, "Please, Grant, don't make me go near them again."

Her panic was real, and with an exasperated sigh, Grant took pity on her, though his words were hardly sympathetic. "If we don't give them what they want, we'll never be rid of them. I'll be right there with you, so you can stop acting like a frightened ninny."

Stung by his rebuke, Tara lifted her chin defiantly, only to find that Grant had known exactly how she would react and had taunted her deliberately. "Nothing's going to happen to you now," he assured her, his gaze more brazenly possessive than that of any of the heathens. "It's later on that you'd best worry about."

Taking a steely grip on her cold hand, Grant twirled her onto the dance floor, but before the fiddlers struck up their instruments once more, he leaned over and said something to Chief Four-bears in his own language. Whatever it was, all six of the savages grinned widely at him and stopped staring at Tara as if she were up for sale.

"What did you say?" Tara asked breathlessly as Grant waltzed her around the floor for the enjoyment of their avid audience. "And how do you know their language?"

Grant ignored her first question and to the second replied, "I've traveled the Missouri enough times to pick up a smattering of several different languages."

After that, she was given no further chance to talk, for Grant splayed his hand behind her back and whirled her around and around in an embrace that was far too tight and shockingly intimate. As their lower limbs came into contact, Tara felt his heated arousal, just as he wanted her to. "Why so surprised, sweetheart?" he whispered into her hair, refusing to allow any space between them. "You've been trying to reduce me to this state for days on end, and your plans have finally succeeded."

Aware that besides the Potawatomies, everyone else in the saloon was watching them dance, Tara tried not to show her acute embarrassment, but with her breasts flattened against Grant's hard chest, she was finding it harder and harder to remain calm. She squirmed for release, but all she gained for the attempt was a warning pat on the bottom, and she immediately stopped fighting, stunned by the radical change in his behavior. For the last two weeks, he had been circumspect in the extreme, but tonight he was treating her like a common trollop.

Tara assumed that this was his way of getting his own back, but to her way of thinking, Grant's brand of punishment far outweighed the crime. All she had done was make him the object of a little harmless teasing. For that, she didn't deserve to face the threat of wild Indians or be humiliated like this in public, and the longer they danced, the more angry with him she became.

"Must you hold me so tightly?" she finally protested, knowing her cheeks were rapidly turning the same shade of red as her hair. "Have you lost all sense of propriety?"

"I'm just trying to convince Four-bears that I have a stronger claim on you than he does," Grant retorted. "Or would you rather dance with him?"

"I would rather dance with a gentleman," Tara hissed angrily, and she had the satisfaction of feeling his spine go stiff as she added for good measure, "or a man like Zeke Dunn. He may be a farm boy, but, unlike you, he knows how to treat a lady."

Without Tara's realizing it, Grant had guided them to another set of doors, and though the music was still playing, he came to an abrupt halt. "Oh, I know how to treat a lady," Grant told her as he pulled her with him through the doors. "And I also know how to treat a woman who doesn't know the meaning of the word."

Once outside, he began striding swiftly down the passage to their cabin, and since he was still holding her wrist, Tara was given no choice but to stumble along behind him. A few moments later, they were in their own quarters with the door locked securely behind them. "I treat her like this," Grant pronounced, giving Tara no time to reply or even think as his mouth came down on hers and he bent her body over his arm.

"And this," he continued, pushing her gown off her shoulders and pulling down her chemise, revealing her breasts. He flicked his fingers casually over her nipples, then lowered his head and took one into his mouth. Instinctively, Tara grabbed at his hair to pull him away, but he responded to her resistance by closing his teeth around her nipple until she gave in and allowed him full suckle.

Tara didn't know which sensation was more overwhelming, the pleasure she was feeling or the shame of it. Grant was making no attempt to be gentle, yet her reaction to his ruthless assault on her senses was stronger than ever. She tried to protest when he unhooked the back of her gown and stripped both it and her chemise away, but she liked his kisses too much to pull her mouth away. When she was naked, she tried to cover herself, and she made a feeble attempt to escape when he carried her to the berth, but when he straddled her hips and she felt the first touch of his warm hand between her thighs, she was too shocked to move.

"This is what you were asking for, Taralynn," Grant reminded her as he probed her silky flesh, watching her expression change from embarrassment to wonder as she discovered how intimate a man's lovemaking could be. It was this unfeigned naïveté that saved her from the consequences of his rage, for Grant was immediately reminded that she had no real knowledge of what a man might do if she pushed him too far. Tonight, he would teach her an unforgettable lesson, but only if she continued to taunt him would he make her pay the ultimate price. He owed Angus Armstrong that much, but no more.

Tara moaned in pleasure as Grant caressed her in ways she could never have imagined. She felt as if her will had been taken away from her as a surging tide of liquid heat rose up inside her and her body writhed helplessly. Vaguely, she realized that Grant was still fully dressed, that he was making no attempt to lie down on the berth beside her but was finding his pleasure in watching her body arch and convulse beneath his expert fingers. For a moment, her mind cried out in rebellion, but then he touched the delicate core of her being, and an explosion of stars burst within her, forcing her to surrender to something she didn't understand and had no strength to fight.

Moments later, Grant stood up abruptly from the berth. Where he came from, a man didn't put a woman's needs before his own. Indeed, Grant couldn't recall a time when he'd made a woman ready for him, then denied himself the pleasure of taking her. This was a new experience for him, and not a very pleasant one, he noted in frustration as he pulled off his frock coat and vest, then threw them both at the wall. Watching Tara climax without him was agony, and he tried to shut the arousing sight out of his mind as he spread out his bedroll, but the image seemed to be branded into his brain.

As he removed his boots and stretched out on the floor, his loins ached with throbbing intensity, and his blood raced like burning fire through his veins. Grant pressed his forearm over his eyes and groaned, a sheen of moisture breaking out on his skin as he tried to resist the natural inclination of his tortured body. In silent misery, he damned Tara with every curse he could think of, damned her for being so incredibly lovely in her nakedness, so tempting in her passion, but most of all he blamed her for being a virgin. If she wasn't a virgin, he wouldn't have to suffer as he had every day since he'd met her, and he wouldn't have to continue suffering for several weeks more.

If she weren't an innocent, he could be inside her right now, grinding his hips fiercely against her slender white hips, hearing her passionate moans as he thrust deeper and deeper into the tight, satiny passage between her thighs. In that instant when his traitorous brain had roused his deprived body to a fevered pitch, Grant cried out, but not from a real or even an imagined fulfillment. The seat of his passion had just been thoroughly doused beneath a deluge of cold water, and the beautiful woman in his fantasy was standing over him, brandishing a small derringer and a now empty pitcher!

"Get up, you miserable cur, or I'll shoot you where you lie!" Tara blazed.

Wrapped in nothing but a blanket, her titian hair tumbled wildly about her face, she was more magnificent in her anger than any Potawatomie warrior and infinitely more anxious than any member of that sorry tribe to draw the blood of her chosen enemy. As he stared up into her glittering green eyes, Grant shivered, but not only in reaction to the damp cold seeping into his clothes. There was absolutely no doubt in his mind that if he didn't do exactly what she said, the little hellion was going to pull the trigger and shoot him in the gut.

Jumping to his feet, Grant held his hands out in front of him. "Okay! I'm up, I'm up." He tried to placate her, but her eyes didn't waver from their target at his waist, and her finger was still coiled firmly around the derringer's black metal draw.

"Take those clothes off," she commanded. "Every stitch!"

Grant's brows rose at the order. "Now, Tara, I know you're upset, but—"

"Do it!"

If she'd shown any sign of nervousness, Grant might have refused, but when it came down to a choice between dying a slow, painful death or taking his clothes off, he would gladly take his clothes off. Since he didn't have a modest bone in his body, he didn't have any idea what she hoped to gain by watching him strip, but he had plenty to lose if she understood what she saw. Unfortunately, unless she dropped her guard, that was a chance he was just going to have to take.

Intent on distracting her, he began talking as he unbuttoned his shirt. "I did nothing to hurt you, Tara, and I could have," he reminded her. "If I was the miserable cur you think I am, I wouldn't have stopped when I did. I would have tossed you down on that bed, spread your legs, and robbed you of the gift that belongs to the man you're going to marry someday. You should be thanking me."

"Take another step toward me, and I'll pull this trigger," Tara said, and she meant it.

Thwarted in his first attempt, Grant switched tactics and moved his hand from his shirt to his pants. In all likelihood, Tara had never seen a man naked from the waist down, and she just might lose her composure once she did. A pitcher of cold water had quickly dampened his arousal, but an innocent should still be taken aback by his size, and he would act swiftly to take advantage of her shock.

"The shirt, too," Tara demanded, not taking her eyes off his face for a second, even though she wanted to.

"This is what humiliation feels like, Grant Collingswood," she informed him tartly as he stood before her naked. "And no matter what I said about you, I didn't deserve to be shamed like this. What you did to me was vile and cruel, and . . ." Tara's voice trailed off when her eyes strayed lower and she saw the twin scars on his broad shoulders. The derringer clattered to the floor when she saw two more carved into the skin beneath his flat nipples.

Grant didn't need her to tell him about cruelty, Tara realized as she stared at him in rising horror. She could see similar scars on each arm below the shoulder, also below the elbow, on his stomach and thighs, and below the knees. He had obviously been the victim of some hideous torture, and she couldn't imagine the kind of pain he must have endured at the hands of someone so vicious that they would attempt to mutilate another human being. It looked as if a knife or some other sharp instrument had been used to cut into his smooth, bronzed flesh with diabolical precision.

Now she knew why he'd been so careful not to disrobe in front of her. She had thought he had vast experience with women, but now she realized that assumption was wrong. Grant hadn't dared reveal his disfigurement for fear that she would be repulsed. No wonder he'd treated her no better than he would a cheap whore.

Yet, even with the scars, his body was magnificent, splendidly, primally male. Standing tall and proud before her, Tara thought him beautiful. With tears in her eyes, she stepped toward him. Sensing she would only wound him more by questioning him about his scars, she reached out her hand to touch the silvered lines on his chest, then followed the healing motions of her fingers with the feather-light caress of her lips.

Nonplussed by her unexpected action, Grant stood still for her tender ministrations for as long as he could, but he was a man, not a eunuch. The feel of her soft lips on his chest was driving him to the brink of insanity, and when her hand slipped below his waist to caress the small scar beneath his navel, he came close to forgetting all about his past debts. "Lord, woman," he groaned. "You have to stop this. You don't know what you're doing."

"Make love to me, Grant," Tara murmured, intent on accomplishing her benevolent mission no matter what his protest. Tonight, she was going to convince him that she thought him perfect, more beautiful than any man had a right to be. Maybe then she would no longer see that awful vulnerability that sometimes appeared in his eyes when he thought no one was looking.

Rapidly losing control, Grant grasped her upper arms and held her away from him, but the tactic backfired in his face. Gazing deeply into his eyes, Tara slowly and deliberately shrugged her shoulders, and the blanket fell away from her. "Make love to me," she repeated softly.

With a pained groan, Grant gave up the fight. He lifted her up in his arms, his lips claiming hers as he walked across the room to the berth. He laid her gently on the mattress, and she reached up with both arms and drew him to her. At that moment, there was no turning back for either of them.

Grant covered her body with his, his weight almost crushing her. Tara pressed herself fiercely against him, loving the feel of his strong body on hers. Passionately, he kissed her, his fingers seeking the source of her femininity, stroking her softness until her hips began to move of their own volition.

She was ready for him almost immediately, and Grant closed his eyes in relief. Soon, very soon, he could rid himself of the throbbing agony in his loins. He was bursting with the need to take her, but he forced himself to hold back, not wanting to breach her maiden defenses until she was far gone in passion.

To his surprise, even as he ordered himself to go slowly, Tara pleaded, "Now, oh, please, now!"

As she pushed her hips up hard against him, instinct took over, and Grant drove into her with one powerful stroke, absorbing her tiny cry of pain into his mouth. He felt her heart pounding violently, but then she arched her back, demanding him to continue, and Grant immediately complied.

Tara gasped as Grant moved within her, and she felt a savage ripple of pleasure. He moved again, and it came again, increasing with intensity at each thrust. Then, as he filled her more deeply than she thought possible, increasing his speed at the same time, she found herself losing control of her mind, body, and soul. The wonder of it was awesome, and Tara moaned as the most incredible sensations she'd ever known engulfed her completely.

Grant wanted her to know the exquisite joy they could reach together, but his own desire drove him to a hellbent rhythm that he couldn't stop. A liquid fire was embracing him, driving him forward toward completion as Tara's hips writhed and undulated beneath his, drawing him ever deeper inside her. Then, more fantastic than any of his fantasies, he felt her loins tighten around him, felt the tiny ripples of her pleasure gripping him, claiming him in a way that he'd never experienced before. In awe, he whispered her name over and over again as the shattering impact of total fulfillment surged through his body, whirling him into a place unknown yet more beautiful than any place he had ever been before.

It seemed like forever before Tara regained the power to think. Snuggled warmly against Grant's side, she would be content never to move again. "That was . . . that was . . ." She was unable to find words to describe what they had just shared.

"I know," Grant replied, not even bothering to make the attempt.

"Is it . . . is it always like that?"

Grant closed his eyes, her husky question setting off a series of arousing shivers along nerves still raw with excitement. "No, it's not," he muttered truthfully.

Grant's voice sounded so strange that Tara lifted her head to look at him. His expression was both disbelieving and perplexed. "Any woman would want you," she told him, assuming he was confused by her uninhibited response to him and unable to accept that a woman of quality would enjoy making love with him. Leaning down, she kissed his shoulder. "These scars don't matter to me at all."

"What?"

Smiling tenderly, Tara laid her head down on his chest. "I know you were worried that I'd be repulsed when I saw them, but I'm not. I did feel quite sick that someone could have hurt you so badly, but the signs of your suffering don't make you any less in my eyes. With or without scars, your body could never be unsightly.''

''Is that why you gave yourself to me?'' Grant exclaimed, sitting up so fast that Tara's head landed on the pillow behind him with a thump. Grasping her arm, he pulled her back up beside him until her face was inches from his chest. ''You thought I wouldn't bed you because I was afraid of how you'd react to the sight of these?''

''Weren't you?''

Grant stared at her for several seconds, then let out a bark of laughter. He didn't know which one of them was the bigger fool. Him because in his supreme arrogance he'd assumed that Tara had succumbed to an overwhelming desire as she'd viewed his manly body, or her because she'd felt such compassion for his pain that she'd handed over her virginity as an act of charity. ''Oh, my sweet little humanitarian, I can't tell you how much I appreciate your loving concern.''

Tara frowned. ''Why are you laughing?'' she demanded indignantly.

Struggling to contain his self-mocking amusement, Grant shook his head. ''I'm afraid you made a slight error in judgment, sweetheart. I'm not ashamed of my body, and, believe me, I've never lacked for women.''

Tara's doubting expression irritated him, and out of wounded vanity, he lashed out, ''As I told you the day we met, seducing a child holds no appeal for me. That's why you remained a virgin.''

As his words registered, Tara sat back in horror. ''No,'' she insisted frantically. ''You wanted me. I know you did.''

''Of course I did,'' Grant agreed. ''But when a man reaches my age, he can control his baser instincts without too much trouble. It was your instincts that were the problem. I did my best to keep temptation out of your way, but . . .'' He held out his hands, palms up, and shrugged. ''In the end, I still got raped.''

''Raped!''

Grant grinned at her outrage. ''What else would you call it when a woman demands that a man take his clothes off at gunpoint, then runs her hands all over his defenseless body?''

"I never!" Tara cried, then choked, for she'd done exactly what he said she'd done. Thoroughly humiliated, she grabbed for the sheet and pulled it up to her neck. "Well, you don't have to worry that I'll ever touch you again," she exclaimed. "From this moment on, you are perfectly safe from all my unwanted attentions."

"I never said I didn't want them," Grant declared matter-of-factly. "And now that your virginity is no longer an obstacle, I plan to enjoy them immensely."

"Over my dead body!"

Grant reached out and passed his hand over her breast, watching as her nipple sprang to instant life beneath the sheet. "Hardly dead," he complimented her hoarsely, then proceeded to show her what pleasure could be derived from a woman who was definitely still alive and kicking.

Chapter

Ten

Having lounged too long in bed, Tara stepped out into the passageway late one bright June morning. Lips turned up in a serene smile, she picked up her skirts and hurried to catch up with Grant before the cook closed the kitchen. Grant had left the cabin ten minutes earlier, trying to appear annoyed with her for enticing him back into bed and thereby making them miss the first call to breakfast. Considering how much he'd enjoyed their sensual interlude, Tara hadn't found his act very convincing, but she could certainly sympathize with his announcement that he was about to keel over from hunger. After this morning's exertions, she, too, was ravenous.

Still smiling like the well-satisfied woman she was, Tara walked swiftly down the passageway. Oh yes, desire was a delicious thing, but she was also in love, helplessly, hopelessly in love with a handsome, exciting, wonderful man. The only thing that worried her at all about her relationship with Grant was that there was still so much about him that she didn't know. All she had to do was be very patient, and eventually he would trust her enough to take her into his confidence.

During the weeks that followed her initiation into womanhood, Tara had arrived at the conclusion that Grant was going to Montana for reasons other than what he wanted people to believe. Even though he had yet to disclose what those reasons were, she did know that he loved her as much as she loved him. He had proved that to her satisfaction every night since that frightening encounter with the Potawatomies.

Since then, the *Ophelia* had ventured farther and farther into an untamed land. The heavily loaded steamer struggled in a constant fight to put league behind league, bumping against hidden sandbars and being tossed to and fro by a current as wild as the country it traveled through. At the sound of the puffing steam engine, herds of deer and elk and antelope careened away from the riverbanks in confusion. Never in her life had Tara seen a more spectacular sight than when she'd watched a huge herd of antelope fleeing across the rolling prairie to escape the alien noise that had invaded their territory.

Tara understood their anxiety, for with every day that passed, she, too, was getting closer and closer to her confrontation with the unknown. However, if things worked out the way she hoped, Grant would be standing by her side when she met her father and brothers for the first time. Then, after a respectable period, Grant would ask for her hand in marriage, and they would spend the rest of their lives together.

"There you are." Looking even more handsome than usual in black, close-fitting breeches and a white shirt with long, flowing sleeves, Grant strode toward her down the passageway.

"The last breakfast gong has yet to sound," Tara said, surprised by the sense of urgency in his voice.

"Breakfast can wait," Grant said, taking hold of her arm. "There's something up on deck that you'll find far more interesting than that warm gruel the cook has been foisting on us for the last several days."

"What would that be?" Tara wanted to know, but Grant simply grinned and hurried her along, just as an explosion of cannonfire rocked the decks.

Face pale, Tara shouted to be heard above the roar. "Are we under attack?"

"No," Grant reassured her. "We're just saying hello."

"To whom?"

"To them," Grant said as Tara gazed over the rail, enthralled by what she saw. Along the sandy river shore, a hundred beautifully formed naked savages were riding bareback on magnificent horses of every imaginable size and color.

"Those are Assiniboin warriors, a proud tribe," Grant informed her, just as he'd identified so many other tribes they had encountered on their journey. "As you can see, they do not run in fear from the boastful salute of our cannons."

"There are so many of them," Tara whispered fearfully, then added half in horror, half in awe, "and not a stitch of clothing amongst them."

"Horse thieves and murderers, all of 'em, and greedy to boot," Slade Plummer declared as he came to stand beside Tara at the rail. "Give those muckers a few pretty beads, some colored cloth and combs, and they'll let you have most anything they got. Me and my partner traded with them for land claims 'til they remembered how fond they be of their hunting grounds. Then they came at us like angry hornets, and we barely made it out with our scalps."

Tara could feel Grant stiffen as Plummer reached out and patted Tara's arm. "Don't you worry, ma'am. Many a man has lost his scalp to them scurvy devils, but soon there'll be so danged many of us, they'll lose all their sting. I cain't wait for the day when every one of them dumb buggers is wiped off the face of this here earth."

Before Plummer knew what had hit him, he was lying flat on his back on the deck, trying to stem the blood flowing from his battered nose. "From now on, keep your hands off my wife," Grant growled over his shoulder as he dragged Tara away from the fallen man.

"Why on earth did you hit him?" Tara demanded, shocked by such unnecessary violence. "He meant me no harm."

In a deadly quiet tone, Grant replied, "No man offends what is mine."

For an instant, Tara had the oddest feeling that Grant wasn't referring to her when he uttered that statement, but then he bent down and kissed her. "Maybe I did overreact, but where you are concerned, I've become very possessive. I don't like any other man to come near you."

Tara laughed. "Believe me, you have nothing to worry about with Slade Plummer. He is crude and obnoxious, and he smells."

"Yes, he does, doesn't he?" Grant retorted, grinning smugly. "And now he'll have a crooked nose to add to all his other charms."

Without the slightest show of remorse for his action, Grant escorted Tara into the dining hall and seated her at their table, where their breakfast was rapidly growing cold. When he saw her wrinkle her nose at the less than appetizing-looking fare set before them, Grant warned, "Eat up, milady, for the plans I have for your delectable person today will require all of your stamina."

Tara adored it when he called her "milady," and she was greatly looking forward to these "plans." "Yes, milord," she replied, and she quite happily dipped her spoon into the thickened gruel.

Unfortunately, as their meal progressed, the conversations of other latecomers to breakfast could be heard, and Grant lapsed into a tight-lipped silence. "A more niggardly lot I never did see," Jack Baker declared as he walked past their table with another merchant. "Like Colonel Gibner tol' his men, the only good Injun's a dead Injun."

Although Grant continually denied it, Tara believed he had far more than a passing interest in Indians. In her opinion, his answers to her questions about the various tribes proved him to be a learned expert on the subject, and she was beginning to wonder if he might have spent some time living among them. Even though that prospect seemed highly unlikely for a man who was supposedly going to Montana to seek his fortune, just as were Jack Baker and Slade Plummer and most of the other men on board, Grant's reaction to their attitude toward the Indians seemed very odd indeed.

Actually, he didn't seem to like any of the topics being discussed this morning, Tara realized. As they listened to a prospector who was heading back to his claim at Last Chance Gulch advising his companions about how much gold there was in the territory just for the taking and what sections of the country were best to commence the search, Tara could sense Grant's disapproval. She couldn't believe he was the type of man who, out of his own greed, would wish to suppress information about the gold strikes to increase his own chances of finding a fortune. But what other reason could there be for his anger?

"If you'll excuse me, Mathilda," Grant stated abruptly, standing up from the table. "I just saw Lloyd Dunn go up on deck, and he wanted to speak with me this morning. I should only be gone a few minutes."

He was wearing the same dark expression as when he'd punched Slade Plummer in the nose. Tara nodded. "Once you're finished, you can find me over there in the ladies' section."

As soon as Grant started walking away from the table, his seat was promptly taken by Rose. As usual, the blond, blue-eyed young woman was fairly bursting with the latest news. "Did you hear? If we don't get hung up on any more snags, we're only a day out of Fort Benton!"

"Really?" Tara exclaimed, her stomach fluttering at the realization that she was so close to the end of her long journey. "Who told you that?"

"Captain Randolph stopped by to ask my pa if he would help load up the wood needed for the last length." Glancing over her shoulder, she inquired, "Isn't that where Grant was heading? To help out?"

"He said your father wanted to talk to him, but he didn't say why," Tara said, relieved to discover that Grant hadn't been making an excuse to leave before his temper exploded.

"The captain wants every able-bodied man on the riverboat within the hour," Rose replied, pouring herself a cup of coffee and grimacing at the taste. "I sure hope those savages don't decide to attack before our men finish loading. I didn't like the looks of them one bit, and I don't aim to be some chief's captive white squaw."

"As far as I can tell, Rose Dunn," Tara teased, "you don't aim to be any man's anything."

That comment produced a burst of sheepish laughter from her friend. "It's not that I don't like men," she admitted. "It's just that I'd like to be one myself. Men get to do all the exciting things in life, while we women sit around and worry after them. The last thing Pa said to us before he went after the captain was to stay put in here where we'd be safe. He says that every time we land."

Since Tara had often entertained the same notion concerning the disparity between the sexes, she said, "If the Indians do decide to attack, none of us will be safe, so I don't see what harm there would be if we went up on the hurricane deck to watch the proceedings."

"Now, that's a fact," Rose acknowledged, stealing a look over her shoulder at her mother as, arm in arm, she and Tara stole swiftly out of the dining hall.

Unfortunately, viewing the loading of cut wood onto the lower decks of the boat was not the most exciting pastime, and after an hour of that occupation, both girls grew tired of it. "At the speed they were riding, those Indians must be miles away from here by now," Tara mused out loud, an adventurous sparkle in her green eyes.

"I don't see hide nor hair of 'em," Rose agreed.

"Wouldn't it be nice to take a short walk on the shore?" Tara inquired. "It's such a delightful day."

"It would be grand," Rose replied. "And I don't see what harm could possibly come to us, do you?"

"I'm sure the captain's rule for passengers to stay on board only applied to when those Indians were near. There's no danger now."

"None that I can see."

A few moments later, they had slipped past the main loading deck and were walking down the rear gangplank which had been lowered to accommodate the cook and his crew, who had left the boat to hunt fresh game. "Isn't this beautiful country?" Tara said as she viewed the boundless waves of prairie grass on the countless hills that stretched before a backdrop of snow-capped mountains. "It's so open and wild and free."

Bending down to pick a pretty pink wildflower, Rose nodded thoughtfully. "I wonder if our place will be like this. If I didn't know better, I'd think we were the last two people left in the entire world."

"It is kind of overwhelming," Tara agreed as they ventured farther and farther away from the river, skipping through grass grown up past their knees. "It's like an ocean on land."

"Maybe we should get back." Rose's words surprised Tara. "If we go much farther, we could be swallowed up in this stuff."

"Why, Rose Dunn, you—" Tara broke off what she was about to say as she felt a strange vibration beneath her feet. "What is that?"

Rose stared down at her shoes. "I don't know."

"Maybe it's an earthquake."

"Do they have such things out here?"

"I don't know," Tara said, but the vibrations were fast growing in strength. Reaching for Rose's hand, she ordered, "C'mon! Let's run."

As the last cord of wood was loaded onto the *Ophelia,* Grant stayed on shore, reluctant to go back on board. After two months, it felt so good to have firm soil under his feet, and with each subsequent landing it became more and more difficult to reboard. Out of the corner of his eye, he caught a sudden movement in the tall grasses leading up to the river, and at the same time, he felt a familiar rumble beneath his boots. As soon as he recognized the two slight figures dashing toward him, he let out an oath and set off to meet them on a dead run.

"Grant! What is it?" Tara screamed as he grabbed her hand, then Rose's, and started running with them back toward the boat. She got no answer to her question. Grant pulled them after him, setting a pace that made her legs burn with pain and her lungs feel as if they were on fire.

Grant didn't stop when they reached the gangplank but rushed them on board. At last, he let go of their hands, and the two gasping women slumped to the deck, while he and the waiting roustabouts pulled in the heavy plank. The instant that task was completed, the bells sounded for full stroking, and the decks groaned beneath the strain of a wide-open throttle as the *Ophelia* lurched away from the shore.

It took a few moments for Tara to recover, but once she'd regained her breath, she heard an awful roaring noise and rushed to the rail. "Oh, my Lord," she exclaimed in disbelief as a mammoth dark shadow came up over the hills and spread out onto the prairie.

Standing beside her, Rose groaned. "My pa's goin' to kill me if he hears about this!"

"He won't hear it from me," Tara said, her voice quivering in fear as she realized what had almost happened to them.

Rose gazed beseechingly at Grant, and he shook his head in exasperation. "All right, if you two have learned your lesson from this, I'll say nothing to your folks."

"I certainly have," Rose replied, and she was gone in a flash, leaving Grant and Tara still standing at the rail.

"It's the running season," Grant said as he stepped behind her, clasping his arms around her trembling body. "Another few minutes and you and Rose would have been trampled to death."

Tara had seen her first buffalo the day before. A mother and two large calves had been wallowing in the mud on the shallow river bank, but those placid-looking animals hadn't prepared her for this awesome sight or the deafening roar of an oncoming stampede. Closer and closer they came, a rampaging sea of dark hides, pointed horns, and sharp hooves that cut down everything in their wake.

"There must be thousands of them," Tara gasped. "Are we safe in the river?"

"Safer than we would be out there," Grant said. "By the time they plunge into the water, we should be deep enough in the channel that we'll only get nudged a time or two."

"Thank God."

"You should certainly thank someone," Grant replied tersely, his own legs feeling shaky as he contemplated how close he'd just come to losing her. On the heels of his fear, came a vivid memory from the past and a blinding anger. Before he could stop himself, he'd wrenched Tara around to face him. "For scaring me like that, I should thrash you to within an inch of your foolish life!"

When presented with a thousand head of stampeding buffalo or the anger of one man, Tara was exceeding grateful for the latter. Throwing her arms around Grant's waist, she hugged him tightly to her breast.

The feel of her soft, curvaceous body pressed against him had the usual effect, and Grant found himself returning her embrace instead of meting out the beating she so greatly deserved. "Promise me you'll never do something like that again," he murmured gruffly.

"I promise," Tara whispered.

"It's over," he assured her as he felt her shiver. "Don't think about it."

But she couldn't help it. She kept picturing herself running through the grass, then falling to the ground and being stamped into a bloody pulp.

Grant didn't need to be told what was on her mind. He could see the same picture, and he had to do something to erase it. Without a word, he picked her up and carried her down the passageway to their cabin.

Tara was reluctant to let go of him as Grant laid her down on the berth, but then she saw the tense, possessive look in his eyes and understood his intentions. She watched him remove his clothes, feeling a mixture of edginess, desire, and desperation as he joined her on the bed. It was as if the only way he could assure himself that she was safe was to surround her with his body, and to assure herself of the same thing, all Tara could do was give herself up to his physical demands.

With quick, impatient movements, Grant stripped off her clothing and pulled the pins out of her hair. After combing it with his fingers, he lowered his mouth gently to her breasts. Tara laced her fingers through his hair and arched herself against his lips. She needed fire and passion, not tenderness.

Grant instinctively sensed her needs and got a little rougher, his caresses less playful. Instead of teasing her thighs apart, he wedged a hard leg between them and began to stroke her with a demanding touch. His arrogant male aggressiveness made Tara tremble with excitement rather than fear, thoroughly eradicating the specter of death which had come so close to claiming her as its own.

With every movement of his body, Grant proved that she belonged solely to him. His kisses were branding, his fingers seeking the pleasure points that only she knew. Tara writhed beneath him in a convulsive plea for release, but he wouldn't allow it. Again and again, his fingers lingered at the feverish core of her, probing and then withdrawing before she could gain fulfillment.

She was dazed and panting by the time he pulled away.

Confused by this sudden cessation in their lovemaking, she opened her eyes and found him staring at her with an almost pagan possessiveness. Then he reached down for something in his saddlebags, his voice husky and hypnotic as he showed her a small vial of amber liquid. "This was given me by a medicine man a long time ago. It is used to prolong pleasure. I never thought I would make use of it, but I'm going to use it on you."

Tara was already so aroused that she would have given him anything he wanted, but his next words inflamed her even more. "At first, you will want to scream with frustration as the sensations overwhelm you, but then your body will explode with the sheer ecstasy of it."

Wide-eyed, Tara watched him pour some on his fingers, but her eyes fluttered closed as he massaged it into her most delicate flesh, then took a little more and worked it up inside her. He was so thorough that she was ready to shatter into a million pieces by the time he was through, only to learn that the pleasure had yet to begin.

He pulled her on top of him and teased his way a little bit inside her, grasping her hips to direct her movements. Tara put her arms around his neck, kissing him hungrily, wanting him deeper, but accepting his firm control. Her last coherent thought was how wonderful he felt—full and hard but also velvety soft.

As he eased himself completely inside her, she drew up her knees and clutched his hips tightly. She didn't know when it happened, but suddenly she was the one in control, setting the pace, moving closer, then drawing back. When she'd aroused them both to the breaking point, he took over again and drove her hard and fast to a shattering, overpowering release. Limp and out of breath afterward, they lay in each other's arms, still joined together, savoring the afterglow.

"I want you again," Grant said after a few minutes. "Only this time, I want it to be slow."

Tara didn't know what was in that oil, but whatever it was, the effects lasted throughout the afternoon. She fell asleep at sunset but sometime after midnight awakened to find Grant seated beside her, caressing her breasts. "You are so beautiful,'' he murmured, gazing lovingly down the length of her naked body. "No woman should be this beautiful."

The element of sadness in his voice made Tara frown, but when she attempted to sit up, he moved his hand down her side, to her belly, then between her still sensitive thighs. "You have touched my heart, Tara."

Pleased beyond measure, Tara whispered back, "I love you," but then, as the throbbing within her accelerated with his touch, she had no breath left with which to speak.

Having seen her climax, Grant was on fire to have her, and she accepted his penetration with a sigh of blessed contentment. "Whatever happens, you are mine, Taralynn. You will always be mine."

As he loved her with his hands, his mouth, and his body, Tara held him close. She reveled in the knowledge that she held his heart. When at last they reached completion together, she fell into a deep and blissful sleep.

The *Ophelia* reached Fort Benton at sunrise the next morning. Upon hearing the landing bells, Tara opened her eyes but found herself alone in the berth. Less than an hour later, she was forced to accept the unacceptable. Grant Collingswood was gone from her bed, the boat, and Fort Benton.

Without explanation or the slightest concern for her feelings, the man she loved had disappeared out of her life, leaving her to face an uncertain future alone.

PART
2

Chapter

Eleven

Montana Territory, June, 1864

Grant rode the stolen mount he'd acquired at Fort Benton long and hard. By midmorning, he was well away from the *Ophelia* and the river and especially Taralynn Armstrong. Today she would discover that the man she'd professed to love had cruelly deserted her, and with that discovery, she would come to regret every moment they'd spent together. Eventually, when she realized that he was never coming back, she'd probably start hating him. As much as that thought bothered him, Grant knew he had no right to expect more from her. He had to forget all about her. Whatever she had felt or would feel for him, Taralynn had no place in his life, nor he in hers.

When the sun stood straight up in the sky, Grant pulled his horse up beneath a stand of cottonwoods as if they were his ultimate destination. Dismounting swiftly, he led the animal between the tall trees until he located the steady stream of crystal-clear water bubbling up from beneath a large rock. As the lathered stallion drank from the wide spring-fed pool which was housed and roofed by a sheer granite cliff, a joyous expression came over Grant's face. With lighthearted movements, he pulled the saddle from his horse, then drew out a leather satchel from his saddlebags.

Going down on his knees, Grant used the glassy surface of the pool like a mirror as he shaved off his night's growth of beard, the first step in a transformation that would have shocked Taralynn to her very depths. If she'd investigated further that day she'd been snooping through his belongings, she would have discovered many things that would have stunned her even more then what she did find. The tenth earl of Collingswood was the least of who he really was.

Stripping off his muslin shirt, dark pants, and boots, Grant dived naked into the cool water. He held his breath and stayed beneath the surface as long as he could, swimming underwater until his lungs were near bursting. When he finally did emerge from the depths and stepped out of the water, he didn't replace his clothes but reached inside a soft leather bag and donned a breechclout and leggings. Having cleansed himself of the white man's world, he was no longer Grant Collingswood, the English lord, or the riverboat gambler, but Star-runner, courageous warrior and respected high chief of the mighty Absaroka.

Squatting in the wet sand at the edge of the pool, Star-runner pulled the rest of his necessities from his saddlebags. On his feet he placed a pair of beautifully embroidered moccasins. As evidence that he had contended with and overcome a desperate enemy in open combat, he drew a necklace of bear claws over his head. He then girded his waist with a buckskin belt and tucked in his tomahawk and knife.

To prepare himself for his upcoming session at council, he tied the tobacco sack which contained the flint, steel, and spunk needed for lighting his pipe to his belt. Finally, he restored his medicine bag, that sacred, inviolate symbol of his manhood, to its proper place next to his bare skin. When again he viewed himself in the clear surface of the pool, his transformation was complete. With the exception of his hair, which was cut much too short for his exalted position in the tribe, he was once more Absaroka.

Off in the distance, he could see the sacred mountains,

and a surge of pure happiness filled him as he thought about his homecoming. He had crossed a wide ocean and been away from his people for eight years, but at last his long exile was over. By nightfall, he would be back where he belonged, among his own kind.

With a running leap, he remounted the roan stallion. Riding bareback as a warrior was meant to ride, he headed for the mountains, and with each passing mile the emotional trappings of civilization fell away from his soul. At long last, he was free again, free to ride like the wind beneath an endless blue sky. As a Child of the Raven, he was part of that sky and the earth below it. He was blood brother to the bear and the mountain lion and the soaring eagle. Yet, even as he raced toward the camp of his beloved people, he remembered a time when he'd had no people, no past, and a future that had struck sheer terror into a young boy's heart.

Chapter

Twelve

At first, the boy was aware of nothing but the pounding in his head as he opened his eyes and found himself lying on a thick bed of buffalo robes. But then, as his eyes grew accustomed to the darkness, he realized that his unfamiliar bed was surrounded by wild-looking people who were all staring down at him, their savage faces gleaming like polished copper in the flickering light from a small cooking fire. He was too frightened to do more than whimper as they poked and pulled at his clothes, and far too weak to fend off so many hands as they stripped him naked. Paralyzed by terror and humiliation, he could do nothing as the curious men, women, and children surveyed every inch of his thin white body.

He could sense their amazement at the birthmark they discovered on his right hip, but he couldn't comprehend their words, for they spoke in a language he couldn't understand. More hands than he could count reached out to touch the small, dark, birdlike marking on his pale skin, and though he tried to squirm away, he was held fast. To escape their probing black eyes and rough hands, he again sought the blessed peace of unconsciousness, but during the next few days, as his brain began to clear, that kind of escape was denied him. Whoever these people were, he soon came to discover that he was considered one of them, and, as such, he was expected to learn their strange ways.

The woman who forced him to drink a vile brew that was meant to restore his strength called him Star-runner, and whenever he answered to that name, she rewarded him with a pleased and kindly smile. At other times, when he failed to understand some word she was trying to teach him, she would scowl fiercely and shake her head, as if he were a great disappointment to her. Although he knew by the dark color of her skin and eyes that he couldn't possibly be related to her or to the three other dark-skinned boys who laughed at his frequent mistakes, he understood that he was nevertheless looked upon as a member of their family.

This was explained to him on the fifth day of his convalescence by a tall, broad-shouldered Indian with white hair and a bronzed face marked with many scars. In a deep-timbered voice, he named each member of the clan, explaining their relationship to each other by drawing a series of pictures on the dirt-packed floor of the tepee. Eventually, the boy understood that this man was called Mountain-lion, and the woman who served their lodge was his daughter, White-fawn. The three boys were her sons by Split-nose, chief of the Fire-bear clan who would soon be returning from the hunt. Swift-bear was the eldest son and had seen fourteen summers, Otter's-heart had seen six, and the youngest was Running-deer, who was less than four seasons old.

On the sixth day, the boy's newfound position in this alien family was reconfirmed by a barrel-chested white man dressed in oily buckskins who entered the tepee and seated himself Indian-fashion near the boy's bed. "Don't know how you came to be wandering 'round in circles out on the prairie, boy, but it's a lucky thing I found you when I did," the man said in greeting. "You were on your last legs, and plum crazy out of your head. I brought you here, because I knew White-fawn would take mighty good care of you, but who'd have ever thought she and her kin would up and adopt you like this? I hear tell ol' Mountain-lion's preparing the ceremony to make ye his grandson, real official-like."

"Who are you, sir?" the boy asked. Desperate for any

kind of reassurance, he reached for the man's large hand, clinging to it as if it were a lifeline.

"I'm no sir, that's for certain," the man said. "Jebediah Fenton's the name. Fur trapper by trade. I wanted to meet you proper before I set out on my trap line, so I'm glad you're back amongst the livin' again. You remember yourself any better now? Can you reckon who you are and where you come from?"

The boy shook his head, knowing he was past the age of crying but feeling the tears well up in his eyes. "I can't remember anything before the time when I awakened to these frightful people in this awful place. I beseech you to take me away from here, sir."

"Ah, it won't be that bad," Jebediah stated gruffly, pulling his hand out of the boy's grasp as he stood up. "Mark my words, in no time at all, you'll be as good as one of 'em for all your fancy way of talkin'. Why, the next time I pass this way, I probably won't be able to tell you from any of the other young bucks."

"But I don't belong here!" the boy cried, struggling to raise himself up out of his bed as he realized that his salvation was leaving as abruptly as he'd arrived. "Please! You have to take me with you."

"Naw, I reckon you'll be better off here," Jebediah said, relenting slightly when he saw the boy's tears. "Don't take on so, son. If you be in your right mind at the end of the season, I'll take you with me down to St. Louie, and we'll try and locate your rightful family."

Reaching into his back pocket, Jebediah drew out a long, black metal tube and tossed it down on the heavy pile of robes. "Maybe this will help you remember 'em. Had it in that dandified coat you were wearin'," he said, neglecting to mention that he'd also found several funny-looking gold pieces and a finely crafted pocket watch that he'd decided to keep for himself.

"My telescope!" the boy exclaimed in delight, but although he recognized the instrument, he had no idea how he'd come to own it.

"Never seen no telescope," Jebediah admitted. "What's it for?"

"To view the stars." Brow furrowing, the boy tried to

hold on to the memory that beckoned to him, but it disappeared before he could grasp it fully.

Jebediah nodded, but once he realized that no more information was forthcoming, he departed the tepee and very soon after left camp. Although the boy waited and waited, he never saw or heard from the old trapper again.

"Star-runner, take off your shirt and leggings," Mountain-lion ordered on the first day of summer.

It had been five months since the ceremony that had made him grandson to this great chief, and in that time Star-runner had learned to obey his elders without question. When he'd balked at swimming in a river that was caked with floating ice, he'd been thrown in and repeatedly dunked. When he'd refused to eat the bloody meat set before him, he'd gone without food for three days. When he'd backed away from the flailing hooves of the horse he'd been given, he'd been given a larger and even more vicious animal.

Having no other choice, he'd learned how to obey, and he'd also learned how to speak the Absaroka language. Anxious to please, he swiftly tore off his clothing and stood before his grandfather naked, except for his moccasins.

"Now, catch me a yellow butterfly," Mountain-lion demanded. "And be quick, for above all else, an Absaroka warrior must be swift!"

Searching the meadow, Star-runner spotted a golden set of wings and sprinted after it. In and out among the trees and bushes, across streams and over grassy places, the small creature darted and flit until, at last, the boy managed to capture it in his hands. Panting to conceal his shortness of breath, he jogged back to where he had started the chase. He offered the pretty butterfly to Mountain-lion, but the man shook his head and smiled at him with genuine affection. "Rub its wings over your heart, my son, and ask the butterflies to lend you their grace and swiftness."

Calling upon the wild creatures to pass on their abilities to him was becoming a familiar duty to Star-runner. Thus far, he had learned to listen as the chickadee listens, to think with the cunning of the fox, and to swim like the otter. The Almighty had given each of his creations some peculiar grace or power, and the Absaroka believed that if a man was disciplined enough in his study of their behavior, he could obtain their skills.

If he was steadfast in his lessons, Star-runner would soon be ready to hunt large game with his bow and arrow and ride his horse with the same skill as the other boys his own age. Although he could not recall how many seasons had passed since his birth, Mountain-lion suspected that he was in his twelfth year, which meant that he was far behind in his studies and must work very hard to catch up. Mountain-lion had made it his responsibility to see that Star-runner would not lag behind for long.

Although he still felt out of place in the Indian camp, he was a smart boy, and his thin body grew stronger day by day. In the beginning, his white skin had burned from overexposure to the sun, but now his arms and legs were almost as brown as the other boys, and his black hair was almost as long. The only thing about him that still set him apart were his blue eyes, and that was something no amount of time would change.

At first, Star-runner had a difficult time adjusting to the rigorous routine of exercise boys his age were expected to follow, but after suffering the contempt of Swift-bear and his friends at every turn, he no longer revealed his fear or exhaustion. The taunting youths were intent on showing him up as a coward, a weakling, and a failure, but his pride refused to let that happen. Someday, he vowed, his skills would be superior to theirs, and he would be the one laughing.

Unlike Swift-bear and the other older boys, Mountain-lion never punished Star-runner for his defeats. He only gave more lessons.

"Tonight will be a special night for you, Star-runner," Mountain-lion said as they walked back toward camp. "Do not speak of this to the others, but bring your wolf's skin and meet me at the riverbank when the moon is high."

That night, Star-runner was surprised to discover that he was not the only boy who had slipped away from the village to the secret camp on the riverbank, and he was even more astonished when he learned that Split-nose, the tribal chief and his adopted father, was cast in the role of their teacher.

The significance of this was told him by Big-shoulder, a boy of ten seasons, one of the few who had befriended him.

"Split-nose sees that we are fast becoming men," Big-shoulder whispered excitedly. "Tonight he honors us with his acknowledgment of our growing skill. If we succeed in the task he requires of us, we shall be praised as his future warriors."

Holding up several peeled sticks to which were tied the small breath feathers of a war eagle, Split-nose spoke solemnly to the eager group of nine. "Young men, there is a new village near us. Our scouts have seen it and counted many horses tied to their lodges. To enter this village and cut a fine horse is to count coup. Paint your bodies with mud until you resemble the wolf's color, and cover yourself with your wolf skin so that you will not be known to our enemy. Bring back some good horses, and I will give a feast in honor of your bravery and courage."

The other boys understood that when Split-nose spoke of horses, he actually meant meat, but Star-runner was unaware that stealing chunks off the drying racks of buffalo meat from a neighboring village was used to teach the skill of counting coup that would be required of him once he came of age. Star-runner took the directive seriously, and when he crept into the neighboring village, he bypassed lodge after lodge, in search of the chief's tepee where he knew the best horses could be found. In this he was correct, for three magnificent stallions were hobbled before the entrance to the chief's lodge.

Stealthily, Star-runner approached the great tepee, keeping his body low to the ground so that his form would not be caught in the light from the chief's cooking fire. Making no sound, he cut the soft rawhide straps that tethered the horses' legs, then mounted the largest of the three, a burnished chestnut. Heart pounding in fear, he guided the horse toward the shadows, wanting to cry out in relief when the two other stallions followed obediently behind. As soon as he considered them far enough away from the chief's lodge, he circled in a wide arc around the enemy village until he was able to head back in the direction he had come without risk of discovery.

Then, holding on to the horse's mane with both hands, he

kicked the chestnut into a full gallop and took off at a breakneck pace for the river. Suddenly, the stallion let out a high-pitched scream, and Star-runner heard an answering whinny off in the distance. Within moments, his small band of horses was joined by ten mares intent on following their chosen stallions.

Back at the secret camp, Split-nose was speaking to his future warriors. "This is a fine band of horses," he decreed as he carefully examined the pile of stolen meat presented for his admiration. Holding up a piece of back fat, he declared, "Ho! This is an especially fine horse. Who stole this one?"

"I did," Big-shoulder answered proudly, and he was given a coup stick. Saying, "I stole this fine horse," he poked the stick into the ground before him while the rest of the group cheered.

Just at that moment, Star-runner rode into the secret camp at the head of a real band of horses, and the cheering gave way to a stunned silence. "For you, teacher," he declared as he slipped off the chestnut's back and humbly presented the leather rein to his adopted father. Bowing his head, he prayed that his accomplishment was as great as that of the other competitors, for Split-nose had yet to look upon him with anything but disdain. Seeing that the other boys had beaten him back to camp and unnerved by the silence that had greeted his arrival, he feared that he was about to suffer for his tardiness and that his gifts to the chief would be ignored.

Split-nose accepted the reins, not showing by word or expression how he felt about Star-runner's gifts. "Run to the village," he ordered sternly. "For what you have done this night, you must call out the men of council to join us here."

In the deafening silence that followed the chief's order, Star-runner felt his knees begin to quake. All the other boys were staring at him, unable to believe what he had done and as frightened as he of the possible consequences. Never before in their memory had one of their group committed an action that required the presence of the full council in order to decide what was to be done about it.

"Go, Star-runner!" Split-nose repeated. "Do as I have commanded you."

Shoulders slumped in defeat, Star-runner did as he was bid. Once again, he had failed, but this time his failure was so great that it required public chastisement. In the time he had been with the Absaroka, he had witnessed only one such tribunal, but it had convinced him he should never commit a similar offense. For violating the order of a chief, Black-lynx, a young man of perhaps eighteen snows, was stripped of his clothing and forced to accept the duties of a squaw until the council deemed him worthy to take up his manly pursuits once again. His humiliation continued for days, and Star-runner shuddered as he recalled the morning when he'd seen Black-lynx being chastised by an angry old woman who was whipping his bare flanks with a willow switch.

As he pictured himself enduring some similar punishment, Star-runner was tempted to run away and take his chances in the forest, but if he did that and was found, his suffering would be even greater than what was already in store for him. If he'd learned one thing about the Absaroka, it was that they detested cowards. Though his fear of the upcoming trial was great, his fear of being deemed a coward was greater.

So, as the moon began its nightly descent in the sky, he returned to the secret camp in the company of the clan's most wise leaders. At council's request, representatives of each military society—the Foxes, the Big-dogs, and the Fighting-bulls—were also called out from their tepees to join the assembly at the river. Avoiding the jeering gaze of his brother Swift-bear, newly elected member of the Foxes, Star-runner returned to his place with the younger boys while the men gathered around the campfire, speaking together in low murmurs.

"What did I do that was so wrong?" he whispered to Big-shoulder when he could stand the suspense no longer.

Pointing to the pile of stolen meat, Big-shoulder whispered back, "We were sent out to steal the meat of our enemy who is not our enemy, but you have stolen their chief's horses. For this crime against our sister clan, I know not what fate will befall you."

It was Mountain-lion who eventually came to stand before the wide-eyed group of frightened boys. "Stand and hear me, Star-runner," he commanded. "Stand before this company of your fellows and the bravest warriors of our clan."

Though he didn't know if his quivering limbs would hold him, Star-runner rose to his feet to face whatever judgment had been decided. Bravely, he lifted his chin, hoping that if he met his fate with courage, the council would show him some mercy. Whatever his punishment, he knew that Swift-bear and his cronies would gloat, but he tried not to think about having to endure that additional humiliation.

"This night," Mountain-lion began solemnly, ignoring Star-runner and addressing his words to the group of young boys, "one amongst you has shown himself to be a true warrior. Though he has yet to learn all the ways of our clan, he has earned his place as a true Fire-bear. He has listened well to his lessons and has borrowed the grace and swiftness of the butterfly, the cunning of the fox, and, above all, the heart of the grizzly. This night he was challenged as a young boy is challenged, but he has answered as a man. From this time forward, the name Star-runner will be spoken in the lodges of the Fire-bears with great pride."

As astonished as he was by Mountain-lion's pronouncement, Star-runner was shocked speechless when Split-nose stepped forward, his normally expressionless face wearing a beaming smile. "As all of you young magpies know, my son Swift-bear has recently joined the society of the Foxes. Tonight another of my sons has been invited to take his place as a member of that elite club of young warriors. Though he has only twelve snows, Star-runner has counted coup and thus earned himself this great honor. If you desire to follow in his footsteps, the rest of you must think long and hard on what has happened here tonight. Never forget that it is the mind that leads a man to power, not the strength of his body."

To the thundering ovation of the gathering, Split-nose walked over to Star-runner and clasped him around the shoulders. "Come, my son. Let us return quickly to the village," he declared, smiling the smile of a proud father. "I want you to be standing by my side with council as we greet my brother White-horse, who has just returned from the

Wolf Mountains with his followers. It is time he meets this young nephew of his who brings honor to our family, and I suspect he shall arrive in our camp very soon.''

Split-nose's prediction was correct, for a group of ten men were waiting for them by the large fires as the gathering came forth from the forest. Laughing at the irate expressions on their visitors' faces, Split-nose inquired, ''Were you not prepared for the descent of our magpies, men of the Big-shields? Do you come to complain of the empty stomachs you must suffer without the fine meat our boys have stolen from your lodges?''

A man of perhaps thirty snows, with the long glossy hair of a revered warrior, answered back, ''My brother mocks us when it is he who must be judged for sending us an eagle disguised as a magpie. It would dishonor us to beg you for the meat your boys have been clever enough to take, but there is no dishonor in asking for the horses stolen from us by one who is a pesky magpie no longer.''

At this, the entire crowd burst out laughing. ''Did you see this brave eagle, White-horse?'' Mountain-lion hooted.

Unamused, White-horse stared at his father. ''Do you condone the shameful tactics of my young brother? Is this the kind of trickery I can expect from the chief of the Fire-bears whenever we come down from the mountains to make camp near his village, Father?''

''There has been no trickery, my son,'' Mountain-lion replied, no longer smiling. ''We welcome your summer visit to us. Your horses were not stolen by some villain but by your young nephew, and even you must commend him for his courage.''

For the first time, White-horse grinned. ''So it is Swift-bear who has outwitted me. In the passing of winter to summer, the boy has fast become a man.''

''Not Swift-bear,'' Split-nose informed him. ''It is your nephew Star-runner who has reaped the rewards for your lack of diligence.''

White-horse and his warriors gazed in astonishment at the blue-eyed youth who was being credited with this great feat. As Star-runner stepped forward into the light of the camp-fire, the men of the Big-shields exchanged questioning glances with the men of the Fire-bears, and then Mountain-lion nodded. By mutual agreement, nothing was said to the boy who stood before them, but in that moment, the truth in prophecy was confirmed. Tonight, this untried stripling had shown the daring and recklessness required in a man who would one day become a great chief.

"It is good that I meet you, Nephew," White-horse said. "Though the way you have made yourself known to me has lessened my sleep after my long journey."

"I am sorry, Uncle. I did not know that the Big-shields were not my enemy," Star-runner apologized as he untied the black tube that was always attached to the belt at his waist. Unbidden, he proved again his worthiness as a future chief by offering a gift to his elder without thought to his own gain. "I beg your forgiveness, and I present my most treasured possession to you to make up for my ignorance."

In praise of this generous gesture, Split-nose clasped him tightly around the shoulders, and even Swift-bear looked at him as if he were proud to call him his brother. For the first time since he'd come among them, Star-runner felt as if he belonged, and for this the sacrifice he had just made seemed well worth it.

"I accept your gift, Star-runner," White-horse said. "Though I am unfamiliar with this treasure."

Stepping forward, Star-runner pulled on the tube until it reached its longest length, then showed White-horse how to hold it. "Now, look up there, Uncle," he suggested, pointing to the heavens.

White-horse gazed up at the sky through the eyepiece. "Argh!" he cried out in shock a moment later. As if the telescope were possessed of powerful spirits, he gave it back into Star-runner's hands.

"What is it, White-horse?" Split-nose asked, shocked by the fear he saw in the eyes of his brother who feared nothing.

"See for yourself," White-horse replied, pointing to the black tube held by Star-runner. "Show these warriors what magic you possess, Nephew."

The black tube was passed from hand to hand until all had seen what was not possible for men to see. Star-runner did his best to explain away their fright and awe, but he did not have the words to convince them that the telescope possessed no magic power. Eventually, he gave up the task and retired to his tepee. The telescope was placed beneath the store of his other belongings, and as time passed he forgot that it was there.

The men of the Fire-bears and the men of the Big-shields did not. As Mountain-lion boasted later that evening to the assembly of elders gathered inside the council lodge, "It is as I have spoken on the night of the big snow! Star-runner has the power to call down the moon! He is the chosen one."

Chapter

Thirteen

It was a day when the chokecherries were ripe and the wild plums were full on the trees. As was their custom each year at this time, the maidens of the Fire-bear clan danced through the forest, waiting to see which young brave would gather the most fruit and thereby win his choice of female partner. At seventeen snows, Star-runner joined in the scramble for berries, and, as usual, he won.

Taller than the other young men his age, Star-runner also had a symmetry of form most pleasing to the feminine eye. His muscles were lean and strong, his long black hair glossy, and his features ruggedly handsome. Whenever his blue-eyed gaze lingered with admiration on a maiden, her stature immediately increased, for Star-runner had already proven himself a courageous warrior.

Riding with the Foxes on their last foray to the Beartooth Mountains, Star-runner and his companions had discovered many lodges that belonged to their enemies, the Blackfeet. The sight of so large a village established on Absaroka hunting grounds had caused them to tremble in fear for their people, but Star-runner had conceived of a plan that would send the Blackfeet back to their own territory. As they'd waited for the cover of darkness, the Foxes had disguised themselves as raging spirits, then stolen into the enemy camp just as a fierce storm had risen up in the forest.

That night, the sky had been black with streaks of mad color racing through it, and as the lightning struck an eerie blaze in the heavens, the Absaroka braves had screamed like those possessed and danced their fierce dance between the Blackfoot lodges. Their enemies had been very frightened as they'd rushed outside to view the masked personages of the thunders, the four winds, and the war eagles vowing vengeance on their tribe if they did not move their village from ground sacred to the spirit world. Luckily, as a few brave warriors had begun to question the manlike appearance of their visitors, a great gust of wind had blasted through their camp, twisting trees like fragile blades of grass and allowing the Foxes to disappear like shadows before the rain.

In the morning, the young men had crept back to the Blackfoot village, but it was gone from the forest as if it had never been. Star-runner had been praised as a hero, and even before the Foxes had returned to their village to regale their people with the story of his great cunning, he had been elected their new leader. Though younger than most other members of the society, he had been given the feathers of an eagle to wear on his lance, and at the celebration that had followed his triumph over the Blackfeet, his companions had pledged him their eternal loyalty.

This feast day, however, was in celebration of love, not war. As winner of the race for ripe berries, Star-runner chose Winter-rose, a lovely girl of fifteen snows, to take back to his tepee. As yet, none of those favored by his interest had been able to capture his heart, for no matter how the women admired him, Star-runner did not respond to their amorous attentions, and no female had yet shared his tepee for more than one night. Winter-rose was determined that she would be the one to bring an end to his unmarried status, for with the coming of womanhood her beauty had blossomed beyond compare.

The next morning, Otter's-heart paced back and forth before his brother's empty tepee, trying to work out what he must say before the sun rose much higher in the sky. Star-runner's lack of continuing interest in the many sweethearts who pursued him was becoming embarrassing for Otter's-heart to explain. He adored his adopted older brother, but even the beautiful Winter-rose had not managed to impress him with her considerable charms. At first light, Star-runner had sent her away from him, just as swiftly as he'd dispatched all of his previous lovers.

Otter's-heart knew this behavior had to stop, or soon he would not be able to thwart the rumor he'd just heard that Star-runner might be a *berdache* and was seeking a lover from among the men. It was time that Star-runner sang before a maiden's tepee and put such evil talk to rest.

"Why so solemn, little brother?" Star-runner inquired a short while later as the twelve-year-old boy came to sit beside him on the riverbank. A serious face was a rare thing for Otter's-heart, who was normally as full of high spirits and mischief as a playful puppy.

"I have come to advise you, Star-runner," Otter's-heart declared in a severe tone. "You may think it is so, but I say it is not enough that you please the maidens under the blanket. Much more is required of a warrior."

"And what would you know of what goes on under my blankets?" Star-runner inquired, holding back his amused smile.

Scowling at this taunt to his manhood, Otter's-heart retorted, "Did you not see Little-moon lead me from the berry patch? She has seen sixteen summers, yet I was her choice of partner. I have learned much of kissing, and soon I, too, shall be admired by the maidens for my great skill."

"Every boy over ten is Little-moon's choice at one time or another," Star-runner scolded. "You would be wise to accept my advice and seek out a more discerning female, or you will learn of itching as well as kissing."

"Hmmph," Otter's-heart grunted. "If you had the gift of wisdom, you would be married by now. Some are beginning to worry that your organ cannot produce manly seed. If this is so, perhaps you should visit Fire-weasel when next she comes, so that she might cure you of this weakness."

Star-runner could see that his young brother was truly concerned about him, so he did not become angry upon hearing such insulting gossip. Otter's-heart was right in saying that it was time that he marry. Marriage was forbid-

den to those who were of ill health or weak and those who
had yet to count coup, but he had already led a successful
war party, had taken an enemy's bow, and had cut out a
horse from a Cheyenne picket line.

For these brave deeds, he had earned the respect of every
member of his clan, yet he would not enjoy his revered
position much longer if he did not take a wife. "You need
not concern yourself, little brother," he assured him, smiling
as he recalled the pleasures he had enjoyed the night before
with Winter-rose. Perhaps he should stop searching for a
female with the power to move his heart and marry one who
enticed the power in his loins. "As Winter-rose can tell you,
I have no need of such a cure."

Greatly relieved, Otter's-heart sighed. "I told Swift-bear
this could not be so, but he said no woman carried your
lance because the one between your legs is yet too small to
hold."

Over the years, Star-runner had grown accustomed to his
older brother's teasing, but this affront was much too ven-
omous to ignore. "Is that so?" he inquired, his voice low
and dangerous.

Otter's-heart nodded. "He thinks you might be a *berdache* and should be asked to step down as leader of the
Foxes."

"And has he spoken of this suspicion to anyone else?"

Suddenly, Otter's-heart realized the import of what he
was saying. Shaking his head back and forth in denial, he
stammered, "Only . . . only to me, Star-runner, and . . . and
we both know he says such hurtful things because he is so
jealous. To be usurped as leader by a younger brother was a
bitter thing for him to accept."

Star-runner was well aware of the motivation behind Swift-
bear's loose talk, but understanding the cause would not
prevent such rumors from spreading. When going into battle,
a man had to have the complete loyalty of his followers, and
even a brother could not be allowed to undermine his authority as leader of the Foxes. "It is good you have come to tell
me of these things, Otter's-heart," Star-runner said as he
slowly stood up, fingering the knife at his belt. "I will think
on your advice, but now I must attend to other business."

Running to keep up with him, Otter's-heart pleaded, "Do

not dishonor me, Star-runner. I have spoken of things that Swift-bear meant for my ears alone."

"You are wrong, little brother," Star-runner said. "Swift-bear knows that your ears are my ears. This was his way of issuing a private challenge."

With a snort of disgust for Swift-bear's cowardly tactics, Otter's-heart complained, "If he wants to prove himself your better, he should do so in the honored way."

"No," Star-runner disagreed. "One brother does not best another before the eyes of the village. We shall take our disagreements to a secret place."

As expected, Swift-bear was waiting outside his tepee. When he caught sight of Star-runner walking toward him, he lifted the flap and spoke to his new bride, Falling-water. "It is time, woman. He comes."

Immediately, Falling-water came outside to stand beside her husband, her brown eyes glittering with satisfaction. "Today you shall gain back what Star-runner has stolen from you. Today you shall reclaim your rightful place as leader of the Foxes," she said.

"Perhaps," Swift-bear agreed. "And today you shall learn if your ambition has gained you a good beating by your husband or the wounds that come with being his widow."

Since the first day of their marriage one moon before, Falling-water had encouraged her husband to challenge his younger brother to a physical contest. Although a confrontation between close kin was frowned upon by the tribal elders, Star-runner had usurped Swift-bear's honored position, and this was the only way he could reclaim what should still belong to him. If he won, Falling-water would once again be revered as the wife of a distinguished warrior and the future chief of the clan. On the next feast day, Swift-bear would paint her face, and she would ride his best war horse at the head of the parade, carrying his lance and dressed in skins as white as the fresh snow.

It did not fit into her plans to make her appearance bearing bruises. "I do not understand your anger, my husband. I desire only that you take back the place you deserve," Falling-water said, forcing the shimmer of water into her eyes in order to soften Swift-bear's heart.

Unfortunately for Falling-water, Swift-bear's mind was no

longer clouded by the sensual fog of first love, and her tears did not move him as they had previously. "A good wife takes what her husband has to offer without complaint," Swift-bear said, as determined to take back his place at the head of his household as he was to regain leadership of the Foxes.

"I do not make this fight with my brother for you but for myself," he informed her tersely. "Such was destined from the time Star-runner entered the lodge of my father. However it ends, you shall be taught a lesson in humility, if not by my hand, by the hand of the mourning spirits."

With a frightened gasp, Falling-water cried, "I speak not of a fight to the death, my husband. A defeat of Star-runner's strength is defeat enough."

In a tone of finality, Swift-bear retorted, "Between warriors, there can be no such defeat without death."

Star-runner heard these words as he approached. "Between brothers, there can be no honor in death. Is your hatred for me so strong that you would bring this shame upon our family?"

Before answering, Swift-bear shoved Falling-water inside their tepee. "You have shamed me in the eyes of my woman, Star-runner. There can be no greater shame than that."

Terrified by such talk, Otter's-heart exclaimed, "If this is so, Falling-water has disgraced you, Swift-bear. It is she who deserves to feel the pain of your anger, not our brother."

"And so she shall," Swift-bear agreed, but the challenge in his dark eyes did not lessen.

Star-runner appealed to reason one more time. "We have many enemies who covet our country, Swift-bear. The Lacota and Cheyenne push us away from the blackened hills, and the Blackfeet try to slay us with the many guns they have obtained from the white traders. All tribes wish to embrace the high mountains and great rivers of our land. They would fight us for the wealth of our game, the fine grasses of our prairie, and the ripe berries on our trees. Must we also fight amongst ourselves?"

"It is your place as my brother that has yet to be proven to me, Star-runner," Swift-bear replied. "I understand that you have powerful medicine that protects you from harm, but you are not of the people. I, too, have medicine, and it is pure. This day I shall know if the sacred power given to me is greater or less than that possessed by one who calls himself Absaroka yet sees through the eyes of the white man.''

"So be it," Star-runner stated quietly. Then he ordered, "Leave us, Otter's-heart, and say nothing of this to anyone."

"We will go to the Valley of the Wolves," Swift-bear suggested.

Star-runner agreed, and the two men separated in order to fetch their horses and weapons. Otter's-heart watched them ride out of the village together, and his heart fell to the ground as he realized that only one of them would be returning. To his shame, he could not help but hope that Star-runner would be the victor. Swift-bear was of his own blood, true, yet it was Star-runner who listened to his dreams and sympathized with his failures. It was Star-runner who did not begrudge the time it took to teach a young boy the ways of a warrior. He excelled at everything he tried yet was never unjust or impatient with those who did not. Though his eyes were not of the people, as Swift-bear attested, in his heart he was a true Absaroka.

The Valley of the Wolves was situated in the place where the two flowing rivers joined their waters and the trees formed an arrow pointing to the sacred mountains. As Star-runner and Swift-bear guided their horses along the narrow trail between pines, a deer ran across their path. Wondering what had caused the creature's flight, Star-runner looked down the hillside and saw a party of warriors riding in the opposite direction.

"Quick!" he whispered to Swift-bear. "Get behind the rocks before we are seen. They are Sioux scouts."

In the face of this threat, all animosity between the two men was forgotten. The land of the Absaroka was surrounded by enemies, and it was the obligation of every man, woman, and child in the tribe to defend their hunting grounds. "If they continue on as they are going, they shall discover our lodges," Swift-bear murmured under his breath. "It is our duty to help them find their way to a more distant place."

With an understanding grin, Star-runner complied with that idea. "In the next world."

Though the odds were three to one against them, they were Absaroka warriors and used to being outnumbered. As if by instinct, they raced down the hillside, mentally dividing their six enemies into two groups of three and choosing which group to attack. Veering to the right, Swift-bear got off the first shot and killed the last man in his group. His second shot was equally successful, but the third man would not die as easily.

A fine warrior, the Sioux let out a war whoop, dropped his rifle, then turned his horse and charged. As a point of honor, Swift-bear could do no less than meet this challenge. Tossing his rifle onto the ground, he unsheathed his knife, let out an answering yell, and rode his horse into battle.

Star-runner's horse was faster than the three he was chasing. When he drew even with them, he got off a shot that pierced the heart of the man riding closest to him. His falling body cleared the way for Star-runner's knife, which sailed through the air and hit his second target dead center. Before he could take proper aim on the third man in his sights, however, the Sioux slipped half off his horse, keeping his body between his mount and Star-runner's bullets.

Off in the distance, Star-runner could hear the sound of other horses, and he realized that this scouting party was not the only one present in the forest. They were soon to be joined by more Sioux, so there was no time to lose. Gaining on his quarry, Star-runner managed to get off a good shot, but though his enemy reeled in the saddle, he did not fall off.

Having no other choice, Star-runner launched himself off his horse and caught the Sioux around the waist, but even though he pulled with all his might, the man would not fall. Aware that help was coming, the Sioux was full of fight, and it was all Star-runner could do not to lose his own grip. Finally, he threw a vicious punch into the man's stomach which forced the Sioux to let go of his horse's mane, and they fell together to the ground.

Though wounded, the Sioux was as powerful as a buffalo bull. As soon as they landed, he lashed out with his fists, catching Star-runner full in the mouth. Taken off guard by the fury of the Sioux's attack, Star-runner tried to defend himself, but he suffered blow after blow to his face and body until a powerful club to his midsection whirled him around. He staggered backward, but somehow he managed not to fall over the edge of the washout that dropped off behind him. Knowing that time was running out, Star-runner pulled his war club from his belt and let out a furious yell.

With the ferocity of a grizzly, he faced his worthy adversary, but his club was no match for the deadly pistol aimed at his chest. Aware that he was about to join his ancestors, he hurled his body into the air as the sound of gunfire exploded in his ears. Strangely, as he landed on top of the enemy who had killed him, he felt no pain from his mortal wound and no depletion in his strength. An Absaroka fought on to his last breath, and so he clasped his hands around the Sioux's thick neck and squeezed.

"There is no need to kill what I have already slain," Swift-bear reprimanded him as he calmed his skittish horse, then replaced his smoking rifle in its scabbard. "If you would stop wasting our precious time like this, Star-runner, we could ride on to warn our people."

Tossing down the reins to Star-runner's pinto, he continued, "You may not have noticed, but more Sioux are fast approaching this place."

Realizing that he was choking a lifeless corpse, Star-runner felt very foolish, but this was not the time for self-recrimination. "My life is yours, Swift-bear," he informed his grinning brother, then grabbed for his horse's reins and vaulted onto the animal's back.

They took off down a long coulee, reaching the Bighorn River only moments before the second scouting party arrived in the valley to see which way they had gone. Never decreasing their pace, they followed the fast-flowing river downstream to a place where a crossing looked possible. The water was dark with churning mud, and there were floating logs and trees swirling about in the flood tide, but the conditions here were better than any other they'd seen thus far, and there was no returning to the safety of their original crossing on the Little Bighorn.

Dismounting their horses, they guided the animals into the swollen water, swimming beside them until they reached the middle of the river. Star-runner's horse was an excellent swimmer, but Swift-bear's mount gave up and began to drift. Star-runner knew that when a horse stopped fighting like that, it would nearly always drown, and it was likely that Swift-bear would go under with it.

Although he was bruised and exhausted, he was also a better swimmer than his brother, and so he let go of his horse. The big pinto seemed to understand and turned downstream toward Swift-bear, who caught it. It took every bit of Star-runner's remaining strength to stay afloat as he struggled against the powerful current, but at last he managed to drag himself onshore.

Swift-bear and the pinto had reached shore much farther downstream, and Star-runner could hear his brother singing as he walked the horse back up the narrow bank. As for himself, he didn't have the strength to lift his head.

"Your medicine is powerful and pure, Star-runner. Because you sent the pinto to me when I needed it, I did not perish in the angry water," Swift-bear said as he sank to the ground next to Star-runner, who was still stretched out facedown in the mud. "My life is yours, little brother."

Fighting to regain his breath, Star-runner got to his knees. "As mine is yours," he managed to reply, but when he tried to smile, his battered face pained him, and a fresh trickle of blood ran into his mouth.

"At least you can still see," Swift-bear groused unsympathetically as he fingered the swollen flesh around both of his eyes. "Until the black recedes from my vision, I will be forced to eat the tough meat provided me by our young brother, Otter's-heart, whose arrows pierce only the old and the lame."

"I, too, must suffer this hardship," Star-runner grumbled, holding up his right hand to reveal his bruised and swollen fingers. "Until the splints are removed from my broken hand, I cannot stretch the bow."

"A sad fate for two such daring warriors," Swift-bear muttered, attempting to reduce the inflammation around his eyes by splashing his face with cold water. "Are you ready to continue on, Star-runner? The urgency of our mission does not lessen with our wounds."

With a resigned sigh, Star-runner nodded, but then he

heard a sound and turned to gaze across the great river. Unbelievably, their flight from the Sioux had gone unnoticed. Even as they watched, the scouting party swerved away from the river and the path to their village. "Either our medicine blends together so strongly that it blinds our enemies, or the Sioux track like old women," Star-runner mused, gasping with the pain from his bruised ribs as he struggled to his feet.

In no better shape, Swift-bear clutched his midriff, startled when his hand came away wet with blood. "They might track like old women, but they have great skill with the knife."

"This is well," Star-runner suggested pointedly as they helped each other mount the remaining horse. "If your woman is kept occupied nursing your wounds, perhaps she will not have the time to inflict any."

Sheepishly, Swift-bear nodded. "After this day, Fallingwater will know her master," he promised. "Her words will not sever the bond we have forged together in battle."

Riding double, their progress was slow, and it took them more than an hour to make the journey back to their village. Unable to bear the knowledge that two of his brothers had left but only one was to return, Otter's-heart had broken his word to Star-runner and poured out his aching heart to Mountain-lion. As anxious as his young grandson to learn the results of what had transpired in the Valley of the Wolves, he and Otter's-heart had kept vigil together atop a high cliff.

Spotting the pinto, Otter's-heart jumped up from his seat on a flat rock. "Look there, Grandfather!" He pointed to the space between the trees, his eyes bright with astonishment. "It is not one brother who returns but one horse."

As the pinto drew closer, the condition of its riders became more noticeable. Star-runner was bent nearly double over the horse's neck, and Swift-bear was slumped heavily on his brother's back. Otter's-heart was concerned by the blood he could see on both men, but Mountain-lion emitted a hearty laugh. "It is good what your foolish brothers have learned this day, Otter's-heart. As they unleashed their fury on one another, it is hatred and jealousy that was slain."

Having witnessed the deadly hostility between his two

brothers firsthand, Otter's-heart was uncertain of the truth in his grandfather's words, but then he saw Swift-bear help Star-runner dismount. Once this task was accomplished, the twosome limped together toward their lodges, their arms wrapped about each other's shoulders. A relieved smile broke out on Otter's-heart's face, matching the wide grin worn by Mountain-lion.

As they walked down from the cliff, Mountain-lion laid his hand on Otter's-heart's shoulder. "Whatever tale they wish to tell to explain their wounds, we shall accept."

"Yes, Grandfather," Otter's-heart agreed, but even though he did not break his promise, he could not help but giggle each time his two older brothers regaled the camp with the grandiose story of how they had saved their village from destruction by slaying an entire scouting party of Sioux warriors.

Chapter

Fourteen

Grandmother Fire-weasel returned from her sojourn with the Black Robes when the berries became too ripe to stay on their branches. Sister of Mountain-Lion, she had never married or borne a child. Tall and broad-shouldered like her brother, she did not braid her long white hair as an Absaroka woman should but had adopted the ways of a medicine man at a very young age. Though no other female in the tribe had followed on this strange path, Fire-weasel was blessed by the healing spirits, and so she was not cast out from the clan.

It was her habit to travel the length and breadth of their hunting grounds in search of the plants and herbs she needed for her stores. On this particular journey, she had stopped to investigate the mission on the Green River, and she had brought back many valuable gifts, including the white man's Book of Heaven, which she presented to the village elders with many shouted alleluias. Showing off the yellow crucifix she wore around her neck, the old woman boasted of her new invincibility and spoke of the prayers she had learned which, according to the Black Robes, would be more powerful than all the entreaties she made to the spirits of the sun and the moon to protect their tribe.

Although skeptical, the men of the village listened to her vehement sermon on hellfire and brimstone, then laughingly sent her away to her tepee which was deliberately kept far removed from the main lodges. Fire-weasel had good medicine, but everyone knew she was slightly crazy, and they did not want her eccentricities tainting their loved ones. As always, the old woman was upset that her great wisdom was scoffed at, but when she stalked off in anger to her own tepee, Star-runner followed swiftly behind her.

As he'd listened to her fiery speech, he had a vague memory of hearing such words before and was tormented by a picture of himself kneeling for long hours before a plaster statue. Even though he could not recall names or people's faces, he remembered snatches of the stern lectures he had once heard in that other life he had thought long forgotten and felt again the pain of being beaten with a hard cane. Somehow, he knew that this punishment was meant to cleanse him of his sins. At one time, he must have been trained in the faith of the Black Robes, but where? When?

He tried hard to recall but discovered that the religion of his past life had been thoroughly vanquished by the rituals of the Absaroka. As he concentrated on the memory of being beaten with a cane, the image was replaced by his recollection of the torture ceremony. For now and forever, he would know the true meaning of sacrifice, and no penance imposed by a priest could be as great as the penance he had imposed on himself that day when the willow leaves had become full grown.

Along with the other candidates, he had entered the sacred medicine lodge. Naked except for his war shield and medicine bag, he had prayed for courage and entrusted himself into the hands of the Great Spirit. Then, after going without food or drink for four days, he had taken up his position before the official witnesses and stood without expression as the attendant cut into his flesh with a knife. When there was an inch-long wound on each shoulder, below his breasts, and under his elbows and knees, the attendant had forced skewers through the wounds and attached them to long leather cords. He was then hauled up off the ground by two of the cords which had been lowered from the top of the lodge. Suspended in air by the strength of the severed flesh in his shoulders and chest, he had then been subjected to the additional torture of having weights attached to the cords dangling from his arms and legs.

Gently at first, then faster and faster, the attendants had whirled each candidate until the agony could be endured no longer. Then, trusting his life into the keeping of the Almighty, each candidate was led outside, where two men would grasp the skewers firmly in their hands and race him firmly around the altar in the center of the viewing area. To the cheers of the watching crowd, the candidate ran until his endurance gave out and he fell to the ground. When consciousness returned, he was then allowed to return to his own lodge, where family and friends were waiting to admire him for his courageous entry into full manhood and his veneration of the Almighty.

Though he had no wish to embrace again the Catholic faith he must have once practiced, Star-runner was anxious to remember the many seasons he had lost. Up until today, he'd had no reason to believe he'd ever recall that past life, but Fire-weasel's words had inspired a flash of memory, and with it had come a burning curiosity to know more.

Fire-weasel was gratified to see that Star-runner had not become as closed-minded as the others since their last meeting. While she bent down to light the fire in the center of her tepee, he sat cross-legged on the ground, waiting patiently for her to complete the task so they could talk. He had first sought her out when he was a young boy, probably because he'd sensed that she did not quite belong to the clan, just as he didn't. Unlike most males in the tribe, Star-runner embraced new ideas, enjoyed thinking thoughts that expanded the mind and the spirit, so he and the old woman soon became fast friends.

"Tell me more of what the Black Robes taught you," Star-runner requested when she sat down across from him.

"At least there is still one warrior whose ears remain open to hear what a female has to say," Fire-weasel grumbled, filling her pipe with tobacco and touching flame to the large bowl. As was the custom between men, she drew on the pipe, then offered it to Star-runner, expelling the smoke from her lungs as she muttered, "I was foolish to have mentioned the devil. It is this nonsense that could not be believed."

Again, Star-runner was overcome by a surge of memory, seeing the image of a grim-mouthed priest ordering him to bare his flanks for whipping so that the evil within him might be purged. "You say the Black Robes speak often of the Evil One, but you have listened well and still do not believe?" he asked, his tone curious.

"Of course, there are created things that possess evil powers," Fire-weasel declared knowledgeably, pleased by this inquiry. As usual, Star-runner was willing to learn and did not fear new ideas. "The owl is possessed of bad medicine, but the All-high rules even him. Of course, everyone knows that Old-man-coyote, to whom the Almighty entrusted most of the work of creation, is responsible for any mistakes in nature. I am thinking that Old-man has played his mischievous tricks on the Black Robes and convinced them that he is this devil they fear so much."

"Maybe so," Star-runner replied thoughtfully, unable to banish the dull pain that had begun to throb inside his head.

Suddenly, as if she had just thought of something that had escaped her before, Fire-weasel let out a loud cackle. Patting her gold crucifix, she exclaimed, "It is a wise woman who can attain pretty gifts such as these yet fear not this Evil One with the red horns. Perhaps I shall go to the Green River again and suggest that the Black Robes hear of the Almighty from me. For their generosity to Fire-weasel, they should learn that the one who created us all speaks not of evil but of love. Perhaps for this kind lesson, they would give me many more pretty things."

Star-runner smiled at her logic, but the pain behind his eyes intensified. "Not of evil but of love," he repeated, struggling to hold on to the picture that had formed in his mind of a blue-eyed woman who wore a gold satin dress and many precious jewels in her hair. Unfortunately, as abruptly as the image appeared, it faded away.

Watching him, Fire-weasel frowned, then blew a puff of hot smoke into his face. She adored this young man as if he were her own son, but they both had duties to their people as well as to themselves. Their country was surrounded by enemies, and to keep it the people had to remain strong. "It is well that you speak of love, Star-runner," she informed him tartly. "For soon you shall feel it. I shall remedy that which you lack this very day."

Immediately, the old woman had his full attention. Eyes wary, he demanded, "Have you been talking to Otter's-heart, Grandmother?"

"What could that young chipmunk tell me that I have not seen for myself?" she demanded, irate at this indication that her knowledge of events did not spring from an all-knowing inner power.

"And what have you seen?" Star-runner inquired suspiciously.

"I have seen that your man root has grown to match your stature as a warrior, but as yet you have found no maiden worthy to receive your seed," Fire-weasel declared, oblivious to the bright red flush that came upon his cheeks as she discussed what no other woman would dare. "Your seed holds the future of our clan, Star-runner, yet again and again you allow it to spill onto the ground."

Speechless with embarrassment, Star-runner could do nothing but stare as the old woman shook a bony finger under his nose. "The summer is growing old, my son, yet you still ignore your duty. You must appease the hunger in your loins, but it is the germ of our posterity that slips through your stroking fingers at night."

As Star-runner squirmed in increasing mortification, she continued relentlessly, "I would not be a great and wise healer if I could not see the way to right this wrong. Therefore, you shall go to the sacred pool below the twin peaks, and there you shall be cured of your unworthy affliction."

The fire that burned in his face was so hot that Star-runner could barely force the words from his dry mouth. "You . . . you forget yourself, old woman," he charged tersely, slamming the pipe she had offered him onto the hard ground as he jumped to his feet. "You shame me with words you have no right to speak and command me to do what is not yours to command."

Unmoved by his anger, Fire-weasel stood up from the fire. "It is not my shame but your own that brings the red heat to your cheeks, Star-runner, and you are not yet so much a man that I cannot demand your obedience. If you do not wish my words to be repeated at the next council of elders, you shall do what you must."

Fire-weasel was the only woman in the clan who was allowed to appear at council, and Star-runner realized that she meant what she said. If he did not comply with her wishes, she would humiliate him before his peers and the wise men of the tribe. The shock of her betrayal contorted his handsome features, but Fire-weasel remained unmoved. "Follow the clear water stream to the twin peaks, Star-runner," she repeated purposefully.

"After this day, our paths shall not cross again," he promised bitterly, then ducked beneath the flap of the tepee and strode angrily across camp to the path that led to the sacred pool.

Fire-weasel watched him until he'd disappeared from sight, then her seamy face split in a grin, revealing the wide gaps between her teeth. "We shall see, my son," she cackled in amusement. "We shall see."

Star-runner's moccasins made no sound on the path of pine needles as he strode swiftly toward his destination. Normally, he would have enjoyed the serenity to be found in the forest, but the whispering breeze that stirred the golden aspens did not soothe him today, nor did the smell of sweet sage and old cedar ease his frustrated rage. He could only guess what kind of "cure" Fire-weasel had in store for him, but he assumed it would be some concoction that would make him so wretchedly sick that he would be unfit to return to camp for many hours, perhaps days. That possibility was the only reason he could think of for her to send him away to the place of restorative waters. Apparently, he would require such sustenance in order to survive his upcoming ordeal.

As always, when he stepped out between the thick trees onto the rocky cliff that jutted out below the snow-capped peaks yet above the bubbling hot spring, he felt as if he were standing at the very center of the world. It was a primeval place, unchanged from season to season, untouched by time. Looking down, he could see the swirling white mists rising up from the mysterious blue waters of the deep pool, bathing the surrounding red rocks and boulders in a shimmering wet veil. Somewhere on the flattened stones at the pool's edge, he would find the vile mixture left for him to drink, but he was not yet ready to commence the search. He had no choice but to suffer, but he would decide when and where the torture was to begin.

In a show of childish belligerence witnessed by no one but himself, he sat down where he was, refusing to venture any closer to the misty pool until he was moved by the freedom of his own will. Closing his eyes, he felt the warm sun on his face and the cold breeze off the mountains ruffling his hair. He listened to the humming of the summer insects in the trees, the calling of a hawk to his mate, the lilting music of a flute.

Star-runner's eyes shot open, searching for the sound that had no place in these surroundings, and when he located its source, his mouth fell open as well. A young, delicately made woman was lying naked by the side of the pool, her slender arms raised above her head as she played on a carved wooden instrument. Her skin glistened with droplets of moisture and was the dark gold of wild honey. Her hair was spread out around her like a luxuriant sable curtain, a fitting backdrop for her high, firm breasts and nipples the color of dusky roses. Even her features were as lovely as a flower, lips as pink and fragile as the petals of a mountain pansy.

As he stared at her in astonishment, the woman stopped playing and sat up, as if she were suddenly aware that she was no longer alone. In growing anticipation, Star-runner waited for her frantic gaze to turn in his direction so that he might see her eyes. For some reason, he knew that if he could only see her eyes, he would know if her physical beauty was matched by a beauty in her soul.

When their gazes eventually met and locked, he felt an explosion deep inside him, a shock wave that killed his anger with Fire-weasel and replaced it with a wild exhilaration. Her eyes were like the sacred pool, clear and fathomless yet warm as the summer sunshine. They were as soft and velvety brown as a deer's and as wide and startled as a fawn's. Slowly, so as not to frighten her any farther than he already had, he got to his feet and began walking down the curving path of wet stones.

"I am Star-runner," he said, as if she should recognize

him with the same depth of certainty as that with which he had recognized her. No one needed to tell him who she was. She was the woman born to be his, just as he was born to be hers.

Later, he would question why she made no attempt to run away as he approached her, no protest when he drew her naked body into his embrace, but the wondrous feel of her in his arms was far too overwhelming for him to ask any such questions of her now. All he knew was that she seemed to understand that she belonged to him, which gave him the right to touch her in any way he chose. Reverently, his hands caressed the wet, gleaming curtain of her dark sable hair, then moved beneath it to clasp her tiny waist.

"What is your name?" he whispered hoarsely. He swallowed hard as she answered him in a voice as sweet and gentle as the spring-wind.

"I am Sliver-of-moon," she said, her big brown eyes peeking shyly up at him from beneath her silky black lashes.

"And how did you come to be here, little one?"

"Grandmother Fire-weasel brought me with her when she came from the Black Robes," the girl said, her naked body shivering like a young asp though she still made no attempt to escape his arms. "The . . . the priests took me in when my family was murdered by the Sioux, but though they were kind, I am Absaroka and I yearned to be with my own people again."

Star-runner nodded, so enamored of her beauty that he was only half listening. It didn't really matter to him how or why she had come, only that she had, for with her arrival his long search for a wife was at an end. As she finished speaking, she turned her sweet face up to him with the innocence and trust of a flower drinking in the morning dew, and Star-runner surrendered to the wild yearnings inside him.

He let go of her only long enough to strip off his buckskins, then he scooped her up into his arms and strode toward the grassy place at the side of the hot spring. Tenderly, he laid her down on the soft bed, then came down beside her. He kissed her slowly, deeply, loving the taste of her as it was destined that he would, loving the feel of her warm breasts in his hands and her slender legs entangled with his.

Eventually, however, he realized that she was not kissing him back, nor was she joining in the sensual dance of love. When he opened his eyes to look at her, he saw that hers were wide open and moist with tears. "Is this your first time, Sliver-of-moon?" he inquired in surprise, for her body was no longer that of a girl but a mature woman.

She seemed unable to do more than nod, her cheeks aflame as she admitted to her innocence. Star-runner felt as if his heart would burst with the blessings heaped upon him this day. He'd had no right to expect that he would be her first lover, yet even this honor had not been denied him. In thanksgiving, he murmured humbly, "Do not be afraid, my sweet flower. I would cut out my soul before I would hurt you."

Reluctantly, he forced himself to slow down, banking the fever in his blood until he could incite the same intensity of heat within her. He could sense her shock as he touched her in places that had never known a man's hands, but her embarrassment soon gave way to the ancient fever that had bound men and women together since the beginning of time. Finding the sensitive bud between her thighs, he began a circular caress that had her moaning in pleasure, and then his patience was rewarded.

Her arms came up around his neck of their own volition, and she arched her back and her hips, offering to him what he needed since she required the same thing—the primal desire to be joined into one. He filled her slowly, gently, caressing her with his hand until he felt the rapture sweep through her in rhythmic waves that embraced his manhood in velvet heat. The pleasure was so great that he wanted it never to end, yet he knew if he couldn't let go soon, he would die of the sweet agony.

He heard her broken cry as ecstasy claimed her, and he groaned in relief, for now he could break the barrier of her innocence without giving pain. He thrust forward, deeper and deeper into her liquid heat until he could go no further, then surrendered himself to the female power that she possessed without knowing and wielded without guile. His last coherent thought, as she claimed him as no other woman had ever been able, was that physical sharing was nothing when compared to this sharing of the spirit. In Sliver-of-moon, the Star-runner of old would die and then be reborn with new strengths, virtues, and wisdom.

It took a long time before the delicious tremors of utter fulfillment drifted away to a pleasant lassitude. When he could breathe again, Star-runner propped his head up on his hand and smiled down at his adored one. "At the waning of the moon, we shall begin our life together," he promised, his heart singing with the joyous future they would enjoy.

"I am your obedient slave," Sliver-of-moon replied in acknowledgment of his words.

Star-runner frowned at her choice of reply. To be a slave was to be chattel, and though she now belonged to him, Sliver-of-moon would be his first wife, a position of high honor. "Slave of my heart," he agreed, but he could find no acceptance of this fact in her face. "Did you not give yourself to me freely, Sliver-of-moon?"

As he watched her beautiful eyes widen in surprise, his frown deepened. "Of course I did, Star-runner. It is my duty to comply with all of your wishes."

"But what of *your* wishes?"

"I wish to serve you well."

The seeds of a growing suspicion took root within him, and his joy was strangled in his chest. "Why do you speak to me of slavery when I speak to you of love?"

Confusion replaced the astonishment in her expression. "I do not understand the questions of my master. Why would a great warrior speak of love to his slave? My body is yours to do with as you will."

"You are not my slave!" he shouted angrily as his suspicions were confirmed, but he immediately felt guilty as her flower face crumpled in misery and two large dew drops spilled from her shimmering dark eyes. In a much softer tone, he continued, "Did Grandmother Fire-weasel tell you that you were to be my property?"

Sliver-of-moon stared at him as if she considered him none too bright for a man who she had been told excelled at so many things. "Would you have claimed my body with your own if I were not?"

Star-runner winced at her question, realizing that what he

141

had considered the perfect union between two lovers she had considered the ritual of ownership between master and slave. She had felt none of the soul-deep awareness that he had, nor reveled in the utter rightness of being with him as he had with her. Their joining had been an ordeal she felt she must endure lest she suffer punishment for disobedience.

Even though he knew this was true, he punished himself further by asking, "So you came to me because you thought it was expected of you?"

"Fire-weasel said you would wish to make this claim and that I must allow it if I did not want to be sent back to the Black Robes. To be amongst my own people again, I agreed to this arrangement. I will stay in your tepee and serve you in whatever way you decree."

With far more tenderness than he was feeling, Star-runner grasped her by the shoulders and brought her up to her knees, facing him. "Your beauty has no equal, Sliver-of-moon. Many warriors would want you in their tepees, not as slave but as wife."

Like all Absaroka women, Sliver-of-moon possessed a wide streak of practicality. "But I have no father or brothers to demand a bride price, Star-runner, and no dowry to bring to my husband's lodge. For this reason, I cannot hope for the honor of wedlock but only the benevolence of a kind master. When Grandmother Fire-weasel described you to me, I knew that you would not be cruel, and so I chose to go with her to the village of the Fire-bears."

In growing despair, Star-runner muttered, "Where I promptly made you suffer the greatest cruelty of all."

To his amazement, Sliver-of-moon placed her small hand on his shoulder. "You have shown me no pain, Star-runner. To stay with you, I would suffer the loss of my virginity again and again."

Her words only made his guts twist together in tighter knots. "I did not mean to make you suffer at all. I wished you to enjoy it as much as I did."

"It was highly pleasant," Sliver-of-moon replied.

"Pleasant." He spat in self-disgust.

Stunning him with the sound of her tinkling laughter, she elaborated, "The pain of your lovemaking was such sweet torture that I felt as if I might die of it. If it be your will, Star-runner, I would die many times over.''

Certain that he could not be understanding her correctly, Star-runner searched her face, but it was her actions that confirmed that his hearing had not failed him. Looking straight into his eyes, she reached down to touch him as intimately as he had recently touched her, caressing him with the circular motions he had taught her such a short time ago. He stifled a low groan of pleasure, not daring to make a sound in case she stopped. He wanted only that which she gave to him freely, and in her innocence she could not know the kind of greed her soft hands inspired in him.

"It is true what Grandmother Fire-weasel said," she murmured as she stroked the length of him with her finger-tips, then bent her head to gaze at his hot, throbbing flesh.

Watching her marvel at the effects of her personal attentions increased them tenfold, and his voice came out in a strangled gasp. "Wh-what did she say?"

"That I would only fear your great size until I felt your mighty weapon bursting within me, filling me with its manly power."

With the last of his control, Star-runner groaned out a plea for her to stop before she felt his manly power again, but having enjoyed the feel of it so much the first time, Sliver-of-moon wished to be filled by him once more. With his wavy black hair and sky-blue eyes, he was the most handsome brave she had ever seen, and also the most kind. This day, she had learned many things, and one of these lessons was how to give sexual pleasure. For his great kindness to her, Star-runner deserved the same consideration.

As she continued her loving assault on his manhood in the tender manner he had taught her, she could not help but be pleased by her swift success. Star-runner soon lost the strength in his muscles, just as she had become helpless and weak when he had caressed the moist folds of her woman's flesh. He collapsed backward upon the soft grasses, and, delighted by her accomplishment, Sliver-of-moon fit herself over his supine body.

When she felt him throbbing inside her, she cried out in satisfaction and sighed with joy as the satin convulsions within her own body returned to pleasure her as they had done before. This new lesson was the most wondrous of all. "Belonging to you is a fine thing, Star-runner," she assured him sincerely. "I should wish to be your slave until the pine leaves turn yellow."

Forever. Star-runner agreed with her. They should be together forever, but it would not be as she expected. He would court her as she was meant to be courted, charm her with the love songs of his flute, shower her with trinkets, and demonstrate the honor of his intentions by killing a buffalo and passing its innards from one brave to another while declaring her name. Sliver-of-moon did not have a father, but he would pay her bride price to Fire-weasel, and it would be the highest price ever paid for a woman by a warrior of his clan.

Chapter

Fifteen

It was four years later, at the time when the plums were bright purple, that Sliver-of-moon presented her husband with a strong, healthy son. On the third day after his birth, Star-runner carried the infant to the naming place on the high summits and lifted him up toward the sun. As he gazed up into the blue sky, he sang the praise song, for at long last the Almighty had blessed him with a child, and his heart was bursting with joy.

Before the moisture in his eyes could be noticed by those who had accompanied him, Star-runner handed the tiny boy to Mountain-lion. "Grandfather, I wish you to be godfather to my son."

With fierce pride for this honor bestowed upon him, the old man accepted the infant into his arms, then cleared his throat so that his voice would ring out clearly to the valley below. Raising the naked baby toward the sky, he exclaimed, "This child shall be named Tall-bear, for the time when his father killed a grizzly who stood taller than a tepee."

Star-runner watched as his son was lifted three more times by the other adult male members of his family. Split-nose was first, and his voice reverberated off the high cliffs as he cried, "Like the fox, Tall-bear, so shall you be cunning and swift. Like him, you shall show great alertness and a keen sense of all that surrounds you."

Swift-bear accepted the infant into his arms and called out, "Tall-bear, may you follow in the same path as your father and honor our tribe with your great courage."

Chest pushed out in pride for being allowed to take part in his first naming ceremony, Otter's-heart stepped forward. With a beaming smile, he lifted Tall-bear over his head. "Tall-bear, may you listen like the chickadee listens and never miss a chance to learn from others. It is the chickadee who is least in strength but strongest in mind of all his kind. He is willing to work for his wisdom, and so shall you prosper if you follow in his ways."

Eyes glowing with heartfelt emotion, Star-runner accepted his newborn son back into his arms. "Tall-bear is a fine name for one who is yet so small," he crooned to the solemn infant who stared adoringly up at him with the big brown eyes of his mother. "This day my heart sings."

With those words, the naming ceremony officially ended, and the men walked together down the mountain path toward their village. Split-nose passed ahead of the others but called back over his shoulder, "Council will wait until you have told your son's name to the women of the village, but then you must come to state your petition. With the Cheyenne moving so close to our village, we have much other business to discuss this day."

"Yes, Father," Star-runner replied, striving not to reveal his trepidation. The snow had fallen on his head only twenty-two times, and the wise men of the tribe could very well hold his young age against him as he entreated them to make him a chief. If they turned down his petition on the naming day for his son, his heart would fall to the ground.

Otter's-heart felt no such anxiety. "Your great deeds are proof of your capabilities, Star-runner. The worry creases in your face are for nothing."

Swift-bear, who already wore the feathers of an eagle in his war bonnet, was not as quick to reassure him. "My advice to you, brother, is to hold your lance high and never lower your eyes. Recount your deeds proudly in a loud voice, so that later none of the old ones can say he did not hear."

As he waited inside the council tepee, Star-runner remembered Swift-bear's advice, and when his name was called he presented a bold front. Chin raised, he lifted his war lance high in his right fist and shouted, "Men of the Fire-bears! I took an iron gun. I took an enemy's bow! I—"

To his horror, the circle of elders burst out laughing. "Why do these young men persist in bringing this torture to our ears?" Pretty-eagle, the eldest of the chiefs, inquired, shaking his head at Mountain-lion, who was trying and failing to control his amusement.

Big-horse, a chieftain of fifty snows, complained gruffly, "One would think we were the enemy the way they point their lances at our faces and shake their fists at us in the manner of war."

Horrified, Star-runner cast a killing glance at Swift-bear, but the young chief was doubled over in laughter and did not see. Seeing the direction of Star-runner's glare, Mountain-lion grinned. Like so many before him, including his traitorous older brother, Star-runner had fallen for an age-old trick.

Striving for a severe look, Mountain-lion chastised him. "No matter what you have heard to the contrary, Star-runner, we old men still have all our faculties. There is no need to shout, and it is proper to petition your elders in a manner of respect. If you dance about like a magpie, we shall see you as such and deny your petition."

Unaware that this reprimand had been repeated so often that it had almost become ritual, Star-runner bowed his head in abject apology. "Forgive me, wise men of council," he entreated humbly. "I was told that you appreciated such spirit in a petitioner and that by speaking in a loud voice I should prove my confidence in attaining what I seek."

Pretty-eagle sighed. "The young men of the Fire-bears seem to get no smarter with the passing seasons. The same story was told when I was young."

Big-horse nodded in agreement. "Tell us, Star-runner. Why should council bestow the honors of a chieftain on a young man as gullible as yourself?"

"And kindly do so in a normal tone," Pretty-eagle added. "Without waving your war lance beneath our noses. Our eyes are not so dim that we cannot see the strength in your body or the ferocity of your spirit."

With much less bravado than he had demonstrated before, Star-runner recounted his deeds to them once more. "I took an iron gun. I took an enemy's bow. I led a war party that killed our enemies. I was shot. I killed an enemy's horse. I brought home twenty horses. I shot a Sioux."

As he came to his last achievement, his tone changed from respectful to sardonic. "I saved a fallen brother and comrade from the Arapahoe." Gazing meaningfully at Swift-bear, he concluded, "Though I should have left him to suffer their cruelest torment."

"This is probably true," Split-nose agreed with a sympathetic chuckle. "But then, if your brother Swift-bear were dead, he would not be here to give you these words."

Swift-bear got up from his council seat and came to stand before Star-runner. With no sign of his earlier laughter, he placed his hands on his younger brother's shoulders and stared solemnly into his eyes. "I, Swift-bear, grandson of Mountain-lion, son of Split-nose, high chief of the Fire-bears, on this day do name Star-runner as the newest chief to serve our noble clan. By his deeds, he has shown himself worthy. In honor of his bravery, a feast has been prepared by our women, for they would share in our celebration of this courageous warrior who has distinguished himself at such an early age."

As the sun stood straight up in the sky, Star-runner, chief of the Absaroka, walked out of the council lodge to the wild hoots and cheers of the whole clan. It was a day above all days in his memory, and his heart sang more joyfully than ever before. Together with his people, he feasted on the fat meat of the bighorn deer and the elk and danced until he could dance no more. As the daylight waned, the fires were lit with the burning embers of sage and primrose, so that by this sweet smell he would always remember the day when his son was named Tall-bear and he was named chief.

"The drums will beat all night in your honor," Sliver-of-moon murmured happily as she walked with her husband beneath the starlit sky. "And in honor of our first son."

Star-runner dropped his arm over her shoulders and drew her more tightly against him, careful not to disturb the babe suckling at her breast. "Tonight the world is all good, and our voices are happy," he replied contentedly. "On a night

148

such as this, I can have no enemies, for there is no room left in my heart for hatred."

Leaning her head back on his shoulder, Sliver-of-moon agreed. "It is a raven's moon, my husband."

Star-runner gazed up at the silver disk shining down on them so brightly. According to legend, the Great Spirit was walking in the forest one night when by chance he came upon a raven's nest. A very conceited bird, the raven questioned the Great Spirit's wisdom in making him so plain that he could not be seen when flying at night. That very instant, the Great Spirit granted the raven his wish and changed his feathers to a brilliant silver, but the color was so bright that the raven's wife and children were immediately blinded.

Seeing the results of his selfish wish, the raven begged to be changed back. The Great Spirit granted this wish also, but to make sure that the raven would never forget the lesson he'd learned, his feathers were changed to silver again one summer night each year. To save his family from the punishment of his vanity, he was forced to fly as high and as far as he could until his brilliance could be looked upon without harm.

Recalling the story, Star-runner wondered if his wife was gently reminding him that, to her, he would always be the gentle young man of seventeen snows who had begged for her hand in marriage, and not the magnificent chieftain who on this day had so many accolades laid on his head that it had swelled to mammoth proportions. With a wry smile, he admitted, "It is hard not to swagger and puff out my chest when my ears are treated to continuous compliments."

Sliver-of-moon smiled back, "Then, for your own good, this wife shall not whisper any more honeyed words into your ears. I would not like it if you would suffer the sad fate of the raven and leave me to lie in our marriage bed alone, if even for one night."

Star-runner threw back his head and laughed, then immediately sobered when he saw the depth of her love for him glowing in her dark eyes. "Do not worry, my sweet one. Unless the pine trees turn yellow, you shall never be alone beneath the blankets, no matter how magnificent a personage I become."

Yet the very next day, Star-runner was forced to leave his

beloved in order to defend his tribe against an invasion by the Sioux. A scouting party had been sighted by their wolves, and so, together with Swift-bear, he rode out at the head of a large group of warriors. On Cloud Peak, they picked up the trail of their enemy coming in from the Blackened Hills. The sign was fresh and heavy, telling them that there were many Sioux to be found ahead of them. Near sundown, their scouts brought back word that they had seen a large war party camped on Goose Creek.

In preparation for the battle to come, the warriors of the Absaroka dismounted their horses to paint their faces and put on their war bonnets. To the sound of beating drums, they tested their weapons and encouraged each other to fight with courage and valor. When all were deemed ready, they sprang back up onto their horses, yelled out the Absaroka war cry, and raced down the hill to meet their enemy.

The battle was fierce, with many horses going down beneath their riders, but even though they were outnumbered, the Absaroka persevered. Beneath their fierce assault, the enemy fell back, fighting desperately but losing ground. Eventually, Star-runner and Swift-bear split their band of men into two groups and attacked their foes from opposite sides, dividing their strength. This tactic caused the Sioux to lose many braves, and in the end they retreated back up the creek bed, until they were able to make their escape into the hills.

Although the Absaroka counted ten among them who had sustained severe wounds, only one of their warriors had gone on to his Father. Because of the clever leadership and strong medicine of their young war chiefs Star-runner and Swift-bear, they had won the day, and as they started back to camp, they were looking forward to a great feast of rejoicing. When their horses reached the apex of the valley, however, their hearts fell to the ground, for they could see smoke rising from the burning tepees of their village.

"Cheyenne!" Star-runner shouted in fury as he urged his mount into a gallop. "While we were engaged in battle with the Sioux, they have invaded our camp!"

Upon discovery of this treachery, every warrior was prepared to fight once again, but as they charged into camp, they realized that there would not be another battle this day.

The smell of death was strong in the air, and an eerie pall of silence hung over the village. In the center of camp, they found the old men who had not ridden with them to find the Sioux. Here they had made their stand against the invaders, and the earth was red with their spilled blood.

Pretty-eagle and Big-horse had died fighting like warriors, but even their great courage was no match for the Cheyenne. Mountain-lion was still alive, though his wounds were grave, and it was he who told the returning braves what had transpired. "The Cheyenne came . . . while we were just . . . rising to start the new day," he gasped. "We fought to our last man, but they overpowered us. They have killed the old men of our village and stolen away many women and children."

"Sliver-of-moon!" Star-runner cried, but Mountain-lion could not tell him what had happened to his wife and son. At that same moment, Falling-water and a number of other women and children slipped out from their hiding places in the forest and ran into the arms of their husbands and fathers. Sliver-of-moon and Tall-bear were not among them.

Though a sick dread weighed down his limbs, Star-runner ran to his lodge more swiftly than he had ever run before. He was relieved to find that the tepee had escaped the fire, but the tanned white hides had been slashed open, and through the gaping slits he viewed a sight that would be forever burned into his memory. Upon the soft buffalo robes of his marriage bed was his beloved, killed by an enemy's spear through the chest, her stiffened arms still clutching the body of her son, whose tiny head had been crushed by the brutal blow of a Cheyenne war club.

Overcome with grief, Star-runner threw himself down on their still warm bodies, but the force of his weeping did not change what could not be changed. His loved ones were gone from him forever, and the pain was like a living thing inside him, clawing his insides with such violence that he drew his knife out of its sheath and began slashing his body to release the agony. The sight of his own blood mingled with that of his dead wife and son did not lessen the grief in his heart, but it did serve to inspire a glaring memory of another time and another woman who was probably still grieving over the death of her firstborn son, heir to an English earldom.

Dazed and bleeding, Star-runner fell backward onto the ground, his brain swirling with all the knowledge that had been denied him for ten long years. His name then had been Grantland William Collingswood, and he had been born on the huge family estate outside London to Lord Roger and Lady Mary Collingswood. Besides his parents, he also had a brother, two years younger than himself, George Roger Collingswood.

Lady Mary had been a devout Roman Catholic, and though she loved her two sons very dearly, she had feared that they would fall prey to the wicked perfidy that influenced so many other boys who attended Eton, and so, on every holiday from school, she had sent for the village priest, who punished Grant and George for their sins, be they known or assumed.

Lord Roger did not embrace the faith of his wife, but his marriage was financially beneficial to his family, and Lady Mary did not interfere with his flamboyant life-style. While she stayed at home, worrying about the welfare of their sons, Roger traveled the world in pursuit of his favorite pastime, hunting. After hearing about the bountiful game to be found in the western territories, he had decided to take an entourage to America and bag a few fine trophies for himself.

Thinking his eldest son wouldn't be a true Collingswood unless he was invested with the same enthusiasm for hunting as his father, Lord Roger, under protest of his wife, had brought the twelve-year-old with him. Once they'd reached St. Louis and organized the expedition, they had traveled in fine style. With twenty wagons loaded down with provisions, two horse carts, four mule wagons, and a firearms wagon loaded with pistols, shotguns, and muzzle-loading rifles, they had ventured far into the wilderness.

During their trek, Lord Roger and Grantland had slept on brass bedsteads in a large linen tent that was set up each night by one of the thirty servants they had hired to see to all their needs. Each morning, Lord Roger had decked himself out in a fresh white jacket and Panama hat, as had his son. For chasing small game, they had brought forty greyhounds to lead the charge over the prairies and valleys of the vast hunting grounds.

As the expedition traveled over the mountains, they had left a path of senseless killing in their wake. The dead bodies of bison were strewn for miles, and many more animals were killed than were needed to supply the party's larder. Grant had been horrified by his father's bloodthirsty approach to hunting, but when he had protested, he'd been chastised for not appreciating the thrill of the chase and the triumph of the kill.

One morning, Grant, his father, and a few other men in their party had found themselves in the path of an approaching herd of buffalo. A million hooves, sounding like the roar of a mighty ocean, had surged up over the land behind them. Unable to avert the stampede by firing their guns, the group had quickly sought cover. Grant had thrust himself as far as he could into a crevice of rock, and because his body was thin enough to fit this narrow shelter, he had escaped being trampled.

The others had not been so lucky, and he'd watched in horror as his father and his hunting companions were cut down, then stamped into oblivion. After he had witnessed their brutal deaths, a flying piece of rock had struck Grant in the head. When he'd regained consciousness, he had been all alone in the prairie with no memory of his past or how he'd come to be there. Half out of his mind with pain and fear, he had wandered about for days until Jebediah Fenton had found him, near death from hunger and exposure.

His memory had now been restored to him, but Starrunner did not gain any peace from this new knowledge of himself. His past life no longer mattered to him, and his present life was over. Without the sweet woman he loved more than his own breath and the bright-eyed son whom he would not see grow into a man, his heart fell to the ground, and he knew it would never rise up again.

PART
3

Chapter

Sixteen

Fort Benton, Montana Territory, June, 1864

"Seein' how close the two of us have become, Matil—I mean Taralynn—I don't mind tellin' you, I was a mite put out when Pa told us the true way of things. I could hardly believe it," Rose admitted as she sat down beside Tara on the berth. But there was no censure in her touch as she reached out to pat her friend's shoulder. "I felt like you'd played me for a fool, but I can see now that there was far less playactin' on your part than on Grant's. You weren't prepared for him leavin' the way he done, were you?"

"I thought he loved me," Tara murmured, using the back of her hand to wipe away the tears rolling down her cheeks. "And I guess that makes me the biggest fool of all."

"He had to have cared something for you, Tara," Rose insisted sympathetically. "Otherwise, he wouldn't have asked my pa to look after you until you reached your folks, or made the arrangements for you to join our wagon train to Bozeman."

"Evidently, he considered that fair payment for my dedicated services to him as a mistress."

Tara was shamed to the core by the knowledge that Grant

had only been using her. She had built up such romantic dreams concerning their future, but he had known all along that their time together would be over as soon as the *Ophelia* reached the headwaters of the Missouri.

"And I reckon you were expectin' a marriage proposal."

Miserably, Tara nodded as another rush of tears spilled over onto her cheeks. "Like a ninny, I believed him when he said I would always be his woman."

Rose knew exactly how Tara felt, for she had been similarly betrayed by a handsome young drummer who had passed through the small town near their farm. Billy Carmichael had pledged her his eternal love, but in truth he had sold her a bill of goods as false as the benefits he claimed could be had from his wonder elixir.

"It don't do no good to blame yourself for the perfidy of a no-good polecat like Grant Collingswood," Rose advised with the voice of experience. "All you can do is take a lesson from this, and don't be so quick to give your heart again."

When Captain Randolph had come to her cabin to tell her that Grant wasn't to be found onshore or off, Tara had wept inconsolably, but she was fast reaching the point where she had no more tears left to shed. Then, as Rose went on to tell of her encounter with Billy Carmichael, anger replaced her overwhelming sense of emptiness and loss. Adding Rose's experience to her own, it became obvious that men were a self-centered lot, and if she wanted to survive, a wise woman must see to her own interests.

Since birth, she had suffered at the hands of selfish men. First there was her father, who hadn't had the patience to wait for her to grow old enough to travel before going in search of his own fortune. Then there was her Uncle Lachlan, who had always looked the other way when his domineering wife had mistreated her. Next had come her fiancé, Louden, who had held a much greater affection for her money than for her. And, finally, there was Grant, who had desired nothing from her but the convenient use of her body.

"Men!" Tara spat bitterly. "Well, I'll tell you this, Rose Dunn. After what I've been through, I'll not let another one of those treacherous creatures take advantage of me!"

"That's the spirit," Rose encouraged her, heartened by

the color she saw returning to Tara's cheeks. "Now, what do you say you and I get off this goldarned boat?"

"I'm right behind you." Tara took a last survey of the cabin to make sure she had left none of her belongings behind. Unfortunately, every place she looked held a vivid memory of the time she'd spent there with Grant. In her mind's eye, she could see him standing tall and handsome before the mirror for his morning shave or stretched out on the floor to sleep. She could see his beautifully formed naked body shimmering in the moonlight as he'd stood before her the first time they made love. Even now, though she knew he was not worthy of her love, her heart fluttered with the remembered excitement and pleasure of that night.

From that time on, everything had been so marvelous between them, so perfect, so incredibly . . . With forced effort, Tara banished those useless thoughts. The man was gone, and it wouldn't do her any good to dwell on what might have been. What she had to do now was concentrate on what lay ahead of her.

She was heading out into a whole new world, beginning a brand new life, and if she had any pride at all, she wouldn't waste another moment yearning after a blackguard like Grant Collingswood. "Are you sure my trunk has been transported to your wagon?"

Rose nodded. "I saw Pa take it ashore myself. It was carted off to the other end of town along with all of our things."

Tara took a deep breath and stood up from the berth to shake out her wrinkled twill skirt. "After these many weeks on the river, it's going to feel so good having firm ground beneath us again."

Rose laughed. "I hope you still feel that way after riding a few hundred miles in the back of a wagon. I can tell you, it ain't all that comfortable."

"At least I'll have the comfort of traveling in much more upstanding company than I have enjoyed on the past leg of my journey," Tara retorted spiritedly as the twosome made their way down the narrow passageway and out onto the main deck.

For some reason, whenever Tara had thought about Fort Benton, she pictured a military stockade, not a struggling hamlet of rude log cabins stretched out on the open prairie. As she and Rose followed the other members of the Dunn family down the gangway, she couldn't help but feel a bit overwhelmed. Every type and condition of man that a continent could produce seemed to be waiting onshore to greet them.

"Lordy!" Rose exclaimed under her breath as a swarthy Mexican extolled the lovely blond color of her hair and fell to his knees on the levee, pleading eloquently for her hand in marriage. "Did you ever see the like?"

"Never!" Tara whispered back, her cheeks flushing pink as a hard-looking desperado with a greasy beard called out a proposal to her that went far beyond the bounds of common decency.

"This ain't St. Louis, that's for certain," Zeke declared darkly, offering one arm to each girl as their party stepped off the gangway and began walking down the rutted wagon track that represented the main street. As if they were a traveling carnival show that had come to town, the crowd of gawking males who were lined up three deep at the landing ambled along behind them. "I'll make sure none of them rowdies gets near you, but you two best stick to me like glue 'til we reach the wagons."

"Thank you, Zeke," Tara said as she slipped her arm through his, trying hard to dispel a recollection from the not too distant past when Zeke had backed down beneath the possessive stare of only one pair of male eyes, especially since he was now faced with forty.

"They're leering at us like they ain't never seen a woman before," Rose complained irately. "And the things some of 'em are saying would make a harlot blush."

Tara took a tighter grip of Zeke's arm, but her free hand was thrust inside her reticule, and her fingers were firmly curled around the handle of her derringer. She supposed she should commend Grant for having been gracious enough to return her weapon so that she had something with which to protect herself since she could no longer count on his services. Of course, the small gun wouldn't be of much help against this host of ruffians, but at least she had the means to stop one of them. As their lewd comments increased in volume, she declared, "I've never witnessed such bestial

160

behavior in my entire life. Are there no authorities to put a
end to this harassment?''

"Out here, men make their own laws," Zeke said, glancing back anxiously at the boisterous crowd. "It's a good
thing our wagons are pullin' out right soon. If we don't get
you gals out of town straight away, you're likely to start a
panic."

"This is outrageous, Father!" Harriet Dunn exclaimed,
glaring over her shoulder at the parade of men dogging their
footsteps. "I did not come two thousand miles to have my
daughter insulted like this, or myself either, for that matter.
Did you hear? That black-eyed scoundrel up there on that
roof actually had the audacity to request that I throw you
over for a younger man."

Her husband grinned. "Well now, Mother, you can't
blame the poor fella for trying. There ain't enough women
in these parts to go around, and you are still one very
handsome gal."

"Really, Lloyd!" Harriet replied tartly, though her blue
eyes sparkled with pleasure at the compliment. "Whatever
their excuse, the behavior of these men is reprehensible."

"Ah, don't pay these gents no mind," her husband advised, no longer threatened by the fact that he and his son
were no match for the raucous crowd trailing behind them.
Although they were doing a good job of intimidating his
womenfolk, they kept themselves to a reasonable distance,
and Lloyd found their bawdy comments more amusing than
sinister. "It don't look like they mean us any harm. I reckon
they're just hard up for a look-see at some decent, God-
fearin' women."

"Indeed!" Harriet retorted piously, only slightly mollified
when they continued on for several more yards and none of
their noisy followers made any attempt to act on their
outrageous suggestions. "If this is the kind of thing we must
deal with once we get to our own place, I shall be on the
very next boat back to civilization."

Although she didn't say so, Tara agreed with Mrs. Dunn's
sentiment. She was beginning to think that all men were cut
from the same disgusting cloth, but at least in the more
civilized parts of the country, they weren't so insultingly
blatant about their physical needs. On the other hand, she

decided upon further consideration, maybe these men should be applauded for their honesty. At least a woman would know exactly where she stood with one of them and wouldn't fool herself into thinking that he wanted anything more from her than a temporary bed partner.

"Hard to believe that this here ramshackle place is the commercial center of the whole territory, ain't it?" Lloyd Dunn remarked, as wide-eyed as everyone else as they took in the sights surrounding them. "Just look at the size of them outfits."

Before the doorway of each trading establishment stood huge freight wagons drawn by a half-dozen span of oxen or mules, ready to start out on their toilsome journeys to the mining camps back in the mountains. "The bull trains ain't all that's amazing," Zeke murmured, gazing incredulously at the number of saloons and hurdy-gurdy houses that lined the single street. Crude hand-painted signs boasted of every kind of pleasure a man could desire, from smooth whiskey and tobacco to gambling and prostitutes. "This is my kind of town."

"Ezekiel Dunn, I won't hear that kind of talk from you," Harriet scolded severely, turning her nose up in the air as they passed by pile after pile of garbage. "This place is a filthy den of iniquity, and we shall leave here as soon as is humanly possible."

"Yes, ma'am," Zeke replied meekly, but his eyes kept straying to the windows of each cabin they passed in the hopes that he'd see one of the good-time girls dancing in the altogether like some of the miners swore that they did. And no matter how his ma felt about it, he couldn't help being a mite envious of the free and independent men in town, who one by one had finally lost interest in following the family and were now inside one of those "evil" dens. At twenty-two, Zeke felt he was more than ready to experience a little decadence in his life, but, unfortunately, he didn't think it would be today.

As they approached the end of the street, a short, barrel-chested man with skin as dark brown as oiled leather and a steel gray beard came forward to meet them. "That there's Ben Fallon," Zeke informed Tara and his sister. "He's the wagon master. Pa says he's been workin' the mountain highway to Bozeman for nigh on to six years.''

"Well, folks," Fallon declared heartily after the introductions. "I'm for standing around jawin' as much as the next man, but we've got a lot of miles to cover yet today. Dunn, your gear is all loaded and your mules harnessed, so as soon as you get your womenfolk settled in your wagon, we can pull out."

Precisely at noon, Fallon mounted his big chestnut gelding and led the small train of six wagons out onto the open prairie. After the lead wagon, the Dunns were placed next in line. Then came the four freight wagons loaded down with supplies ordered out of St. Louis by the farmers and merchants who were settled in and around the Gallatin Valley. Neither Tara nor Rose dared ask why it was necessary for the teamsters who drove the other wagons to be so heavily armed, but as they soon found out, they realized it was a very good thing that they were.

By midafternoon, the sun was baking hot on the prairie. Tara was dozing on a feather tick to the rocking motion of the wagon when she heard the first shot and Zeke's yell. "Injuns, Pa! Hell 'n tarnation, what do we do!"

Before Zeke received an answer to his question, Ben Fallon galloped past, bellowing orders from atop his huge gelding. "Circle 'em up, boys! Them bloodthirsty Sioux are almost upon us, and we're gonna have a helluva fight on our hands!"

As the covered wagon pulled to a stop, Lloyd shouted, "Harriet, pile them mattresses up on the sides, then you gals get down as low as you can behind 'em. You'll be a far sight safer stayin' inside there than out here on the ground with me and Zeke."

To Tara's amazement, Mrs. Dunn didn't lie low but opened up the gun box and pulled out an old muzzle loader. In a perfectly calm voice, she said, "Rose, dear, I'd better work the powder while you do the shootin'. Your aim is so much better than mine."

"Yes, Ma," Rose replied in the same matter-of-fact tone, and then both women crouched down at the back of the wagon and prepared to defend themselves.

Chapter

Seventeen

Star-runner knew he was being followed as he rode toward the twin peaks, but the knowledge did not cause him any fear. Indeed, he was glad to see that his presence had been discovered by the scouts so soon after his arrival in Absaroka territory. It told him that the young men of his tribe were still diligent in their duties. From what he had learned in his travels up the Bid Muddy, the future of their nation was in more danger now than ever before, for it was not only their lifelong enemies who coveted the wealth of their land but the white man as well. In search of gold, he would come and keep coming in greater and greater numbers.

Star-runner was glad that he would be present to help guide his people through these changing times. Though he knew there was no way to stop this invasion of fortune seekers, he would do his best to assist his tribe in defending what had always been theirs. His understanding of the white man's world would be of great help when the time came for their government leaders to try to negotiate a legal takeover of Absaroka lands. Such tactics were already widespread in the more settled territories, but in this case the Indian agents and Army officers would not find it so easy to take advantage of the red man's naïveté and ignorance. This time, they would be dealing with a man who knew exactly what they were after.

A moment later, Star-runner's mouth was no longer set in a grim line of determination but in a joyful smile. Over the rise of the next hill came the welcoming party, and even from a distance he could recognize Swift-bear and Otter's-heart. Star-runner burst out in laughter when he saw how they had dressed for the occasion, as if they were on their way to confront a great and powerful enemy.

The party was at least fifty strong, and they were all dressed in bright colors and wearing wonderful war bonnets of eagle feathers that waved in the wind. Riding pinto ponies, they charged down the hillside, whooping loudly as they surrounded Star-runner's roan stallion. As if they were in danger of their "enemy" fighting back, they cut their horses in toward him, then turned them abruptly away, daring him to shoot at a target that would not stand still.

Grinning widely, Star-runner allowed them their fun, for they were a beautiful sight to behold. Their finery glistened in the sunlight as they rode swiftly over the plains, and sunlight glinted off the gay paint on their beloved faces. The wind rushed through the magnificent feathers on their bonnets and swirled around their prancing horses in exhilaration. As he watched their performance, Star-runner could think of nothing else but that it was good to be home, so very good.

"Do you not fear us, pale face?" Swift-bear demanded as he cut inside the others and began riding parallel with Star-runner's stallion. "Do you not quake with the knowledge that your scalp might soon decorate our lances?"

"Your lance could use some new decoration," Star-runner agreed. "It sports the same feathers and scalps as it did when I left. Have you not accomplished any brave deeds in the meantime?"

Swift-bear laughed. "Is this any way to speak to the chief of the Fire-bear clan? My young brother does not know his place!"

Star-runner was happy to hear of Swift-bear's rise in prominence, but before he offered his congratulations, he inquired, "Our father is not well?"

Otter's-heart broke away from the surrounding band of riders and flanked him on the other side. "Split-nose lives, Star-runner," he announced in a voice that no longer held the cadence of childhood but the richness of maturity. "And even now our mother slaves to welcome you with a feast worthy of a warrior who has traveled across the wide ocean. She is certain that your body has wasted away from ingesting the white man's bad food, and she intends to feed you until your stomach bursts."

As he heard this, Star-runner's eyes were filled by many images all at once. His adoptive mother, White-fawn, had always worried after his stomach, but there had been so many others who had cared about him as his real family in England never had. All the dear faces he had missed so greatly swam before his eyes. He knew it was too much to hope that Mountain-lion had survived the grave wounds he sustained from the Cheyenne attack or that Fire-weasel had lived beyond her seventieth season, so he did not inquire after their welfare, but he yearned to know how everyone else had fared during his long absence.

"Where is our young brother Running-deer?" he asked, surveying the other horsemen. "Was he not allowed to ride with you?"

The answer to his question was given by a tall, handsome man with flowing black hair who rode a black and white pinto with the effortless grace of a seasoned warrior. "What rules does a chief follow but his own, Star-runner?"

Both Otter's-heart and Swift-bear roared with laughter when they saw the astonished look on Star-runner's face. "Running-deer is no longer that stripling you remember but a respected chief, just as you were at his age."

"Forgive me, brother," Star-runner apologized, hardly able to believe that this fierce-looking man was the fourteen-year-old boy who had wept so sweetly at the burial of his wife and son. "I did not recognize you."

"Much has changed since you left us," Running-deer stated, and he would have said more but for Swift-bear's warning glance.

"You shall have answers to all of your questions when we reach our village," Swift-bear promised. "But for now, let us ride like the wind, as we did when you and I were first joined with the Foxes.''

Star-runner could think of nothing he would enjoy doing more. Kicking his horse into a fast gallop, he took off across the prairie. "As I recall, Swift-bear," he yelled back over his shoulder, "I was always in the lead, and you were left to follow."

With that challenge, the race was on, but this time the competition was not exclusive to Star-runner and Swift-bear. Otter's-heart kept pace easily with his two older brothers, and Running-deer outdistanced them all. At the top of a flat rise of land, the foursome pulled up their horses, but not because their urge to compete was over. The sound of gunfire was unmistakable.

"Is it coming from our village?" Star-runner inquired anxiously, the bitter taste of painful memory clogging his throat.

"Our village lies to the east," Swift-bear assured him quickly, sensing the direction of his thoughts. To confirm that his brother worried needlessly, he pointed to the valley below. "Our enemy the Sioux are in pursuit of another quarry for a change."

Gazing down at the small circle of canvas-covered wagons under siege, Running-deer said, "Perhaps one day the white man will learn that to settle here is to be killed." With a disinterested shrug, he proposed, "Let us away to our village and the homecoming feast."

In the past, Star-runner would have left the settlers to fend for themselves, just as Running-deer suggested. An Absaroka did not enter another man's fight, but in this instance, he simply could not turn his back and ride away. He should not care, but he did.

Taking a firm grip on his reins, he glanced over at Swift-bear. "Will the chief of the Fire-bears lead his warriors into battle without knowing the reason until the fight is won?"

Swift-bear's astonishment was apparent, but there was no hesitation in his answer. "If my brother has reason, it is reason enough."

Star-runner looked to Otter's-heart and Running-deer to see if they were of the same opinion as Swift-bear, and his heart sang when he saw the unquestioned loyalty on their faces. It had been eight years since he'd left them, but among his people some things did not change. "I have reason," he acknowledged quietly, then dismounted to paint his face.

As soon as Star-runner was ready, Swift-bear raised his lance high in the air and emitted the war cry. Instantly, the fifty warriors behind him lifted their shields in preparation for battle. When the signal was given to charge, they rode as one toward the valley, for they were Absaroka, and together they were like an angry buffalo which never retreats, which nothing can stop.

Chapter

Eighteen

When the first round of bullets hit the wooden wagon bed, Tara was too paralyzed by fear to move, but as she watched the Dunn women, she realized she'd be far less frightened if she had something else to occupy her mind besides the gruesome thought of being scalped. She doubted she could actually shoot another human being, even an Indian, but she did know how to fire a gun. At Laurel Glen, she had often followed the hunt, and even though she was a woman, she was considered a commendable shot.

"Is there another weapon I might use, Mrs. Dunn?" she shouted in order to be heard above the explosive exchange of gunfire around them.

"There's my daddy's old flintlock revolver, but it's been known to misfire," Harriet shouted back, wiping a streak of sweat off her forehead as she jammed more powder down the muzzle of her old-fashioned gun. "You'd best not chance it, Tara."

But when Tara crept up to the front of the wagon and peeked out of the canvas, she took exception to Harriet's warning. Their small train was surrounded and greatly outnumbered by the attacking band of Sioux. To her way of thinking, it was better to die by her own hand than by that of one of those screaming devils outside, and so, keeping her head down, she crawled back toward the gun box. Before she could lift the heavy lid, however, she smelled smoke and looked up in time to see a half-dozen burning arrows sear through the white canvas.

Within moments, the top of the wagon was enveloped in flames, and those inside had to choose between death by fire or death by bullet. The smoke from the burning canvas was so thick that Tara didn't see Mrs. Dunn and Rose scramble out of the back of the wagon, and her eyes were watering so badly that she had to feel her way along in order to reach the front. She finally managed to struggle up and over the wagon seat, but her long skirt got caught on a nail.

She tried to keep low as she tugged frantically on the material, but a bullet whizzed by her ear and another ripped through the flaming canvas by her head, sending a cascade of orange sparks over her back and hair. Luckily, none of them was hot enough to burn through the fabric of her blouse, and she was able to beat out the ones in her hair before it caught fire.

Tara realized that her luck would not hold if she didn't get down off the wagon and find cover. With her red hair and white blouse, she made a bright target, and sooner or later one of those bullets was bound to find its mark. She was very close to panic when, with a last vicious yank, she finally ripped the material of her skirt free from the nail. Then, just as she was preparing to jump to the ground, she heard a bloodcurdling yell right behind her. She whirled around in time to see the tomahawk raised over her head, and by instinct she lifted her arms to ward off the attack.

But the blow never came.

Instead, she heard an odd gutteral sound, and she felt herself scooped up into the air, then swept across the back of a horse. The arm that held her around the waist was like steel, and she opened her mouth to scream, but with the awareness of her coming death, her brain had ceased to function, and no sound came out. Unfortunately, her eyes were wide open, and as she twisted and fought to escape the steely arm around her middle, she caught a glimpse of the malevolent savage who would bring about her murder.

His hateful features were disguised by a hideous coating

of war paint that made him look like the personification of everything evil, and his head was covered by a war bonnet of long feathers. Around his neck, he wore a disgusting necklace made out of claws. In desperation, Tara tried to scratch at his exposed face, but he immediately prevented that action. He jerked her flailing arms behind her back, then kept them there by pinning her body more firmly against his hard chest. The beads on his breast shield dug painfully into the skin of her back, but she knew that pain would be nothing compared to what was yet to come.

She shut her eyes, but the image of a heavy tomahawk raised over her skull remained, and it was followed by a ghastly picture of this savage, grinning in triumph as he pulled away a piece of her scalp, then lifted his hand to show off his bloody trophy. Even after that happened, she might still be alive, so he would club her again . . . and again . . . and again.

Her eyes were still tightly closed when her captor brought his horse to an abrupt halt, and before she could gear herself up to defend herself, she was unceremoniously dumped onto the hard ground. The wind was knocked out of her, but she refused to die without a fight. Her fingers closed around a rock, and she grasped it firmly as she struggled up onto her knees. "Come ahead, you despicable coward," she gasped. "And . . . and . . . I'll bash your head in!"

Beneath the layers of war paint, she thought she saw the savage smile, which made her even more livid. "Then I'll come to you, you murderous pagan!"

"Stay here, white woman!" the Indian barked down at her in a voice that scorched her already singed hair, then he wheeled his mount and galloped away.

English! The devil had spoken to her in English! Even though Tara had understood what he'd said, she was still having trouble believing that she wasn't about to be brutally murdered. Warily, her eyes followed him as he rejoined the battle, and it was then that she saw something that had entirely escaped her notice before. The Indian who had scooped her up off the wagon seat was a member of a much larger group, but his companions weren't shooting at the wagons. They were attacking the Sioux, and in the face of their fierce assault the Sioux were retreating!

171

At the same time as Tara's brain registered that she had just been rescued by an English-speaking heathen, both groups of Indians had disappeared into the hills. For several moments, she just sat there, too stunned to get up off the ground, but she could hear Ben Fallon's voice booming out the fact that she hadn't been seeing things. "I ain't never heard of a Crow taking on another man's fight, but we all can be mighty glad their party of warriors arrived when they did. Bless their scurvy hides. If not for them, we'd all be goners by now."

When she finally did muster the strength to walk back to the smoking circle of wagons, Tara saw the dead Sioux, tomahawk still in hand, draped over the seat of the Dunns' wagon. As she gazed up at the grizzly corpse, a bubble of hysterical laughter rose in her. According to scripture, the Almighty worked in strange and mysterious ways, and she had certainly been given proof of that today. In the space of eight short hours, she'd been cast out by one man who she thought had loved her and saved from death by another who should have hated her.

Chapter

Nineteen

"So this is the reason we have entered a battle that was not ours and forsaken a sumptuous feast in favor of a burnt and skinny rabbit," Swift-bear declared with a knowing grin, his eyes following the progress of the Dunn wagon as it entered the Gallatin River Valley. "The white woman belongs to the Fierce-ones."

Star-runner nodded, yet his expression was surprisingly challenging as he responded to his brother's statement. "Now that I have seen her to safety, I am free to return to our village, for my debt to their chief is paid."

"It is well that you have found the means to lift this heavy burden from your shoulders," Swift-bear acknowledged solemnly, though his dark eyes were sparkling with amusement. "Yet I saw the rock the flame-haired woman was prepared to throw at your head in exchange for your rescue of her from the Sioux. She must share the same bad temperament as their chief, Red-beard."

Glaring, Star-runner corrected him. "It is true that she has his fighting spirit, for she is his daughter."

"Ah," Swift-bear murmured. "The passing seasons have done much to change your outlook on Red-beard's disposition."

Otter's-heart did not understand this exchange between his two older brothers. All men of his clan were aware of the red-headed warriors who inhabited this section nearest their hunting grounds and of the fierce green-eyed chief who led them, but he was unaware of any debt Star-runner might owe to this man. For the most part, the Absaroka avoided confrontations with the whites, but this small clan was the exception, for they behaved nothing like the majority of their tribe. The men who lived in this valley were as skillful with horses as any Indian, and when they were victims of a horse raid, they raided right back, their war cries as triumphant as those of the Absaroka.

Because of their great courage and skills, the Absaroka referred to them as the Fierce-ones, for unlike other whites, they knew of tribal honor and followed a code of justice that the Absaroka could respect. After several seasons, they had even adopted the Absaroka custom of counting coup. From then on, many members of the Fire-bear clan had felt the fist of a flame-haired warrior, while just as many others had restored their honor by stealing into the valley and touching their well-respected enemy or stealing his property.

"Why have I no knowledge of this debt?" Otter's-heart demanded. "Is not the obligation of one brother obligation to us all?"

Swift-bear grinned. "Star-runner was very young when he contracted this encumbrance to his honor. As I recall, he had just joined the Foxes and was most anxious to distinguish himself."

Star-runner waved his hand, suspiciously anxious to forestall his brother's next words. "We do not have time for such reminiscing, Swift-bear. Our people are waiting to welcome me home from across the big waters, and I have much more interesting news to relate."

Running-deer caught Swift-bear's eyes, then pressed for the remainder of the story. "After two days of waiting, our women have cast your feast to the birds, Star-runner, so why hurry? Of course, my stomach growls with the pain of what it will not have, but now my mouth waters for knowledge of why I have done without such sweet sustenance."

In a sage tone, Swift-bear put in, "I, too, feel this hunger,

Running-deer, but when I think of Star-runner's fight with the chief of the Fierce-ones, my soul is well satisfied."

"A soul such as yours deserves nothing but pain," Star-runner grumbled, but his taunt only made Swift-bear grin more widely.

"It was Star-runner's wish to steal the pure white stallion belonging to Red-beard," Swift-bear began, ignoring his brother's scowl as he continued. "In order to verify this feat, I and Big-shoulder stayed behind to watch from the hills as Star-runner crept down into the valley. Their outriders did not see him coming, for he moved in silence like the mountain cat, and he managed to spirit the great stallion away right out from under their noses."

Running-deer and Otter's-heart were properly awed by this recounting of such bravery, but Star-runner knew how the story ended, so he did not take pleasure in their compliments. As Swift-bear continued with the tale, he thought back to that long-ago day, recalling each moment in vivid detail. He had considered himself quite clever for pulling off the daring theft, but that was before he'd looked over his shoulder and seen the man riding after him.

Mountain-lion and Split-nose had seemed very large to a boy of thirteen moons, but compared to them, his pursuer was gigantic. Not only that, but the energy of the sun seemed to gather in his orange hair and then shoot out of his glowing green eyes in intense rays. Because of his anger, his face was the color of ox blood, and the full beard framing his mottled complexion was like a burning fire.

Although his horse could not match the speed of the white stallion, the chief of the Fierce-ones spurred on his mount with the force of his rage, and within seconds he caught up with the stallion. Star-runner was prepared to die beneath a blow from one of his mammoth hands, but instead, the bearded man plucked him off the stallion and tossed him over one stupendously broad shoulder.

Seconds later, he found himself sailing through the air. To his humiliation, he ended up facedown in the muddy water of a creek, his ears ringing with the first words of English he'd heard spoken in two years. "A grand try, laddie, but Angus Armstrong has a keen eye, and you'll not be takin' what's mine. A good hidin' is what you deserve, but a face full of mud ought to dampen your enthusiasm just as well.''

As soon as the man stepped down from his horse, Star-runner charged, deciding that with his friends watching, he would rather die than give up the stallion without a fight. Unfortunately for him, Red-beard thwarted this plan with amazing ease. As if he were fending off the bothersome attack of a flea, the man placed one hand inside Star-runner's belt and lifted him up off the ground. Then, after dispensing a good, swift kick to the backside, he tossed him back into the creek. ''Be off with you now, laddie, or you'll be eatin' mud all day.''

''It . . . is . . . my right to die like a man, Red-beard,'' Star-runner sputtered, drawing his knife as he struggled back to his feet. ''I am not a boy but a mighty Absaroka warrior.''

Red-beard's bushy brows rose when he realized what he was hearing. ''Who taught you to speak English?''

Taking advantage of the man's surprise, Star-runner attacked, and this was how he had earned the debt he had been unable to pay back for so many years. With one quick movement of his hand, Red-beard snatched the blade away and broke it in half over his knee. ''For takin' me on, I give you back your life, mighty warrior. Now be off with you, before I change my mind and break you in half with my bare hands!''

Star-runner stared at him in astonishment. Red-beard had the strength of ten warriors, and his medicine was so powerful that he could grab the blade of a knife without harm to himself. More awed than frightened, Star-runner backed slowly away, but before he lit out for the hills, he challenged his muscle-bound enemy one more time. ''I'll be back for that stallion, Red-beard. You may have the eyes of the fox, but I have his cunning. A man's strength is in his mind, not his body.''

He'd never come face to face with Angus Armstrong again, but he had eventually managed to steal his white stallion. He considered it one of his proudest accomplishments, the best part being the knowledge of how the theft must have enraged his old enemy. He could only imagine the man's fury if he ever found out that the same Indian who had stolen his favorite horse had also stolen something even more valuable—his daughter's virginity.

"So now your debt is paid," Running-deer said at the end of the story, trying hard to keep a straight face. "In exchange for your life, you have given Red-beard the life of his daughter."

"I say that our brother had no need to feel any such obligation," Otter's-heart pronounced loyally, earning himself a pleased smile from Star-runner. It was swiftly replaced by a thundering scowl as he added, "For the great wounds he suffered to his dignity and pride, I say it is Red-beard who owes him."

"And I say, if you don't want your dignity to suffer in a like manner, you will keep silent about what you have heard here today," Star-runner commanded.

Otter's-heart clamped a hand over his heart. "You wound me, brother. When have I ever been known to carry tales?"

Then, with a mischievous glint in his eye, he picked up his reins and galloped off. "If we ride long and hard, Running-deer," he shouted back gleefully over his shoulder, "we can arrive in our village in time to make the next council session."

"So we can," Running-deer replied eagerly, and he kicked his mount into an equally fast gallop.

"They wouldn't do that to me," Star-runner groaned softly.

Swift-bear shook his head in silent mirth. "Of course not. Would your young brothers show you so little respect?"

The question was barely out of Swift-bear's mouth when he heard a gutteral curse, and then he saw Star-runner, the great and mighty chief of the Absaroka, go charging through the trees, hot on the trail of his departing siblings. Swift-bear lifted his reins and gave his mount a gentle nudge with his moccasins as he prepared to follow. "After so many seasons away from us, I sincerely hope my brother has not forgotten the hazards of riding through such a dense forest."

Chapter

Twenty

Gazing out the back of the wagon, Tara surveyed her surroundings with growing wonder. As she viewed the high mountains, virgin forests, and lush valley spread out before her, she knew in her heart why her father and brothers had left the tame landscape of Connecticut in order to settle here. Such untamed land as this would have appealed to their highland souls, just as it was now appealing to hers.

As she breathed in the brisk mountain air, Tara felt a freedom of spirit greater than any she had yet experienced, and also a curious sense of homecoming. She had studied enough geography to know that the highlands of Scotland were as rugged and wild as this place, but she hadn't realized that she would feel this elemental kinship with a similar setting. It was as if the land itself was embracing her, stimulating the adventurous side of her nature that had been forced into dormancy for so long by her domineering aunt. As her gaze traveled upward to the snow-topped peaks and beyond to the wide blue sky, she felt an exhilaration in her soul and a soaring energy that made her think she could handle any trial that came her way.

"Look, Tara!" Rose exclaimed as the wagon drove around a curve in the muddy track and they got their first glimpse of the Triple-A Ranch. Atop the cedar shake roof of the ranch house, she counted five stone chimneys, an unheard of number of fireplaces to be found in one dwelling. "I'd say your menfolk have done right well in Montana. That's one fine house they've built for themselves."

To some, in comparison to the white stone mansion at Laurel Glen Farm, the framed stables and barns, and the neatly fenced paddocks surrounding them, the ranch would seem an extremely rustic place, but Tara loved it on sight. As the wagon passed by a wide, rolling green pasture, then a series of sturdy outbuildings, her gaze centered on the huge house, and her heart began fluttering with anticipation. Inside that sprawling two-story log structure, built like a fortress at the base of a wide hill, was her real family. At long last, she was finally going to meet them.

Anxiously, she smoothed down her skirts, then nervously fingered the cameo brooch at her throat. "Do I look all right, Rose?"

"You always look all right," Rose retorted in mock exasperation. "And it's a might galling, Taralynn Armstrong. Nary a hair out of place even during an Indian attack, while I looked as much a fright as a scarecrow."

As she was meant to, Tara laughed, but Rose's soothing tactics were unnecessary. Moments after bringing the wagon to a halt, Lloyd Dunn came back to the wagon to inform them that no one appeared to be home. "Out riding the range, most likely," he surmised. "According to Ben Fallon, they run a mighty large herd, so it's my guess your pa and brothers won't be back to the house much before nightfall."

As soon as she heard that, Harrlet declared, "Well, Tara can't remain out here by herself for the entire day. We've made arrangements to stay in Bozeman until our cabin is built, and it's not that far away. You'd best travel on with us, dear, and spend the night in town. Then tomorrow we'll send word to your pa to come there and fetch you from our boardinghouse."

"Oh, no." Tara negated that suggestion at once. "Now that I'm finally here, I can't possibly leave. Please don't worry about me, Mrs. Dunn. I'm sure I'll be just fine for these few hours."

Harriet was not so easily convinced, but Tara pointed out

that she would be perfectly safe as long as she did not venture out from the safety of the house, which looked as impregnable as a military stronghold. Perusing the place, Harriet allowed reluctantly, "I suppose that would be all right, but lest you forget, these hills are crawling with wild Indians and Lord knows what other kind of varmints. I'm certain your father would much rather you come with us than wait here alone."

Eventually, Tara managed to persuade the good woman that she would be perfectly safe for such a short while, and before the family left, she promised Rose that she would come into town for a visit as soon as she was able. After Zeke had deposited her trunk inside the front hall of the house, she stood on the wide veranda and watched as the Dunns continued on their way down the valley. She suffered a twinge of panic when their wagon disappeared from view, but she did not regret her decision not to go with them. She was an Armstrong, after all, and that meant she must be strong-hearted as well as strong-willed.

Since leaving Connecticut, she had come to know that she was far more capable than even she had imagined. She might be young and a mere woman, but she had outrun the agents sent out to find her, survived a hazardous trip up the Missouri River, escaped death by a buffalo stampede, and lived through a Sioux Indian attack. Not to mention . . .

Tara closed her eyes. *No! You will not think about that bounder!* she ordered herself. *You will not think about him or pine after him or waste one more minute of your time asking yourself fruitless questions.*

With a resolute toss of her head, Tara turned around and marched inside her father's house. Her fortitude was badly shaken, however, when she stepped through the wide arch off the center hall. What she saw looked more like a den for wild animals than the main room of a house. She had never seen such disarray and filth in all her life!

Rose had exclaimed over the number of fireplaces the house sported, and this room had one at each end, but they both contained at least a year's worth of ash in their grates, and the fire bricks in front of them were so dusty that she couldn't even tell what color they were. From what she could see, the furniture looked solid, but every stick of it was covered by soiled clothing, dirty dishes, and the discarded bones of some half-eaten game. Thoroughly dismayed by this evidence that the men in her family were a slovenly lot, she feared what else she might discover about them as the day wore on.

She didn't get the chance to worry long about it or explore any farther. Upon hearing an unearthly yell, she ran out of the room and back onto the veranda, her eyes going very wide as she gazed across the open fields. "Oh, my heavens," she whispered, one hand clasped to her throat. "Just look at them!"

Shouting like banshees, they rode parallel to one another, each on a horse of a different color. As they thundered across the wide section of grass, their strong white teeth gleaming in the sunlight and their shaggy red hair flying out from their heads, they reminded Tara of the Four Horsemen of the Apocalypse she had read about in scripture.

"And to wreak God's vengeance, they were given authority over a quarter of the earth, to kill by the sword, by famine, by plague and wild beasts," Tara quoted from the Bible in an awed whisper, then held her breath as the fearsome riders galloped straight for her at breakneck speed.

In a whirl of dust and pounding hooves, the first rider pulled up short by the porch railing and jumped effortlessly down from the saddle. "Good day to you, lass," he greeted, seemingly highly pleased with himself, but whether it was for scaring her witless or winning the race, Tara didn't know. With his dark brown eyes and auburn hair, he was devilishly handsome, and the young devil was well aware of it.

With a flourishing bow worthy of the royal court, he introduced himself. "James Armstrong at your service."

"I saw her first!" the next rider to reach the porch complained as he vaulted out of the saddle. "And a lovelier sight I never did see," he concluded, grinning widely as he stared up at Tara with adoring blue eyes as if she were a gift sent down especially for him from heaven. "Now that I'm here, fair maiden, you can forget you ever saw my young brother. I'm sure you prefer an older man, so the only name you need remember from now on is Neal Armstrong."

"Now, that would be foolish," the third arrival proclaimed, flipping himself backward over the rear of his horse, then landing right side up on his feet. With a sweep of his hand, he pushed a thicket of dark russet hair away from his green eyes and spoke through a smile enhanced by two of the largest dimples Tara had ever seen. "I may be the youngest, but I'm also the best-looking. Most call me Rob, but you, dear lady, can call me Robbie."

Tara was delighted by their antics, but her gaze was fastened on the fourth rider as he pulled up his big white stallion by the rail and dismounted. "Don't mind these rapscallions, miss," he advised gruffly, not really looking at her as he tied his reins to a metal ring stuck into the ground. " 'Tis been so long since they've been off the place that they've forgotten how to behave around the gentle sex."

"It's all right," Tara murmured, unable to stop staring at him. Though he had to be well past his middle years, Angus Armstrong's back was straight as an arrow, and his big body was as fit as that of a man half his age. In contrast to his weathered brown face, his full red beard was like a bright wreath, and it gave him a jovial look that wasn't matched by the intensity of his dark hazel eyes as he glanced up and met Tara's curious gaze.

"Guid God!" Angus intoned softly, the Scot burr very evident in his voice as he grasped onto the porch railing to steady himself. "Is it you, sweet lass, or do my eyes conjure ghosts?"

"Pa!" Neal inquired, staring first at his father whose usually ruddy face was devoid of all color and then toward the young, very proper-looking lady who had brought on his sudden malaise. There was something familiar about her, all right, and Angus had recognized her on sight, but Neal was damned if he could place her. "Who is this girl?"

Angus shook his head, his eyes growing moist as he stared at this beautiful replica of his long-dead wife. He blinked once, twice, but the vision did not fade away. "Ellen," he moaned, his fingers turning white on the rail as he looked into eyes as green as highland moss and long, splendid hair that glowed like fire. Even her lips were the same tender pink as his beloved's, the top one sweetly bowed, the lower sensually full.

Swaying, he closed his eyes and let the glorious memories wash over him. They had both been so young in those long-ago days before their beloved Isle of Kell had been stolen away from them by the English and their parents brutally murdered . . . so young and so very much in love. He could see her now, his sweet Ellen, running through the heather to meet him at the end of the work day, her wild, wind-tossed hair billowing around her shoulders like a fiery cloud.

"And why do ye tarry so long in the fields, my dear husband? Dinna know that your supper risks a-burnin'?"

"And what of you, lass?"

Her laughter was throaty and far too mature for a girl not yet fifteen, but this girl was his bride, his bonny Ellen, and he was a lucky man, for she thoroughly enjoyed a good tumble in their marriage bed.

"Aye, my fine brawny mon, I burn for you, too. So why do ye still tarry?"

"I tarry no longer, lass!"

Angus was lost somewhere in the past, and, shaken by the dazed, faraway look in his eyes, his sons went looking for someone to blame. Tara gulped as the atmosphere around her suddenly became charged with hostility. Like a company of loyal soldiers, her three brothers rallied around their dazed leader, their gazes not nearly as welcoming as they had been until now.

As his father continued to stare sightlessly off into space, Neal demanded in a voice that could cut steel, "Pa? Who is she!" When he still got no answer, he turned on Tara. "Okay, you tell me, lady. What the hell kind of business do you have with my father?"

"Family business," Tara mumbled nervously, thoroughly intimidated by the murderous tone of Neal's voice and the antagonistic expressions on all three of her brothers' faces. "I mean your father no harm."

Of course, as soon as she'd heard the name Angus had called her, Tara had realized why his reaction to her was so odd. Apparently, she greatly resembled the mother who had died giving birth to her. It was just as obvious that her father had loved his wife very deeply, and Tara didn't know if her resemblance to the deceased Ellen was a good thing or bad. In the last few moments, the man seemed to have aged ten years.

With a shudder, Angus came back to the present, and his eyes focused on Tara's face. "What is your name, lass?"

"Not Ellen," she finally managed to say, hating to cause him any more pain than she already had but fearing his reaction to her real identity. Would he want a daughter who would be a constant reminder of the woman he had lost? Would he even believe her when she told him? "My name is Taralynn, Mr. Arm—I mean Fa—"

Not knowing what she could call him, Tara stopped speaking, then started again, but beneath the intense scrutiny of four such fierce-looking men, she began to stammer. "I . . . my name is . . . Taralynn . . . Taralynn Armstrong . . . your daughter, sir, and . . . and I've come all the way from Connecticut to meet you. You see, I didn't die as a babe, as you thought. They . . . they only told you that I did to . . . but . . . but it was not true."

The brothers gawked at her as if she were some kind of half-wit, but Angus's face seemed transformed by an inner glow. "My wee bairn," he breathed joyfully, accepting her halting words without question. "All grown up and as beautiful as her mother."

Seconds later, he bounded up the stairs to the porch. In an instant, Tara's feet were swept off the floor and her body crushed against a hard, burly chest. "By the saints! 'Tis a miracle, to be sure," Angus murmured into her hair, fairly cracking her spine as he clasped her close to him and whirled her around and around. When at last he placed her back on her feet, Tara was stunned and completely out of breath.

Keeping one arm about her slender shoulders, Angus used the other to make a sweeping gesture to his sons. "Come on up here, lads, and give your young sister a proper welcome," he ordered in a booming voice. "Then we'll go inside and break out the good Scotch whiskey and lift a wee dram to celebrate her homecoming. 'Tis a grand day, I'm thinking, a very grand day."

Tara could see that her brothers weren't quite as ready to accept her into their hearts and home as their father seemed to be, but not one of them refused his order. By the time they had all finished hugging her and bestowing dry kisses on her flushed cheeks, she was certain that several of her ribs had been broken. Then, as James grasped one of her elbows and Robert the other to escort her inside the house, she felt as if her arms were being pulled out of their sockets.

"Ain't this purely amazin'?" James asked Robert over the top of Tara's head, a telling grimness around his mouth as they whisked her down the front hall. "As Pa says, 'tis a miracle. After all these years of grievin', he has his little girl returned to him from the dead."

"Hard to believe," Robert agreed sarcastically, a dangerous glint in his emerald eyes as he gave Tara's arm a painful squeeze. "And to think she's come all this way from Connecticut to finally take her proper place as our own dear *sister*. You did say Connecticut, didn't you, Taralynn?"

"Yes," Taralynn replied, but she could tell that they didn't believe her. Even so, no matter how these great louts felt about her, no lady deserved such rough treatment. She tried to wrench her arms free from their hold, but her brothers were far too strong, and at her first sign of protest they quickened their pace down the hall until her toes were barely skimming the floor.

A moment later, they were inside the main room, and she was shoved none to delicately down upon a couch that was piled high with soiled clothing and worse. "So, Taralynn," James growled in a deadly low tone. "Why, after all these many years, have you decided to foist . . . come home to us?"

Glancing back over his shoulder to make sure that Angus was still out of earshot, Robert suggested, "Or maybe you had some help arriving at this unwise decision? When he's imbibed more than his share of ale, our pa has this tendency to talk about the wee daughter he lost and all the fine plans he had for her if she had but lived. Why, most every barkeep from here to Bannock has heard the sad story a time or two."

"And what with you being too young at the time to realize who you rightly belonged to, somebody else must have told you the tale," James determined, sending his father a brilliant smile as Angus entered the room and crossed over to a small cabinet. As Angus bent down behind it to begin the fruitless search for some clean glasses, James turned back to Tara and hissed, "Now, just who would that be, you little—"

"Stop it!" Neal commanded under his breath, gripping James by the shoulder as he came to stand beside him. "Look at this portrait, then tell me who else she could be!"

First James and then Robert peered into the small silver frame Neal held in his hand. "That's what Ma looked like when Pa met her," Neal whispered. Then he muttered to himself, "I knew I'd seen her somewhere before."

"Lordy!" James gasped in astonishment.

Seeing the resemblance, Robert concurred with his older brother's opinion. "Great God in heaven!"

Tara gazed up at the threesome staring down at her, her mouth dropping open in amazement as James whooped, "Well, I'll be! We really do have ourselves a baby sister!"

"That we do," Neal agreed somberly, and then Tara found herself the subject of the most incredible conversation she had ever heard in her life.

Robert shook his head and sighed. "Now, what the devil are we going to do about it? She ain't exactly what you'd call a mud fence."

"And that figure," James groaned, eyeing Tara's full bosom as if he were in great pain.

"Once word gets out," Neal complained gruffly, "all the men in the territory will be sniffing after her like dogs in heat."

James scowled. "Then those bastards will find themselves looking down the barrel of a shotgun. No man lays a hand on my sister unless I approve of him."

"And I," Neal declared.

"Between the three of us, we'll protect her," Robert stated smugly. "Now, what do you lads think of Charlie Young?"

"I've always liked Charlie," James said. "He's a good man. Built up his herd from scratch, and now he's got a right decent spread. How 'bout it, Neal?"

"We could do a whole lot worse," Neal decided. "I'll agree to Charlie. He's young and strong and should give her some fine sons."

"And if our scruff cattle are allowed to graze on his northern pasture, it wouldn't be a bad bargain at all," James added.

"Then it's settled," Robert concluded. "Charlie gets first crack at her."

After listening to them, Tara wondered if there was something about her that made all of her relatives think they had the right to dictate her future. "I hate to disappoint you gentlemen," she declared tartly. "But I am not in the market for a husband. Indeed, I doubt I shall ever marry!"

They all looked at her as if they'd forgotten she was still there, let alone that she might have her own opinion to offer. After several moments of tense silence, James inquired, "Not even if we could get our hands on some of the best grazing land this side of the Bighorn?"

"Not even then," Tara snapped indignantly. These brothers of hers were outrageous, absolutely outrageous.

"You'd throw over a great catch like Charlie?" Neal demanded.

"Completely over!"

Robert tried for an irate expression, but his dimples spoiled the effect. "Wouldn't you know it? It's just our kind of luck to get stuck with a sister who is so damned bullheaded."

"And independent," James lamented.

"But gorgeous," Neal reminded them. "But then, that's to be expected. All we Armstrongs have great looks."

Snorting at their nonsense, Angus walked over to the couch, carrying a tray and five somewhat spotty-looking mugs filled to the brim with an amber brew. With a beaming smile, he handed Tara the cleanest one of the batch. "Best beware, lads. If she's as much like your dear departed mother as she looks, she's got a temper to match."

His tone was so hopeful that Tara couldn't help but laugh. "As it happens, when pushed . . ." She paused to give her brothers a pointed look. "I do have a perfectly frightful temper."

"The curse of the Armstrongs," Neal stated with a pleased grin, then saluted her with his mug. "Welcome to the family, Red."

"Hey!" James patted his unkempt auburn locks. "Red is *my* name."

"I thought it was mine," Robert noted with a frown.

Neal shrugged his shoulders. "Now that you mention it,

I've been called that a time or two myself. Sorry, Sis, but since the name fits us all so well, I'm afraid you'll just have to share it. Is that okay with you?"

Tara swallowed a giggle along with her first sip of whiskey. As the liquid burned down her throat, she gasped for breath. Eyes watering, she willed herself not to cough. If she planned to hold her own with this threesome, she could see that she would have to take whatever they dished out and dish back in equal measure. "That's just fine with me, Red," she assured them when she recovered her voice.

Angus's smile encompassed them all. " 'Tis indeed a grand day for our family," he murmured hoarsely, wiping his teary eyes with the back of his shirtsleeve. "The best day ever, I'm thinkin'."

Chapter

Twenty-one

Seated at the head of a long wooden table, Angus speared his knife into a thick slab of beef, then said to Tara, "When he bowed down to her wishes and changed his name to Wainwright, I knew that my brother would cowtow to Margaret on almost anything, but I didn't figure he was capable of this kind of disloyalty. If I had known the extent of his wife's power over him, I never would have left you with them as a bairn. I would have waited until you could travel with us."

Hazel eyes glowing fiercely, he brought the knife to his lips and chewed off a healthy chunk of meat. "At least Lachlan had the backbone to tell you the truth before he died and you got hooked up with that Louden fella. From what you've told me, he sounds like a male version of Margaret."

Tara nodded in agreement, too shocked by the activities going on around her to give her father's words her total attention. For all their good looks and inherent vitality, the Armstrong males had the table manners of a pack of hungry mongrels. As if they had gone without food for days, they reached and grabbed for the bowls and platters placed before them by their cook, Barney Gibson, a wizened old man with whiskey breath, a greasy stubble on his face, and grimy fingernails.

Tara had realized very shortly after the meal had started that if she didn't dive into the fore, she could well end up with an empty plate, but that thought didn't bother her in the slightest. The food looked charred and inedible, the serving plates were only passably clean, and not even that much could be said for the cook who was now slumped on a chair at the foot of the table half asleep. Unless something was done to remedy these deplorable conditions, she would gladly starve.

No matter how badly they behaved at mealtime, however, she liked her father and all three of her brothers. True, they were rowdy and rough and had few social graces, but along with a sparkle of devilish mischief and good humor, honesty shone from their eyes. She'd been with them less than one day, yet she felt as if she'd known them all her life, and as soon as they'd been convinced of her identity, they'd started treating her as if she had always been a cherished member of their family. Of course, it would take some doing to get used to their outlandish teasing, but even though such behavior was strange to her, she could see it was their way of conveying affection.

"You did good standing up for yourself like that, Red, and coming all this way on your own. For all her trying, it looks like Aunt Margaret didn't squash your Armstrong spunk, that's for sure," Neal commended her as he heaped his plate high with what looked like boiled brown potatoes. "I was only twelve when we left Laurel Glen, but I remember how bossy Aunt Margaret could be. I avoided her like the plague."

"Me too," Jamie agreed, stretching full length across the table to scoop up a handful of hard biscuits. "But somehow that old battle axe found me out every time I broke one of her precious rose bushes, and she took after me with a willow switch."

"I was six when we left there, and all I can remember about her was her voice," Robert recalled with his mouth full. "She always sounded like a screech owl."

Angus sighed. "I knew she disapproved of the boys' highjinks, but I never thought she'd treat a lass of mine the same way, especially when she always wanted a daughter of her own. I thought she might spoil you prissy and fill your head with a lot of her blue-blooded nonsense, but I figured I could deal with that problem well enough once I had you back under my roof.''

''You might still have to,'' Tara replied quietly, especially if he expected her to develop these atrocious table manners. ''I'm afraid some of those prissy habits are still with me.''

Robert scoffed through a mouthful of greasy brown gravy, ''Ah, that don't matter a bit. We get so few refined ladies in these parts that any man who sees you is going to think he's died and gone to heaven. Whether you act all prissy or not, you'll have so many offers of marriage, you won't be able to keep 'em all straight.''

James wiped his mouth off with the back of his sleeve. ''Just look how sappy we acted when we saw you standing out on the porch. You had us doing somersaults and standing on our heads without your sayin' so much as a word.''

Tara still wasn't saying much, but her brothers were so busy filling their mouths that they didn't appear to notice. As her gaze traveled from man to man, then around the room, she smiled to herself. If Aunt Margaret had taught her anything of worth, it was how to run an efficient household, and this was one household that was in dire need of order.

In all her eighteen years, Tara had never felt needed by anyone. Thus far, her fancy education and domestic skills had been without purpose, but these men and this house cried out for a female touch. It was going to take some time and clever effort, but she was going to see to it that this filthy lions' den was changed into a proper home for human beings. They might not like it, but it was high time her unkempt and disorderly brothers became slightly more domesticated. Civilization was fast encroaching on their wild and woolly domain, and in order to meet it successfully, they were going to have to learn a few social graces that their ''prissy'' sister was more than qualified to teach.

As she considered that amazing realization, Tara's feeling of contentment grew. At long last, she had found a place where she might truly belong and a family that admired her for herself, not for her ability to continue the family line. Though they'd teased her unmercifully about the number of marriage proposals she would supposedly receive in the very near future, her brothers had also made it clear that she was under no obligation to marry anyone. As an Armstrong instead of a Wainwright, she could finally become her own person, not merely a lovely showpiece meant to enhance the financial interests of her family.

It was Angus who first noticed that Tara wasn't eating, and a red flush worked its way up his neck as he figured out why. Over the past two decades, he'd forgotten that a woman required certain amenities at the table, and his three sons had long since dismissed every lesson their blessed mother had ever taught them. As he watched his genteel daughter eyeing the proceedings with distaste, he thought about his Ellen and what her reaction would be if she could see what a poor job he'd done with the lads.

But it was never too late to start correcting the error of their ways, he determined, and he cleared his throat loudly to gain everyone's attention. "Neal, before you grab the last slab off the meat platter, would you please pass it to Tara, and Jamie, it wouldn't hurt you none to cut the meat off that bone before you start gnawing at it. Robert, when dining in the company of a lady, a man does not spit what he don't like on the floor."

"Huh?" all three men answered in unison. Then they followed their father's gaze down the table to their sister, who was sitting primly in her chair, hands folded politely in her lap as she watched them gulp down their supper.

At one time or another, every one of them had come upon a woman who had demanded some semblance of manners and decorous behavior, but they'd never entertained one of those respectable types in their own home. Then it dawned on them that this particular woman was here on a permanent basis. As Tara watched their facial expressions change from confusion to resigned understanding, she almost burst out laughing.

"It's okay," she assured Neal, since she had no idea how to gloss over Robert's filthy spitting habit. "I'm really not hungry."

"You might be if these vittles were fit to eat," Angus complained, glaring at Barney, who had assumed they were going to spend the night at the line camp and thus had to be rousted out of a drunken stupor in order to fix their meal. "This meat is as tough as an old boot."

"Perhaps tomorrow I might show Mr. Gibson a way to tenderize the lesser cuts of beef," Tara volunteered, putting the first phase of her plan into motion. "To keep out of my aunt's way, I spent a lot of time in the kitchen with the cook, and Mrs. Valentine taught me a few things."

With a wistful sigh, she added, "Of course, I could only watch her. Even though I longed for the chance, I was never allowed to make a meal for the family. A Wainwright woman was considered much above such mundane duties as cooking and baking even if she knew how."

She could see her brothers exchange eager glances which told her that her suspicions were correct. They would be willing to make some concessions if there was even a chance that the quality of their edibles might be improved. Tara forced herself not to smile as Neal reminded her, "Well, you're an Armstrong now. If you want to turn your hand to the stove, go right ahead."

"Then you wouldn't mind if I trespassed into your kitchen tomorrow, Mr. Gibson?"

Jamie shot the besotted cook a meaningful glare. "I'm sure Barney'd be glad of the help. Wouldn't you, Barn?"

"Yes, ma'am," Barney agreed without need of any prompting. If it meant less work for him, he'd accept help from a snake, and Taralynn Armstrong weren't no viper. With a wide smile that showed off his missing teeth, he admitted, "I ain't much of a cook, but I'm the only man on the place who don't get all riled with their rantin' and ravin'."

"I thank you, Mr. Gibson." Tara smiled sweetly.

Grinning, Angus leaned back in his chair, not as easily fooled as his sons. Aye, his young Taralynn was much like her mother, using charm and a gentle manner to get what she wanted instead of forcing her demands on them like so many other women would have done. If he didn't miss his guess, before the lads knew what had hit them, this green-eyed minx would have them all dressing up for dinner and eating off sparkling clean plates.

"I'm proud of the way you managed this whole situation and powerful grateful to Lloyd Dunn for looking after you the way he done," Angus said as an overwhelming jolt of sentimentality and love for her hit him in the midsection. "If you hadn't been under the protection of his family on that long ride up the river, we might never have learned the true story, for like the lads here said, women of quality are in mighty short supply once you get out of the states, but we're full up with no-goods and ruffians. If you had been on your own amongst all those scalawags, I hate to think what might have happened to you."

Tara could feel the guilty flush rising up in her cheeks as she recalled what had indeed happened to her at the hands of just such a scalawag. Things were going so well with her father that she hated to lie, but she couldn't bear to tell him the whole truth, either. Ever since she'd arrived, her family had put such emphasis on her ladylike appearance and demeanor, but they wouldn't continue to think of her in such a favorable light if she told them that she'd shared bed and board with an unscrupulous riverboat gambler.

"I did have some assistance from another quarter," she admitted finally, intending to stick to the facts as closely as possible but leaving out those portions that would damn her in their eyes. Hastily, she relayed the story of her escape from Amos Snedeker and Grant's offer of protection, but she did not say how very dearly she had paid for his dubious help.

"Like most others on board, Mr. Collingswood was on his way to the goldfields to seek his fortune. I'm afraid that when the *Ophelia* landed at Fort Benton he left rather abruptly, so I wasn't allowed to thank him properly."

Her eyes held a fiery glint as she said the last, but her voice held only a vague distress. "Since the territory is so large, I doubt if I'll ever see him again."

"Collingswood," Angus mused thoughtfully. "Did you say Collingswood?"

Tara was startled by the question. From the look on his face, it appeared that her father might recognize the name. "That's right," she confirmed hesitantly, fearful of the sudden strain in his expression. Was it possible that Grant's womanizing ways were so legendary as to have spread this far?

"Was this man a foreigner?" Angus asked, controlling

some strong emotion with visible effort. "Was he an Englishman?"

"Why, yes," Tara said, now more confused than ever. "How did you know?"

Ignoring her question, Angus demanded, "What else did he tell you about himself?"

Deciding that information concerning Grant's English background was the least hazardous of the things she could say about him, Tara replied, "Well, as strange as this sounds, he was indeed a titled gentleman, the earl of Collingswood, to be exact, or at least he would have been if he hadn't given up the title to his younger brother George. George, he felt, was better suited for the responsibility that position entailed. You see, Gra—Mr. Collingswood—had traveled extensively in America, and eventually he'd concluded that he much preferred his life here to that which he'd enjoyed in England."

In the oppressive silence that followed her words, Tara grew more and more uncomfortable. Apparently, it was not only her father but her brothers, too, who knew something of Grant, for they all looked ready to commit violence. When she could stand the tension no longer, she inquired nervously, "Have you met the man, Father?"

"I have no desire to meet that devil's spawn!" Angus raged, pounding one fist on the table. "And it's a good thing for him that he left off his protection of you at Fort Benton. If he'd accompanied you here, he would be the one in need of protectin'. For what his kin had done to me and mine, I would take great pleasure in killin' him."

Upon hearing that announcement, Tara's eyes widened in astonishment, but thankfully she didn't have to wait long for further explanation. Seeing her confusion, Neal said, "Since she wanted you to think you were her daughter, Aunt Margaret wouldn't have told you the story of how our family came to live with her and Uncle Lachlan at Laurel Glen, but it was the earl of Collingswood who forced us out of Scotland."

"It was?"

Neal nodded. "For centuries, the Armstrong clan had lived on the Isle of Kell, unbothered by the politics of England, but unbeknownst to us, our ancestral chief had sold our land to pay off his debts to the throne, and what we had always considered our own belonged now to the ninth earl of Collingswood.''

At Tara's gasp, Jamie picked up the story. "And Roger Collingswood, your man's father, I reckon, had a passion for hunting. He built himself a fine hunting lodge on the far end of our island and imported a herd of red deer. Unfortunately for us and all who lived there, his deer and our sheep competed for pasture, and our sheep were winning the battle."

"So what did the earl do then?" Robert exclaimed sarcastically. "He slaughtered our animals and evicted us from the isle!"

"Aye, but we would not leave meekly on his say," Angus recalled bitterly. "So to crush our rebellion, the earl sent the English soldiers to burn down our homes and force us out. Those of us who survived the battle were near starvation by the time we made it down to Glasgow. Both of your grandfathers died protectin' their homes, and my mother threw herself into the fire rather than leave her husband. Several more of the old ones expired on the hard journey south, for there was no food to be found anywhere. Your sweet mum was carrying Robert at the time, and she delivered him out in a barren field without even a midwife to help her."

Tara bit her lip as she saw the moisture gather in her father's eyes. "No matter, we made it to safety. My Ellen was never the same afterward."

After a long hesitation, Angus continued, "Eventually, I earned enough money working the docks to cable my brother in America. Lachlan sent us enough for our passage to Connecticut, but a man who is used to livin' and workin' for himself canna take much pride in beggin' off the leavings of his brother. For six years, I worked for Lachlan, training the fine horses in the Wainwright stables, but I dreamed of the time when I could take my family west and settle on my own land, land that could never be stolen away from us as long as we had the strength to hold it. We saved every penny and had almost enough when your mum discovered she was carrying you . . .''

Again, Angus's voice trailed away, and this time it took

him even longer to recover from the pain of his memories. "After all she had suffered, my sweet lass just wasn't strong enough to survive another birthin'."

"Oh, Father," Tara cried softly, feeling her own eyes fill with moisture as she watched the single tear roll down her father's face and into his beard. "I'm so sorry."

Angus pulled himself up and cleared the huskiness from his throat. " 'Tis no reason for you to be sorry, lass. 'Twas that deuced bastard Collingswood who caused her death, not you. Before he came to our isle, my Ellen was a fine strappin' lass who had no trouble deliverin' her bairns, but he kill't her with his greed and his selfishness, same as he kill't my parents and Ellen's kin, too. Same as if he took a gun and shot them all, he's responsible."

"And his son best be glad we weren't there to meet your boat," Neal added. "For all his gallantry to you, we don't look kindly on any Collingswood."

Tara swallowed hard, remembering Grant's reaction when he'd discovered her name. Now, after hearing this story, his strange behavior made sense. Wrongly, she'd assumed his reluctance to make love to her was out of fear of her reaction to his scarred body, but all along he had been thinking about her reaction to the knowledge that his father had taken the bread out of her father's mouth, exiled her family from their homeland. No wonder he'd departed the boat so abruptly at Fort Benton.

Concerned by her ashen complexion, Robert soothed, "Don't fret, Tara. There was no way you could have known who he was, and it sounds like he's a far different sort from his father."

"Hah!" Neal scoffed. "Any man, even the lowest form of vermin, can act the gentleman to impress a pretty lady."

It was Jamie who posed the question that kept niggling at Tara. "Well, whatever kind of man he is, I can't see an English gent working from dawn to dusk on a claim. So if he didn't come out here seeking gold, what's he doing in this part of the country?"

"I don't know," Tara replied thoughtfully.

"And it's not likely we'll ever find out," Robert declared, catching Jamie's eyes, then looking toward Angus.

Seeing his father's agonized expression, Jamie got the

message. "So, Tara, you mentioned that Dunn has an unmarried daughter. Is she anything much to look at?"

"Rose is very attractive," Tara said, as anxious as her brothers to move on to another subject. "She's blond and has the most lovely blue eyes."

Jamie grinned. "Well, then, since we've got so much in common already, I think I just might have to take a ride into Bozeman one of these days and meet up with this gal."

"Don't bother making a wasted trip," Rob advised. "I'm heading that way first thing in the morning."

"Then I'll probably see you there," Neal inserted smoothly. "Since I'm spending tonight in town."

When the dust finally settled back down, Tara and Angus found themselves alone at the table. "Maybe I should have warned them that Rose doesn't have much use for men," Tara worried out loud, making a face as she took her first swallow of Barney's coffee.

Angus emitted a hearty laugh. "Naw, when it comes to bonny lassies, the lads don't take much heed to warnings. They'll be too busy performin' to notice any lack of appreciation on your friend's part."

Tara shook her head as she pictured the upcoming confrontation between Rose and her three brothers. "I don't think so, Father. Rose is very outspoken."

Angus laughed all the harder. "Well, then, lass, I'll say it again. This is turning out to be one very grand day for the Armstrongs, especially for those who need to be taken down a peg or two."

Shyly, Tara suggested, "There are a few Armstrongs who seem to think quite highly of themselves."

Angus gazed warmly into her eyes. "Aye, and if I'd have had it my way these past eighteen years, that trait would be common to us all."

Tara smiled impishly. "Please, Father, you need not despair on my account. I'm sure I shall attain it in very short order."

Angus grinned and rolled his eyes toward heaven. "Aye, daughter, of this I have little doubt."

Chapter

Twenty-two

Stepping away from his brothers, who remained standing at the entrance to the tepee, Star-runner knelt down beside the old man resting on a thick pile of buffalo pelts. Mountain-lion was asleep, but even in slumber there was no escape from the constant pain he endured. His copper skin was gray with ill health, his breath labored and raspy. Because of the continual strain of gritting his teeth, the scars of those many long-ago battles were carved more deeply into his aged face, and the effort to go on living had chiseled wide furrows into his noble brow.

Star-runner had not thought his beloved grandfather could survive the grave wounds he had sustained during the Cheyenne massacre, but, according to Swift-bear, the old man had refused to die, and because of his great courage none in the clan had been able to bring himself to cast him out. Although he was now an ancient one and could no longer hunt or assist in moving camp, his wisdom was too highly respected for anyone to question his reluctance to pass on to the spirit world as his sister Fire-weasel had done five seasons before. Thus, when the clan broke camp, Mountain-lion was placed on a travois and carried with them from place to place.

"I have returned, Grandfather," Star-runner whispered, reaching down to grasp one gnarled hand in his. As he unclenched the crippled fingers, he blinked back tears, for he who had always been so strong was strong no longer. "I am here."

Mountain-lion opened his eyes, and in them Star-runner could see the end of pain and the beginnings of total peace. When asleep, the old chief was already among the spirits, and only by sheer will did he hold on to the old life when awake. It was inevitable that his tired and lame body would soon follow his soul down the path to the other side, whether or not his spirit was willing. "I am here," Star-runner repeated desperately, hoping Mountain-lion would show some sign of recognition before he crossed over.

He need not have worried, for as soon as his grandfather's rheumy eyes refocused, he smiled a greeting. "At last," he grunted in satisfaction. "Soon I shall be free to go, for with your coming, Star-runner, the prophecy will be fulfilled."

Star-runner sighed, half in exasperation, half in fear of what he knew must soon happen. "Did you endure this great torment all these years just for this, Grandfather? I came back as I promised you I would. Could you not trust that I would obey your last words to me?"

With the force of his remaining strength, Mountain-lion squeezed Star-runner's hand. "Your conceit has not altered with the passage of time, my son," he scolded him fiercely. "I live to fulfill my own destiny, not yours. Just as you must now follow the path set down for you, I follow my own trail. All in my dream has come to pass, and now your trial begins."

Star-runner glanced up sharply at Swift-bear, who nodded and then gestured to Otter's-heart, who immediately ducked outside the tepee. Seconds later, he returned, followed by all the chiefs and wise men of the clan. Solemnly, they formed a half-circle around Mountain-lion's deathbed, then seated themselves as if at council.

"The seasons are long since I have spoken with the white buffalo bull, but with Star-runner's return he has again spoken to me," Mountain-lion whispered.

In the reverent silence that followed this announcement, Otter's-heart built a small fire in the center of the circle, and

Running-deer lit the pipe. All those gathered knew that Mountain-lion would not speak again until each man had smoked of the sacred tobacco, but even though the company was anxious to hear his next words, this ceremonial process could not be hurried. As the pipe was passed from man to man, Star-runner clasped his grandfather's hand tightly, his mind traveling backward in time to that terrible day when he had first been given the incredible story of what had transpired during the winter of the big snow, the night of the icicle wind.

With his wife and son dead at the hand of his enemy, Star-runner had cried out for vengeance against the Cheyenne, but to his amazement no warrior would follow him to the enemy camp. Outraged by their disloyalty, he had demanded that they accompany him to see Mountain-lion, certain that the courageous old chief would convince the men of the clan to ride out into battle. Once they had seen the great wounds Mountain-lion had sustained in defense of their women and children, they could not help but ride with him to seek revenge.

Yet, when he had bent down by his grandfather's bed and pleaded with him to call out for an immediate reprisal against the Cheyenne, even Mountain-lion had denied him. "Our warriors have remembered my dream, Star-runner," the wounded man had informed him, then gone on to describe the prophecy that involved him yet had deliberately been kept from his ears.

In Mountain-lion's dream, a white buffalo bull had foretold of a great warrior who would come among the Fire-bears, a courageous chief marked by the sign of the raven and with the power to call down the moon. Because of the small telescope Star-runner had possessed as a boy and the birdlike birthmark on his hip, it was assumed that he must be this exalted warrior. Though Star-runner had scoffed at this description of himself, Mountain-lion had remained adamant in his belief. "We named you Star-runner because we knew that one day you would chase the stars on your sacred quest across the great wide waters."

"But Grandfather, I have no knowledge of this quest, nor have I any wish to chase the stars."

"In this you have no choice. The white buffalo has shown me a fearful enemy that only you can vanquish."

"The Cheyenne is this enemy!" he had insisted, but his grandfather had shaken his head, then reclined on his bed.

"Our warriors will not follow you again until you return from your sojourn amongst the white man, my son. When this journey is complete, you will be cleansed and ready to help us in our time of need."

"I am ready now!"

With the understanding that comes from suffering and the wisdom of age, Mountain-lion had decreed, "No! You must chase the stars across the wide waters and not return until your helpers have taught you all that you will need to vanquish our enemies and protect the heart of our people. When the blood spilled here today has returned to the earth, we will dance in the sun and sing songs of your coming. The torment in your heart cannot end until you do this thing that I have dreamed."

The next day, Star-runner had gazed down at the body of his beautiful wife, Sliver-of-moon, and his precious newborn son, Tall-bear, dressed in their best clothes and placed on the burial scaffold. Tears streaming down his cheeks, he had listened to the women of his clan call out to his loved ones, "Go now! You are gone, turn not back, we wish you fare-well."

In the tradition of deep mourning, he had gashed his arms and legs and cut off his long black hair. Then, covered in his own blood, he had followed the tribal custom of absenting himself from camp in order to grieve, but in his case, given no other choice, his absence had lasted much longer than a full season. After dispensing all of his valuables among the people, keeping nothing but his medicine, weapons, and some clothing, he had ridden away from the camp and the sacred mountains.

Three months later, he had been known in the northern territories as Grantland Collingswood, a ruthless drifter, lightning fast with a knife, whose eyes were as blue and frigidly cold as a winter sky without sun. Eventually, as he'd worked his way east, he earned enough money on various jobs for passage aboard a vessel that would carry him across the wide ocean. No matter what situation he would find in

England, he was determined to return to Montana in as short a time as possible, to prove to his superstitious clan that they had been wrong to cast him out. He was not this all-powerful champion of Mountain-lion's prophecy; he was simply Star-runner, brave warrior of the Absaroka, and his place was with them.

As the pipe was passed to him, Star-runner was jolted back to the present. After all this time, he had expected his people to have forgotten all about the circumstances under which he had left them, yet they were still insisting that he was this mystical hero destined to rescue them from some great evildoer. Moreover, they maintained that Mountain-lion would remain trapped inside the painful prison of his ruined body until Star-runner agreed to accept his destiny as their savior. Although he was no more convinced now than he had been when he'd left that he was this omnipotent chief about whom Mountain-lion had dreamed, he was prepared to do whatever was required of him to relieve his grand-father's suffering.

After expelling the last puff of smoke from his lungs, Star-runner laid down the pipe and faced the tribal council, his eyes on his adopted father, who had told him the reason why Mountain-lion had refused to give up his spirit for all these many seasons. In a resigned tone, he said, "I am ready to listen, and ready to serve my people, in any way that I can."

With a sigh of relief, Split-nose nodded, then gazed deeply into his father's eyes. Mountain-lion responded to his son's visual question by raising his free hand off the bed. "Tell him all I have learned," he ordered weakly. "Before my eyes grow to weak to see."

Split-nose proceeded to recount the events of the past season. True to Mountain-lion's prophecy, a great unknown enemy had risen up against the people, and already many had died by his brutal hand. "His white raiders come in the night like deadly shadows. They have attacked us and the lodges of other tribes, but also the camps of the white miners, who now, because these savage murderers disguise themselves as Indians, believe it is our people who have killed them. Your uncle White-horse and his wives and children are now slain, as is your friend Big-shoulder, who was murdered while he rode through the valley of horses. As my father has dreamed, the blood of many chiefs has now reddened the ground.''

Swift-bear asserted angrily, ''It is our belief that the leader of these vicious raiders wishes to incite us to break treaty and declare war on the white man.''

''But war would bring the soldiers down upon us, and their weapons are too strong,'' Otter's-heart explained, the frustration he felt sharp in his tone. ''If we raise our hand against the whites, we shall bring about our own destruction.''

''Not if we retaliate in secrecy, like these evil raiders,'' Running-deer argued. ''Are we to lie down like old women while they seek to destroy us?''

''They seek the gold that lies beneath us,'' Mountain-lion whispered harshly, his fingers tightening around Star-runner's hand as he struggled to rise up on his bed. ''For this wealth, our unknown enemy would slay both white and Indian alike.''

''Yet we do nothing to stop him!'' Running-deer raged.

''Our anger is a useless weapon,'' Split-nose chided, but he could see that his words had little effect. The young braves of the tribe were spoiling for a fight, and soon he and the other wise men of the council would not be able to control them. In retaliation for the attacks upon their people, they yearned to make war, and it was becoming more and more difficult to convince them that revenge against the whites would bring about even more useless slaughter. As yet, Swift-bear had not thrown in with their cause, but with each subsequent attack more pressure was brought to bear upon the newly elected chief of the clan.

Aware of the growing unrest among the young warriors, Mountain-lion berated their rashness. ''Before we can stop our enemy, we must know him. As is known to all of you, this is the task set to Star-runner in my dream. He must . . .''

As he felt Mountain-lion's hand go limp in his grasp, Star-runner glared up at his younger brother. ''We have no more time to waste arguing, Running-deer. I have sworn to listen to all my grandfather has to say. Let him say it.''

Mountain-lion's voice was so weak that Star-runner had

to lean down to hear him. "You . . . you must find our enemy. This . . . is your duty, my son."

"I will find him," Star-runner vowed, his face contorted in grief as he watched the approach of the inevitable. "I promise you, Grandfather. I will find him and destroy him."

Mountain-lion's head fell back on the bed, his dark eyes glowing with the last spark of life. "It is well, my son. The white buffalo has . . . come to lead me . . . on the spirit trail. Do you see him, Star-runner?"

"Yes, Grandfather," Star-runner assured him, unashamed of the tears that rolled down his cheeks. "And he only appears to lead the most high among men."

As the shudder of death passed over him, Mountain-lion smiled for the last time. "I have kept my promise to him."

"And I will keep mine to you, Grandfather," Star-runner whispered fiercely, but Mountain-lion had already departed the lodge to follow the trail of the sacred white buffalo.

Chapter

Twenty-three

The small town of Bozeman had sprung up like magic soon after gold was discovered in the territory. It was situated between the Yellowstone and Gallatin rivers in a beautiful valley at the head of a mountain gorge. The stroke of the miner's hammer, the clatter of hooves, and the creak of wagons told of the changes that had come over the valley, where before the coming of the white man naught was heard but the zephyrs that whistled through the noddling pines on the mountainside and the rippling waters of brooklets as they glided over their pebbly bottoms.

Now that quiet was gone. All was bustle, all was life. Cabins, stores, and hotels had been built up overnight. Saloons, billiard tables, and monte banks occupied the business corners, and clapboard houses filled the spaces between.

As the mines began to yield up their golden treasures, businessmen assumed an air of the well-to-do, and those who had been in the habit of spending their nights in the gambling halls yearned for retirement in the more peaceful avocations of life. Marriage brought children, and with them came their parents' concern for safety. In a place where many recognized the laws of neither God nor man, a sheriff was appointed to keep the peace. A school was started and a church founded.

On the first of August, the respectable ladies of the town, under the guidance of Mrs. Bertina Riley, the self-proclaimed leader of the community's fledgling society, organized a supper dance to celebrate the newly completed construction of a town hall. According to Bertina, a citizens' forum was the next step in the long process of instilling civilization in a primitive place. Of course, she did not say that in return for putting up the money to build the required hall she fully expected her foppish husband, Frank, to be elected the first mayor of the township.

Even those who didn't put much faith in Frank's chances to win an election, miners and merchants, townsfolk and farmers, anyone who lived near enough to town flocked in for the dance, and though the festivities were not scheduled to start until evening, by early afternoon the main street was congested by a steady stream of incoming horses and wagons. No matter what the excuse for a gathering, whether it be a wedding, a dance, or a funeral, attendance was high, for with so much distance between settlements, homesteads, and mine claims, people were always yearning for the chance to exchange news and enjoy the company of others.

Greatly looking forward to the occasion, Tara had risen at dawn, and by midmorning she had finished with her cooking and was ready to leave for town. Her brothers, however, subscribed to the philosophy that a party wouldn't start until they got there, so they felt no need to rush. At least, that was the excuse they gave for their dawdling as Tara bustled up and down the polished floor of the hallway between their rooms, anxious to hasten their departure.

"James Armstrong! You can't possibly wear those filthy old things!" Tara squeaked in horror as she arrived at Jamie's doorway and found him whacking the seat of his favorite pair of pants to remove a heavy layer of dust. Pointing to the freshly laundered and pressed dress trousers she had laid out on his bed, she inquired tartly, "What, pray tell, is wrong with those?"

"They ride up way too high in my crotch, Tara," Jamie informed her bluntly, hoping the reference to his privates would prevent her from pursuing the subject and he wouldn't have to don such fancy duds. "I don't aim to be wearin' no ball-crunchers whilst I'm dancin'. That would hinder my grand style."

After living in this all-male household for close to two months, Tara was no longer shocked by her brothers' crude remarks, especially when they were used to prevent her from winning an argument. Although her siblings didn't know it, she had caught on to that ploy early on. Even so, she had also discovered the wisdom in compromise and how best to achieve one. Donning the innocent expression of an angel, she sympathized with Jamie's predicament. "I can see how that would be a problem. Of course, I know quite a few women who will be disappointed when you show up in those baggy pants, but then, that's their problem, isn't it?"

Jamie frowned quizzically. "Why would they be disappointed?"

With an impish twinkle in her eye, Tara told him, "Because your manly form happens to be much admired by the ladies, and those droopy drawers don't show off a thing."

At first, Jamie seemed shocked that the female of the species paid any attention to how a man wore his pants, but then he looked down at himself, and his expression turned thoughtful. As Tara marched across the hall to Robert's bedroom, Jamie was already changing. Thankfully, the only problem she encountered from Robert was a stubborn cowlick that refused to stay down, but she solved that by applying a few drops of her bath oil to his comb.

"What if some gal notices that I smell as pretty as she does?" Rob complained, but she was able to mollify him by saying that the refined gentlemen of her acquaintance often adorned themselves with sweetly scented hair oils.

As rough-and-tumble as her three brothers were, Tara had soon discovered that they were all endowed with a large streak of vanity, and Tara had shrewdly taken advantage of that fact, using compliments instead of censure to achieve her aims. Though they still had their lapses, her siblings no longer chafed at the idea of bathing on a regular basis or wearing clean clothes. Indeed, just last night, her brothers had washed up and changed out of their work clothes before appearing at the table for the evening meal, and not one of them had spit anything vile on her newly washed floor.

All things considered, Tara was quite pleased with their progress, especially when she arrived in Neal's room and found him dressed very nicely in a white shirt, string tie, and black pants. Though Tara could find nothing wrong with his appearance, her sensitive nose picked up a distinct aroma of the barnyard. Upon further investigation, she noticed the telltale mud caked on his boots. Without further ado, she searched beneath his bed until she found what she was looking for.

"But those are my old ones," Neal informed her doubtfully as she held up a pair of black boots. "I thought you wanted us to get all decked out in our Sunday best."

"I do, but since you're wearing black, these boots will match so much better," Tara said, trying not to grimace as she helped him remove the dirty pair he had on. "Believe me, Neal, women never fail to notice such things."

"They don't?"

"No, they don't," she declared emphatically, then ran down the hall to her own room in order to wash her soiled hands. As soon as she was finished with that unpalatable task, she rushed back out again, certain that if they were ever going to make it to town in time for the dance, she would have to continue urging her languorous siblings to a faster pace, but to her surprise, when she opened her door they were all standing right outside.

Shaking his finger at her, Neal pulled out his pocket watch and grumbled, "Geez, Red. With all your lollygagging, we're going to miss half the fun."

"Women!" James exclaimed in disugst. "They don't think nothin' about it when they keep a man coolin' his heels for hours."

"How much longer do we have to stand around waitin' like this?" Robert demanded as he slicked his hand over his cowlick. "We should have been on the road by noon."

"I'm so sorry for the delay," Tara apologized, lips twitching as she marched ahead of them toward the stairs. They were impossible, truly impossible. "But as you all must know by now, a woman takes longer to ready herself than a man because she has far more to do. What with choosing the perfect dress to wear and fixing my hair, the time just seemed to get away from me."

"That's what they always say," Rob groused as he and his brothers trouped dutifully behind their laggard of a sister.

Once they had exchanged a few words with their father, who was staying behind to see to the chores, the group gathered around the wagon. After a lengthy discussion, it was finally decided that Neal would drive and that Tara would share the wagon seat while James and Robert guarded the baskets that contained their supper. Having ridden with Neal before, Tara held on with both hands and offered up a heartfelt prayer for deliverance as the wagon lurched to a start and careened down the road.

Three hours later, a very white-faced Tara arrived safely in town, but as soon as her grinning brothers had lifted her down from the buckboard and deposited her at the Fair Winds Hotel, they took off for the nearest saloon, where drinks were being sold for half-price in honor of the occasion.

As she and Rose stood at the wide front windows in the hotel vestibule and watched them bound down the steps and then stride swiftly across the crowded street, Rose groused, "At the rate they're going, all the menfolk in town will be three sheets to the wind before the fiddlers ever start playing. My poor feet are already complaining, and I haven't danced a step."

Since it had been her experience that very few men in the territory excelled at dancing even when they weren't worse off for drink, Tara sighed, "Mine, too."

"I sure do hope Jamie doesn't ask me," Rose said, though Tara noticed that her friend's gaze didn't waver away from James until he had ducked inside the doors of the Rusty Nail Saloon. As soon as he was out of sight, Rose charged, "Even when he's not under the influence, that clumsy brother of yours has two left feet."

Since the only evidence Rose had for that assertion was the square dance held the previous month at the Dunn barnraising, Tara inquired, "Why, then, may I ask, if you felt that way, did you dance with him so many times at our last get-together? As I recall, Neal and Robbie tried to cut in on you quite a number of times."

Rose's blush gave Tara her answer, but when she laughed, Rose retorted indignantly, "I figured I'd be in even more trouble with them two, seeing's how they half maimed Gladys Olson. That poor gal still walks with a limp."

Rose scowled at Tara's knowing nod, but she didn't pursue the subject, which made Tara think that the relationship between her best friend and her brother Jamie was even more serious than she'd already surmised. And since the two of them rarely had anything good to say about each other, Tara could hardly wait for tonight's festivities to begin. Like most people who had settled in this vast wilderness territory, Tara had come to appreciate any form of amusement, and she was finding the stormy courtship of James Armstrong and Rose Dunn highly entertaining.

"If you like, I could warn him off you tonight," Tara suggested, and she was immediately rewarded by Rose's exclamation, "Don't you dare!"

Annoyed that Tara could see right through her defensive tactics, Rose glared at her and turned away from the window. As they went to join the other women seated together in the hotel parlor, she whispered, "And if you even hint to him that I think he's wonderful, you'll wish you were never born, Taralynn Armstrong!"

Tara shrugged off the warning with a knowing smile. Once Rose had set her sights on Jamie, his fate had been sealed. It hadn't taken Rose long to figure out that the only way to catch a scalawag like Jamie was to keep him guessing.

"How long do you intend to keep up this merry chase?" Tara asked.

Rose grinned. "Only until he catches me."

Giggling, the two girls linked arms and entered the hotel's parlor. "Come sit here, girls." Harriet Dunn gestured to a red velvet settee across from her chair.

"If you need to freshen up later on in the day, my dear," Harriet offered Tara, "Lloyd has kindly reserved us a room upstairs for the night, and of course we'll expect you and your brothers to join us for supper at the hall. I've brought along more than enough food for all of us."

"That's very kind of you, Mrs. Dunn, and I do need a place to change into my dress, but I think I've finally mastered a few of those dishes you taught me," Tara replied, happy to report that she no longer had to rely on the generosity of her nearest female neighbor in order to provide a decent meal for her family. Those first few days after her arrival at the ranch had been very humbling for her, and a huge disappointment to her brothers to learn that though she'd watched the preparation of so many recipes in the kitchen at Laurel Glen, she was a perfectly awful cook.

"I am most proud to announce," she added dryly, "that the fried chicken I have prepared for our supper tonight won't make anyone sick, and my biscuits won't chip anyone's teeth."

Harriet beamed at her. "As I always say, all it takes to succeed at anything is lots of practice."

"And patience," Bertina Riley declared with a righteous sniff as she joined the growing circle of women. Her ample figure was encased in a stiff-necked, black taffeta dress which Bertina felt befitted a person of her high station in the community, but Tara thought it made her look very much like a plump crow.

Since the woman's voice also carried a close resemblance to that raucous bird, Tara had hoped for a few minutes' respite before being subjected to it, but, as usual, that wish was to be denied. As soon as she'd made Tara's acquaintance and learned of her esteemed social background, Bertina had begun fawning over her, and, without being rude, Tara couldn't find a way to stop her.

Perching her weighty body on the very edge of a cane chair, Bertina gushed, "You have every reason to feel proud of yourself, Tara. Taking charge of any household, especially one that has gone so long without the tender influence of a woman, requires infinite patience. I'm sure you often feel like giving up, but please do not despair. The changes you have wrought in your unruly brothers after so short a time are truly remarkable."

Turning to Harriet and Mariah Daniels, the hotel owner's wife, she exclaimed, "Why, just the other day, Neal doffed his hat to me on the street, and James assisted me over a deep rut without my even having to remind him of his proper duty."

Tara was hard put not to laugh when she saw Rose roll back her eyes, but she managed to respond to the compliment with a weak smile and a weaker "Thank you."

Hoping to steer the conversation into another vein, Tara

addressed her next comment to Letitia Bates, whose husband operated a trading post along the Bozeman trail. Since their property was nearest to the border of the Crow hunting grounds, the couple was privy to the latest news concerning the disturbing accounts of that normally friendly tribe's retaliation on those who were found trespassing on their land. Having lived side by side with them for many years, Tara's father and brothers refused to believe that the tribe had suddenly turned against them, but all the evidence was pointing in that direction. "I understand that another group of miners was attacked last week on the Yellowstone. Is that true, Mrs. Bates? And were the raiders Crow?"

Letitia nodded, her pale cheeks flushing slightly at the unexpected attention. A short, nondescript woman with mousy brown hair and downcast eyes, Letitita had very little self-confidence, and normally her gregarious husband, Victor, did her talking for her. Unfortunately, Victor was across the street with all the other men, which left Letitia to describe the most recent murders that had taken place at a mining camp upriver from their trading post.

"The only witness left alive insists that his attackers were that same band of renegade Crow who slaughtered Ezra Field and his partners. All three of those poor unfortunates who died were not only shot but scalped and mutilated," Letitia stammered in horror. Then she recited the words her husband had used at breakfast that very morning. "I fear an Indian war is about to break out, and to maintain our own safety when surrounded by those bloodthirsty savages, we must call upon the Army for protection."

Seeing that statement garner several affirming nods, Letitia spoke more forcefully. "We simply cannot allow this type of activity to continue, or we may all lose our lives."

"The way I heard it," Mariah put in, "even though they were warned, those miners were encroaching on Crow lands, just like that last bunch, and for their greed they were killed. They knew the consequences of trespassing, but they chose to take the risk."

Once again, Letitia relied on the wisdom of her husband for a response. "But . . . but the Indians have no use for all that gold, so why should they mind if we pan for nuggets on their territory?"

"Why indeed?" Bertina asked, still shivering from Letitia's description of the latest incident. "Those men were causing no harm, and it's not as if the Crow held a deed to their property. They only own it because they say so and ruthlessly attack anyone who questions their right."

"They do have a signed treaty with our government," Tara reminded her. "I would say that's a deed of sorts."

"But even if the miners were trespassing," Letitia said, trying to remember her husband's recent speech to his customers word for word, "that's not grounds for murder. Such savagery tells me that those heathens are determined to exterminate any and all whites in the area, including us."

Mary Baker, wife and mother of five young children, shuddered as she imagined her home burned to the ground and the mutilated bodies of her babies strewn among the ashes. "Letitia is right. None of us is safe as long as these hideous attacks go unpunished. We should call upon the Army to intervene on our behalf."

"I shall ask my husband to pursue that undertaking this very day," Mariah declared stoutly. "After all our efforts here, I would hate to wake up one morning and see our hotel aflame and our guests lying murdered in their beds."

"Your suggestion is sound, Letitia," Bertina agreed. "And I shall set Frank to write a letter to the commandant at Fort Ellis as soon as possible."

Since her opinions appeared to be accepted as gospel by the other women, Letitia's physical stature underwent a visible change. By straightening her slumped shoulders and lifting her chin, she increased her height by more than two inches, and her stammer was completely gone as she said, "I must warn you ladies that there are some who do not agree with our position. Why, just yesterday, I overheard a young man, who has started up a ranch in the Absaroka Mountains, saying that he had heard of several similar attacks on the other side, supposedly by these same raiders."

"Attacks on the Crow?" Tara inquired curiously.

"That's what he said," Letitia confirmed, though her expression implied that she doubted the truth of the man's story.

"Why would Crow attack Crow?"

Again, Letitia had a ready answer. "Well, this rancher put

forth the incredible idea that white men, disguising themselves as Crow, are behind these murderous raids for the
very purpose of starting a war. If it came to that, he said the
government would nullify its latest treaty with the Crow and
force them off their tribal grounds. Then these alledged
criminals would be free to mine for gold on Crow land
without fear of reprisal.''

"I suppose that theory is possible," Tara allowed, but the
other women scoffed at such a far-fetched conjecture.

"As my Victor says," Letitia asserted, basking in the
glory of her newfound position as an authority on the subject, "what white man would want war when it would bring
about so much needless slaughter to his own kind? After all,
gold isn't worth anything to a man who isn't alive to spend
it.''

"How true," Bertina affirmed. But since she found the
matters of war and killing extremely distasteful, she put an
end to the discussion by saying, "Enough on a topic that is
best left to men. Taralynn, we are all dying to see that lovely
dress you are planning to wear tonight. We realize that it's
been two months since your arrival amongst us, but since so
few of us, other than myself, have ever been as far east as
New York City, your dress must still be considered the
height of fashion. Isn't that true, ladies?''

If they didn't want to endure Bertina's scathing censure,
the other women in the parlor would be wise to agree, which
they did with commendable sincerity. Once Bertina had
deemed that Tara had been graced with a suitable number of
compliments, she excused herself in order too commence
her own toilette for the evening. "Such an auspicious occasion as this occurs far too rarely in our town," she explained
before departing for her home. "I might not be able to match
Taralynn's fashionable attire, but I do intend to look my
very best. As you all know, Franklin sets such store by my
appearance.''

"At least someone does," Rose muttered under her
breath, but several women heard, and since Bertina had left
the room, they could afford to laugh.

Harriet tried to look disapproving, but there was a noticeable twitch on her lips. "I do wish that woman could hear
herself," she finally said, shaking her head. "She denigrates

the Indians for giving themselves rights without our agreement, but Bertina is guilty of the very same thing. Just because her husband owns the general store and manages the land office, she has proclaimed herself our community's social conscience, but I can't recall casting a vote in her favor. Can any of you?"

With a cheeky grin, Rose declared, "Might makes right, Ma, and Bertina Riley outweighs all of us, including her poor husband, by at least a couple of stone."

At that, Harriet lost her battle with laughter. "That's a very unkind thing to say," she attempted to admonish. But since all the other ladies were smiling, she admitted, "But, unfortunately, so very true."

Chapter

Twenty-four

For Star-runner, making the transition from Indian to white man and back again was simply a matter of changing his clothes. As an Indian, he led a band of warriors who could not be identified with the markings of any tribe. Whenever they received word that the gold seekers were encroaching on Absaroka territory, his raiders would ride into their mining camps and destroy their sluices. Without resorting to bloodshed, he and his warriors had thus far been highly successful in frightening the miners away from their hunting grounds, though they had yet to confront the band of vigilantes who continued their murderous assaults on Indian and white man alike.

To increase his chances of discovering who was behind these attacks, Star-runner switched identities. Calling himself Grant Collingswood, he moved with ease among the boom towns and settlements, and no one questioned his interest in the vicious raiders who preyed on the mining camps. To be convincing in his guise as a rancher, he had located an isolated tract of grazing land in the Absaroka Mountains and had built a small cabin for himself. Over the summer, he had purchased enough cattle and horses to make it look as if he were running a viable ranch operation.

Unfortunately, on his stock-buying trips, he had learned that few whites were willing to believe that the recent attacks on the miners weren't being conducted by a renegade group of bloodthirsty Crow out for white scalps.

Although he'd provided more than enough facts to prove otherwise, he'd been unable to convince anyone that the Crow were also victims and were not on the verge of declaring war. He couldn't even persuade Victor Bates, a man who made his living by running a trading post that dealt with both whites and Indians. It was at the post that he had heard about a dance being held in Bozeman, and he'd decided it would be wise for him to attend.

Of course, there was a good chance that Taralynn Armstrong might be in attendance there, too, since the Triple-A Ranch was within a reasonable distance from the town. He also realized that Tara would probably make quite a scene if she spotted him, but needing the information such a gathering might afford him, Grant was prepared to take that risk.

Knowing Tara, it was doubtful that she'd told anyone about their love affair, and if he could keep it that way, he wouldn't lose his credibility with the other settlers. If he was to keep his vow to Mountain-lion, he had to be accepted as one of them, leading a double life. But it was going to take some doing to persuade Tara that he'd given up gambling to become a cattle rancher. If he was able to convince her, however, he could spend some time with her again, and that he would enjoy immensely.

With this pleasant thought in mind, he entered the town hall, where the dance was already in progress. As if by some second sense, he knew she was somewhere inside. He spotted her almost at once. Her flaming red hair was like a beacon that immediately drew his eyes. Seeing her held in the arms of another man, Grant felt a powerful surge of jealousy. Knowing he had no right to feel the way he did, he still experienced a searing pang of betrayal. Tara was his woman and should be dancing with no one but him.

Pleading exhaustion, Tara lifted her skirts and limped off the dance floor before she could be claimed for the next Virginia reel. Sighing, she noted that the mauve satin trim of her hem was coated with a thick layer of sawdust. Though the women in town had proclaimed her dress lovely, Tara had quickly determined that this event was no place for mauve satin and white muslin. Her dancing partners were far too exuberant, and the thin material of her skirt was already torn in several places, while her tight-fitting bodice, having been splashed by a falling glass of elderberry punch, sported a stain that would be impossible to remove. Though the dance was barely half over, her dress was already ruined, and if things continued this way, she'd be down to her petticoats before the night was over.

Fanning her flushed cheeks with her hand, Tara glanced around, trying to locate one of her brothers as she made her way toward the front doors of the hall. The crowded room was stifling, and she was in desperate need of a breath of fresh air, but the men in her family didn't allow her to go anywhere unescorted. Unfortunately, all three of her brothers were dancing, and she didn't feel inclined to wait for the musicians to stop playing before gaining some relief from the heat.

Just as she got near enough to the front doors to bask in a rush of cooler air, the fiddlers changed tempo and began playing a waltz. Before Tara could complete her escape outside, she was grasped around the waist and swept back onto the dance floor. It took her several moments to regain her bearings, but once she did she was struck by another attack of dizziness that had nothing to do with being whirled around and around and around.

"You!" she squeaked accusingly, staring up into eyes as blue as a summer sky, eyes she had prayed never to see again. Her footsteps faltered, but Grant didn't allow her to sink into an unceremonious heap at his feet. His grasp tightened around her waist, and he smiled down into her stunned face.

"Good evening, milady. You're looking quite lovely to-night, as usual." He greeted her as if it had been not months but minutes since they'd last seen each other.

Tara would have told him in no uncertain terms what he could do with his compliment, and his arrogant self, but she wasn't given the chance. Before she could open her mouth to berate him, Grant swung her around so quickly that it was all she could do to keep her balance and her breath. A second later, they were out the double doors, and Grant had pulled her into the narrow alleyway between the town hall and the general store.

"Why, you—"

Grant cut off her words with his mouth. As expected, she was spitting mad, but he could deal with that problem later. At the moment, all he wanted to do was kiss her as he'd done so many times in his dreams, reacquaint himself with the delightful texture of her skin and the sweet curves of her slender body.

Beneath the intoxicating pressure of his mouth, Tara was helpless to do anything. As much as she'd like to deny it, she loved the way Grant kissed, and probably always would. Even knowing who he was, what his family had done to hers, her treacherous body still yearned for his touch. She felt the greedy heat of his mouth all the way down to her toes, and her loins tightened in remembered response.

Suddenly, it no longer mattered what he had done to her in the past. All that mattered was what he was doing to her now. With a tiny sigh of pleasure, she melted against him, and he rewarded her surrender by thrusting inside her mouth with his tongue. As she touched her tongue to his, caressed it, quivers of joy started at the base of her spine and raced along her nerve endings. Being in his arms and kissing him again felt so good.

The sensation of his hardening body pressing against hers was poignantly familiar. She'd lived this moment in countless dreams. Forgetting all about right and wrong, she allowed his hands on her breasts, the intimate movement of his thighs against her hips. Lost to everything but desire, she clasped him to her, pretending for a moment that he was everything she'd ever wanted him to be.

By the time he released the hooks at the back of her dress and bared her breasts for his touch, Tara was panting, and when his hands cupped her, lifting her weight in his palms, stroking her nipples with his thumbs, she moaned in undeniable pleasure. Only Grant was able to inspire this wondrous feeling inside her, this yearning, this ecstasy . . . only Grant.

Then, just as suddenly as he had pulled her into his arms, Grant held her away from him, breathing hard as he stared down into her luminous green eyes. "Well, well," he murmured thickly. "Some things never change, do they?"

"What?"

Grant gazed down at her creamy breasts gleaming in the moonlight, his tone husky as he viewed the rosy nipples still tight from his recent caress. "That was some welcome, sweetheart. If I didn't know better, I'd assume you had forgiven me for the callous way I left you."

"But you . . . do know . . . better," Tara managed haltingly, shamed beyond measure by her wanton response to his lovemaking. Within seconds, he had her half naked and groaning, as if nothing had changed between them. As her reason returned, the heat of passion was replaced by the consuming fire of her anger, and she struggled, rather belatedly, to break out of his hold.

Grant refused to let her go. "Yes, I do," he admitted in a soothing tone, smiling as he sidestepped the kick she directed at his shin. To avoid further injury, he wrapped his arms around her and dragged her stiff body back against his chest. "If you would just settle down for a minute, I could explain why I left you."

"I know why!" Tara exclaimed hotly into the crisp material of his shirt, almost crying in frustration at not being able to inflict any physical damage and thoroughly humiliated when her oversensitized nipples immediately tightened into pointed nubs at contact with his body. "You're Grant Collingswood, a . . . low-down son of a murdering coward!"

Before he could inquire about that amazing comment, Grant felt a vise close around his arm, and it was practically wrenched out of its socket as he was jerked backward. Caught off balance, he heard an outraged growl, and then a fist smashed into his midsection, cutting off his breath.

"Get your hands off her, you damned bastard," a man shouted, just as his companion slammed two arms down across Grant's shoulders. Doubled over in pain, Grant struggled for breath, but another body blow forced him to his knees. "Make sure she's decent," the first man ordered as he and a third man dragged Grant out of the alley and dumped him on his face in the center of the main street. "For what you've done to her and our family, Collingswood, you're going to wish you were never born."

Grant tried to rise up and defend himself, but a boot caught him in the jaw, and he was knocked flat again. Before his eyes were closed by a series of brutal punches that made him see stars, Grant saw the color of his attackers' hair, and it didn't take much to guess who they were. From past experience, he knew what he could expect from these three. Like the Absaroka, the Armstrongs were well known for protecting their own. For accosting their sister, he'd be lucky if they let him live.

"This one is for taking advantage of an innocent girl, Collingswood!" the first brute informed him as he punched him in the gut, then pushed him toward the next taker.

"And this one is for pawing her!"

Given no time to recover between blows, Grant was passed from one Armstrong brother to the next as they told him all about his father's crimes against their family and what he could expect if he ever approached Tara again. While they attempted to beat him to a bloody pulp, a crowd gathered, and after hearing what the Armstrongs had to say, they championed their cause. His ears were ringing, and his breath came in agonized rasps, but Grant could still hear their damning remarks as they encouraged the brothers to finish him off for his perfidy.

Because of something that had happened decades before in another country, a highland eviction undertaken by his father, he was now labeled as an unscrupulous man without honor. Even if he managed to escape the wrath of the Armstrongs with his life, Grant Collingswood was not to be trusted, and the story of what had happened here tonight would spread like wildfire. The last coherent thought he had before losing consciousness was that by next week his presence wouldn't be welcomed anywhere in the territory.

Chapter

Twenty-five

With one stroke across the throat, the squaw was dead. Slade Plummer smiled down at her naked corpse. She'd been pretty good for an Injun, Slade decided. She had screamed nice and loud when he'd yanked her thighs apart and forced his engorged organ deep inside her tight passage. And those times he'd chawed down real hard on her nipples for fighting him, her begging could be understood in any language.

Yup, she'd been real nice, given him a fine time right up until the end, and that was why he preferred attacking the Indians to the miners. He usually got the chance to relieve his lust on some sweet young piece of flesh before he and his men burned down their lodges and cut out. No matter what the boss said, Injun cunt felt as good on the inside as any other kind.

With a last gratified look at his leavings, Plummer ducked out of the tepee and gestured for one of his men to set the thing on fire. "You know how the boss feels about live witnesses, Sweeney," he barked at the man who'd been waiting outside for him to finish his business. "You checked to make sure we got 'em all?"

"This romp weren't hardly worth the effort," Mike Sweeney complained as he swung his lean, lanky body onto his horse. "All we rounded up were three sick men, a young kid, and a couple of wizened old crones."

Plummer shrugged his beefy shoulders. "Like the boss says, it don't matter how many as long as they is good and dead."

Sweeney laughed and pointed to the blackened frames where four Absaroka tepees had once stood. "Dead and gone," he confirmed.

"Good," Plummer grunted as he pulled himself up in the saddle. "That carcass ought to rile 'em," he said, nodding toward the wiry male body staked out in the center of the camp. "I hear tell those scurvy Crow set real store by their old warriors. Think they's wiser than most."

"Now, that ain't sayin' much for 'em, is it?" Sweeney barked, and the other riders laughed at his joke.

After taking a last glance around the burning camp, Plummer ordered, "Make it good, boys. If the weather don't hold fair, this may be our last raid 'til spring."

Mike Sweeney and the eight other riders pulled their rifles out of their scabbards. In unison, they took aim at the old man stretched out on the ground and then shot, all at the same time. When they were finished, their victim was still alive, so they took aim again and sent another volley of bullets into his twitching body.

Plummer walked his horse over to the riddled corpse. "Think we left 'em enough evidence this time to tell 'em who done it?"

Sweeney took off his hat and tossed it onto the ground. "Don't know any tribe that does its tradin' at Randolph's Mercantile."

As they rode out of camp, Sweeney shook his head. "It never fails to amaze me. Young or old, no matter how much pain we give 'em, those damn Crow braves don't make a sound whilst they die."

"That's cuz they ain't human," Plummer reminded him, then noticed a puff of white smoke rising up from the top of a distant hill. Digging his heels into his horse's flanks, he took off for the river, shouting, "Better split up and ride like hell, boys."

Two hours later, Plummer arrived at the place where he

was to meet his employer. "We almost bought it this time," he complained. "One of their scouts spotted us on the way out, but we managed to outrun 'em."

With no show of emotion, the man he had come to meet tossed him a sack of gold coin, then remounted his horse. "To your continued good health, Mr. Plummer," the man said as he drew up his reins. "And time off for good behavior."

"You care if we stay around these parts for a spell?"

The man's smile sent a cold shiver down Plummer's spine. "Just make sure none of you comes near me. Some of you don't have the best of reputations, and I can't afford to be seen talking to you. If this latest incident doesn't bring results, however, I'll call upon you again."

"Yes, sir. We won't come within a mile of you, 'less you want to make contact."

The man nodded. "I'll be very displeased if I have to put off my plans until spring. The settlers are all for calling in the Army, but they won't interfere until the Crow start an outright attack. Who would've thought those damned heathens would have such a long fuse? I expected them to retaliate long ago."

"Like you always say, boss. Those muckers is dumb."

The man's expression turned thoughtful. "But maybe not as dumb as I thought," he admitted. "I sent two more groups of miners into their hunting grounds this past week, and before I could send you boys in, they were run off by a band of Crow. All those scurvy savages did was pull down their sluices and frighten them off."

"Don't worry, boss. After the way we left that last bunch of redskins, they're sure to come around," Plummer assured him.

The man didn't look too certain. "A couple of months back, I would've agreed with you, but something or someone is keeping those young bucks in line, and until they mount an attack outside their hunting grounds, the Army won't step in."

Plummer nodded in commiseration. "By this time, I was hopin' we'd be up to our necks in gold nuggets. The boys are happy with their wages, but I know there's a fortune out there, just waitin' for me to claim it."

Plummer blanched at his slip of the tongue and hastened to correct himself. "I mean us, boss, just you and me. I swear I ain't told another soul about that rich deposit me and Jeb found when we strayed over into Crow territory."

"That's good," the man returned quietly, his pale eyes as cold as ice. "You know how I feel about men with loose tongues. I'm sure you wouldn't want to end up the same way as your partner."

Plummer shook his head. "No need to concern yourself about that," he promised swiftly. "I ain't as fond of corn liquor as old Jeb was."

"Once we've rid ourselves of those heathens, you'll have money to buy all the corn liquor you can drink or anything else you might want."

Plummer grinned at that possibility. "So what do you want us to do next?"

Shrugging, the man picked up his reins and wheeled his horse around. "I'll be in touch, Slade. In the meantime, you and the boys do what I told you and lay low."

Chapter

Twenty-six

Keeping their horses concealed beneath the branches of virgin pine on the hillside, Otter's-heart and Running-deer could watch the comings and going at the Triple-A Ranch without being seen. After three days of surveillance, they knew that the formidable enemies who inhabited the stronghold rode away from it each day, soon after the sun rose, leaving the flame-haired woman of their clan alone with only one weak old man to protect her. Of course, several outriders occupied the bunkhouse, but they were diligent in their work and rarely came near the house.

"Remember, Star-runner made a successful raid on the Fierce-ones when he had not yet seen sixteen seasons," Otter's-heart reminded his younger brother, his watchful gaze focused on the wide front veranda of the ranch house. "And today, the snow flies in our favor. We shall be gone before anyone knows we have come."

Running-deer agreed with this assessment of the situation, smiling up at the huge white flakes floating down from the sky. "If it continues like this, the falling snow will cover our tracks."

"Just as the woman who captures the morning sun in her

hair will entertain our brother during the long nights when he cannot ride against our enemy,'' Otter's-heart said.

Black eyes gleaming hotly at his brother's complimentary description of their victim, Running-deer spat, "For besmirching Star-runner's honor and hampering his plans to find the evil one, the woman will be lucky if he does not beat her as severely as her brothers beat him. If his horse had not carried him back to his cabin, he might have died from his injuries.''

Otter's-heart nodded grimly. "It is his right to beat her.''

"One right among many,'' Running-deer added pointedly.

For the first time all morning, Otter's-heart smiled. "Oh, yes, I think Star-runner will be greatly pleased by our gift to him. He has been too long without a woman.''

Running-deer smiled back. "In time, he will come to appreciate our generosity.''

Remembering the expression on Star-runner's face as he had described his recent confrontation with the Fierce-ones, Otter's-heart was assured that he and Running-deer were doing the right thing. "For all his anger toward her and her clan, the flame-haired woman has created an unquenchable fire in our brother's loins.''

"He will deny this,'' Running-deer warned, although he shared Otter's-heart's conviction.

Otter's-heart shrugged off this possibility. "Once she is his to do with as he chooses, his denial of this need will be as nothing in comparison to his lust.''

"Then he will thank us,'' Running-deer concluded happily, straightening in the saddle as he noticed movement on the veranda. "Look, she is there.''

With a quick glance at his brother, Otter's-heart tightened his hands on his reins. "Ready?''

"Ready,'' Running-deer confirmed as their horses moved silently forward through the trees.

Wrapping her woolen shawl more securely around her shoulders, Tara took a deep breath, amazed by the amount of snow that had fallen overnight. According to her family, there was a strong possibility that by the end of the day several more inches would cover the ground, even though it was not yet September. In preparation for the possibility of being snowed in, they'd loaded hay onto several wagons and driven out to the north pasture. If the snow became too deep, the stray cattle that still remained out on the open range wouldn't be able to find food. The hay would sustain them until they could be rounded up and brought into the cow pens, where they would stay until spring.

Tara wasn't thrilled by the thought of being trapped in the house for several days, perhaps weeks at a time, but Angus had told her that some winters they got as much as eight feet of snow. She couldn't imagine that amount of accumulation in one place, but if the flakes kept falling as fast and thick as they were this morning, she might soon find out. Remembering what Jamie had said as he left the breakfast table, Tara grimaced. "Don't worry, lass. We might be trapped here from late September to early May, but we still manage to keep ourselves busy and have a good time."

"Doing what, I wonder?" Tara asked out loud.

Since Barney was the only one still home, and he was asleep in the kitchen, Tara didn't expect an answer to her question, but she got one. She heard a guttural grunt close behind her and opened her mouth to scream. Before she could utter a sound, however, a hand was clamped securely over her mouth, and a steely arm snaked around her waist. Terror-stricken, she tried to escape the arms that held her before she was dragged off the backside of the porch, but the only thing her flailing hands could reach was a smooth, sticklike object that snapped in two and slipped through her fingers when, instead of her captor, she mistakenly struck the corner wall of the house. Immediately thereafter, a heavy buffalo robe was dropped over her head, and she was wrapped up so tightly inside it that she could barely breathe, let alone escape.

Panting with the effort to find air, she felt herself being lifted over the porch rail, then hoisted up and draped face-down over the back of a horse. As the animal broke into a gallop, her struggle for breath became secondary to enduring the pain as her helpless body was jangled and jounced about for what seemed like forever. When the bone-jarring agony finally ended, Tara moaned in gratitude, but as she was lifted into a sitting position across a hard pair of thighs and the heavy robe was drawn away from her face, an even greater horror greeted her eyes. She had been kidnapped by a savage!

She heard the whinny of a second horse, and her head whirled toward the sound. Two savages! Two black-haired, black-eyed, grinning devils who looked so pleased with themselves that Tara wanted to be sick.

With one glance at the triumphant expressions on their cruel faces, Tara knew that screaming would be useless, and any attempt she made to defy them would be ruthlessly squelched. She could see that they were both young, perhaps near her own age, but their half-naked bodies seemed impervious to the cold, and the muscles of their chests and arms were lean and whipcord hard. Even on horseback, they appeared to be much taller than the other male members of the tribes she had seen while traveling up the Missouri and as fierce-looking as the Sioux who had attacked their wagon train.

As she felt the rippling power in the thighs beneath her and the pitiless grip of the muscular arm wrapped around her middle, Tara's mind reeled with the thought that she had been saved from certain death on the wagon train only to endure another assault which could be far worse than dying. Indians were known for taking white female captives, and her heart pounded in terror as she realized that she was about to become an unwilling slave to these brutal heathens. As her imagination conjured up one terrifying image after another, her teeth began to chatter, and her eyes brimmed over with tears, though she didn't dare make a sound for fear of what they might do to her.

Just as she was about to succumb to total despair, another image came into the picture, the image of a man laughing in amusement at her ignorance. *Grant! Oh, Grant, help me, please.*

Get a hold of yourself, Tara, she could almost hear him say. *I taught you enough about Indians to know that they despise weakness of any kind. Be strong.*

If she wanted to survive, Tara knew she couldn't let these red devils see her fear, but even as she straightened her spine and held up her chin, the silent tears continued to roll down her cheeks, and her teeth chattered violently.

After what she and her family had done to him, Grant

wouldn't be coming to rescue her. She was alone, and it was cold, so bitterly cold. The wind whipped her face as they sped through the thick pine forest, and her shivering increased as snowflakes melted in her hair and ran down the back of her neck.

It must have been more than a half-hour later when they crested a peak, and her kidnappers reduced their pace to begin their ascent up the side of the mountain. The Indian holding her said something, and Tara flinched as if he'd struck her, but her reaction seemed to amuse him, for he grinned over at his companion and started talking in a language that she would have sold her soul to understand.

"She will be an easy one to tame," Otter's-heart said, a strong measure of disappointment in his tone.

Running-deer stared over at the small, frightened woman seated in front of his brother, noting the proud tilt to her head and the stiff way she held herself in the saddle. As difficult as the position was for her to maintain, she would not allow any part of her body to touch Otter's-heart. "I do not think so," Running-deer disagreed. "She knows she will gain nothing for her struggles now, but that it is not to say that she will go meekly to her fate."

"I hope you are right, for Star-runner needs a challenge to occupy his mind. The snows must melt before he can take up his sacred quest once more, and the rage within him must be banked lest it destroy him."

"Our father believes that this rage is not only for the Fierce-ones who attacked him unjustly but for himself. Since his return from across the wide waters, our brother's soul is torn between two worlds, and this woman is the cause of his inner turmoil. It is possible that Star-runner carries love for her in his heart, as well as desire, and to make her heart sing, he must leave us."

Otter's-heart scoffed at this suggestion. "He is an Absa-roka warrior and she a mere woman. She has no say in where they live if he chooses her as his mate. It is the way of a woman to follow her man."

"But she is not one of our women," Running-deer reminded him. "And Star-runner has told me that in the white man's world women do not meekly follow their husbands' bidding but oftimes expect him to defer to her wishes."

Upon hearing this, Otter's-heart shook his head. "Then they are fools, for between men and women there can be only one master."

"Ah," Running-deer sighed knowledgeably. "That is why you rush so swiftly to the side of Singing-moon whenever she calls to you. You wish to show her who is master."

For this comment, Running-deer earned a severe scowl, and Otter's-heart kicked his horse into a furious pace which he kept up until they ascended the steep trail between Bear Claw Mountain and the higher elevations of snow-capped peaks. A few hours later, they broke through a stand of trees and descended into a hidden valley. A cold, frothy mist hung in the air, waking Tara from the stuporous daze she had enjoyed for the last several miles.

The first thing she saw when she opened her eyes was a log cabin, and her pulse leapt with a tiny beat of hope. Indians lived in tepees, not cabins. White men lived in cabins, and if they were planning to leave her here, maybe there was some other purpose behind her abduction than enslavement. Even if that was the case, her captors' next actions indicated that she should not expect kind treatment. As if she were a sack of flour, she was tossed over one man's shoulder, and once they were inside the cabin, she was dumped unceremoniously onto the hard, dirt-packed floor.

Immediately, she fought to get loose from the confines of the buffalo robe, but the leather ties that bound her would not give way. Breathless with effort, she did manage to push herself up into a seated position, where she was finally able to view the cabin's rustic interior and the man who inhabited it. Although his back was turned to her, she could tell by the jerky motions of his arms that he was not too happy about her arrival. He never looked at her directly, so she had yet to see his face, but he kept stabbing the air viciously in her direction.

He was a tall dark-haired man dressed in buckskins, and he conversed fluidly in the same language as her captors, which made her think he was an Indian, too, maybe a renegade who operated outside the tribe. Somehow, as she watched him and listened to the deep, intense timber of his voice, Tara sensed that he presented a much greater danger to her than the two who had dropped her on his doorstep.

With that realization, her panic increased, and she renewed her struggles to free herself.

"How could you do something this stupid?" Star-runner demanded. "Don't you know what will happen if the Fierce-ones discover who has taken her?"

"No one saw us," Running-deer assured him. "And our tracks disappeared soon after we made them."

"It is not a stupid deed but a brave one that we have done this day out of our great love for you. We have brought you what you need most, my brother," Otter's-heart announced grandly, making a sweeping gesture with his arm toward Tara, who was now stretched out full-length on the floor, trying frantically, though without much success, to escape the encasing folds of the buffalo robe. "If this woman has dishonored you in the eyes of the whites who would have helped you find our great enemy, then she deserves the lessons you shall teach her. If you've lost your taste for vengeance on her, so be it, but do not tell us you have lost your desire for her. Even now, we can see it in your eyes."

"Accept our father's wisdom in this, Star-runner," Running-deer pleaded, noting that the furious expression had not diminished from their brother's face. "Lie with Morning-sun-woman and see if her touch does not help to soothe the bleeding places in your heart."

Star-runner was incredulous. "Split-nose put you two up to this!"

Otter's-heart nodded. "And we shall not defy him by returning her to Red-beard's lodge. If you refuse our gift to you, you can take her back yourself."

"Which I cannot do until the storm has blown itself out," Star-runner retorted irately, throwing up his hands in frustration. "By now, the trail is well nigh impassable."

With a negligent shrug, Otter's-heart strode swiftly toward the door. Running-deer was right behind him. "To make it safely to our own camp, we must go now," he mumbled apologetically, then pushed Otter's-heart through the doorway before Star-runner could make up his mind to stop them.

"I can think of worse ways to ride out this frigid storm than between the warm, giving thighs of a pretty woman," Otter's-heart shouted back over his shoulder, but his words were met by the resounding slam of the cabin door. An indignant expression on his face, he remounted his horse. "One would think such a respected chief as Star-runner would show us the proper gratitude for the kind favor we have done him this day."

Running-deer groaned as he reached for his reins. "In reward for our kindness. I will be content if he has forgiven us by the time the leaves turn green once more."

Chapter

Twenty-seven

The moment she broke free of the confining buffalo robe, Tara scrambled to her knees, but she sat back down again quickly when she heard the man swear. As she listened to a long litany of expressive curses, she understood that he was lividly angry, but since he spoke in English she also knew that the curses were not directed at her, and that gave her some small measure of hope. Yet, when he stopped swearing but continued to ignore her presence as if he'd forgotten her existence, her fear returned. The malevolence radiating from him was so intense that it raised the hairs on the back of her neck.

When she could stand the silence no longer, she inquired softly, "Please, sir, who are you? And why have I been brought here?"

At the sound of her voice, Star-runner turned around. "Guess," he bit out tersely, his gaze intent on her face.

Tara's jaw dropped as she stared at him, overcome by a jumble of confusing images that completely disoriented her. At the sight of his sky-blue eyes, she remembered the devil-may-care gambler who had been her companion and lover while on board the *Ophelia*. As she gaped at the elegant set of his broad shoulders, the high cheekbones and aristocratic features, she recalled his English title. An instant later, her gaze noted his overlong hair, well-worn buckskins, and beaded moccasins, and she couldn't tell who she was dealing with.

This was a Grant she didn't know, yet another in his seemingly endless switches of identities. Less than a month ago, he had been trying to establish himself to the people in town as a rancher who had started a small cattle operation in the Absaroka Mountains. As soon as she recalled that, her gaze softened with concern, her eyes searching his face for any sign of the bruises her brothers had inflicted on him. Noting the slight bluish discolorations that could still be seen below his eyes, she winced.

Suddenly, it didn't matter who he was pretending to be this time. Beneath all of his disguises was the man she had fallen in love with and couldn't seem to stop loving even after his desertion. The night of the dance had confirmed that in her mind as well as something else. Whatever her father and brothers thought, Grant was not to blame for the sins of his father, and it made her sick to think about the pain he'd been made to suffer in punishment for a crime he'd never committed. "Oh, Grant," she murmured softly as she got to her feet.

"I tried to stop them," she whispered apologetically, tears brimming in her eyes as she staggered toward him. "But they wouldn't listen to me."

Wrapping her arms around his waist, she laid her cheek down upon his shoulder and let the tears fall. "I was so worried about you—so desperately frightened. I thought you might die. You were bleeding, and your face, oh, your poor, battered face."

Of all the reactions Grant had expected, this one was the last. "Come now," he chided, standing stiffly in her grasp. "I was there. Remember? You didn't say or do anything in my defense. You let them think I had assaulted you."

"I wanted to stop them," Tara murmured miserably. "But Neal handed me over to Lloyd Dunn, and before I could persuade the man to let me go to you, my brothers had tied you on your horse and sent it off on a gallop out of town. I tried to make them go after you, but they wouldn't, and they wouldn't let me go, either."

Grant stood stock still in astonishment as she sobbed against his shoulder and begged him brokenly to forgive her. He didn't want to believe her. Only a fool would believe her, but even though he knew she was a consummate actress, he couldn't stand to hear her crying, and before he could stop himself, he was seeking her mouth.

God help him, he thought, as he drank in the sweet taste of her. No matter what kind of problems she'd caused him in the past or would cause him in the future, she was the only woman he wanted, the only woman who could ease the ache that had been plaguing him for months. "You may be a liar, but I still want you," he admitted bitterly against her soft lips.

"Oh, Grant," she whispered, going up on her toes to kiss him. "This isn't a lie. As much as I'd like to, I can't lie about my feelings for you."

"At least your body can't," he corrected.

"It's not just my body that wants you," Tara insisted, and the look in her eyes was his total undoing.

In an explosion of longing, his tongue plunged deeply into her mouth, indulging himself and her with the full force of his passion. He was starving for her, and he tasted his fill, while she clung to him, her rapid heartbeat entwining with his. The kiss went on and on, the mindless pleasure continued, until at last he lifted his head to gasp for air.

"You are mine, Tara," he whispered hoarsely, blue eyes glimmering with intensity as he repeated the words he had said the night before he'd deserted her at Fort Benton. "Whatever happens, you will always be mine."

"Yes," Tara whispered back. "And nothing else matters."

For a time after that, nothing else did. His need for her was too strong, and he bent down and scooped her up into his arms. In three strides, he had crossed the room and was laying her down on a pile of soft furs. His hands were shaking as he stripped off her clothes, then his own, but somehow he managed to accomplish both tasks in a matter of seconds. As he came down next to her warm, naked body and drew her against him, he groaned, "It's been too long since I've touched you and tasted you and felt your naked flesh burning sweetly into mine."

"Yes," Tara murmured in pleasure, nuzzling her face against his hot, smooth chest, breathing in the glorious smell of his skin. "It seems like it's been forever."

Their lips came together. Grant ran his tongue over her lower lip, then drew it between his lips and sucked. The sheer sexuality of it made her whimper, and he immediately lowered his head farther and opened his mouth over her breast. He kissed her nipple fervently, applying enough suction to draw it up against his teeth. He tickled it with his tongue, then fanned it to pulsating hardness with his warm breath.

He deserved this much from her at least, this one last mutually satisfying session of lovemaking before he told her the true way of things. He wanted to take her tenderly, slowly, until she forgot about everything but the feel of him loving her, but she didn't want to wait. The instant his lips touched her again, she was hungry for all of him. Her mouth crushed his, and the quick darting of her tongue stole his breath away. Her supple body moved suddenly against his, entreating him in the womanly way that was as old as time, destroying his control. She opened herself like a flower in desperate need of life-giving rain, and the frustration that had eaten away at him ever since he'd last kissed her in a dark alley tightened into a roiling storm of need. He desperately wanted her hands on him, her lips on him, but when her soft fingers moved to the heat of his desire, something inside him snapped.

His mouth ravaged hers. His tongue plundered, and his fingers were urgent as they swept over her back, the curve of her hip, the backs of her thighs, and anywhere else he could reach. Rolling her beneath him, he plunged into her heat, capturing her cry of pleasure with his mouth as his control shattered into a thousand separate pieces of excruciating yet wondrously pleasurable sensation.

Driven by the same wild, uncontrollable hunger as he, heedless of the consequences, Tara arched her hips to meet his thrusts. When Grant was with her like this, the future seemed far away and unimportant. Love for him poured out of her, free and unfettered and so strong that he had to feel it, had to know. She was certain that he did, for he was saying her name in cadence with his thrusts, his voice raw with emotion. Then, when the pleasure became too much to take, he threw back his head and surrendered, just as she did. With a long, low, primal groan, he filled his woman with his hot, rich seed, and she closed her eyes, replete in the knowledge that at long last she was back where she belonged.

It could have been seconds or it could have been hours before Tara drifted back from the glorious place Grant had taken her. Since her body was still glowing with languorous warmth, she rather suspected that she hadn't been floating for that long. Turning her head, she found that they were lying side by side, his face so close to hers that their noses brushed. Smiling tenderly, she brushed her lips across his mouth, and he opened his eyes. "Methinks you missed me, milady," he said, a teasing inflection in his voice.

"And methinks my fine English lord has lost some of his charming gentility since coming to the territory," she retorted, wrinkling her nose as the bristle of his beard scraped against her cheek. "I can understand that, but whatever happened to my dashing husband, the riverboat gambler?"

Grant was expecting questions, but when he felt the soft press of her breast against his rib cage, he decided to postpone the inquisition. As long as the snow kept falling, they had all the time in the world for conversation, but an aroused portion of his body wasn't as willing to be put off. Grinning with anticipation, he responded to her question. "He's right here, Mathilda, and most anxious to fulfill his marital duties, for when he neglects his insatiable wife, she has a tendency to make her complaints public."

Tara giggled at his teasing, her green eyes sparkling as she remembered that night on the boat when he'd confronted her for spreading rumors about his lack of sexual appetite. "She has no reason for complaint now," she admitted with a contented sigh.

Shifting slightly, Grant moved his hand to cover her breast. "And he's going to make certain she never does," he assured her as his other hand slid down her body, his palm cupping the soft mound between her thighs, his fingers caressing.

Tara moaned as he parted the moist folds of her woman's

flesh and slid one finger deep inside her. "So soon?" she gasped as his fingers teased her, moving in and out, lingering, then withdrawing, as her body quaked with a renewal of the tremors that had so recently been abated.

"As many times as it takes," Grant murmured hoarsely, his blue eyes aflame as he watched her body writhing in pleasure at his touch. She knew about this kind of pleasure, but there were so many others he could teach. By the end of their confinement together, she was going to know the full extent of a man's passion, the total intimacy that could be shared between two lovers, and then, no matter what happened, she would never be able to deny that she was his.

As the quaking intensified to a fever pitch, Tara's thighs fell apart helplessly, and she reached for him. When he refused to end the sweet torture, her eyes flew to his face, and she pleaded, "Please, Grant, now!" afraid he meant to send her over the edge alone.

He smiled at her then, a slow, seductive smile that sent the blood racing through her veins, and he kissed her once more before positioning himself between her thighs. With agonizing slowness, he lowered his head, and his hot mouth closed around a straining nipple. Tara felt an insistent tug at her breast, but she didn't cry out until he thrust inside her and established the same delicious rhythm both above and below. When he had pushed her to the point of screaming frenzy once more, he came with her, and his hoarse shout joined with her cries as they fell over the edge together.

"Let it be a long winter," Grant whispered in gratification once he could think again, but Tara heard him, and he felt her body stiffen under his.

"I can't stay here all winter!" she exclaimed anxiously. "My family will be sick with worry. When they find me gone, they'll assume the worst. I know it's going to be difficult to face them, but you have to take me back as soon as this snowstorm is over."

"That's where you're wrong, sweetheart," Grant informed her, a ruthless glint in his eyes as he returned her startled gaze. "For, you see, I am Star-runner, chief of the Absaroka, and you are my woman. In the way of my people, that makes you my possession. From now on, I'll decide what we will do and when we're going to do it."

Chapter

Twenty-eight

"What are you saying?" Tara frowned in confusion, a tiny shiver of anxiety snaking down her spine as she gazed into the wintry blue eyes staring back at her. Sometimes she felt certain Grant loved her, but at other times he said or did things that made her feel as if she were dealing with a mysterious stranger, and a dangerous one at that. After the wondrous experience they'd just shared, she couldn't understand the abrupt change in his mood or the aggressive expression on his face. "What's the purpose behind this latest disguise?"

When all she got for an answer was an irritating smile, Tara sat up in bed, dragging up the fur robe to cover her bare breasts. "Grant?"

"It's no disguise this time, sweetheart."

"Well, I don't know what else to call it, since you're always announcing that you're someone other than who I think you are," Tara blazed hotly. "First I find out that you're an English lord, then you tell me you've given up your title to become a riverboat gambler, only you plan to retire from that profession in order to seek your fortune in the goldfields. But did you ever follow through with that plan? Oh, no, the last time I saw you, you were trying to convince people that you were a rancher. And now, of all things, you say that you're an Indian. Is it any wonder I'm confused?''

Grant grinned. "I suppose not."

Irked by his amusement, Tara charged, "I'm beginning to think you're half mad and really have no idea who you are."

That inspired a laugh. "I assure you, I'm as sane as the next man, and I know exactly who I am."

"Then why, pray tell, are you pretending to be all these different people?"

"I have my reasons," he informed her arrogantly.

"Would you mind explaining them to me?"

His tone was calm, but his eyes flashed at her question. "Yes, and you'd be wise to remember that a warrior doesn't have to explain himself to his woman."

Ignoring the last part of his sentence, Tara persisted. "What possible reason could you have for disguising yourself as an Indian?"

"It's not a disguise," Grant repeated, starting to lose his patience as he sat up beside her. "I am an Indian, an Absaroka warrior, and a chief of the tribe."

"An Absaroka warrior and a chief of the tribe," Tara mimicked sarcastically. Then, unable to help herself, she burst out laughing. Of all Grant's chosen identities, this one was definitely the most ridiculous. Rolling her eyes, she observed dryly, "And, of course, you would be a chief. After all, what English lord would accept a position as a lowly brave? That would place you far beneath your accustomed station."

Grant allowed her to mock him because he knew something she did not. After a time, she'd have no other choice but to believe him. In the weeks to come, he was going to teach her her proper place, and he was going to enjoy himself immensely during the process. She was nothing like Sliver-of-moon, could never be like her, but she would serve his needs. As Split-nose said, he had been too long without a woman, and even a white woman was better than none.

"I've never thought about it before, but I imagine that sooner or later blood lines do tell," he admitted with a self-deprecating shrug. "As you know, my white father was the earl of Collingswood, and he brought me with him on a hunting expedition. He died in a buffalo stampede, but I escaped being trampled by squeezing my body inside a rocky crevice.

"A few days later, I was found wandering around the plains by an old trapper who took me to an Absaroka camp. When I woke up from my daze, they had already adopted me into their tribe. I was named chief at a young age, and my name has been sung in our lodges since the time of the big snow. I had only seen twelve seasons when I first counted coup, which is considered quite a feat in my tribe. For my great courage and cunning, I was invited to join the Foxes, a military club for warriors, the highest honor any young brave could receive."

Smoothing a hand over his chest, he continued, "I took part in the sun dance when I had seen sixteen seasons, and as you can see by my scars, I triumphed well over the pain. Rather than signs of torture, these marks are banners of my bravery, and my heart sings with pride as I view them."

A heavy knot of dread coiled within her as Tara listened to him talk, and it tightened more and more as she heard the alien inflection in his voice and his odd use of terminology. Suddenly, she had the funny feeling that he was telling her the truth, and, recalling those two young savages who had kidnapped her, that feeling intensified.

But then, just as she was about to accept his incredible story, she saw the devilish twinkle in his blue eyes, and she knew that he was trying to deceive her once again. While on board the *Ophelia,* Grant had demonstrated his in-depth knowledge on the subject of Indians, but he was crazy if he expected her to believe that his expertise sprang from being one of them. Grant Collingswood was no more Indian than she was, even if he did know so much about their primitive customs and was friendly toward them. However he'd attained the knowledge, it wasn't firsthand.

As soon as he stopped talking, she demanded angrily, "I can't understand why you are doing this to me. Is this some kind of stupid revenge for the beating my brothers gave you? I told you what happened. Can't you forgive me?"

Before she knew what hit her, Tara found herself lying flat on her back with Grant straddling her hips. Although he made no attempt to hurt her, her arms were pinned down over her head and her legs clamped between his powerful thighs. Belatedly, she tried to struggle, but she was unable to do more than arch her feet and stare up in astonishment at his face. "Why are you doing this?" she demanded again, but much more fearfully.

In his eyes was that wild look she had glimpsed so many times in the past but had never fully understood, and this time it did not fade away before she got the chance to analyze its cause. The story he'd just told her was true! This was the man who existed beneath all the layers of camouflage. This was the real Grant Collingswood, and as impossible as it seemed, he was no English gentleman, no devilishly charming rake. This man was exactly who he claimed he was, a savage renegade.

That realization must have been reflected on her face, for he grinned and nodded his head. "As I've already told you, I do this because I am Star-runner, chief of the Absaroka, a tribe known to the white man as the Crow, and I have claimed you, Morning-sun, as my woman."

The chilling words were barely out of his mouth when Tara was struck by another realization. "That was you! Back there on the wagon train—you were the one who saved my life! That grinning heathen was you!"

His amusement faded abruptly, and a dark shadow passed over his face. In a deadly tone, he said, "No enemy attacks my woman and lives. That Sioux was lucky I allowed him to die a swift death. If there had been time, I would have castrated him, and his scalp would now hang from my belt."

Tara's eyes fluttered closed in shock, unable to accept that she had fallen in love with a man who was capable of committing such uncivilized acts, capable of killing . . . and scalping . . . and . . . worse. *Renegade!* her mind screamed, recalling the terrible rumors she'd heard about his tribe. Was Grant part of those brutal attacks on the miners? Could he kill and mutilate without conscience? "My God, this can't be happening. I can't believe this is happening."

"By the time the leaves turn green once more, you will believe whatever I choose to tell you," he assured her. "Your obedience to my will shall be as much a part of you as drawing breath. As my woman, your whole purpose for being is to serve my needs."

At such an outlandish announcement, Tara's eyes flew open, and anger replaced all her fears. She didn't care what kind of man he was or what threats he made, for she was no longer the naive girl she'd been when they first met. She had learned so much since coming to the territory, and she was no longer so easily intimidated. No matter what hardships she must face, and she had already faced several, she had a deep inner strength to draw upon, and she would survive whatever happened to her.

"The man I belonged to no longer exists," Tara challenged, meeting and holding his gaze. "I am not your woman. I'm not your anything, and if you keep me here against my will, my family will kill you!"

"Maybe."

"Or I'll murder you myself."

Star-runner smiled. Her rebellion pleased him immeasurably. Eyes gleaming with anticipation, he responded to her defiant words. "I can see that you're going to require a great deal of training to be worthy of the honor I am bestowing on you, but we'll have plenty of time at our disposal. When the leaves turn green on the trees again, you shall be as docile as a lamb."

"If you believe that, then you're as stupid as a goat."

"As randy as one," he acknowledged with a hateful grin, shifting his hips to make her aware of his renewed arousal. "But then, one of your most important duties as my woman will be to ease that condition whenever it arises . . . which, because of your squirming, it has."

Tara attempted to buck him off her, but he squashed the effort by bringing more of his weight down upon her hips. "You can take your condition and go to the devil," she hissed at him, her cheeks flaming in outrage as he nuzzled the cleft of her thighs with his swelling manhood.

"Your education as a squaw might be lacking in other areas, but in this one you are already an expert," he complimented her, deftly turning his cheek to avoid being scratched by the flying hand she had managed to pull out of his grasp. By the time he'd managed to recapture it and subdue the mutinous female body attached to it, he was breathing hard. It was a good thing he would always be her physical superior, for he doubted if he'd ever be able to break her spirit.

"Wildcat," he complained good-naturedly. "Your family should be happy that I've decided to take you off their hands."

Temporarily defeated, Tara called him a vile name, and he laughed.

"My brothers have named you well, Morning-sun-woman," he declared, smiling affectionately down into her face. "In anger, your eyes blaze as brightly as the sun, and your hair glows like amber fire. Just looking at you warms my blood, and from now on your passion will burn only for me."

Tara was complimented by the beautiful name but took no pleasure in the rest of his speech. "Keep manhandling me like this, and you'll feel the heat of my anger as well."

His grin widened. "I think I am going to enjoy having a wife who does not always surrender meekly to my wishes. You challenge my body, but you also challenge my mind, which will make our union all that much more exciting."

"Wife!" Tara gasped in shock. "You intend to marry me?"

"As quickly as possible, and in the way of the white man, so no one will question my rights of ownership," he said. "Otherwise, the next time I meet up with your family, they'll probably murder me."

Her relief at this announcement was obvious, but when he saw the dawning joy in her expression, a muscle leapt in his jaw. "Do not misunderstand my reasoning. I make you my wife only because I have been too long without a woman in my lodge," he growled furiously. "By the time the winter is over, your belly will be swollen with my child, and our marriage will ensure that I keep what is mine. A warrior needs strong sons."

"And a woman to care for him," Tara murmured softly.

"To cook and keep his clothes clean," he gritted harshly. "And to give him children."

Tara's doubts about the kind of man he was began to dissipate as she heard the desperation in his tone, as if he needed to convince himself as much as her into believing that theirs wouldn't be a love match. For some reason, he wanted her to think him ruthless and cruel, an unfeeling savage, but he wasn't. Somehow, no matter what he did to prove otherwise, she just knew that he wasn't. From the very beginning, she'd sensed a deep loneliness in him along with the wildness, and even if her attempts to domesticate him took forever, he would never be alone again.

"Fine, strong children," she agreed. "Born out of love."

Star-runner reacted to the tenderness in her tone as if he had been slapped, and his features tensed with the pain of remembering another woman in another time, a sweet, doe-eyed woman who had borne him a healthy son. "I don't need your love! A man may require the heat of the sun in order to live," he spat contemptuously. "But in my heart I will always prefer the serene beauty and gentle light of the moon."

Tara didn't understand the significance of this avowal, but the words had a profound effect on him. Abruptly, he let go of her wrists and practically vaulted off the pile of fur robes. He tossed her dress to her as he pulled on his buckskins. "Get up," he ordered curtly. "Now that you have eased my lust, you can satisfy the pangs of hunger in my stomach. It is your place to serve me."

Still bemused by his marriage proposal, Tara obeyed his directive and got dressed. For the moment, she was content to let him go on thinking that she had accepted her supposed place in his life, but he was not going to find it so easy to keep her there. In the meantime, she had a thousand questions that needed answers, and in order to get them she knew she'd have to behave as if she were going along with him.

An hour later, she was able to place a respectable meal on the table, and the astonishment on his face as he bit into the soft biscuit he had dipped in her hearty beef stew was highly gratifying. She waited expectantly for his compliment, but none came. Grumbling at his rudeness under her breath, she ladled some stew into a small wooden bowl and carried it to the table. Like him, she was famished.

She sat down opposite him at the table, but before she got the spoon to her lips, Star-runner slapped it away. "A squaw does not eat until her man is finished, Morning-sun."

"What?"

"Nor does she sit down with him unless she is asked."

Star-runner finished his bowl and reached for hers. "Get me another biscuit."

Tara shot him a murderous look. "Since I am not your squaw, you can damn well get it yourself!"

Star-runner stared at her for a full minute. Tara was beginning to feel smug at calling his bluff, when he said in a low, level voice, "If you ever want to see your father and brothers again, you will learn to obey me. This land is vast, and my people know every mountain and valley. If I choose to, I can keep you in a place so far removed from civilization that no one will ever find you."

For a few seconds, Tara was cowed by this threat, but then she remembered something that Grant knew nothing about. It might take them a while, but her family would find her. Once they discovered the broken arrow her captors had left behind on the porch, they would be able to identify the tribe responsible for her kidnapping, and they wouldn't give up the search until they found her. Of that she was certain, but she was just as certain that she'd never have a better opportunity to explore her relationship with Grant than she had right now. Until the weather cleared, it would be impossible for her family to commence their search, which meant that she had days, perhaps weeks, to accomplish her purpose.

With that goal in mind, she pretended to be frightened. "You . . . you wouldn't really do that to me, would you?" she asked tremulously, and the self-satisfied smile she got in response made her want to hit him.

"To keep what is mine, I will do whatever is necessary," he told her, gratified when she made no retort but clasped her hands together beneath the table and lowered her eyes submissively. She was learning. At last, she was finally learning who was the master in this relationship.

A week later, however, Star-runner had to acknowledge that he'd overestimated his power over her. On their first night together, he'd intended to enforce his superior position in bed, but Tara had taken as much pleasure in his ruthless lovemaking as he had. The next night, to his greater chagrin, she had retaliated by unleashing all of her seductive talents on him. The pleasure she'd offered him with her soft mouth and clever hands had been too much to withstand, and he'd been reduced to her willing slave.

Of course, he'd loved every minute of it, but it still galled him to admit that she was his equal beneath the blankets. Nor was the situation much better when she was out from under them. He didn't quite know how she'd accomplished it, but more and more often lately, every order he gave her came out sounding an awful lot like a request, and the more anxious she was to please him, the more willing he was to please her, too.

Indeed, his plan to subjugate her wasn't working out his way at all, and this morning's occupation was a prime example of his failure. Instead of rousting her out of their robes at first light to prepare his breakfast, she had looked so warm and contented that he'd left her there and clumsily prepared his own meal. His corn mush and fried biscuits hadn't turned out that badly, and he was so proud of them that he was actually considering serving her breakfast in bed so that she could taste them.

Unfortunately, before he'd convinced himself of the stupidity of that idea and returned the wooden tray to the kitchen, Tara woke up and cried out in delight, "Oh, Grant, did you make that for me? What a sweet man you are."

Star-runner mumbled something about the Indian's disapproval of any form of waste, but Tara didn't seem to care what had prompted him to share with her. Like a greedy child, she reached for the tray and in a very short time had eaten every morsel of mush in her bowl and every tidbit of biscuit. "That was wonderful," she complimented him once she had finished, her smile so beguiling that he found himself returning it. "Who would have thought an English lord would be so handy in the kitchen?"

Over the last several days, he'd discovered that forcing her to forget his white identity was useless. No matter how often he corrected her, she always called him Grant, but maybe that was because she didn't realize how completely he'd rejected everything from his past life. "Anything I know about cooking, I learned from the women of my tribe. The only thing I learned in England was that I no longer had a place there."

Tara lifted her arms over her head and stretched, smiling

as she felt his warm gaze following her languorous movements. Taking advantage of his distraction, she probed the subject that he rarely talked about. "But why didn't you? After all, you were the firstborn son, the rightful heir to all the Collingswood holdings. Why would you give all that up to live a life like this?"

Star-runner succumbed to temptation and joined her beneath the blankets, unaware that he'd reverted to the aristocratic accent of his youth as he spoke of things and feelings he'd never told anyone else. "I had no choice. A man's rightful place isn't determined by his birth but by the emotion in his heart, and my heart was empty. My father would have scoffed at that philosophy, as did my mother. When she saw that I was still alive, she expected me to step right in and claim my position as head of the family, but I had no interest in doing so."

"Why not?"

"After enjoying the total freedom to be found in these mountains, I couldn't stand being so closed in, fettered by responsibilities that held no meaning for me. Every time those wrought-iron gates of our family estate slammed shut behind me, I felt like I was being imprisoned."

"I know the feeling," Tara said, thinking back to her restrictive childhood at Laurel Glen. She had yet to suffer a single pang of regret over leaving, so Grant's decision no longer seemed that mysterious. "And that's why you gave up your title."

Surprised by her easy acceptance of his motivation, Grant admitted, "That was one reason, but not the most important one. I couldn't take something that was no longer mine. No matter what his place in the birth order, my younger brother George was the rightful earl. Maintaining our family heritage was his prime reason for being. He deserved the title, not me."

"But you stayed in England for several years after that. Why?"

In the blink of an eye, the English accent was replaced by the melodic cadence of the Absaroka. "A warrior must abide by his duty or be forever dishonored in the eyes of his tribe. My father had left behind many debts, and I was not free to leave until I had assisted my brother in restoring the family fortunes."

"If you felt obligated to do that, then you still must have loved them."

Without a trace of bitterness, Star-runner said, "I felt the fealty of shared blood, but that is all. To be happy, a man needs much more than that."

"Yes," Tara murmured softly. "So does a woman."

Hearing the plea in her voice, Star-runner gazed deeply into her eyes. "When I returned to England, my family was foreign to me, their traditions were no longer mine. I am Absaroka."

"And I am a white woman."

"A refined eastern lady."

Tara could sense him distancing himself from her, so she reminded him, "But also a captive squaw. Yours to do with as you choose."

"Yes," Star-runner said, then grinned wolfishly as he pulled her naked body against his. "And right now, I choose to make love to you."

"I would like that," Tara said as she offered him her mouth. "Perhaps we have much more in common than you think."

"Perhaps," he agreed, but even as they lost themselves in the fiery passion they aroused so easily in each other, they were both afraid that something far more important was missing, and though they both yearned for it, it might never be theirs.

Chapter

Twenty-nine

By the second week of their confinement together, the snows began to melt, and it was no longer impossible to travel. Knowing how much Grant cared for his tribesmen, Tara felt obliged to tell him about the broken arrow his Indian brothers had left behind and what her father would do once he found it and figured out who had kidnapped her. "I realize that where we go and what we do is your decision, but if my family is unsuccessful in their search, they'll probably call in the Army to help."

Grant's reaction to this news was far different from what Tara had expected. He didn't look angry or even annoyed. His expression was blank and his tone brittle as he pronounced, "Then you'd better hope we can find a preacher to marry us before that happens. We'll head for Bozeman in the morning."

Tara realized that Grant would never go down on bended knee to request her hand in marriage, but she refused to accept such an arrogant proposal. Over the past several days, she thought she had made a great deal of progress with him, but she could see now that Grant still expected her to cowtow to his every wish like an obedient squaw. With an indignant tilt to her chin, she inquired, "And if I don't choose to marry you?"

"Then, to save themselves, my people will be forced to destroy yours."

Tara stared at him in disbelief. "For refusing your suit, you would have my entire family murdered?"

"Yes."

Her horror was obvious, and the accusation in her eyes cut into his soul. As he watched her digest his ominous words, Star-runner lost all interest in the selfish game he'd been playing with her. This was no longer a game. Out of concern for his happiness, his brothers had brought him the woman he wanted, but if he couldn't persuade Tara to marry him, their kind gesture would cost them their lives. His guilt was like a hideous snake, striking his innards with piercing agony. His people thought him a savior, but his inability to hide his passion for Tara could bring about their destruction.

"If the Army is brought into this affair," he said quietly, "my people won't stand a chance. Our weapons are like nothing to their guns. The long knives won't wait to hear that we're not responsible for the deaths of those miners, and for the added sin of kidnapping a white woman, they will slaughter every man, woman, and child in the tribe. Our guilt or innocence won't matter to them, and whoever is behind these attacks on my people and yours will have what they want. The gold beneath our hunting grounds will be theirs for the taking. If we have to kill a small clan like the Fierce-ones to keep that from happening, we will."

"The Fierce-ones?"

"That is the name we have given your family, for the men of your clan fight as well as any Indian. In our many dealings with them, they have earned our respect as mighty warriors."

"That's why you . . . " Tara's voice trailed off as she slumped back in her chair. "Your recognition of my name had nothing whatever to do with your being a Collingswood, did it? You knew who I was because of these many confrontations?"

Star-runner nodded. "And out of respect for your father, Red-beard, I did not wish to dishonor you. Many seasons ago, he chose not to kill me though it was his right, and in return for this favor I vowed to protect you from all harm."

Before she could stop herself, Tara bit out, "With the exception of the harm that you inflicted on me yourself."

To her surprise, his face flushed with heated color. "Eventually, you wore down my strength, and I lost my will to resist you. You were much too beautiful, and whenever I came near you I couldn't seem to think rationally. I wanted you too badly to honor my vow." She almost didn't hear him as he dropped his face into his hands and whispered bitterly to himself. "And, damn it to hell, I still do."

Her legs were shaking terribly, but Tara managed to stand. "I will marry you, Grant . . . er . . . Star-runner, as soon as possible."

His head snapped up, and he searched her face. The compassion in her eyes was unmistakable, but there was something more there that he didn't wish to identify. "To save your family?" he suggested bitterly.

"And yours."

A muscle in his cheek twitched as he jerked his hand toward the bed. "Then you'd best get some sleep. The pass will be open, but our journey tomorrow still won't be easy."

"Very well." Tara left the table and walked across the room. "But I'm warning you right now, Chief Star-runner, once we're safely married I'll want to know exactly what kind of trouble you and your people are in and what we can do about it. These raids on the mining camps concern me as well as you. None of us, white or Indian, wants war."

Reluctantly, an admiring smile turned up the corners of his lips. "I will gladly tell you what I know, though your kind concern can be of no help to my people. The only thing that will help them is if I can find the leader of the vigilantes and prove to the settlers that he is at fault for these brutal murders, not the Absaroka."

"Have you been able to find any clues to his identity?"

"That was the purpose behind my being a rancher. I was hoping that once I was accepted as one of you, I would be privy to the kind of information I need. Unfortunately, you and yours thwarted that plan very nicely."

Tara flushed at his sarcasm but didn't back down from her offensive stance. "You might not know this, but the Fierce-ones have as much respect for the men of your tribe as you have for them, and working together we just might find out who is responsible for these crimes against your people far quicker than you could on your own.''

He gave her a quelling look. ''If you recall, I am not on the best of terms with your family.''

Tara lifted her chin disdainfully. ''As my husband, that will soon change.''

Star-runner fingered his jaw, remembering what her brothers had given him in exchange for a little kissing and petting. Wincing at the twinge of pain he still felt whenever he took a deep breath, he wondered what his punishment would be for carrying her off their ranch and marrying her . . . and then there was the matter of his being a Collingswood.

''Somehow, I doubt this will improve things,'' he grumbled before wrapping himself up in a warm robe and stretching out on the floor.

Angus subjected the man who was claiming to be his daughter's husband to an intense study. Flanked by James on his right and Neal on his left, with a shotgun pointed at his heart, the man didn't reveal the slightest sign of fear. Indeed, he was smiling with genuine amusement. As much as it galled Angus to admit it, it looked like Grant Collingswood was a man of courage. In appearance and build, he was much like his father the earl, but there the resemblance ended. The younger Collingswood radiated a deep inner strength that Angus couldn't help but admire, and this forced him to entertain the notion that the son was nothing like the father.

Even so, after the hell this young man had just put them through, Angus could happily murder him, though all three of his sons had already volunteered for the job. Tara might have been part of the family for only a couple of months, but every one of her brothers would lay down his own life for her. Angus knew, as he glared at the man who had carried her off right from under their noses, that he would do the same.

''Very clever of you to leave that broken arrow behind for us to find,'' he admitted cuttingly, noting Grant's well-worn buckskins and the hand-beaded sheath that had recently housed a very lethal-looking knife. This lad was cut from a far sturdier cloth than his father, but Angus had yet to determine what kind of fiber made up the whole. "We were going to take out after the Crow as soon as the pass to their hunting grounds was clear."

Keeping a careful watch on Grant's face, he added, "'That tribe's been takin' the blame for quite a bit o' trouble around here lately. We were more than willin' to believe they had a hand in this, too."

Grant's eyes frosted over with cold, conveying a far different message from his words. "Now that Tara and I are married, there is no need to send you down any more false trails. I am the man who took her, and I intend to keep her."

Warning Tara with his gaze to let her family continue operating on the assumption that he had abducted her himself or she would live to regret it, he continued, "No matter how you feel about our relationship, Armstrong, it's too late for you to do anything about it now. Our marriage is legal."

"We'll see about that," Angus retorted, but his tone held a curious lack of anger.

Grant inclined his head in deference to the older man's skill at maintaining his control.

"Take him into the main room, lads," Angus directed, then turned his attention back to his daughter. "For the last time, Tara, I want you to go upstairs. Now!"

Tara refused. She had not survived a horrendous three-day journey through a raging blizzard, said her "I do's" to Grant in the back room of a smoky saloon, then traveled another grueling two days on horseback only to be sent to her room when she finally arrived at her destination. As long as Neal and Jamie had Grant's arms pinned behind his back and Robert had a shotgun aimed at his chest, she wasn't going anywhere, even if she was on the verge of collapse from exhaustion. "Until we get this situation settled, I'm staying right here. After all, it is my future that is at stake, and I will have my say in any decision that's made."

Angus scowled ferociously at her, but she didn't back down, and he had to fight to hold back a grin. For all her lack of size and the fatigue that showed in every line of her small body, the lass was as stubborn and wayward as his sons. Angus saw that the fact hadn't escaped the notice of her new husband. Though the man hadn't been given much to smile about since his arrival, Tara's challenge to her father's authority had Grant's lips twitching with amusement.

As much as he appreciated the humor in that himself, Angus growled, "For what you've done to her, Collingswood, I should have your gut shot and allow her the pleasure of watching you bleed to death."

"My thoughts exactly," Neal agreed, though he took a wary step backward when the subject of his pronouncement turned those cold blue eyes in his direction. "I don't know how things are done where you come from, Collingswood, but out here, if a man forces his attentions on a woman, her family has every right to revenge. For kidnapping Tara and besmirching her honor, you should be shot."

Tara thanked Robert with a grateful smile when he revealed that he, at least, was willing to listen to reason. "Maybe so, Neal, but out here we don't judge a man until we've got all the facts."

Tara wanted to stamp her foot in frustration when, instead of being grateful for Robert's attempt at fairness, Grant went out of his way to antagonize him. "I wish I had known that the night you ambushed me," he drawled mockingly. "It might have saved me some cracked ribs and a couple of black eyes."

To Tara's amazement, all four of the men in her family looked sheepish. "Don't blame the lads for something that was my fault," Angus advised. "For too many years, I've let my hatred for your father eat me up on the inside, and a lot of my bitter poison spilled over on them. By thrashing you, they thought they were doing right by me and our clan."

The grip his captors had on his arms was too strong for Grant to shrug off, but he shrugged off the need for any apology. "I understand the ways of vengeance," he allowed in a tone that was almost gracious.

Angus's bushy brows drew together over his eyes. This young buck was not only impressively arrogant, but he had a strange way of thinking for a lorded English gentleman. Of couse, Tara had told him that Collingswood had given up the title, but that fact only added to Angus's curiosity about him. If he didn't know better, he would have sworn that the man was born and bred in the territory. And those piercing blue eyes. Angus couldn't put his finger on where he'd seen eyes like that before, but there was something disturbingly familiar about them. "So if I take a shotgun to you for running off with my daughter, you won't look badly on me, eh?"

Grant's reply to his threat was nonchalant. "You will do what you must, just as I have done."

James laughed at this assertion. "No one forced you to abduct Tara!"

"True," Grant acknowledged evenly. "I wanted her, so I took her."

As he heard the satisfaction lurking behind that answer, James could barely tamp down his fury. "You gave her no choice in the matter, did you? You bedded our poor girl, then forced her to wed you."

Before making his answer to that charge, Grant's gaze landed briefly on the "poor girl" in question, annoyed by the embarrassed color that suffused her cheeks. Even now, his blushing bride would have preferred it if her family thought she would go to her marriage bed as pure as the driven snow. Just like the last time he'd had one of these confrontations with the Armstrong males, she kept her eyes downcast and said nothing in his defense.

With a contemptuous twist of his lips, he switched his attention back to his inquisitor, ignoring the increased pressure being applied to both his arms as they were wrenched higher up on his spine. "Let's just say that there is a strong possibility that my seed has already taken root within the womb of your sister, and since I'm still paying for my last run-in with this family, marriage to her seemed a most advisable course."

Angus's lips curled back from his teeth in an animal rage. "If you think some words on a piece of paper are going to save your damned hide, you're dead wrong. If you forced her, I'm going to flail the flesh right off your bones before unmanning you!"

Grant gazed knowingly at Tara, reminding her of the recent conversation they'd had concerning the Sioux brave who had attacked her. "Why so shocked, Taralynn? As I've told you, I have much in common with the men of your family. We oftimes think the same.''

Jamie growled. "We don't have anything in common, Collingswood, and none of us would think to hide behind a woman's skirts like you're doing.''

"I'm thinkin' that once we're done with you, you'll be fit to wear one yourself,'' Neal taunted angrily.

"Oh, please,'' Tara gasped in exasperation. "I don't want to hear another single word about torture and killing!''

"Didn't I predict this would happen?'' Grant asked, sending her a pitying look. "Out here, the laws of vengeance are much harsher than they are back in civilization.''

"You're right there, Collingswood,'' Neal proclaimed fiercely. "Though I doubt you'll take much pleasure in being right about that once we're finished with you.''

Jamie concurred with his brother. "And our brand of vengeance is swift.''

"Take him outside,'' Angus ordered.

In as dignified a tone as possible under these humiliating circumstances, Tara exclaimed, "That won't be necessary, Father. Grant didn't force me to do anything. I went with him quite willingly.''

Angus stared at her. "You've got a soft heart, lass. You're not just saying that, are ye?''

"Of course she is,'' Neal inserted before she could answer the question. "Taralynn is a lady of quality, and no lady would condone torturin' a man, no matter how well deserved. Violence offends her delicate sensibilities.''

As she heard that, Tara was reminded of all the other ridiculous rules and regulations that had been applied to her as a "lady,'' and she swiftly concluded that she no longer wished to be considered one. Moreover, she believed that all these primitive masculine rituals concerning vengeance and honor were ridiculous, and she would not tolerate such nonsense as it pertained to her situation.

"I can speak for myself, Neal,'' she declared tartly, then stepped forward and snatched the shotgun out of Robert's startled hands. "And this senseless male posturing has gone on quite long enough. Grant is well aware of your displeasure with his conduct, and I'm sure you've convinced him that you're men of exceptionally high honor.''

"Tara!" all three of her brothers exclaimed as one, but Tara was already turning her ire on her husband.

"As for you, employing a bit more tact wouldn't have killed you! By your childish attitude, one would think you were hoping that my family would make me a grieving widow before the ink is even dry on our marriage certificate."

"Childish!" Grant growled, the offended expression on his face matching that of the other put-upon males in the room.

Ignoring him and her brothers, Tara gazed intently at Angus. "Now, Father, I would appreciate it if you would stop threatening my husband and give him a proper welcome into this family. So what if our courtship and marriage were slightly unconventional? This is what I want. You have always done whatever you pleased, and your three sons are as unruly and headstrong as they come. I'd damned well like to know why I should be any different."

"But Tara!" James sputtered in astonishment at her use of profanity. "The bastard just up and stole you without giving you any say in the matter at all. You can't tell me that's the way you wanted it."

Tara stepped forward, pushing James aside as she slipped her arm through Grant's. "What's done is done."

Reluctantly, Neal dropped his hold on Grant's other arm. "We can't have you married to a Collingswood!" he blustered, but one glance at his father deflated that argument. "Pa! You're going along with this?"

"If Tara loves him," Angus said, "so be it."

Grant's mouth gaped open at Tara's instant retort. "Of course I love him. I love him very much, and he loves me."

His new son-in-law didn't seem nearly as certain about the state of his heart as Taralynn was about hers, but Angus didn't consider it his place to comment. Besides, if his daughter had made up her mind that Collingswood loved her, he didn't give much for the man's chances of holding out against her. For a time, since he'd considered her too young, Angus had attempted to protect his heart from Ellen, but the winning lass had slipped inside his defenses with nary any trouble at all.

"She's very much like her mother," Angus commented sympathetically.

Caught off balance by Tara's vehement declaration, Grant muttered, "You may think so, Red-beard, but I have found her to be much like her father."

Angus frowned as something clicked in his memory. "What did you just call me?"

Grant threw Tara a killing glance, blaming her for his slip of the tongue. His mind was still spinning from hearing her announce that they loved each other as if she didn't have any doubts in the world. During the time it took him to control his whirling emotions, Angus had remembered the blue-eyed stripling who had stolen his prized stallion.

"You've grown up some mighty Absaroka warrior," Angus observed gruffly. "But you're still a bane to me, lad. Is there anything else you'll be takin' of mine before you're done plaguing me?"

Grant straightened his spine and lifted his head, an implied threat in his proud stance. "I cannot return the white stallion to you, Red-beard, but he has sired many strong foals. If you want, I can include a few of them in the bride price."

"For the likes of that horse, you'd best include more than a few!"

Surprised by the man's amused response to his real identity, Grant grinned. "For the likes of your daughter, one or two is more than fair."

"What the devil are you two talkin' about?" Neal demanded, confused by the almost affectionate interplay between his father and Grant.

Angus relieved his son's curiosity with a booming laugh. "We shouldn't have taken on so, lads," he proclaimed jovially. "Tara didn't get herself tied to no bloody English dandy. She up and married a Crow."

That explanation didn't help any, and Jamie said so, his brown eyes conveying his astonishment. "As in Injun?"

Grant was staring at Angus every bit as hard as his sons, not sure if he was hearing right. Was it possible that Angus was more willing to accept an Indian as a proper husband for his fair-skinned daughter than a white man?

"Right you are, Jamie," Angus said, and he clapped one arm over Grant's shoulder. "And I for one can't wait to hear the story of how a sniveling, pantywaist *berdache* ended up as a warrior of that proud tribe."

Chapter

Thirty

The next morning, Tara was awakened by the absence of Grant's body heat. Before opening her eyes, she tried to snuggle closer beneath the patchwork quilt but discovered herself alone in the big four-poster bed. Startled, she opened her eyes and found Grant standing at the window, staring out at the distant mountains. It was the dawn of a cloudless September day, and Tara knew that once the sun began heating the earth, the last of the snow that still remained in the aftermath of the blizzard would melt away. She hoped her new husband wouldn't disappear with it, but, according to the faraway expression on his face, he was already somewhere else.

The day was going to be a warm one, but sometime during the cold night, the fire had gone out in the fireplace, and Tara could see her breath. Seemingly impervious to the chill in the room, Grant stood naked. Drawing the covers up over her bare shoulders, Tara took advantage of his lack of awareness to watch him, a blissful smile on her face. Her wedding night had been all any woman could want. Grant was capable of giving her incredible pleasure, bestowing magic with his slightest touch. She would always desire his body, think of it as one of God's finest creations, but it was the man inside that beautiful body whom she loved.

She knew it, and so did he, though he had yet to admit that he felt the same way about her. Yet Tara knew he did. As much as he tried to fight the truth, his body conveyed that message to her every time they made love, and one day he would give her the words as well. All she had to do was continue loving him and be patient.

Grant emitted a ragged sigh, and a deep sadness came over his face. Unmindful of the cold, Tara pushed back the covers and padded over to him. Stepping up behind him, she pressed the front of her body against his back, then slipped her hands beneath his arms and crossed them over his chest. "What's wrong?" she inquired softly, placing a gentle kiss on his shoulder blade.

"Nothing."

His body was tense, his spine stiff, and Tara felt it stiffen more as she splayed her hands across his flat stomach. Maybe she should leave him to his private thoughts. He definitely wasn't in a very receptive mood, but when he was in pain, everything in her demanded that she try to comfort him. "What are you thinking about?"

His chest rose and fell with his harsh breathing. "My people and yours. Your father and brothers do not think like most white men."

Tara smiled against his smooth skin. In all the time she'd known him, Grant had never seemed uncertain about anything, but after their initial hostility, her family's easy acceptance of him had thrown him completely off balance. "Does that really surprise you so much? My family lives side by side with yours in this wilderness, and they have had to adopt the same means of survival as your people. Besides, the highlanders of Scotland have always been a fierce and noble breed."

"In some ways the Fierce-ones may be the same, but in most they are different," Grant insisted.

"Maybe," Tara allowed. "Yet you have always known that they were men of rare courage and integrity. Why would you expect that to change now?"

He shrugged his shoulders indifferently, but his tone was raw with suspicion. "I am not the kind of son-in-law Red-beard was hoping for, yet he accepts me into his clan. I don't understand it, unless he mistakenly assumes by my blue eyes and English name I am more white than Indian."

Tara knew she was taking a risk, but she could sense the turmoil going on inside him, and she was almost certain of the cause. "Would it be so wrong for you to acknowledge both sides of yourself? You are white, just as you are Indian."

"No," Grant bit out tersely, pushing her hands away from him as he turned around to face her. "No matter the color of my eyes or my skin, I am Absaroka, and those whites who would seek to destroy my people are my enemy. I will never be one of them!"

"The Fierce-ones admire your people, and they have resided in peace with them for many years," Tara reminded him. "Must they be considered your enemy just because their skin is white?"

"If it came to war, the Fierce-ones would side with the whites against us."

Tara shook her head. "How can you say that after the discussion we had last night? When we told my father and brothers the truth of what has been happening on your hunting grounds, they believed us, and they offered to help you find who is really responsible for these despicable raids."

With an almost desperate belligerence, he insisted, "If these attacks continue, war is inevitable. To save themselves, the Fierce-ones will align themselves with the Army and the other settlers. Your family might sympathize with our plight, but when the call to battle comes, they will take up arms against us."

"You're wrong, Grant Collingswood. My family would fight on the side of justice."

"I would like to believe that," he replied, jaw tensed at the deliberate emphasis she'd put on his white name. "But I am a realist, and I cannot afford to take such a dangerous risk."

"So you're going to refuse their offer of help?" Tara cried in disbelief. "Even knowing that if we can find the man responsible for these crimes there won't be a war, and all this talk of taking sides won't matter?"

"Between white and Indian there will always be sides," Grant stated curtly, his mouth thinning cruelly. "I have already chosen which one I'm on, and now you must choose. Do you love me enough to be Morning-star-woman, or will you remain Taralynn Armstrong?"

"Taralynn Collingswood," she corrected, but that only seemed to provoke him further.

"We may be tied together in the way of the white man, but an Absaroka recognizes no law but tribal law. It is not Grant Collingswood but Star-runner who requires your answer."

His tone and expression were savagely ruthless, yet Tara experienced an abrupt surge of compassion for him. As an Absaroka war chief, Star-runner had sworn to protect his people, but even as he committed himself to fulfill this solemn duty, he was fighting an inner battle that might well destroy him. He loved her, a white woman, but a warrior could not allow himself to be torn by mixed loyalties. To maintain his honor as an Indian, he had to cut all ties with her world, even if it meant losing her—and part of himself as well.

As he demanded arrogantly for her to make her choice, Tara could see the torment in his eyes, and her heart ached for him, but he would not welcome her pity. Knowing this, Tara lifted her chin at a defiant angle and gave him her answer. "Until such time as we discover who seeks the destruction of both our peoples, I shall be Morning-sun-woman."

"And afterward?" he inquired without revealing any emotion.

If there was one thing Tara had learned about her husband, it was that he could not back down from a challenge. "Afterward, we shall decide if you are brave enough to accept all of yourself and all of me."

Though they tried, neither one of them could stare the other down, but it was Star-runner who brought an end to their visual combat. Lifting his hand, he cupped her bare breast in his palm, smiling at the instantaneous tautening of her nipple. "Until that day, I am happy to settle for the part of you I have now."

Not to be outdone, Tara lowered her hand and cupped him

between the legs. "As am I, mighty warrior," she promised seductively. "As am I."

As they approached the camp of the Fire-bears, Star-runner brought his horse even with Morning-sun's mare. "It will go easier for you if you don't reveal your fear of them."

"I'm not afraid," Tara retorted indignantly, unaware that he could see the white-knuckled grip she had on her reins. "Like any new wife, I'm just a little nervous at the prospect of meeting my husband's family. What if they hate me?"

Star-runner could not lie to her, but he did try to spare her the complete truth. "They will respect you as the woman I have taken to share my tepee."

"And save their insults about my white skin for when my back is turned," Tara judged perceptively.

With a resigned sigh, Star-runner nodded. "Perhaps, but once they get to know you, they will accept you."

"And if they don't?"

"They will."

Tara saw no purpose in prolonging a futile argument. "I certainly hope so," she sighed, then took a deep breath for courage as she spied the crowd of people gathered to greet their arrival.

"Welcome, brother," Swift-bear declared. "It is well that you have come."

Split-nose agreed, giving Tara a cursory glance, then dismissing her presence as unimportant. "When our scouts discovered your cabin empty with no sign to follow, we became anxious. We knew not where to build our signal fires."

"Has something happened?" Star-runner inquired.

"Not yet, but soon," Otter's-heart predicted, though his attention was not on Star-runner but on the woman riding by his side. The flame-haired one did not appear to recognize him, and considering their last encounter, he felt that to be a good thing. "Unless the snows reappear in the passes, our enemy will return to ride against us. Last night, our scouts reported a small group of miners making camp on the Yellowstone."

Running-deer added his concern to that of the others as Star-runner dismounted. "It is as if the vigilantes have the means to encourage their prey to come amongst us where the blame for their slaughter might be laid upon our heads.''

Distracted by Running-deer's observation, Star-runner assisted his wife off her horse but quickly returned his attention to more consequential matters than her introduction into the camp. If his brother's words were true, he might finally have discovered a clue to the identity of their enemy. There were many in the territory who sold supplies to the miners and directed them to places where they would be most likely to discover gold, but the snowstorm had severely hampered all travel. For these new arrivals to have journeyed so many miles into the Absaroka hunting grounds, they must have set out from a nearby outpost. Fort Bates was the only place close enough for these men to have ventured this far, which meant that the leader of the vigilantes might be operating from there.

For the first time in months, Star-runner felt a glimmer of hope that he could keep his vow to Mountain-lion. Brow furrowed in thought, he considered the best means to investigate this possibility and was therefore unaware of his wife's growing impatience until she inquired tartly, "Are the women of your clan always ignored like this, or is it only I who must endure such rudeness? Perhaps none of your people wishes to make my acquaintance, but I would still like to meet them."

Since Star-runner wished his clan to be more knowledgeable in the ways of the white man, he had taught all three of his brothers a respectable understanding of English, and so they grinned at her chastisement. For Star-runner to have brought the flame-haired woman to their camp, he must have decided to keep her for his mate, but to their amusement, it appeared that he had yet to teach her a woman's proper place. Considering his own difficulties in handling his willful sweetheart, Singing-moon, Otter's-heart was quick to say, "It is a sad thing that the noble sons of Split-nose have a weakness for women who cannot keep their sharp tongues quiet and do not hesitate to speak of their displeasure in public."

Irritated, Swift-bear growled, "Speak for yourself, little brother. Beneath my tutelage, Falling-water has become a meek and docile wife."

To his vast annoyance, all three of his brothers burst out
laughing, but before he could respond violently to their
insult, Star-runner soothed wryly, "We laugh at ourselves
as much as you, Swift-bear. Of all of us, only Running-deer
has yet to demonstrate his inability to master the weaker
sex."

With a self-disgusted snort, Running-deer admitted,
"Then you have yet to view the hobbles that the daughter of
Gray-eagle has tied about my legs. If ever I roam too close
to another girl's tepee, you shall see how swiftly my progress
is hampered."

Otter's-heart sighed, "Singing-moon allows me no progress at all."

His good humor restored, Swift-bear nodded questionably
at Tara. "If she refused your offer of slave, what offer did
she accept?"

Star-runner cleared his throat uncomfortably. "In the
eyes of the white man, we are married."

Otter's-heart hooted. "Married! For all your fine talk of
vengeance, it is she who has gained retribution."

Split-nose sighed, "It seems I have failed with all four of
my sons. Because of the example I have set in controlling
their mother, they do not know how to take command of
their lodges."

This time the laughter encompassed them all, except for
Tara, who jammed an elbow into Star-runner's ribs, her
green eyes glittering with temper. "Why is everyone laughing? What are you saying about me?"

To Tara's surprise, her questions were answered in halting
English by a handsome young man with sparkling brown
eyes and a highly sheepish grin. Eyes narrowed in suspicion,
she studied his face, certain she had seen him before.

Otter's-heart took a wary step backward. "Do not be
angry with our poor brother, Morning-sun-woman. It is
punishment enough for him to know that even though we
brought you to him in bonds, a lowly slave to his needs, he
lacks the strength to be a worthy slavemaster."

"Slave!" Tara cried, her eyes flying to her husband's. "Is
that what you told them I am to you?"

Another young man came forward to reply to her outraged
question, and she thought she recognized him as well. "This

is the boast Star-runner has made," Running-deer said, "but has lived to regret. He now considers you one of his finest possessions."

At his brothers' dubious attempts to aid him, Star-runner rolled his eyes upward in exasperation and got a sharp kick in the shins for the effort. "Well, you're not going to think so for long!" Tara promised, then turned accusing eyes on the smiling twosome who had stepped forward to explain what had so amused them. "You're the ones who kidnapped me!"

Chest puffed out in pride, Otter's-heart flung his arm over Running-deer's shoulder and admitted loftily, "I and my courageous brother here were happy to ease the fire you have started in Star-runner's loins. He did not show his gratitude to us at first, but he has since come to realize the benefits of our action. Now that he has brought you into his lodge to appease his bothersome lusts, he can devote his attention to more worthy matters."

Running-deer nodded in agreement. "We are most thankful to you for giving Star-runner your devoted service under the blankets. We can see by his face that you keep him well satisfied."

"Oh!" Tara gasped, but before she could gear up to launch a physical attack for this mortifying affront to her female dignity, Star-runner bent down and hoisted her up and over his shoulder.

"Put me down!" she screeched in outrage, but Star-runner kept right on walking.

As he watched his brother striding away, Otter's heart glanced at Running-deer in confusion. "Morning-sun-woman does not seem to understand our compliments to her beauty."

Running-deer shook his head, equally bewildered. "Perhaps we did not use the English words correctly."

Swift-bear confirmed this possibility. "Tomorrow, we shall ask Star-runner how to tell his woman that she is most worthy to receive his seed."

Otter's-heart grinned and pointed to the lodge they had designated for Star-runner's use. As his brother disappeared inside, they heard a muffled scream and then silence. "I predict that Star-runner shall soon reap the harvest of his planting.''

A noticeable wetness in his eyes, Swift-bear nodded. ''A warrior needs strong sons. I cannot say the name of the small one departed from us, but I know his spirit will soar in happiness when his grieving father stands on the mountain and lifts a new babe to the sun.''

''Yes,'' Running-deer agreed. ''And on that day, we shall have a great feast to honor the woman who has healed our brother's heart.''

Chapter

Thirty-one

Star-runner and his brothers rode out of camp at first light but arrived at the mining camp on the Yellowstone too late to save the miners. At long last, however, they were in time to lay chase after the ruthless gang of cutthroats who had slain the six prospectors. As usual when pitted against an enemy, they were badly outnumbered, but that didn't stop them from attacking once they caught up with the band of twenty white men who had disguised themselves as Absaroka.

"Hah!" Swift-bear shouted as his arrow pierced the heart of one swiftly fleeing enemy. "To be like us, they wear our beaded quivers, but they have no skill with a bow."

Otter's-heart shouted in glee, "For the bloodshed suffered by our people, they shall now shed blood."

"Do not slay all," Star-runner warned as he shouldered his rifle. "Those left alive must tell us the name of their leader and explain his guilt to the white settlers. Else they will not believe us."

"Not all will die, but most," Running-deer retorted vengefully, kicking his horse into a swifter gallop as he took after the two white riders who straggled farthest behind. Within a few minutes, one man lay like a rotting log on the ground, and his bloody scalp adorned Running-deer's belt. Not waiting to show off his trophy, Running-deer remounted his horse and set off after his next victim.

As Otter's-heart directed a steady stream of arrows in the wake of their pursuit, Star-runner and Swift-bear veered off the path in opposite directions, intending to head off the band of riders before they were able to cross the river and complete their escape out of Absaroka territory. Unfortunately, as the two brothers broke through the line of trees running parallel to the grassy riverbank, their arrival was greeted by a burst of gunfire. Unknown to them, the vigilantes had stored a case of rifles beneath a thicket of wild pigweed, and they had foolishly ridden right into their trap.

The last thing Star-runner saw before he dived for cover was Swift-bear tumbling off his horse. Pinned down behind a large outcropping of rock, Star-runner could not seek to rescue his fallen brother or determine the extent of his injuries. All he could do was return the enemy fire as best he could and pray that Otter's-heart and Running-deer would retreat into the forest to seek reinforcements before he took a bullet.

It was not a bullet that felled him, however, but a flying chip of granite that broke off from the rock as a volley of bullets hit it. One second he was firing his rifle, and the next he felt a blinding pain in his head and dropped senseless to the ground, oblivious to the triumphant exclamation of the man who found him lying there a few minutes later.

"Would you just looky here," Slade Plummer declared gleefully to his remaining companions as he stared down at Star-runner's motionless body. "Last time I saw this young fella, he was calling himself Grant Collingswood. I always knew there was something strange about him, but who woulda figured he was one of them cussed red devils hisself? Now I know why them dumb sons-a-bitches didn't react like the boss wanted. This Injun lover was givin' 'em council and tellin' 'em what to do."

Mike Sweeney yanked a revolver out of his belt and took aim. "Well, he won't be passin' out any more of his damned advice."

Before Sweeney could pull the trigger, Plummer reached out and grabbed his arm. "Naw, we ain't goin' to kill him yet," Plummer said. "I know for a fact that the boss will want to make his acquaintance before we send him on to his maker. He's been itchin' to find the cattywampus cuss that's been keepin' them Crow in line, and I aim to please him. I reckon he'd pay us a nice bonus for our trouble."

An appeal to Sweeney's greed was a guarantee for success. "Then let's pack him up and get the hell out of here. It won't be long before them others are back with reinforcements."

"Done," Plummer agreed. Then he added with a snarl, "And when it comes time to plug this snake, I'll be doin' the shootin'. I came out at the short end of our last run-in, but I'll be gettin' my own back this time."

Sweeney shrugged. "Sure, Slade, it don't make me no nevermind what you do with him."

Plummer grinned vengefully. "Well, before I'm done with him, he's goin' to mind plenty."

Chapter

Thirty-two

Tara watched closely as White-fawn removed a tight canopy of hard hide from over a fire hole, then lifted the frame over which another, smaller hide had been stretched. "Smoking is the last step in the process we use to soften our clothing," White-fawn explained as she beat the still warm piece of doeskin to remove the smoke. "This deer hide will now remain as white as the fallen snow and will feel as smooth upon your fair skin as the dress you wear now."

Tara had to admit that she liked the soft leather garment White-fawn had given her to replace her unpractical long skirt and tailored blouse, but now that she had witnessed the amount of work it took to finish just one hide, she doubted if she'd ever own another dress like it, especially if she were expected to make it herself.

White-fawn folded the small square of tanned leather, then stretched out another hide over the frame and rubbed it with what Tara noted in distaste was the innards of some recently butchered animal. Unaware of Tara's reaction to her work, White-fawn completed her task, then relit the fire. "Because of these methods known to no one but our own tribe, the hides used to build our tepees will resist the wind and the cold yet stay forever pliant. For the snowy whiteness of our lodges, we are the envy of all our enemies.''

Tara smiled in acknowledgment, though her brain was beginning to swirl with all the information she had attained during her first morning in the Indian camp. Before riding out of camp with his brothers, Star-runner had deposited her in the lodge of his adoptive mother. Since White-fawn was the only woman in the clan who could speak and understand English, he had asked her to teach his ignorant bride what was expected of an Absaroka woman.

Thus far, Tara had determined that the life of an Absaroka squaw was a never-ending sequence of hard work and drudgery. As far as she could tell, the women were responsible for just about everything that needed to be done. They cooked all the food, processed the hides needed for their clothing and the construction of their homes, fetched water, and tended to the animals, while their menfolk looked on with the indifferent dignity of their elevated station as masters and warriors.

For the moment, Tara was willing to keep her opinions concerning this unfair distribution of labor to herself, but her husband was going to receive an earful once he returned from wherever it was he had gone in such a great hurry. By midafternoon, however, with her shoulders aching beneath the yoke of the water skeins she was helping to carry up from the river, her patience reached the end of its tether. Pointing to a group of nearby youths who were playing a game that looked much like blindman's bluff, she exclaimed, "Why should they be allowed to amuse themselves while we work like slaves? You are no longer a young woman, White-fawn. Why aren't they helping you? Have they no respect for the wife of a great chief?"

To Tara's amazement, White-fawn looked shocked at the question. "If not for their constant vigilance and protection, I would not be old or young. I would be with those whose names I cannot say."

"Protection?" Tara glared at the laughing boys. "How could these youngsters hope to protect you?"

"They are young, but they are all seasoned warriors. Most of them have already seen their twelfth season, and many have counted coup," White-fawn explained patiently. "To keep us safe from our enemies, they must patrol our borders and put their own lives at risk. To defend their mothers and sisters, they would willingly face death.''

Seeing the disbelief on Tara's face, White-fawn lowered her water skeins and directed Tara to sit down beside her on the green grasses of the riverbank. "Look more closely at those scamps you see as useless, Morning-sun. Then tell me what you see.''

Tara followed White-fawn's direction, and as her eyes studied the slender, brown, half-naked bodies, her feelings of irritation changed to incredulity. "Some . . . some of them look as if they've sustained bullet wounds.''

White-fawn nodded. ''Many of our enemies no longer fight with bow and arrow. They make trade with the whites and come against us with guns. To withstand this threat, our young men must be clever and strong and very skilled with their weapons. Those who are not rarely live to be old enough to marry. Knowing this, do you still begrudge them their time of play?''

"No," Tara whispered, thinking of Grant and the kind of hardships he must have had to endure in his childhood, and how difficult it must have been for him, with his pampered background, to adjust to his new life, where mere boys must shoulder the grave responsibilities of men. Grant had not said much about that period of his life to her, but in order to understand him better, she wanted to know all about his past.

"Please, White-fawn," she entreated. "Tell me of Star-runner and how he grew to be a man.''

Until Split-nose required his end-of-day meal, White-fawn's time was her own, and so she began the story that was much favored among the women of their clan. She told of the day that Star-runner had come to stay in her lodge and the summer night when he had stolen into the village of their sister clan and stolen all the horses of their chief. As if she were speaking of a son she had borne from her own loins, White-fawn boasted of Star-runner's swift passage from boy to man, from warrior to chief, but when that telling was eventually done, her face fell into somber lines, and her voice dropped to a whisper. "For Star-runner, those happy days are finished. We do not speak of our loved ones who have gone on to the other side, but the heart of my son still bleeds for those he has lost.''

Tara frowned when she heard this, and she swallowed a sudden constriction in her throat. ''Those he has lost?''

White-fawn remained silent for a very long time, her lovely face reflecting the course of her inner struggle. Finally, she said, ''I can see the love you have for my son shining in your eyes, Morning-sun. Perhaps I will be forgiven if I tell you of the day his heart fell to the ground, in the hopes that you may help to raise it up again.''

''I would do anything to help him,'' Tara said, though she wasn't certain that it was in her power to do so. The sadness she had sensed in her husband had not been dispelled by their marriage. In fact, Tara felt as if their union had only added more frequency to his inner turmoil, a conflict that went much deeper than his confusion about his dual identity.

Something in her expression or tone must have reassured White-fawn, for she reached out and patted Tara's hand as if she felt a strong compassion for her. ''Now that your destiny is entwined forever with his, it is your right to know.''

''Know what?'' Tara asked tentatively, feeling as if she were about to hear something that would have a profound effect on her future, and not necessarily a good one.

''Many winters ago, on the night of the icicle wind, my father, Mountain-lion, had a dream about a mighty chief who was marked by the sign of the raven,'' White-fawn began in a reverent tone. ''This great warrior would be the one to save us from a terrible enemy. Very soon after that, Star-runner was brought to our camp. When we saw the birdlike marking on his hip, we knew immediately who he was, and thus, in the eyes of our clan, his future was destined.''

As Tara listened to White-fawn recount the tale of some mysterious prophecy concerning her husband, she grew more and more concerned about him, for it was as if White-fawn believed that her adopted son had been endowed with a mystical power that almost gave him the stature of a god. ''As season followed season, all in the dream came to pass, until the day arrived when Star-runner had no choice but to chase the stars across a wide ocean as was described in my father's dream.''

White-fawn's features were contorted by grief, and for a

moment Tara feared she would not continue, but then she said, "While the men of our clan were off fighting the Sioux, the Cheyenne stole into our camp. They killed our old men and carried off many women and children, but this was not the fate to befall Star-runner's beautiful wife, Sliver-of-moon, or Tall-bear, his sweet newborn son. Star-runner returned to find his loved ones both slain."

"Oh my God," Tara cried out in horror as White-fawn hastened to complete the terrible story.

"The agony of his grief was so powerful that he suddenly remembered all of that other life whose memories had so long been denied him. Then, when he had seen to the burial of his family, my father told him what else he must do to fulfill his great destiny as the savior of our people."

Tara closed her eyes as a tide of pain washed over her, barely listening as White-fawn told of Star-runner's journey across the wide ocean. All she could think about was the fact that her husband had been married before and that his first wife had given him a child. At long last, she knew the source of her husband's despondency and the reason for the self-directed anger he felt whenever he came too close to admitting his love for her. Now she knew what was preventing him from saying those words to her, and it was her heart that fell to the ground.

Grant could not love her as she wished him to love her because he still loved Sliver-of-moon. He could take Morning-sun into his bed but not his heart, for that would be a betrayal. Suddenly, the ambiguous words he had spoken to her that day in the cabin made perfect sense. *A man may require the heat of the sun in order to live, but in my heart I will always prefer the serene beauty and gentle light of the moon.*

As she acknowledged this painful truth, Tara wanted to throw herself down upon the ground and weep until she had no more tears left to shed, but she could not give in to such weakness. She might never find a place in Grant's heart, but if she wished to continue being considered fit for his bed, she had to remain strong. With her insides ripped to shreds, she lifted her chin and requested more punishment. "It has been eight long years, but Star-runner still bleeds. Was Sliver-of-moon so very beautiful?"

White-fawn replied in a near whisper, glancing over her shoulder to make certain that no one could hear her as she again broke with sacred tradition and described a woman who had gone on to the Father. "As beautiful as the lake without ripples, the path without stones, the summer sky without clouds."

Tara bowed her head at the lovely poetic description that could never be applied to her. "I see."

White-fawn scowled as she noted the defeated slump of Tara's shoulders. In a no-nonsense tone, she ordered, "We have tarried too long in talking, Morning-sun, and you still have much to learn. Come, we must ready the meat for our cooking fire before the men return from their raid on the Yellowstone."

Nothing else White-fawn could have said would have produced such a drastic change in her downhearted pupil than the information that Grant might be in danger. "Raid!" Tara exclaimed fearfully. "What kind of raid? How dare he go off like that without telling me what he was up to!"

White-fawn smiled a smug smile, pleased by this evidence that even though she now knew exactly what she was up against, the flame-haired girl could not hide her deep caring for a man who had yet to concede that he shared a mutual feeling. Nor did she bother to concede her righteous anger at his refusal to inform her of his manly pursuits. Those foolish men often forgot that their chosen activities brought bad consequences to their women, but White-fawn could see that Morning-sun would not let Star-runner forget.

Whether he realized it yet or not, Star-runner had chosen his new wife well, for although she was white, Morning-sun had a greater strength of character than Sliver-of-moon, who had lived and died as a sweet and docile child. No, this woman with the flashing green eyes would not keep meekly in the background of her husband's life. She would challenge him to greatness, anger him to think harder about his approach to problems, and thus be his spiritual helpmate as well as his lover.

As White-fawn hurried her new daughter-in-law along the path from the river, she said, "I shall not speak of this again, Morning-sun, so remember my words. There is strength in the high waves that churn up the lake, challenge in the path that holds many sharp stones, and great beauty and power in the clouds that fill the summer sky. A wise warrior knows this.''

It took Tara several seconds to digest White-fawn's speech, but once she did, her smile was as radiant as the sun for which the Absaroka had named her. "Then perhaps I should give my husband a lesson to remind him of what he already knows."

White-fawn's laughter was merry. "It is the way of our tribe that when a boy has difficulty learning, his teachers must be patient and give him many more lessons. Eventually, he always learns."

Tara grinned at this advice. "To be worthy of such a mighty warrior as Star-runner, I must learn to follow the ways of his tribe."

"For one so young, you are wise, Morning-sun," White-fawn complimented her.

"Or very foolish," Tara murmured to herself as she readjusted the heavy wooden yoke upon her sore shoulders and followed the older woman back to camp.

A loud commotion was going on in the council lodge when they arrived, and, like the other women, they stopped what they were doing in order to find out what had happened. As they joined the gathering, White-fawn introduced Tara to her daughter-in-law, Falling-water, wife of Swift-bear, but the young woman was weeping so copiously that she barely acknowledged Tara's presence. It was obvious that something was very, very wrong, but Tara had no choice but to wait patiently as White-fawn questioned the other women, then interpreted their answers.

"The evil ones were there on the Yellowstone when my sons arrived, and in the battle that followed Swift-bear was wounded. Running-deer returned with him to seek the aid of our medicine man, though Swift-bear's wound is very grave."

As sorry as she was to hear this, Tara couldn't help asking, "But what of Star-runner and Otter's-heart? Where are they?"

White-fawn's expression was stoic as she said, "Star-runner also fell in battle, but the evil ones did not leave him behind to die. They carried him with them as they fled away from our hunting grounds. Otter's-heart followed to see where they would take him. If his vigilance is not discovered, he will return to tell us."

Trying desperately to contain her panic, Tara asked, "Did Running-deer say how badly Star-runner was wounded?"

White-fawn shook her head. "Running-deer arrived too late to witness the wounding of his brothers. All he knows is what Otter's-heart told him before leaving to follow the vigilantes."

Voice rising, Tara cried, "I don't understand this. Why? Why would the vigilantes take him and not Swift-bear?"

White-fawn could not meet Tara's gaze. "Otter's-heart said that the leader of the evil ones called Star-runner by his white name. Grant Collingswood was known to them."

Tara dropped her head into her hands. "As they must be to him," she moaned. "They took him away to make certain he was dead and could not identify them."

As Running-deer stepped out of the council lodge to report that Swift-bear would recover from his wound, he heard the last of Tara's words and immediately stepped over to her. "No! If they wished to kill Star-runner, they would have already done so," he assured her grimly. "Your husband still lives, Morning-sun, and soon Otter's-heart will return to tell us where they have taken him."

A few minutes later, the medicinal ceremony on behalf of Swift-bear was completed, and he was carried to his own lodge so that his wife and mother could keep vigil at his bedside. Running-deer went back inside the council lodge to continue the recounting of the cunning trap that had been laid for him and his brothers on the Yellowstone. The other women took up their domestic duties once more, but Tara remained exactly where she was, her eyes focused on the trail between the tall trees. When and if Otter's-heart ever returned, she would be there to greet him.

Chapter
Thirty-three

Head lowered sheepishly, Otter's-heart avoided the eyes of his elders as he escorted Morning-sun inside the large tepee. Women were not allowed to take part in council, yet Morning-sun would not be denied entry. As the wife of Starrunner, she felt she had every right to know what had happened to him and what the clan meant to do about it. Otter's-heart laughed in self-derision as he recalled that he had once thought her too faint-hearted to be worthy of his brother.

In truth, this small flame-haired woman was much like Grandmother Fire-weasel. She was far too outspoken and very stubborn, but at least Otter's-heart had managed to extract a promise from her that she would not offer any of her own opinions to the grave matters under discussion. Grandmother Fire-weasel had stalwartly refused to make even that much of a concession to male authority.

To Otter's-heart's great relief, as he and Morning-sun sat down at the edge of the tribal circle, he heard only a few dissenting grunts, and no one openly expressed disapproval of a woman's presence in the lodge. Just as it had been with Grandmother Fire-weasel, the council of warriors took one look at the fierce expression on Morning-sun's face and resigned themselves to the fact that if they wished to get on with the grave business at hand, they would be wise not to confront her.

In Swift-bear's absence, his father, Split-nose, reclaimed the title of tribal chief and stepped forth as the spokesman of the clan. "What can you tell us of Star-runner, Otter's-heart? Does he yet live?"

Otter's-heart stood up to give his report, and since he had promised Morning-sun that she would receive the news about her husband at the same time as the others, he spoke in English. "The wound to his head was not serious, Father," he began, clearing his throat uncomfortably as Morning-sun emitted a loud gasp of relief. Pleading with his eyes for her to be silent, he continued, "The evil ones have taken him to Fort Bates, where they were warmly welcomed by the white trader whose head shines with no hair."

Split-nose frowned as he translated Otter's-heart's words to those who had yet to master the white man's language. Then, with a sympathetic glance at Tara's ashen face, he continued speaking in the way that she could understand. "No-hair is well known to us as a fair trader and an honest man. Why would he welcome these men who prey upon the innocent?"

Black eyes gleaming with rage, Otter's-heart confirmed his father's suspicion. "Soon after our brother was presented to him, it became clear that he is the leader of the evil ones. Those who ride against us answer to him."

A shocked hush fell over the gathering as this announcement was translated to them, and once again the bothersome woman among them broke in with an unwelcome exclamation. "Victor Bates!" Tara cried in astonishment. "He's the man behind all this killing?"

This time, to ensure her silence, Otter's-heart shifted his leg and gave her a mindful kick with the side of his foot. "This news is not the worst of it, Father," he admitted, ignoring Tara's indignant expression. "To hide their own guilt, the evil ones presented Star-runner as a prize to the angry mob of white settlers who are gathered within the strong walls of the fort. No-hair convinced the crowd that Star-runner was leading the Absaroka against them so that he might keep the gold that lies beneath our hunting grounds for himself. In the furor that greeted this news, I was able to get near enough to hear some of what was being said, but then the soldiers closed the front gates."

"Soldiers!" Tara burst out, renewed panic in her eyes. "Bates has brought in the Army?"

"Yes. He prepared well the trap set for Star-runner," Otter's-heart hissed between clenched teeth as his father relayed his words to the other warriors, but Tara didn't respond to his message.

"Oh my God," she exclaimed hysterically. "If the Army thinks he's responsible for the murders of all those miners, they'll hang him without waiting for a civilian trial!"

Split-nose shot his son a withering glare but directed his comments to Tara. "If you wish to hear more of your husband's plight, Morning-sun, you will stay silent. Star-runner would not appreciate this display of female weakness, and the tribal council has no patience for such outbursts. We realize that you are unfamiliar with our ways, and thus we have allowed you to attend this session of council, but if you do not keep your tongue quiet, we will no longer speak in words you can understand."

Chastened by Split-nose's stern rebuke, Tara reluctantly subsided, but as if she had already transgressed much too far across the boundaries of sacred tradition, the discussion continued in the Absaroka language. Otter's-heart spoke at some length in a tone that sent shivers of fear down her spine, and then the tribal elders murmured anxiously among themselves for several more minutes. Finally, Split-nose held up his hand and issued a decree that seemed to be greeted with approval by all in attendance except Otter's-heart and Running-deer. Frustration etched across their features, they both began speaking at once.

Tara couldn't decipher a thing that was being said, but when the two young men clenched their fists, dropped their hands to their sides, and stomped angrily out of the lodge, she knew that the tribal council had arrived at some decision that boded ill for the future welfare of her husband. Without a moment's hesitation, Tara scrambled to her feet and ran after them.

As she caught up with them, she demanded, "What's

wrong? What did they say that made you so angry? Please, you must tell me!''

Otter's-heart dismissed her entreaty with a jerky wave of his hand, but Running-deer paused long enough in his tracks to say, ''The elders believe it is our brother's destiny to face this trial alone. Star-runner's confrontation with our most fearful enemy was foreseen by our grandfather in the winter of the big snow. The sacred white buffalo bull spoke to him in a dream, and his words have all come to pass. To interfere now would be to go against the prophecy given to us by one of the all-powerfuls.''

''What?'' Tara cried out in horror, but she could see by the agonized resignation on their faces that even though they loved their adoptive brother, neither Otter's-heart nor Running-deer would go against the convictions of their elders in order to save him.

His voice raw with emotion, Otter's-heart bit out, ''We can do nothing, Morning-sun. If we cross out of our hunting grounds and ride to the fort, the whites will see it as an action of war, and this is what we have been trying to avoid all along. To save our brother, we would risk the total destruction of our tribe, which is exactly what the evil one desires.''

Tara realized that arguing with them on this point would be useless, and with Grant's life at stake she couldn't afford to waste time on futile arguments. ''Well, I can ride to the fort without risk, and I will,'' she vowed tersely as she whirled around and began running toward the horse Otter's-heart had hobbled next to the council lodge.

At first Otter's-heart and Running-deer were too startled to realize what she intended, but as they watched her mount up, they were prodded into action. As Tara dug her heels into the horse's flanks and charged past them, Running-deer managed to snag the reins and bring the racing stallion to an abrupt halt.

''Do not be so foolish, Morning-sun!'' he scolded harshly, wrapping one arm around her waist and hauling her down off the horse. ''No-hair has inspired a frenzy of blood lust amongst the whites. Anyone who speaks out in defense of Star-runner will be greeted with hatred. Your husband would not want you to risk your own life to save his.''

Otter's-heart nodded, his face contorted in grief as he said, "Our brother is a brave warrior. He will not hide behind the skirts of a woman but must fight his own battles. If he dies at the cruel hands of our enemy, he will face death with great courage. This is the way of the Absaroka!"

"To desert him at a time like this is the way of cowards!" Tara cried out contemptuously, squirming and kicking for release. "If the rest of you men were anywhere near as brave as he is, you wouldn't be standing here bemoaning his cruel fate. You'd be figuring out some way to help him, regardless of some silly dream."

Having grave doubts about his clan's fatalistic decision to forsake one of their own, Running-deer insisted desperately, "All in the prophecy has come to pass. Star-runner does not need our help. He has returned from his sojourn across the wide waters with the powerful weapons he needs to vanquish our enemies."

"Bates has taken his weapons away, and the Army will take away his life," Tara retorted fiercely, but then the hopelessness of the situation overwhelmed her, and her voice dropped to an agonized whisper. "The only thing that might help him now is the strength of his people, but their fear for themselves is so great that they refuse to display their own might."

Otter's-heart was outraged by Tara's low opinion of his tribe. "We are Absaroka, and our spirits are strong! We fear nothing!"

Unconvinced, Tara shook her head, her eyes moistened by helpless tears.

Before Otter's-heart could launch into another tirade, Running-deer took a firm grip on his arm and pulled him back a step. Addressing Tara in a forbidding tone, he demanded, "Would you have us make war against your own kind, Morning-sun? To save Star-runner, would you have so many others die? Do you think our brother's heart will sing because we helped him to live when saving his life means we will lose the heartland of our country?"

As she read the torment on his face, the anguished pain in his dark eyes, Tara was finally able to comprehend why the council of elders had arrived at their decision. Those men were not cruel and unfeeling but gentle and wise, and they believed that the future of their race was at stake here. They might never fully understand the ways of the white man, but they had the intelligence to realize that in order to survive as a people, they could not stand in the way of his coming or begin a fight they would inevitably lose.

"I understand your concerns, Running-deer, but no one need die," Tara stated fervently as an idea came to her that might save Grant without further risk to his clansmen. The more she thought about it, the more certain she was that it stood a good chance of working. "Please, if you want to save Star-runner's life, take me back to the council lodge so that I might speak of my plan to the elders. Please! You must make them listen to me."

Running-deer and Otter's-heart exchanged dubious glances, but when they noted the fierce expression on the pale face of their brother's wife, they surrendered to her wishes without further argument. Like Grandmother Fireweasel, this green-eyed woman would not be silenced.

"Come then," Otter's-heart said, his voice cutting. "Tell my people how they may cast off the truth in Mountainlion's prophecy and withstand the force of a whirlwind without being destroyed by its wrath."

Chapter

Thirty-four

As he was forced up the stairs of the hastily constructed gallows and his wrists were tied to the wooden railing surrounding it, Star-runner heard the beloved voice of his grandfather echoing in his mind. *All in my dream has come to pass, my son, and now your trial is almost over. Your helpers have brought you what you will need to protect the heart of our country. When the evil one is vanquished, our people will dance in the sun and sing songs to your bravery.*

But I have failed, Grandfather! I must die, yet the evil one lives.

Even as he listened, Mountain-lion's voice faded away until it was no more than a whisper of remembered sound. *Do not despair. Today you shall bask in the restorative warmth of the sun.*

Eyes closed, Star-runner felt the promised heat, but then the burning became too painful, and he lifted his lids to find himself staring once more into the cruel face of his enemy. "How did you like that, Collingswood?" Victor Bates inquired mockingly, relishing the fact that he had provided the Army with the perfect scapegoat for his own crimes.

In stoic silence, Star-runner straightened his spine and drew back his shoulders. Ignoring the blood that trickled down his naked chest, he glared hatred at the man standing in front of him. Since Bates could not sustain such eye contact for more than a second, Star-runner knew him for the sniveling coward he was, and Bates knew that he knew, which only increased the man's need to inflict more pain.

"Give him another taste of that whip, Plummer," Bates ordered as he scanned the approving faces in the vengeful crowd gathered around the scaffold. "Our friends here aren't going to be satisfied with a simple lynching, even if the Army is. For all the killing he's done, these righteous folks want this bastard's blood, and since the hanging party won't start for another few minutes, we've still got time to give them what they want."

Slade Plummer fingered the crooked section of his nose, recalling the last meeting he'd had with Grant Collingswood aboard the *Ophelia*. His disfigurement was a permanent reminder of why he hated the half-naked man standing so straight and proud at the edge of the raised platform. Once he got done with him, Collingswood would have no pride left.

Lips wet with anticipation, Plummer grinned at his prisoner. As luck would have it, several of the Army guards had agreed that the leader of the vigilantes should feel a little pain before his neck was stretched, and so they'd turned him over to Bates and his men. Among the six of them, they'd managed to tie Collingswood's arms behind his back, but his legs still remained free. Since Slade had suffered a painful kick to the jaw once already today, he made certain he stood well out of range of those legs as he raised the bullwhip over his head. This time, he promised himself, Collingswood would be the one to end up on his knees.

"Always pays to keep your customers happy, boss," Plummer chuckled gleefully, then lashed out as hard as he could with the whip.

A spurt of bestial pleasure shot through his loins as he watched the leather strap bite into his defenseless victim's chest. As he noted the blood welling up beneath the smooth skin, he lashed out again with an expert hand, then again, until the strip of reddened flesh split open. Just as Bates had predicted, the sight of blood drew cheers from the angry crowd, and Plummer didn't need any further urging to give them more of what they wanted.

Unfortunately, Collingswood didn't provide much in the way of extra entertainment. When the whip cut into his skin, his muscles quivered involuntarily against the pain, but the man never blinked. As if he truly were an Injun, Collingswood took his punishment without moving or uttering a single sound, just like all the other long-suffering redskins Plummer and his men had either maimed or abused before sending them off to the happy hunting grounds.

Since Slade had been told that Collingswood didn't come by his Injun blood naturally, he was curious to know just how much pain the arrogant devil could actually take before breaking. However, as he drew back his arm with the intention of slicing into a much more vulnerable part of his target's anatomy, a booming voice rang out inside the compound. "You there! Stop what you're doing immediately, or die where you stand! That man has been judged guilty by an Army tribunal, and the Army will mete out his punishment."

As the furious commandant pushed his way through the disappointed crowd and directed the men in his battalion to station themselves around the scaffold, Bates and Plummer ambled toward the steps leading down from the platform. Before descending, however, Bates called back spitefully, "You should consider yourself fortunate that Colonel Eisely's a man of such high honor and efficiency, Collingswood. If he hadn't completed the arrangements for your execution in such a timely manner and interceded on your behalf, you'd be standing up here without a scrap of flesh left on your bones to hang."

Slowly, Star-runner brought himself out of the altered state that had kept him oblivious to the pain. The first thing he noticed as he allowed himself to start thinking again was the searing agony across his chest and the weakness in his legs. Inhaling deeply, he leaned back, resting most of his weight on the railing behind him. Pride kept him from succumbing to the urge to drop his head onto his chest and slump forward, to shield his eyes from the strong morning light. According to the sun's position in the sky, it was almost noon, the time chosen by the Army for him to die.

As a war chief of the Absaroka, he must face death with courage.

Without expression, he gazed down upon the angry mob who had come to witness his hanging. Not a man or woman among them had been willing to listen to him once Bates had told them that he was the leader of the renegade group protecting Crow land from the greedy trespassing of the miners. No one had believed that he wasn't responsible for every one of the murderous raids that had occurred over the past several months in the territory, especially when Slade Plummer showed them the mutilated body of the most recently slain miner and testified that he knew who had done it because he'd witnessed the brutal slaughter firsthand. Ironically, since Plummer had wielded the knife himself, the man hadn't been lying, and his graphically damning testimony had clinched the verdict of guilty in the minds of all three judges in the Army tribunal.

After that, every one of Grant's protests had fallen on deaf ears, and he had been labeled a traitor to his race, a man whose skin might be white but who possessed the murderous heart and filthy soul of an Indian. Knowing he was about to be hanged for crimes he hadn't committed was hard enough to take, but the knowledge that Victor Bates had succeeded in his evil plan made him sick. Bates was not only going to go free of his crimes but reap a bountiful reward for his deeds.

As that unacceptable thought rose to taunt him, Starrunner swayed beneath a crushing tide of defeat. Because he had failed in his mission, his brother Swift-bear was dead. The deaths of many high chiefs would go unavenged, and their gravesites would be raped in a relentless search for gold. Because of his failure, the Absaroka would eventually lose their lands, and he . . . he was going to die without ever telling Tara that he loved her.

God help him, but he loved her! As much as he'd tried to deny it, the moment of truth had arrived. Faced with his own death, he could finally admit that he adored her spirited nature, her tart tongue, the way her green eyes sparkled when she defied him and shimmered with desire when he made love to her. Now that she was forever out of his reach, he could admit that his feelings for her went much deeper than what he'd felt for Sliver-of-moon, and had been since the first.

But then, as a tide of misery washed over his soul, he was saved once again from a fresh onslaught of agonizing pain by Colonel Eisely's voice. As he and two other soldiers stepped up on the platform, the colonel ordered, "You may position the rope, sergeant."

Jaw clenched, Star-runner didn't flinch as a thick hemp was looped over his head and the noose adjusted for a proper fit around his neck.

"Do you have anything else you wish to say before we pass sentence?" Colonel Eisely demanded as he watched Sergeant Moore throw the other end of the rope over the beam of the gallows.

"Only that I acted on my own," Star-runner insisted, as he'd done so many times since his brief trial. Of the three officers who had judged him guilty, Eisely had seemed the most objective, and so he appealed to the man's high sense of ethics one last time. It no longer mattered that he was spouting lies, for only a lie would help the cause of justice and save his people. "The men riding with me were not Crow but renegades dressed up to resemble that tribe, just like I am. To get to their gold, I needed the Army to force them off their hunting grounds."

Distracted by a distant noice, Eisely acknowledged Star-runner's statement with a brief nod, but then the sound grew in strength, and he turned away from the condemned man, his gaze searching the surrounding hills. "What the hell is that?" he inquired of his sergeant. "A buffalo stampede?"

Sergeant Moore gazed over the walls of the fort, shivering as the hair on the back of his neck prickled. "I don't rightly know, sir," he muttered uneasily, just as the crowd of people below him became aware of the sound and ceased their shouting.

As everyone tried to identify the ominous rumble reverberating down from the hills, their vengeful mood changed to one of fearful anticipation. "Drums!" a man shouted as the noise intensified. "Injun war drums!"

An experienced military officer who had led several successful campaigns against the Plains tribes, Eisely had recognized the sound a few seconds before it had been identified by the civilians, and his reaction was immediate. "Troops! Take your posts!" he ordered, and his men immediately scattered to comply with his command.

Remaining where he was on the raised platform, Eisely kept his gaze on the horizon, but he didn't need his eyes to tell him what was coming. The war drums beat closer, sounding as if they came from every direction, and their rhythm was magnified a thousand times by the accompanying throb of galloping horses, their hooves pounding against the hard earth.

The crowd standing below the scaffold watched with horrified eyes as up over the surrounding slopes came the first line of charging horses. Within minutes, every hilltop and rise was filled with Absaroka warriors decked out in full battle regalia. Like an angry swarm, they spread out over the landscape, brandishing their weapons and shouting war cries, and all the while the drums beat louder and louder until they sounded like the malevolent thunder preceding a violent storm.

Suddenly, the drums ceased beating, and the advancing horses were reined to a halt. An unholy pall fell over the countryside. On the hills, the feathers of countless war bonnets fluttered in the breeze. The sun danced off a myriad of shiny breastplates and glanced off the points of a thousand spears.

The awestruck men and women standing inside the fort gaped at the barbaric splendor spread out around them, then quaked in terror as they realized that they were not just surrounded but hopelessly outnumbered. The soldiers in Eisely's battalion were in position at their posts, weapons at the ready, but everyone knew that if they were to fire a shot, they would be faced with a certain massacre. Afraid of doing anything that might touch off their own destruction, no one moved.

To those waiting for their fate to be decided, it seemed like hours before several horses separated themselves from the rest and began a slow descent of the nearest rise. Through the open gates of the fort, the crowd could see the flag of truce flying high over the head of a resplendent chief who was positioned at the head of this small group of riders. He was closely followed by three others, but it was obvious to all who saw him that he was the all-high. His war bonnet of eagle feathers was so long that it swept the ground, and his raised hand was enough to keep the restless surge behind him at bay. It was that hand alone that controlled the primitive force which had yet to unleash its terrible power down upon them.

As he watched the regal party make their approach, then rein in their horses a few hundred yards from the fort, Eisely knew that his only hope for survival rested on his ability to bargain wisely during this parlay. "My horse, sergeant!" he ordered, forgetting all about the man he'd been ready to hang as he descended the stairs. Praying that he would somehow be able to avert the massacre of all the souls under his command and the settlers seeking his protection, he prepared to meet his opponent on neutral ground.

Left alone on the platform, Star-runner stared out at the hills, and his heart felt as if it would burst from his chest. He had instantly recognized his father and two brothers as they'd broken away from the others and ridden toward the fort, but the rider who captured his full attention was neither warrior nor chief, but a small, feisty woman with flaming red hair. Then, as if that wasn't enough of a shock, he noticed a movement off to his left and turned his head to witness the late arrival of another group of men, four of whom galloped forward to join the party already gathered beneath the white flag of truce.

"I'll be damned," Star-runner swore in bemusement, swallowing the sudden lump in his throat as he watched his in-laws join with the rest of his family, who were patiently awaiting their parlay with the commandant.

Flanked by a military standard bearer and a civilian interpreter, Colonel Eisely rode out of the gates, his arm raised in a gesture of peace. As he made his approach, his eyes never wavered from the resplendent Absaroka chief, though he noticed at once, with a jarring bit of shock, that the dignified personage seated astride a magnificent pinto stallion was in the company of not only his own kind but four fierce-looking Scotsmen and a beautiful white woman!

Strangely, as he guided his horse into position and got a closer look at his dignified adversary, Eisely felt his hand falter, then return smartly to the space above his temple. A

West Point-trained officer, Eisely had a healthy respect for authority, and he could see by the determined expression on the chief's face that he would brook no interference in whatever course he had set for himself and the warriors of his tribe. Eisley's salute was not returned, and he felt as if the dark eyes staring back at him could see into his very soul, uncovering all of his weaknesses. Deeply disturbed by that intense stare, Eisely gulped down his fear and offered up a silent prayer that he would be able to find the right words to appease this mighty leader, for there was no doubt in his mind that he was no match for the man.

Then, to the colonel's surprise, instead of speaking through the interpreter, the chief announced, "I am Split-nose, father of Star-runner. I have come for my son."

Without another word of explanation, the Indian delegation, along with their white companions, walked their horses around the startled threesome who had ridden out to meet them and continued on their way toward the fort. Never changing speed from the slow, deliberate gait he had set when he'd first cut away from the masses filling the hillsides, Split-nose led his party straight through the front gates. The crowd parted wordlessly before them, presenting no resistance as the silent parade came to a halt beside the gallows, and their magnificent leader dismounted.

After mounting the stairs, Split-nose pulled out his knife and cut the rope draped around his adopted son's neck, then the bindings at his wrists. No words were spoken between the two men, but all those watching could see the wealth of emotion contained in one slight nod of greeting. Briefly, Split-nose clapped his copper-skinned hands on his son's shoulders as if to assure himself that he was well, then gave a rueful shake of his head. "Your woman has the heart of a grizzly, my son," he murmured under his breath, though his expression showed none of the amusement he felt. "We did our best to shake her off, but her sharp claws dug into our pride, and her fearful growls sent us racing for our horses. We are here because she would not allow us to be elsewhere."

Try as he might to preserve the majestic solemnity of the moment, Star-runner burst out laughing. "I am sorry, Father," he apologized. "I have done my best to tame her, but

I have yet to succeed. Perhaps I should beat her, but I fear she would only strike back.''

Split-nose grunted in sympathy with Star-runner's domestic quandary, then attempted to lighten his son's heavy heart by announcing, ''Swift-bear lives, and his medicine ensures his return to good health.''

''Thank God,'' Star-runner breathed as he watched his father descend the stairs in the same stately manner as he'd arrived. After mounting his horse, he gave Star-runner one last affectionate glance, and then, with a final show of pagan ferocity for the benefit of the wide-eyed crowd, he raised his lance threateningly in their direction before he and his other two sons silently departed the way they had come.

Star-runner's adoring gaze bypassed his father and brothers-in-law and settled on his woman, Morning-sun. Unaware of the besotted smile on his face, he remembered the words of wisdom that had come to him as he mounted the gallows.

Today you shall bask in the warmth of the sun, Mountain-lion had promised, and Star-runner directed his grateful thoughts to the heavens.

You were right, Grandfather. As always, you were right.

Since it was obvious that Grant had eyes for only one person and had completely lost interest in anything else going on around him, Angus Armstrong raised himself up in his saddle and proclaimed, ''You people best listen up while you still can, for if you lay another hand on my son-in-law, you'll be answerin' to me.''

If that wasn't enough to convince everyone, he made a sweeping gesture of his arm encompassing the hills. ''As well as to them. The choice is yours.''

When his challenge was greeted by several moments of respectful silence, Angus chuckled. ''Now, laddie, if you can take your lovesick eyes off my daughter for a minute, the floor is all yours.''

Reluctantly, Grant pulled his gaze away from Tara, but the exultation he felt didn't lessen. His amazing wife and their extremely intimidating family had created an atmosphere in which he could now defend himself. He opened his mouth to speak, but before a word came out, his declaration of innocence was rendered totally unnecessary.

As soon as he'd seen Colonel Eisely back down, Victor

Bates had known that it was only a matter of time before his guilt was uncovered, and he wasn't prepared to wait. Having decided that his only hope for freedom was in taking a hostage, he stepped forth from the crowd and captured the one person he felt certain would ensure his escape.

After pulling Tara off her horse, he held a knife to her throat and hissed, "Sorry, Collingswood, but I don't plan to listen to any boring speech. I want safe passage through the mountains, and if I don't get it, your pretty woman here is going to die."

Chapter

Thirty-five

Except for the labored breathing of the man seated behind her on the horse, Tara could hear nothing. The forest around them was quiet. Behind them, the steep mountain trail was empty of followers, and all looked clear up ahead. She and her desperate captor were completely alone in the wilderness.

Before forcing her up into the saddle and taking her hostage, Bates had demanded a safe passage out of the territory, and ostensibly his request had been met with total compliance. The men in her family, the soldiers in the fort, and the Indian tribe surrounding it were far behind them now, and it appeared as if Bates truly was going to make his way to freedom.

Yet appearances were deceiving, Tara knew, amazed with herself for feeling so calm, especially since Bates probably planned to kill her as soon as she'd outlived her usefulness to him. But then, Bates didn't know her husband like she did. Sooner or later, Star-runner, war chief of the Absaroka, would come for his woman, and when he did, Victor Bates was a dead man.

Of course, that comforting knowledge didn't mean that Tara was going to just sit back and wait to be rescued. For the pain he'd inflicted on so many people, especially her husband, Bates deserved to die, and Tara relished the thought of killing him herself. A tiny gasp slipped out of her mouth as she contemplated this newfound aspect of her personality, and then she smiled. In the space of four short months, she had changed so much that she barely recognized herself. That naive gentlewoman who had traveled to the territory from her cultured home in Connecticut no longer existed, and in her place was a stout-hearted woman who would do whatever she had to in order to survive.

At the moment, of course, her captor had her at a decided disadvantage, but eventually she would be able to reach the knife strapped to her thigh without drawing his attention. She hoped that opportunity would present itself before Grant's arrival. As far as she was concerned, her poor husband had already been through quite enough for one day, and she didn't want him to tax himself unnecessarily on her account.

After another grueling hour in the saddle, Tara's brain started to wander aimlessly, and she almost missed her chance. The trail was descending through a dangerously narrow ravine, with a smooth granite wall on one side and a steep rocky incline on the other. For what she had in mind, the location was perfect, and she took action while action was provident.

Filling her lungs with air, she opened her mouth and screamed.

With his body pressed in between two boulders, Starrunner heard a sound that curdled the blood in his veins. An instant later, his terror was replaced by an overwhelming rage that sent a powerful surge of adrenaline to every limb in his body. After all he and Tara had been through together, he couldn't stand to lose her now. Yanking his knife from his belt, he let out a bloodcurdling yell of his own and raced up the treacherous trail toward his woman and the man who had hurt her.

He covered the distance in seconds, but when he arrived he found Tara and Bates grappling at the very edge of a steep, rock-strewn precipice. He didn't dare throw his knife for fear of hitting her, yet he couldn't just stand by and watch as Bates overwhelmed her with his greater strength and hurled her over the rocks to her death. Heart in his throat, he worked himself into position, but then, just when he was near enough to join the life-and-death struggle, Bates gained the upper hand.

"No!" Star-runner shouted, launching himself into the air at the same time as Bates gave Tara a brutal shove backward.

Arms flailing uselessly, Tara felt herself falling, but an instant later she cried out in pain and shock as she was knocked sideways by the force of her husband's flying body. Star-runner wasted no time assuring himself that she was all right but pushed himself off her supine form and charged at his enemy.

"When you made off with my wife, Bates," he snarled as he landed a vicious blow to the side of the man's head, "you sealed your fate."

As she heard the sound of cracking bone, Tara scrambled back to her feet, but her anxiety was completely unnecessary. Before Star-runner could back up his first blow with another, Bates lost his footing. A grimace of abject horror on his face, he clawed at the outcropping of rock beside him, but the surface was too smooth for him to get a hold. Tara watched in appalled fascination as he fell backward, just as she had fallen moments ago, but for Bates there was no last-minute reprieve. She heard his screams echoing off the steep sides of the ravine, and then there was silence, deathly silence.

Grant stepped forward and carefully drew Tara away from the dangerous edge of the cliff. "It's all over," he assured her grimly as he gathered her into his arms. "He's dead."

"I was so scared," Tara admitted, wrapping her arms around his waist. "If you hadn't arrived when you did, I'd be the one lying at the bottom of that ravine."

Feeling the shudders that wracked her slender body, Grant tightened his hold, trying to withstand the savage wish that he'd been able to do much more damage to him before Bates had fallen over the side. However, instead of dwelling on his frustrated need for vengeance, he focused his attention on the shaken woman in his arms. Cupping her chin in his hand, he gazed down lovingly into her eyes. "I was scared, too. I love you so much, and when I heard you scream like that, I thought Bates had already hurt you. He didn't, did he?''

Tara stared back at him, the message of her own love clear in her eyes. "No. I screamed in the hopes of catching him off guard so I could reach for my knife. And my plan would have worked, too, if he hadn't dragged me with him when he fell off the horse."

Completely secure in the safety of Grant's arms, she added impishly, "But Bates was the one who should have been scared. Between the two of us, he never stood a chance."

Amazed by her quick recovery and the ferocious expression on her face, Grant could only shake his head. He had married a beautiful woman but had got himself a magnificent warrior in the bargain, and he didn't quite know how to handle it. "Not a chance," he agreed gruffly, reaching out his hand to touch a shimmering strand of her hair, remembering how it had gleamed like fire in the sunlight when she'd ridden down the hillside to his rescue.

"As my father said, you may be a mere woman, but you have the heart of the grizzly and the claws to match."

With an indignant little sniff, Tara complained, "I don't think Split-nose intended that as a compliment. I'm afraid he doesn't find me a very suitable daughter-in-law. He thinks you should beat me until I remember my proper place."

Grant was able to smile for the first time since his fear for her gave way to his total astonishment. "You can see how well that method worked with my mother."

Tara frowned. White-fawn did indeed wait upon her husband hand and foot, yet she didn't appear to be the least bit fearful of him. Still, she knew that in the Indian nation males were considered superior, and their women were required to subjugate themselves to male authority. "He actually beats her!"

Blue eyes sparkling, Grant admitted, "No, but he uses an equally effective method."

"What method?" Tara inquired suspiciously.

"He keeps her well pleased under the blankets."

Tara replied with a meek "Oh."

"Which is exactly how I plan to keep you in line," Grant promised purposefully as he scooped her up in his arms and rose to his feet. Striding over to the horse, he lifted her up into the saddle, then mounted behind her. "But before I get started, we have to get back to the fort. Otherwise, I'm going to be in a great deal of trouble with my in-laws."

"How did you ever persuade them to stay behind while you came after me?" Tara asked.

She regretted the question when Grant pushed her soft bottom against his hard groin and irately informed her, "We struck a bargain. If I'm not back by sunset, they're heading out after us, and if anything has happened to you by the time they catch up, I lose my manhood."

Tara gave a long-suffering sigh. "I've tried my best, but I'm afraid I haven't had very much success in domesticating them."

Against her back, she could feel Grant's chest rumbling with silent laughter. "About as much success as you're going to have with me," he predicted.

With a smug little grin, Tara retorted, "We'll see."

Looking forward to her efforts, Grant allowed that comment to pass and proceeded to tell her all that had transpired since the morning. "Slade Plummer and the rest of Bates's crew will stand trial for their crimes, and Colonel Eisely has given us his word that the government will abide by their last treaty with us. For the time being, at least, our hunting grounds still belong to us."

"If Mountain-lion was here, he would be so proud of you," Tara stated softly. "Songs of your bravery will be sung for many seasons to come."

Grant stiffened for a moment, then surrendered to the inevitable. "White-fawn told you about my grandfather's dream?"

"She did."

"Then I imagine she also told you about my wife and son and how they died?"

"Yes," Tara admitted hesitantly, fearing his reaction to the realization that she knew all about his past. "She wanted me to understand you better and felt I should know how much you have lost."

Grant pulled her back against him and began kissing the side of her neck with exquisite tenderness. "I love you, Tara."

302

"I love you, too," she murmured, but he heard the painful catch in her voice, and he had to say something to ease the lingering doubt in her mind.

"Her name was Sliver-of-moon, and I loved her, too, but my feelings for her were completely different from what I feel for you. She was a child, a sweet, docile child. My thoughts were her thoughts, my way her way," he stated hoarsely, unused to discussing himself and his feelings. "We were children together, but none of us can stay children forever. When she was killed, I lost my innocence and the sweet babe born out of it. I will always carry a special place for them in my heart, but my memory of them doesn't hurt me anymore, and I never want it to hurt you."

Tara closed her eyes and brushed the last of her anxious tears away with the back of her hand. "As long as I know that you love me, nothing can hurt me," she declared confidently.

Grant blinked away the moisture in his own eyes and hurried to inject a lighter note into the conversation though his arms were tight around her. "As long as you obey me, I won't have to hurt you," he teased, and he was rewarded by a sharp jab in the ribs.

"Okay, okay," he laughed, and he began the negotiations that he hoped would take the rest of his lifetime to complete. "You don't have to obey me, but when we don't agree on something, could we keep the argument private? After all, I am a mighty Absaroka warrior, and I do have a certain reputation to maintain."

"Of course, I would never jeopardize your dignity," Tara returned magnanimously, secure in his love and blissfully content with her proper place in his life. "White-fawn has taught me my duties as the wife of such a noble chief, and I intend to follow her wise instructions quite closely."

Upon hearing this, Grant groaned pitifully, "I guess what my father says is true. We men of the Fire-bears are truly cursed, for our women refuse to recognize us as their masters, and thus we do their bidding like lowly slaves."

Giggling at his ridiculous supposition, Tara retorted imperiously, "Then make haste, slave, for I would have you make love to me the moment we arrive back home."

To her surprise, Grant pulled up the reins and dragged her

with him off the horse. "We need wait no longer," he murmured against her lips as he carried her toward a lush thicket of soft grasses and laid her down upon it. "My home is wherever you are, for my heart belongs solely to you."

"As mine does to you," Tara replied breathlessly, then lifted her arms and welcomed her husband into her loving embrace. As she felt his hands working their magic on her eager body, she sighed, "Oh, yes, at long last, we are both home."

Epilogue

It was the time when the birds made their nestings and the leaves sprouted green on the trees. Once again, new life had come to the mountains, and the clan of the Fierce-ones had gathered to celebrate along with the clan of the Fire-bears. Standing at the top of the sacred summit, Star-runner presented his newborn daughter, Flaming-star, to both families, then lifted the smiling baby up to the sky and began singing the praise song. The Almighty had blessed him with more than any man could wish for, and he gave thanks to him in a strong voice.

"It is well," Split-nose declared, dark eyes shimmering with moisture as he listened to Star-runner's song. Then, as if he were having great difficulty forming the words, he turned to the young woman responsible for this time of great joy. "Although our women do not take part in the naming ceremony, I do not begrudge your presence here today, Morning-sun. You have given my son back his heart, and for this I shall always be grateful."

Knowing how much such an allowance had cost him, Tara's reply was gracious. "Thank you, Split-nose. I do not always follow the ways of an Absaroka woman, but I will promise to do my best not to shame my husband in the eyes

305

of his tribe. I am grateful that you could take part in this ceremony that is usually reserved for male children.''

Split-nose nodded. ''These are times of swift change,'' he said. ''And the Absaroka must be wise enough to change with them. You are a mere woman, yet you have taught me many useful things.''

''Just as I have learned many things from you.''

Split-nose predicted, ''With you as her mother, Flaming-star shall possess the heart of a warrior.''

''I hope so,'' Tara replied, forcing back an amused smile as Split-nose shook his head in rueful resignation. ''To survive in this wild land, she will have to be strong. All of us have to be strong.''

Split-nose gazed down at the lush green valley spread out below them, and a deep sadness came into his dark eyes. ''As we change, so does everything around us. Someday we may lose most of our beloved country to the gold seekers, but because you and Star-runner are allowed to own land, we can always be sure of our welcome when our people visit these sacred mountains.''

''Yes,'' Tara replied, awed by the majestic beauty of their surroundings and humbled by the depth of love she could sense in the people around her. ''If Grant and I have anything to say about it, the Five-Star Ranch shall never pass out of our family's hands, and what is ours, Split-nose, is also yours. Until the pine trees turn yellow, this land shall belong to the Fire-bears.''

Seeing that the noble chief was so deeply touched by Tara's words that he might not be able to maintain his proud bearing, Jamie entered their conversation and declared jovially, ''Your clan isn't the only one to benefit from the generosity of these two. For a wedding gift to me and Rose, they just up and gave us the deed to Laurel Glen. Come the next high water, we'll be going back east, where I plan to raise the finest horses any man has ever seen.''

''Ain't . . . isn't life funny?'' Rose asked, slipping her arm around Tara's waist and giving her friend an affectionate squeeze. ''The refined lady of the manor will be making her home in the wilderness, and the uncultured homesteader's daughter will be living out her days in a mansion. I cain't hardly believe you'd turn down your inheritance to stay in a rude log cabin in the middle of nowhere.''

Eyes on her husband and infant daughter, Tara smiled in contentment. ''Everything I've ever wanted or needed is right here.''

Rose stepped over to Jamie, smiling a similar smile. ''I know how you feel. Why else would I have gotten myself hitched to a farmer?''

''A gentleman farmer,'' Jamie corrected, which made Tara laugh.

''Oh, Jamie, I wish I could be there to watch while you and Rose turn Connecticut society on its well-cultured ear. Aunt Margaret will probably roll over in her grave.''

With a mischievous sparkle in his brown eyes, Jamie grinned. ''We'll be keepin' you informed of our progress, Red, and we'll expect you to do the same by us. Even though we'll be separated by a lot of miles, we're still a family, and that's gonna be for always.''

''That's a promise,'' Tara said as Grant joined them to begin the walk back down into the valley where White-fawn and Falling-water were waiting to serve them a magnificent feast in honor of the occasion. Beaming with pride, he handed young Julie Ellen Collingswood over to Tara, then wrapped his arm around his wife's slender shoulders. ''What's a promise?''

Cradling her daughter in her arms, Tara went up on tiptoe and kissed Grant's cheek. ''That whatever happens in the years to come, we'll always be a family.''

As their eyes met, Grant's features softened, and he tugged on her hand, holding her back as the other members of their family departed down the narrow trail. ''Always,'' he pledged solemnly, wishing he could capture this precious moment in time for eternity.

Standing together with her husband and child, Tara looked up at the circle of snow-capped peaks that surrounded them and murmured in awe, ''This place is so beautiful. It feels as if we're standing at the center of the world, that all in the past and all in the future comes together right here.''

''Maybe it does,'' Grant agreed, though his gaze was focused on a different image from the one Tara was seeing. Off in the distance, high above the virgin trees of the ancient forest, where the puffy white clouds touched the sky, he saw a white buffalo bull pawing the air, and next to him stood a tall, broad-chested warrior with the scars of many long-ago battles etched upon his handsome face. He was dressed all in white and wearing a war bonnet of eagle feathers that fluttered gently in the spring breeze. When he lifted his fine head, his fierce dark eyes were very bright, conveying the truth of spirits and the wonder of dreams.

Now that you understand with your heart as well as your mind, my teachings are done. Farewell, my son, until the time when you shall walk with me upon the wind.

Eyes shimmering with moisture, Grant lifted his hand, but Mountain-lion was already gone. "Farewell, Grandfather," he whispered. "Thank you and farewell."

Author's Note

Much has been written about the Indian tribes of the Northern Plains, but while conducting my research for this book, I discovered that they were not only a fierce and warlike race of people but a gentle and fun-loving one as well. The more I learned about them, the more I wished to create a safe haven for them and all of their beautiful traditions. Unfortunately, the Five-Star Ranch exists only in fiction. In reality, when the buffalo went away, these innocent people were suddenly cast from plenty into poverty. They were stunned, but their unrelenting faith kept them believing that the buffalo would return, that the white man would feel shame for his wantonness, and that their camps would one day be clean of famine and disease.

This never happened.

The days of the buffalo are gone forever, but, unlike most other tribes, the Absaroka do not hate the ground that holds their lodges. They can still look at the mountains and drink clear water, walk the same paths as the elk and the antelope. By working with the white man instead of against him, they were able to keep the heartland of their country. As Plenty-coups, one of the last chiefs who could still remember the old life, put down in his memoirs, "Instead of holding the country that they love, those other tribes fought the whites and lost all, taking whatever the white man would give. And when the hearts of the givers are filled with hate, their gifts are small."